TO: Denise ♡

♡, Helen

# High Drama

—ɯ—

*A Novel*

Helen Murdock-Prep  5-26-'15

This is a work of fiction. Names, characters, places and incidents either are the product of the author's imagination or are used fictitiously.
Any resemblance to actual persons, living or dead, is entirely coincidental.

Copyright 2014 by Helen Murdock-Prep
All rights reserved. Printed in the United States of America. No part of this book may be used or reproduced in any manner whatsoever without written permission, except in the case of brief quotations embodied in critical articles or reviews.

Library of Congress Cataloging-in-Publication Data
Murdock-Prep, Helen
High Drama: a novel / Helen Murdock-Prep
p. cm.

ISBN: 1502534061
ISBN 13: 9781502534064
Library of Congress Control Number: 2014917498
CreateSpace Independent Publishing Platform
North Charleston, South Carolina

1. Teenagers- Fiction. 2. Theater- Fiction
3. Private school students- Fiction
4. Man-woman relationships- Fiction
5. Acting-Fiction 6. Rich people- Fiction
8. Teacher-student relationships- Fiction

Cover Design/ Cover Photo: Molly Prep
Model: Katie Fletcher
www.HelenMurdock-Prep.tumblr.com

This
is a
love letter
to
Kerry Prep

And to
Molly,
my
Little Love

# A Note To Readers:

The author has worked with hundreds of students in many schools in her career. However, HIGH DRAMA is a work of fiction, and none of those students or their families are portrayed in this book. Names and characters are the product of the author's imagination. Any resemblance to actual events or persons, living or dead, is coincidental. Although some real people, places and plays are mentioned, all are used fictitiously.

"All the world's a stage..."
–Shakespeare

# February 28th
## 1:45pm
## Samuel P. Chester Academy
## Main Building

"**L**isten Amber," I say. "Before we begin, there are a few things you need to know right off the bat about putting on a musical."

Amber tucks a strand of her silky, Japanese straightened hair behind her ear and says, "Okay, Mrs. Graham, but do I have to write this down? Because my promptbook is in my locker." She flips her dark hair over her shoulder as she points vaguely down the hallway.

I smile confidently and say, "No Amber, just listen."

We chose Amber as our student stage manager for *Oliver!* because Tony, the tech director, said that although she's only fifteen, she's very organized and reliable; perfect qualities for the job. She seems a tad on the serious side though, but maybe my goofy ways will help loosen her up a bit.

"I promise we'll have lots of fun," I continue. "But first I have to warn you about this ancient theatrical curse that plagues all high school theater productions."

She looks at me warily. "A curse?"

I nod, but then backtrack and say, "Well, maybe more like a jinx. Or a prophecy. Just listen."

I switch to a spooky kind of voice to playfully ham up my delivery. "I predict *Threeee* Terrible *Thiiiings* are going to *haaappen* when we *begiiin* rehearsing for the *plaaay*."

"Uh huh," she nods tentatively. "What are they?"

She readjusts her glasses as she looks around uncertainly. Not a good sign. Yikes, I don't want to lose my audience before I've even started. Maybe the spooky voice is too much. I drop the voice, but continue to camp it up by slapping one hand over my heart, then raise my right hand high as if I'm about to take an oath.

"Here they are," I announce dramatically. I tick them off, one finger at a time: "One: a cast member will break a bone. Two: another will get mono. And three: someone will die."

Amber gasps and looks at me with alarm.

I drop my hand, (and the act), and say quickly, "Oh, geez! Sorry, Amber. I don't mean a *student* will die, I mean more like somebody really *old*– like a grandparent or someone."

She stares at me soberly. She's not catching my playful spirit. I think I really scared her. Well, that backfired.

"It's okay, Amber," I hurry on. "I was just telling you this because these three things always seem to happen every time I direct a high school musical, and I just wanted to, um, prepare you."

She shifts her books from one hip to another, then begins to chew on her lip.

"Uh huh," she says again.

As if I haven't messed this up enough already, I limp forward, still trying to explain. "My point is, even though we'll be rehearsing for the musical, real life will still happen."

She looks at me dubiously. "Real life will still happen," she echoes. She lowers her chin, the way psychiatrists do when regarding a deranged patient, and says, "Well, that's good. But

Mrs. Graham, isn't like, real life *always* happening?" She looks around the hallway as if to check.

"Yes, yes, Amber, exactly!" I say excitedly. "That's the point! *Of course* real life is always happening, but when a cast is working hard in rehearsals, they sometimes forget that. And then they act all surprised and shocked when something bad happens– like someone gets sick or breaks a bone."

I decide to drop saying "or dies" again; that didn't go down too well.

"And I can guarantee you, Amber, when one of those things inevitably happens, the entire cast will freak out and gasp, 'But what about the *play*?' So I guess my real point is to assure you that the show will go on *despite* the 'Terrible Three.'" I crook my fingers and make those little air quotes for emphasis.

"In fact," I say, "the show is *always* performed, Amber. Maybe you've heard the expression: 'the show must go on?' Well that means, no matter what..."

Amber interrupts, "Excuse me, Mrs. Graham?" Her eyes are blinking rapidly behind her glasses, like she's gearing up for a seizure. "I'm sorry, but I think I'd better write this all down." She begins to scratch about in her gum wrapper purse for a pen.

"No, no, that's okay, Amber..." I trail off. I reach forward to still her arm. Dear Lord. I blab on waaaay too much. See? This is why I need a script for my life. I'm great when I have the words already written out for me, but I stink at explaining stuff on my own. She probably didn't follow a thing I said. Me and my big mouth!

Apologetically I say, "I know I talk too much, Amber. I just wanted to tell you my Three Terrible Things theory, that's all."

Can you say "beat a dead horse?"

I let go of her arm and busy myself trying to smooth my curls back into place. Maybe I'll try to have my hair straightened like Amber's.

"Okay, yeah, I get it, Mrs. Graham. You're saying bad things happen, right? But we'll deal with them, right?" She's looking at me closely, waiting for me to confirm she's got it.

Eloquently put! Simple and direct. Maybe I'll learn a thing or two from Amber about brevity.

"That's it. You've got it, Amber." I give her a big thumbs up. "Just so you know," I add awkwardly. Why can't I just *stop*?

"Mm hmm. Okay, I have to go to French now, Mrs. Graham, but I'll see you next week at auditions. Thanks again for asking me to be the stage manager."

Then she quickly turns on her heel and walks away, her Ugg boots cushioning each step in a rubbery silence.

"Sorry, again, Amber!" I call out after her. "My bad. That didn't come out the way I meant!" I close my eyes, mortified by my own insensitivity.

"That's O.K.," she calls back. With a dismissive wave of her hand she says, "I just hope that last one doesn't happen to me."

Oh snap. She heard the death part loud and clear.

# March 3rd
## 9am
## Home

Samuel P. Chester Academy sits atop a massive hill in the über-rich suburb of Harding Cove. It has all the external beauty you'd expect of a wealthy private school: imposing iron gate at the entrance, tree-lined driveway, four-story brick building complete with required ivy clinging to its sides. This ivy-encrusted cliché was founded by Mr. Samuel P. Chester himself in 1918.

Weird thing: although now deceased, Mr. Chester's subsequent headmasters all bear an uncanny resemblance to him: bald and portly, with those wire-framed glasses. You can see this plainly on display in the front entrance hall of the main building. Chronologically placed, the headmaster's pictures all line the hallway, but other than listing their different dates of service, they all look like the exact same guy. Every other picture or so, a bit of facial hair may appear in the form of a mustache or a dapper beard, but underneath, they all sport the same sweet, round baby face. It makes me wonder if it wasn't, maybe, a requirement for the job!

The campus itself consists of four buildings, and unfurls through acres of forests, fields, a pond, and two streams. It takes a solid minute drive to arrive at the school buildings proper, so I can only imagine the amount of time and energy it takes to maintain it all.

When Jackson and I first arrived for our interview last year, we exchanged dumbfounded glances at its manicured elegance. We come from middle-class public school backgrounds, where every playground was worn down to dirt and crab grass, so this was our first glimpse at how the wealthy among us live.

For some reason, once we were ten feet inside those iron gates, I could only whisper. What is it about the precise and organized arrangement of nature that reduces me to speak in hushed tones?

We spotted several lawn crews here and there mowing away on those fancy lawn tractors. The fields didn't look like they needed mowing actually; like tight carpets, vacuuming came more to mind. Grounds crews swarmed the rolling acres like ants, rooting out errant weeds or unsightly imperfections. No random wildflowers allowed. Unassigned beauty forbidden!

"If this place is run the same way the grounds are tended to, we may be in big trouble," I whispered to Jackson.

Swinging into the large pebble-filled parking lot, Jackson asked, "How do you mean?"

I turned my face to look out the window. "This may be too rigid a setting for us, Jackson. Especially if the kids are handled in the same perfectionist way. I like a more rough-and-tumble kind of atmosphere."

"Kelly, look at me," he sputtered.

Alarmed, I turned back to see my handsome, blue-eyed husband looking pale, and worse, really ticked off.

"What?" I asked, shocked back into my normal voice.

He threw the car into park, then turned to face me. With more than a flicker of annoyance he said, "You knew this was a rich private school, right?"

I nodded, still unsure why he seemed so mad at me.

"So what did you expect?"

"Well," I began primly. "I guess I just didn't expect it to look so...so..." I looked back out the window and flapped my hand at the surroundings trying to come up with the right word.

"Intimidating?" Jackson offered.

"No," I sighed. "Fake."

Jackson let out a slow breath of air. He tipped his head back so it rested on the driver's side window; his soft brown curls splayed out in a halo around his head. He's normally a very low-key guy. What the heck?

"Kelly," he began calmly. "You were excited when we got this interview, right?"

"Yeah," I said in a kind of wobbly voice. It sounded like this was going to be one of Jackson's buildup speeches– where he starts off low and slow, but like a lawyer, ends up shouting out his final point.

"If you don't think you want to do this, you have to tell me now," he said. "But I'll warn you in advance: we *need* this job, Kelly." He slapped his hands in frustration on the steering wheel, then said, "Come on, Kel! We talked about this. I thought we were in agreement! I can't believe you're put off by the *grounds*; how superficial is that?"

But I wasn't really listening. Because straight ahead, just to the left of this modern looking, massive glass sports arena, I had spotted a tiny building. A tiny building that was calling my name. Huddled to the side like a forgotten old shoebox, the perfectly rectangular, slightly disheveled-looking structure sat adorably alone. Its brick facade punctuated by an ancient glass window with its familiar "O" shaped opening, read: "Box Office" in old-fashioned lettering. Above the box office sign was a marquee. Lain into the brickwork itself, spelled out in a bumpy mosaic, were the most magical words: "The Little Theater."

"The Little Theater," I whispered reverently. It was calling to me. It needed me.

I grabbed Jackson's arm, and gushed, "Yes, yes, you're right, Jackson– we *did* talk about it, didn't we? Well come on then, let's go– why are you just sitting there? This will be fine. This'll be great! I can't wait!"

Then I scrambled out of that car so fast, with Jackson following in total bewilderment.

And that's how I came to fall in love with a theater.

—⟋⟍—

Just got off the phone with Headmaster Hank; the librettos are finally in, so we're all set! I'm glad we chose *Oliver!* as our first musical here. It's full of great music and lots of characters– perfect for this academy. We did a comedic play last semester, (*Arsenic and Old Lace*), but the buzz is that the students can't wait to do a musical. Jackson and I will co-direct, with Jackson acting as musical director as well. This means I'll stage most of the scenes with dialogue– the "book" part of the show– and I'll also run the business end. He'll teach all the songs and play piano during the performances.

We haven't met the choreographer yet, but Headmaster Hank, the current head honcho at Samuel P., assures me she's on board. We'll meet her at the first production meeting tomorrow. With an elegant name like Lillette Brewster, she at least has a name that gives her intrigue. If I can read her by her name, I predict she'll be classically trained with a quiet, grande dame assurance about her. One of those long, willowy dancers who looks like she subsists entirely on yogurt. Intimidatingly skinny, but with sinewy muscles like iron. You know, the kind of dancer who has never cut her hair so she can perpetually sweep it back into a dancer's bun. I'll bet she's wonderful, and I'm looking forward to meeting her.

Our tech director will be the same guy who's been here for the last few years: Tony Glynn. Everyone in the school loves him. I think in part because he's tall and handsome. I know that sounds shallow, but everyone from Cinderella to Lois Lane falls for it. This guy is movie star gorgeous and has that Lone Ranger cowboy thing going on to boot. With his confident swagger, set to the music of the tools on his work belt clattering around his waist, all he needs to complete the picture is a splintered toothpick hanging indifferently from his curvy lips. You can almost see a chalky cloud of dust follow him as he scuffs by in his boots; he's got that much mystique.

When I first saw him, I thought, *Whatever happened to the geek-guy stereotype of all the tech guys I've known in theater? Quiet guys, helpful as heck, but still struggling inexplicably with acne into their twenties?*

Tony breaks the mold, I guess. He has thick, straw-colored hair that he wears a little long for my taste. Like he got this notion of how his hair should look from Brad Pitt in *Troy* circa 2004, and just stuck with it. Okay, it isn't quite that long, but almost. He wears it in a stumpy ponytail sometimes (yuck!), and I've actually caught him surreptitiously combing it as he walked down the hallway when he thought nobody was looking.

On the whole, he does his job well, but he's pretty aloof to Jackson and me. I can't put my finger on why. I've asked Jackson if he felt it, too, but I think he took it in the wrong way. Like I was bringing it up because I was attracted to Tony or something. (Absolutely not.) So I dropped it really fast.

Maybe I'm just resentful of how close Tony seems to be to the parents and the students. I've watched him turn on the charm with them, and they all swoon. Like I said, they all seem to adore him, read, almost *idolize.*

We've only been here six months, and Headmaster Hank told us they go through directors like Dunkin' Munchkins, so maybe Tony's reserved toward us for self-protection or something. You know how you don't want to get too close to people if you find they're always leaving you? Maybe that's the reason he keeps us at arm's length. Or maybe the truth is I'm just feeling jealous about being left out of the "Tony kingdom." Hopefully, the more we work together on *Oliver!*, the more comfortable we'll all feel.

One final note: Someone told me last semester that Tony started out as an actor. This could explain a lot– he's a handsome tech guy because he's a former actor. And maybe he's treating us kind of coolly because he'd prefer to have *our* jobs. Yeah, maybe that's it. Maybe *he's* actually jealous of *us.*

Plausible, right?

Oh, who cares! See where too much training in script analysis gets me? Always looking for character clues and motivation, that's me. The point is, the handsome hunk will design the set, head construction, and appoint stage crew students to do lights and sound.

Wait! One more thing! I just remembered this, and I can't possibly leave it out: when Tony was building the set for *Arsenic and Old Lace* last semester, he took his shirt off during construction to show off his hot bod. Yes, in front of the *students.* In front of all of us, really. He strutted around brazenly unconcerned that some of the girls were breaking into fits of giggles. When a couple of stage crew boys started to peel off their tee shirts too, we finally stepped in.

Tony probably has some exhibitionist tendencies– what actor doesn't?– and veers towards being a narcissist. There's that theater training again; I can't help it. Trying to figure out what motivates people's behavior is simply the curse of being a Theater major.

We'll just keep an cye on him during this show to make sure he doesn't give us all another lesson in anatomy.

Auditions are in two days, right after school. Yippee!

# March 4th
## Production Meeting
## Samuel P. Chester Academy

With the librettos for *Oliver!* weighing down my arms, I thank Headmaster Hank in the main office and scoot down the hall. Before I meet everyone over in the Little Theater, I duck into the bathroom for a quick look-see.

The ancient washroom still has those wavy mirrors posted on the wall; the ones that distort your face like they came from a fun house– one step up, really, from a sheet of aluminum foil.

My face in this mirror looks just about the same as it did when I left the apartment. My crazy, auburn curls give the illusion that I'm having a wildly good time, even when I'm standing still. Maybe it's all the movement from my spiraling ringlets that makes me look like I'm in constant party mode. Sort of the way curvaceous women always look like they're ready for sex even when they're standing passively in line at the supermarket.

My nose looks larger in this mirror, and that's a plus, because it's a squashed little nub of a thing. Small and freckled, it earned me the nickname "Pug" in middle school. Even back then, I looked like a downgraded version of Keri Russell, but I didn't mind. I think she's adorable, and if my looks lean in her direction, I'm happy.

My one terrible facial feature is my lips. Despite my prolific use of assorted lip balms, my lips are perpetually chapped– a curse of my dry, Irish blood. And by the way, I've never had that peaches and cream complexion the Irish are famous for, either. I've got the cream part all right: super white, glow-in-the-dark, never-tans-only-burns skin. The only time I get the "peach" part is when I artificially apply my Revlon "Deep Rose" liberally with a make-up brush.

I run a quick swipe of cherry ChapStick around my lips, and give myself an encouraging smile.

"This will be great," I tell my wavy reflection. "I love theater. I love kids. I love that I'm here."

With a light step, balancing the box of librettos and my production book, I turn away and walk over to the Little Theater next door.

—ɯ—

Tangy Bollywood music greets me as I walk down the aisle towards the stage with the scripts. Center stage, next to a big, black 1990's Boom Box, gyrates a short, fleshy looking young woman attempting to do a belly dance. Maybe. I'm not certain. She wears her limp, blonde ponytail slightly askew, giving her the kooky appearance of a flailing ostrich. Her cropped tee shirt barely conceals her chubby belly, which is the color of pizza dough. It undulates in time to the blaring music, and my brain says: *Can't be.*

Lillette?

I mime a small "turn it down" motion with my hand as I plop my stuff on the edge of the stage. She skips forward, snaps the music off, then stands breathing heavily through her open mouth, hands on her ample hips.

"Hi," I say, looking up at her from the orchestra pit. "I'm Kelly Graham. Are you Lillette, the choreographer?"

*Please-say-no, please-say-no, I know it's mean but, please-say-no.*

Still unable to catch her breath, she smiles and nods her head.

"Oh, uh huh," I say, not missing a beat. "Nice to meet you."

She puts her hands to her chest and wheezes out, "I just started belly dance classes; it's trickier than you'd think!" Her bright blue eyes pop open wide.

I smile and nod. I hop onto the stage from the pit and go to shake her hand. It's warm and squishy as a lump of Play Doh.

"Jackson and Tony will be here any minute," I say. "Then we can start. We also have a student stage manager, but she won't be joining us today."

Lillette wipes the sweat from her upper lip with the back of her hand and flings it to her side. "Great," she says brightly.

Making friendly conversation I ask, "Where do you study dance, Lillette?"

"Oh, all over," she throws her arms around like she's swatting away a swarm of gnats. "'Delightful Dance,' 'Grand Jeté Junction'..." She gives me a big smile and points down at the floor. "The stage is my home."

She reaches up, splits her ponytail in two and tightens it with a tug. After giving it a satisfied little pat, she suddenly sweeps down to touch her toes. I watch as she dangles there for a second like an inert puppet, before she jerks herself back up and says, "Oh! Do you know 'Miss Tina's Tappers?' In Middlestone? That's where I got my start. I was only two when I started Tap there." She does a sloppy shuffle ball change and beams at me. "Ta-da!" she sings.

"Dancing at two years old, really?" I drawl. "At two, I think I was just perfecting walking."

They say sarcasm is lost on children, but luckily it's lost on an innocent like Lillette, too. My uncharitable tone goes right over her head.

"Yep, I was advanced for my age," she reassures me. "Always have been. Pre*cocious,* that's what my mother said." She taps out a spastic little rhythm, but stops abruptly. "That's nothing like pre*menstrual,* by the way; in case you thought they were related."

Oh snap. I give her a little half smile. Are we doomed here, or what?

Just then, Jackson and Tony enter the theater together–Tony on his cell, Jackson lugging a huge box. If my looks lean towards Keri Russell, Jackson's veer towards Harry Connick, Jr.: lanky and handsome, with a jaunty, laid-back vibe.

At the moment, though, Jackson is looking anything but relaxed. He's red-faced and sweaty as he struggles with what is obviously a very heavy box. Tony glides ahead of Jackson majestically like a king with his menial servant in tow.

As they approach, I say, "Jackson, Tony, I'd like you to meet our choreographer, Lillette."

Jackson drops the box on the edge of the stage with a crash, then, panting, offers his hand to Lillette. Lillette rushes forward and shakes back a quick, "Hihowyadoin'?"

Tony continues to talk on his cell, but holds up a finger and mouths, "Just a sec."

Lillette's eyes focus on Tony and she does what practically every other female does when they meet him: she melts. Her eyes slip to half-mast and her left hand begins twirling her skinny ponytail until it resembles a lasso. I watch with some embarrassment for her, as she openly stares hungrily down at Tony from the stage. She actually licks her lips.

Tony abruptly closes his cell, stuffs it into his shirt pocket and offers his hand up to Lillette.

"Sorry," he says warmly as they shake. "Tony Glynn."

Instead of letting go, Lillette holds on to his hand tightly and says breathily, "That's all right– I could see you were busy." She gives him a little curtsey and adds, "I'm Lillette Brewster." Her face, already pink from exertion, now deepens to a vibrant, glowing red, the exact color of a maraschino cherry.

Jackson and I exchange glances, and Jackson bats his eyes at me behind their backs.

Tony coughs and gives his best "aw shucks" smile and turns to Jackson. "Is that box too heavy for you? Did you want some help?"

Jackson blinks. His incredulous expression reads, *You mean you want to help me now? After I just put the damn thing down?* But he just wipes his brow and says coolly, "No; no, it's fine right here. It's just a bunch of props: caps for Fagin's boys, mugs for 'Oom-Pah-Pah,' bowls for the opening number, stuff like that. I'll store it later back in the pen."

The pen is a locked cage backstage stuffed with props and furniture from previous shows. Already crammed to the hilt, it's unfortunately our only option for storage at this point.

Disregarding what Jackson just said, Tony hefts himself onto the stage and hoists the box up onto his shoulder like Charles Atlas. Lillette practically swoons at Tony's unnecessary display of machismo. Then I notice that my husband's face has clouded over darkly, and his mouth is set in a grim line. I know he's annoyed that Tony just ignored what he said.

I call out hastily, "Uh, thanks, Tony, but you can put that box down, now. Jackson will get it after the production meeting."

"Nah," Tony grunts. "It's not heavy. I'll just take care of it now." He slips backstage like a mighty stallion, and we all stand there, frozen.

Ooh, if that wasn't just a bout of penis-sparring, then I don't what is. I've seen my brothers trying to one-up each other like this, and it isn't pretty.

I break the silence by asking Jackson, "Can you rip open this box for me and pass out the scripts?"

He grabs the box roughly off the stage and starts for the stairs. It's so silly that he's proving to us he can carry a big old box, too, but I don't say anything. Male vanity is a mysterious continent I'm not interested in exploring. If it restores Jackson's wounded pride to haul another box up a bunch of steps to show off his alpha position, who am I to interfere?

Tony returns, and we start the meeting by sitting cross-legged on the stage. As Jackson passes out the librettos, I can see him still trying to regain a little male dignity by thrusting the script at Tony aggressively. But Tony is completely oblivious. He's chatting with Lillette, who giggles deliriously over the good fortune to be seated so close to him. And look! Matching ponytails!

Although Lillette is not at all what I expected, and she is obviously on shaky ground with her dancing abilities, she's got a sweet, earnest quality about her that I decide then and there is good enough for me. I'll just back her up with a student dance captain if I need to, and I'm sure everything will be just fine.

I suddenly feel myself fill up with excitement. This happens every time I do a show. I am so thrilled to be sitting at our powwow discussing *Oliver!* If Lillette can claim the stage as her home, then I can, too. Ever since I was a little girl, I have loved two things in equal measure: teaching and performing. They are languages I was simply born understanding. I know just what to do, and I love teaching students how to do it, too. My brothers tease me to this day that as a kid I was bossy and demanding, but really, these are perfect qualities for a life in the theater.

Everything seems bright and hopeful again. Jackson seems to have licked his wounds and moved on, and Tony has deflated to a completely benign state. He's leaning towards Lillette, charming her by looking truly interested in hearing all about her belly dance classes.

To be honest, it's not Tony's fault he's so gorgeous. And Jackson shouldn't take it so personally that Tony was probably the strongest boy in gym class. And not to make a federal case about it, but it really *is* Tony's job to do the stage crew stuff.

With a stab of good will, I wonder if my feelings are wrong about Tony. We just need more time to get to know him better. My overactive imagination and tendency to overanalyze everything has gotten me into trouble before, so maybe I just imagined his earlier indifference. He doesn't seem indifferent to us *today*. In fact, I think he's maybe trying to assert himself as being a helpful guy. I'll try not to be so paranoid. (And Jackson should work on his jealousy issues.)

We get down to business– Jackson leading us through all the basics: dates and times for auditions and rehearsals, first read-through, budget for costumes, possible set designs. All goes smoothly.

But then...

"I'd like to sit in on auditions," Tony says when Jackson is through.

Jackson seems taken aback. Oh, shoot– here we go again.

But really, I'm kind of surprised, too. Tech crew usually has nothing to do with casting. That's the job of the directors.

"No, I don't think that will work, Tony," Jackson says in a firm voice. "Kelly and I will cast, and Amber will be in charge of sending the students up to the fourth floor in groups of..."

"It's just that I know these kids," Tony interrupts. "I could be of help."

"Yeah, I see your point," Jackson says equitably. "And thanks, but I don't think it's necessary."

I can tell when Jackson is trying to dismiss someone nicely, but Tony is not having it and keeps pushing. I settle back for round two of penis-sparring. En garde!

"It may not be necessary," Tony says tensely. "But I've got three years on you, Jack. My relationship with these kids and their parents predates you. I know who is capable of handling a role and who isn't."

Well. That's a little blunt. Direct. Aggressive. All of the above.

"That may be, Tony, but so do we," says Jackson. "We know a lot of the students from last semester, and I think we can find our way on our own. I have no doubts you'll be a great team leader with your stage crew students, but we don't need your help in an acting capacity. It's not your job. Okay, now Lillette..." Jackson turns his attention to Lillette, but I can see the fire rise in Tony's eyes. He's trying to hide it, but I can tell he's really pissed. He crosses his arms in front of his chest and stares down at the stage floor like a pouty little kid.

I agree with Jackson; what he says makes sense. Tony is out of line here. It's not his job to cast the show or have anything to do with the acting/directing part.

Jackson ties it all up, then reiterates that Lillette will meet us for callbacks on the second day to put the kids through a simple dance routine. Tony hops down off the stage and takes off with a sulky "so long"– the lobby door slamming behind him.

That's too bad, but there *is* a pecking order in the the-ater. The chain of command begins with the director, and it's everyone's job to represent the director's vision. Period. Period, period, exclamation point! Tony may not like it, but if he's a guy of the theater, he knows it's true. I mean, I can see that even Lillette, with her limited expertise, gets that. Because despite her...er, salt-of-the-earth personality, Lillette is truly enthusiastic and says she'll work out a dance combination to put the students through at callbacks.

But I wonder– how did she qualify for this job?

—ᨠ—

Jackson and I hang the audition sign-up sheet by "Announcement Wall" in the main building by the cafeteria, then make a mad dash through the bitter cold winds to the parking lot.

It's freezing out for March, and as we run across the lot, the wind steals my breath, and for a second I can't breathe.

"Start it, start it," I plead through chattering teeth, as we settle into the car.

When we're finally miles away, cruising towards our apartment, and the heat has thawed my mouth, I ask, "What did you think of Lillette?" No way am I bringing up Tony.

Jackson smirks.

"What?" I say.

"Were you surprised by the choice?"

"Yeeaah," I say as I pull off my hat, my curls springing merrily to life.

"Don't you know who she is?" he asks coyly.

"Stop baiting me, Jackson. Spill," I demand, turning in my seat to face him.

He continues smirking out the window.

"Who is she, Mr. Dramatic Silence? Tell me!"

With a sly, side-eyed glance he says, "That's the headmaster's niece."

"Really?" I say, taken by surprise. "Noooo way." I didn't see that one coming.

"Yup. So tread carefully, Frau Direktor," Jackson warns.

I lean my head back and consider this. Frowning, I ask, "Isn't that nepotism?"

Jackson lets out a snort and says, "Yes. But who, these days, doesn't partake? Everyone from politicians to people in the entertainment business work this way now. Headmaster Hank is the top dog at a *private* school. I really don't think it counts here. I imagine he can probably do anything he wants."

"I guess," I pause. "But I wonder why he didn't mention it to me?"

"Probably for that very reason," Jackson shrugs. "He doesn't want to *advertise* it."

"Then how did you find out?"

He wiggles his eyebrows and smiles, "I have my ways."

"Tell me, Jackson!"

—⟋⟍—

Turns out, Jackson happened to be in the Academy's main office the morning Headmaster Hank was on the phone with Lillette. Lillette was apparently begging to do the choreography, because Jackson overheard Headmaster Hank saying, "As your uncle, Lillette, I want to give you every opportunity, but I only know you from your dance recitals. Isn't choreography a specialized field requiring other skills?" Apparently he kept trying nicely to dissuade her, but after a long series of "uh huh, uh huh's," finally, browbeaten to a pulp, Headmaster Hank acquiesced.

Jackson said the funniest part was the comical way Lillette's voice came through the receiver so loudly.

"It sounded like that scrambled up chatter you hear when cartoon characters talk to each other on the phone. It was all garbled up, but you could hear the force of her inflections loud and clear. Everyone in the office couldn't help but hear it, too."

"Then why didn't you mention this to me earlier, Jackson? It would have been nice to have a warning."

"I was hoping she was just excessively passionate, the way Bob Fosse was or something. I didn't think someone with such limited talent would fight so hard for the job."

True. But I think Lillette may be a little blind in this department. Obviously no one has ever mentioned to her that this may not be the right career path for her. But actually, who am I to talk? I'm not even an actress anymore.

"Well, it all makes sense, now," I say. "I definitely see the family resemblance. It's hard to dismiss the fact that she has the same, uh, family, um...shape."

Jackson's mouth opens in mock shock. "Nasty, Mrs. Graham! Ooh, you're a nasty girl!" He reaches over and tries to poke me in the ribs.

"I said it nicely," I protest as I bat his hand away. "She happens to look *just* like Headmaster Hank, that's all."

"And she's very taken with Tony," Jackson says as he winks.

"Maybe we'll have a show romance blossom," I smile and flutter my eyelashes coquettishly.

"I don't think so," Jackson says, his face clouding over. "Isn't Tony married?"

"Is he?" I never noticed a wedding ring.

"Why does that surprise you?" Jackson says as he sweeps the car into our apartment complex.

"I don't know. I guess because his wife never came to see *Arsenic and Old Lace.* Or at least Tony didn't introduce us to her if she was there. He just seems like a loner, that's all."

I don't want to bring up all the weird underpinnings of hostile alpha-squabbling I saw between Jackson and Tony today, and it seems as though this conversation may veer into that direction. I'm glad we're home. I'll make a break for our door, and hopefully the subject will be dropped.

"Yeah, well, I'll find out about his marital status, if for no other reason than to save Lillette's virtue," Jackson says chivalrously.

"My hero!" I exclaim as the car comes to a rest in front of our apartment. I give him a big smile, then slip my hand under the door handle and brace myself for a blast of icy wind.

### 7pm, Home

Our garden apartment stands many towns away from Samuel P. Chester Academy, in a modest little village called Shoreview. In the miles we travel back and forth to the academy each day, Jackson and I watch the landscape change dramatically, from our town's tiny track homes snuggled together side-by-side, to the stately manors and hidden mansions of Harding Cove.

Once approaching Harding Cove, other than the silky paved roads that we drive along, all other signs of civilization disappear. Dense, dark woods flank either side of the road, held back by large stone walls covered with moss and ivy. Antique signs mark the crossroads with quaint names like, "Pebble Path" and "Stony Ridge Lane."

Like Hansel and Gretel making their way through an unknown forest, our journey through this splendor holds some Brothers Grimm anxiety for us as to what may lie ahead. I think this comes from sensing a lot of money and power holds this beauty captive and in its control.

Each time we leave the academy, while dazzled by the lush flora and fauna of that world, I feel more myself as traffic lights and 7-Elevens jump back into view. By the time we pull up here, into our humble little complex, I always feel myself breathing freer again.

I love our apartment. It suits us. And it's *ours*. When we first moved in, it came partially furnished with a stinky couch doused with Kool-Aid stains, and a beat up looking coffee table circa 1994. We supplemented the "Early American Welfare" look with a queen-sized mattress, thrown bohemian style on the floor. Two bamboo chairs, garbage-picked from our neighbor's curb, and a funky floor lamp from Kmart completed the post-college look.

But the coolest feature, and the one we were most taken with at the time, was the sliding glass doors that led out to the 8' X 8' slab of concrete that served as our patio. We loved that we could walk right out those doors and enjoy our own automatic, maintenance-free backyard. There was enough room for our essentials: a grill, two beach chairs, a cooler, and a rubber plant, now, unfortunately, "dead."

There was a weird improvement though, if you want to call it that, implemented by the woman who had the place before us. She ran a babysitting service out of the apartment, and had upgraded the floor to ceiling blinds that covered the sliding doors. Her idea of an "upgrade" was made entirely with the little kiddies in mind, because she chose the child-friendly, riotous primary colors of red, yellow and blue. It made the living room look like a clown jail. I honestly love those colors– just not all at once and in an alternating pattern!

We didn't care *too* much, though. As theater brats, we're used to bold theatrical statements, so we chose to see it as scenery left over from the previous production. And those were the early days, when we didn't let stuff like that really get to us. We were still distracted by the big, huge fact that we got to sleep together every night. Every night! We were so in love, it was a love fest– a love *feast.* We were all each other needed.

We have since updated the place, of course; the blinds are gone, the couch replaced, the bed tucked into a proper bed frame, but the coffee table remains. Repainted by me in a fit of creativity, I hand-lettered the quote, "Be yourself; everyone else is already taken" across the top. Oscar Wilde said that. I thought it would be the perfect whimsical reminder, (lest we forget!), as we munched on our microwaved frozen TV dinners and watched Judge Jenny.

A word about the food. I know it's not politically correct to be eating frozen food when the world's gone mad eating green and fresh, but food is secondary to us. I once heard someone say you either eat for pleasure or for survival. We both fall into the "survival eaters" category. Our interests lie elsewhere, mainly in our creativity. That's not to say there aren't chubby creative types, it's just that we are not all that interested in food to begin with. I make sure we eat lots of fruit and veggies, too, because they are the ultimate fast food. How easy is it to grab a couple of bananas and apples as we dash off to rehearsal?

In fact, we hardly ever have to shop for food. About once a month, we take a field trip over to our local big box supermarket and head straight for the frozen food aisles. Like trekking over to a favorite room in a museum, we are attracted to these aisles by the minimalist appearance of the uniform glass cases. It's all so modern and shiny and a bit surreal. Boxes and boxes of food stacked up on top of each other, wearing a photo of what's concealed inside. We know it's so unnatural that our choices are based entirely upon these glossy photographs of our hidden food-to-be, but we can't help ourselves. Jackson has pointed out that these pictures should be called "phony-phood-photos," because they are staged to exaggerated, glistening perfection. Of course the food never tastes as good as the phony-phood-photo advertises, but it's convenient for us. And sort of fun. So the snap shot wins!

Shopping is more like entertainment for us. We take our time, strolling leisurely up and down the remaining aisles, while Jackson serenades me with show tunes.

This is a holdover from his childhood, when his grandmother told him Robert Goulet, a Broadway actor, was discovered singing in a store. The seven-year-old Jackson took this to heart, and while checking out the Chips Ahoy in the cookie aisle, he'd sing softly in his little boy soprano. He said he always looked around to see what effect this was having, and was watchful for approaching agent types ready to offer him a part. Because he was only seven, he pictured those caricatures of agents he'd seen in cartoons: big-jawed guys chomping on cigars waving contracts from Ajax Agency. In reality, all he got was fond glances from mothers and giggles and snickers from kids his own age.

I don't even know if the story about Mr. Goulet's discovery is true or not. I suppose I could just search on Google to find my answer in 1.74 seconds, but I'm not ready to let go of the romantic aspects of the story. Not only for Mr. Goulet, but for Jackson, too. It's endearing to me that my husband believed such an old-fashioned story. To this day, when we push our silver cart up and down the wide aisles of the Super Stop and Shop, Jackson sings beautifully and with total sincerity. I guess he's still waiting for his big break. I hold little hope that we harbor some famous music agent in our scruffy little town of Shoreview, but who knows? Maybe. Because I honestly don't think Jackson or I will ever go back to the grind of pounding pavement again. We hated making the rounds, a.k.a. *auditioning*. The real job of the actor is, in reality, to audition. All the time. For the rest of your life.

For an actor's entire career, the way to get each new acting job is to audition again and again and again, year after year, job after job.

And here is another reality about this business that can't be ignored: in the professional world, you are typecast. Period. *And,* you are rejected from the majority of those auditions with no work on the horizon for months, even *years* at a time.

Sadly, the rejection probably has nothing to do with your talent. It's a subjective call, mixed in with trillions of other factors. Among them the fact that there are already way too many skilled actors, and maybe– too bad– the casting director was just looking for something else that day. They can afford to be picky, and look at one hundred, or a thousand actors if they choose. Because they'll get that many. They'll get *two* thousand actors lining up in the rain for a chance at a part. Look at *American Idol!*

I remember when our professors told us the grim statistics: barely 15% of actors in Equity (the stage union) work each year. And even then, very few can make an actual living at it.

While Jackson and I loved our acting training at the university, there weren't any classes offered to help us cope with this kind of tough living. We could have used a "Surviving Rejection" class, or even a "Learn-to-Love-That-Damn-Audition" class, now that I think about it.

I admit it: I detested auditioning. Like a strange and rushed one-night stand, afterward I was always left with a vague feeling of humiliation.

Let me demonstrate– here's how it went: I showered, dressed and arrived at the audition site– usually a creepy building/crappy studio/darkened theater. I waited patiently to be called with fifteen other girls who looked like a slight variation of myself, all holding identical portfolios full of headshots and resumes. When I was finally called, I was handed a script and had thirty seconds to try to understand what the director was looking for. Then I did my best– screamed, laughed, cried, emoted,– brought the character to life as I stood across from an indifferent stage manager reading opposite me in his junky frayed sweater. This self-same stage manager, would read the script in a bored monotone, and then, even then, when I *knew* I was brilliant, I was dismissed with the usual, "Thank you, next!"

As I made my way dejectedly back down to the street, I always felt a bit used and dirty.

Because if you are a true and talented artist, this construct is inherently debasing. Constantly putting yourself out there as this *product* is just really hard on the old ego. *You* are the commodity. It's hard to separate your work self from your self-self. And it's hard to keep picking yourself up, rejection after rejection.

Or maybe Jackson and I just felt this way. The quest for jobs had so little to do with our training and talent; it was grinding us down to dust. We'd learn we didn't get the part because of some arbitrary reason, like we were too tall, skinny, thin-lipped, pug-nosed, riotously curled, whatever. There's that typecast thing again.

We didn't want it anymore. I admit freely now that I wasn't cut out for it. It was too hard on both of us. The few jobs we did get barely paid a thing. Even Jackson's short stint on a soap opera didn't pay enough for him to quit his waiter job. We were already hungry, skinny and pale, and the mindless task of being on that wait staff was grating our souls to shreds. So when Jackson heard about an opening for directors to put on the plays at a local middle school, we sent in our resumes. Although we had BFAs in theater, we were still a little thin on experience. We snagged that first job, I think, on sheer enthusiasm. And maybe our credits as summer drama camp counselors didn't hurt either.

That's how we discovered our true calling. We both loved playing theater games and putting on shows with the kids. It was so rewarding to inspire them and then watch them grow.

I didn't miss auditioning, but I did miss acting. Still do. But then I discovered that in showing the students how to act, I got to act in snippets myself. It has become who we are now. It's all very gratifying, and it helps to be getting a paycheck for doing something we love.

We still have to supplement our job at Samuel P. Chester with our "day jobs," but luckily our day jobs no longer include being waiters. In fact, we really like our day jobs, now. Our friends, Lisa and Larry, hired us four years ago to work at their music shop right here in Shoreview. "Melodies" is a mellow, artsy kind of place that attracts musicians and mommies in equal measure. Larry knows his musical stuff cold, and Lisa provides that loving touch to the mommies for guiding their kids to the best music teachers around. The bulletin board by the front door is crammed with business cards from musicians of all types, and posters for local bands hyping their shows.

This is Jackson's true, laid back crowd, and I like it just fine, too. Mostly because Lisa and Larry have been so good to us. They're a little older than we are, having skated over the line into thirty already, so they like to guide us with their big sibs' advice.

They honestly go absolutely crazy when Jackson and I tell them some of the wacky stories about what it's like to work at a wealthy private school, so we try to keep it to a minimum. Because, believe me, they have very vocal opinions (usually negative) about Samuel P. Chester Academy. I have to admit, it's been a revelation to me, too, to see how the wealthiest among us operates, but some of the stories are so crazy they almost seem funny. I have to remind myself, as we go into this rehearsal process, to keep my sense of humor and pray it doesn't get too loopy again.

I wonder what's in store for us this semester?

Please, God– don't make it anything we can't handle!

Auditions tomorrow– three o'clock.

# March 5th
## 2:45pm
## Samuel P. Chester Academy
## Auditions

I pass the sign-up sheet to Jackson. It's filled with the scrawled names of the students spaced apart in ten-minute time slots.

"Nice turn out," Jackson says as he clicks on his piano light.

We're using a small stuffy practice room up on the fourth floor in the main building for the auditions while the piano in the theater gets tuned. Jackson places the sign-up sheet on top of the piano, then starts playing scales. They must have hauled this ancient piano up here seventy-five years ago and figured it was too much trouble to ever move again, so here we are. I sit down next to Jackson on the piano bench, lower my voice and lean close to his ear.

I murmur, "Do you know what just happened to me?"

"No," he says. "But you're going to turn me on if you whisper into my ear like that. Please try to control yourself, Mrs. Graham– we have auditions to get through first!"

"Ha, ha," I say as I nudge him good-naturedly. "You wish!"

I cross over to close the door, then lean my back against it as I say, "I was on the way up here, using that creepy back staircase as a short cut. You know, the one where the colony of mice was found?"

Jackson continues playing scales with one hand, but gestures with the other in a circular motion, as if to say, *Yeah, yeah, speed it up, speed it up.*

"Well, just as I got to the landing, Taffy's mother appeared."

"Our *student* Taffy, from *Arsenic and Old Lace?*" Jackson asks in confusion.

I pull a face. "Of course, Jackson. How many 'Taffy's' do you know?"

Jackson stops playing and looks at me. "What do you mean, her mother *appeared?*"

I walk back over to the piano and rest my arms on top. "Well, I mean it was *like* she appeared. She was sitting so quietly on the dark landing that I almost tripped over her. I was totally startled, but she just popped up and said, 'hi!' like she was waiting for me."

"Weird," Jackson says. "Kind of stalker-ish."

"Exactly!" I say. "Anyway, I just nodded hello back, and kept walking. She calls after me, 'Do you have a minute?' But before I can answer, she starts running up the next flight of stairs after me, trying to catch up."

Jackson turns his full attention on me and asks with concern, "What did she want?"

"I couldn't tell at first, because she was going on and on, bragging about Taffy and all the voice lessons and dance classes she's been taking since she was three, and about how talented everyone thinks she is. But then, finally she gets to it. She says, 'Taffy is a senior this year,' and I say, 'Uh huh.' So she says, 'And I hear you give the leads to the seniors; I heard that's your policy.'"

Jackson starts to shake his head. He's already figured out where this is going.

"Now the lightbulb goes off, and I brace myself. She says brazenly, 'So you'll give her a part, right?'"

Jackson snorts. "What did you say?"

"I was stunned for a second, but then I said brightly, 'Of course! Absolutely! I cast everyone.'"

Jackson laughs. "Good one!"

"I know, right? Technically we *do* cast everyone. I just didn't specify as a lead or not! But can you believe her nerve?"

"Kelly, she's a mother– it's not like we haven't seen this before. She's just going to bat for her kid."

"Are you kidding?" I bristle. "I would have *died* if my mother ever went up to my high school when I was seventeen and stalked my director to bid for a part."

"Did she offer you her body?" he asks as he cracks his knuckles.

"Eeeew, no! You pervert!" I slap him playfully on his arm.

"Then be glad that's all that happened, Kel." He begins plunking out "Three Blind Mice" with one finger.

"And did the mice nibble on your toes?"

"Cut it out, Jackson. No, they didn't. But I'm never using that short cut again. Way too creepy."

"Fine," he says, rifling through his stack of music. "But how did she know you'd go that way?" He plucks a song out and lines it up in front of him.

"I have no clue," I say. "Maybe she really *was* stalking me. It's a total mystery."

"Yeah, like why she named her daughter 'Taffy.'"

I start laughing.

"C'mon," he laughs back. "What was she thinking? Why would you name your kid after a sticky, cavity-inducing candy?"

Sensibly, I offer, "Because of its sweetness? People name their kids all sorts of food names nowadays: Apple, Clementine..."

"Honey," Jackson adds.

"Cookie."

"Cherry."

"Basil."

"Meat Loaf!"

"That's a nickname, Jackson."

"Yeah, but you know, what's next? Corn On The Cob?"

"Hey! 'Cob' is actually a cute name." I try it on for size. "Cob Graham. That's a cute name for a little boy."

"I don't think so, Kelly. Boys don't want cute names. If we're going with a food name for my son, I prefer a masculine name, like Haggis, or Anchovy. Mutton. Tabasco! Oh, wait! I've got it: Jam. Jam Graham."

"No way, Jackson!"

"Yeah, yeah, that's it," he insists mischievously. "And when he grows up, he can be in a rock band, and everyone can call him Jammin' Graham!" He bangs out a rhythmic beat with his hands on the side of the piano that sounds suspiciously like "Wipe Out." I guess Jammin' Graham is going to be a drummer.

I laugh and say, "I can't believe you'd curse your own son like that. You ought to know firsthand, Jackson; *you* have a food name. Didn't all the kids call you graham crackers?"

"That was a nickname, Kel."

I slide back next to him on the piano bench and throw my arms around his neck with abandon. "Can I have a nibble, Mister Graham Crackers?"

"Very unprofessional, Mrs. Graham. What if the children see?" He cups my face in his hands and kisses me softly on the lips. I feel a flash of desire rush through me, and I kiss him back passionately.

"Now we're back to where we started," he says hoarsely. "You're too much woman for me, Kel." He gives my butt a squeeze, and I jump off the bench with a yelp. He gives me that sexy look that melts my insides, and says rakishly, "Later. I promise."

He turns his attention back to the piano and attacks it with gusto. The musician's equivalent of a cold shower.

*Me, me,* I think to myself. *I want to be those keys.*

"Now go tell Amber she can start sending the kids up five at a time. We've got auditions to run!" he bellows as he bangs away on the keys.

"Okey-doke," I say as I walk on liquid knees to open the door.

"Oh, and Kelly?"

I turn back around.

"Yeah?"

"Don't send them up by the back staircase."

"Right," I smile.

—⚉—

"Hey, guys," Jackson greets our first five auditionee's personably. "Thanks for coming."

The students clump together at the doorway, but don't come in right away.

"Come on in, people, don't be shy; it's just us." He plays a bit of fanfare music to break the tension and they nervously file inside.

"Please hand your audition sheets to Mrs. Graham, then take a seat," he directs.

I reach out to take their sheets one by one, trying to make eye contact so I can give each of them a reassuring smile. The only one who avoids my gaze is a pretty girl who has an air of defiance about her. Could be nerves; we'll see. I know two of the kids in this group from *Arsenic and Old Lace,* but the other faces are new.

I peruse their audition sheets while Jackson continues giving instructions. "We need the entire sheet filled out, contact information and everything. Did everyone do that?"

They all nod mutely.

"All extracurricular activities and conflicts listed there?"

They nod again. Poor things. They look scared to death.

"The time commitment for *Oliver!* is for the next eight weeks. Rehearsals begin right after school at 3pm, starting this Monday, and go to 5:30pm. Evening rehearsals will begin two weeks prior to opening night," Jackson rattles off. "There are some Saturday rehearsals, to be announced. We don't need the entire cast present for every rehearsal."

While he's talking, the kids start to fidget; one kid bounces his leg up and down rapidly, another is zipping the locket she wears around her neck back and forth. A small girl with green eyes chews resolutely on a large wad of pink gum. It flashes around and around, appearing every now and then like clothes in a dryer.

"We cannot cast you in this musical if you are unable to attend rehearsal due to other activities. You guys get that, right? You can't be in two places at once, so if you're already committed to something else, that's fine, but we won't allow you to make yourselves crazy trying to please two teams, got it?" He smiles and they nod.

"Gum?" Jackson holds out a scrap of paper and hands it to the gum girl, who blushes as she crumples it up and quickly stuffs it in her pocket.

"Can I go first?" That's the pretty girl who may or may not have a defiant streak in her.

Jackson says, "Sure. What's your name, please?"

Pushing her long, brown hair off her shoulders, she says without smiling, "Delaney Barnes."

Says here on her audition sheet she's a junior, and played Kate in *Kiss Me Kate* as a sophomore. That means the director in charge last spring cast a sophomore as the lead. Like we said, we try to give the leads as often as possible to the seniors as it's their last shot before graduating. She did not audition for

*Arsenic and Old Lace,* so maybe she can sing, but can't act. I've never heard a word about her.

"I'll be singing Nancy's 'As Long As He Needs Me,'" she informs Jackson crisply.

Jackson shuffles through his music for a second, then says, "Okay, got it."

With her hand resting confidently on the piano, she nods at Jackson and proceeds to belt it out. The small room springs to life, saturated in the sound of her soaring voice. Like a pro, she bites her way, aches, keens and fights her way through a terribly difficult song. What a range of emotion and musicality for a teenager!

Jackson lets her sing the entire song– unheard of at an audition. But I think he's feeling just as amazed as I am. What a talent.

When she finishes, Jackson looks at her and says, "Good job, Delaney," and we all politely applaud. "Do you take voice lessons?"

She tips her nose in the air and says smugly, "Since I was seven."

The four other kids look like the wind has been knocked out of their sails.

But I'm wondering: why the conceited attitude?

Jackson turns briefly to make eye contact with me, then turns back to Delaney and asks, "Can you come back at three o'clock tomorrow for callbacks?"

She gathers up her purse and her backpack and says a short, barely audible, "Yes." No smile. No delight, joy, relief. No reaction whatsoever. She's taking it almost stoically.

Or is that the cool face of entitlement?

How can she show such a wide range of believable emotion while she sings, only to turn it off when she addresses us? Is she, *gasp*, giving us *attitude?*

I scribble my notes on the bottom of her audition sheet: "Possible Nancy. Amazing range. Acting ability?" Then I add and underline: "Possible trouble?"

I do not want to take on a prima donna.

"We'll see you then, Delaney," Jackson says as she moves to leave. I notice she casts a quick glance over her shoulder, but her hair conceals what I think might be hidden there: a smug smirk of superiority. I'm sure Jackson didn't see it.

He smiles and turns to the ashen-faced remaining students, sitting wilted on their chairs. Rubbing his hands together he asks enthusiastically, "Okay, who's next?"

**7:15pm**

"Last of the day," I report to Jackson. "Thomas is coming up by himself, and I sent Amber home." Thomas is this adorable kid who ended up in *Arsenic and Old Lace* because his sister dared him to try out. He started out so shy, but grew to be a really engaging performer and a leader for the cast.

"Excellent," Jackson says as he takes a deep pull on his water bottle. "Long day, but really good."

"Yeah," I agree. "But FYI Jackson, guess who was downstairs hanging out with the students as they waited to audition?"

"Who?"

"Tony."

Before he can say anything, Thomas enters room 404 with a boisterous, "'ello Guvner!"

Thomas now carries a natural confidence about him that is neither pushy nor arrogant. He's just this funny looking, quirky, happy kid. Skinny as a pencil, freckles splashed across his nose, there is a vitality to him fueled by great energy and charm. Without taking any credit for this, I do have to note he is a changed kid because he was in a play.

"'ello, Thomas," Jackson greets him with the latest handshake: a triple fist bump.

Thomas shoves a lock of his thick, brown hair off his forehead and asks, "Before I sing, can I read a poem I wrote?"

Jackson and I exchange glances. Our bemused expressions say, *why not?* We love it when students express themselves, so how can we say no– especially to a student who shows initiative?

"Sure, Thomas, that's fine," Jackson says. "But first tell me what you'll be singing for us today."

Thomas loosens his academy tie and says, "'Pick a Pocket or Two.' You know, for Fagin."

Jackson smiles indulgently, "Yes, I know."

Thomas rolls his eyes up to the ceiling. Grinning broadly he exclaims, "Doh! Yeah, yeah, I thought you may have heard of that one. But you know, just in case you hadn't, I turned into 'state-the-obvious-man!'" He thrusts his hands onto his hips and puffs his chest out like a comic book hero.

"Well, we appreciate that, Thomas." Jackson jokes along with him. "So I guess that makes me 'Play-the-notes-in-the-right-order man!'"

They both laugh and Jackson asks, "You okay with the key it's written in?"

Thomas gives him a salute, clicks his heels together, and bows. "Absolument, my liege."

How cute is this kid? I find myself hoping fervently that he can sing this part. I'd love to cast him as Fagin.

"Whenever you're ready," Jackson says.

Thomas turns his back to us, then shakes his hands several times to his sides. He makes a funny noise with his mouth that sounds something like "Wubbah wubbah wuh!" His skinny shoulders raise up to his ears as he takes a deep breath, then come back down slowly until he stands perfectly still in a neutral position. Without warning, he sweeps around and falls to his knees. Clasping his hands in a begging position, he says fervently,

"Please, dear Grahams,

Let me be in your play!
I'll do all that you ask,
And just as you say.
I can emote,
And enter on cue,
I'll sing the high notes,
And some really low, too.
I'll be no trouble,
I'll show up on time!
I'll try to grow stubble,
On this chin of mine.
I just gotta act;
I'm born to sing,
It's a point of fact,
'I'd Do Anything!'"

He springs to his feet and takes a sweeping bow. Jackson and I laugh and applaud delightedly while he continues to bow to the left and to the right, mopping his brow and blowing kisses to the invisible crowd.

"Thank you, Thomas, very clever," Jackson says. "We especially love it when students grovel! Now let's hear you sing. And..."

The poem is just icing on the cake, because Thomas opens his mouth and performs the song beautifully. He prances and mugs his way flamboyantly through the song, just as Fagin would. I'm so relieved! We have a Fagin.

"Thank you, Thomas, that was really good. Can you come back tomorrow after school for a callback?" I ask.

His face bursts into a smile the size of Rhode Island. "Yes! Yes, absolutely! I'll be there! I just have to be part of this show! Thank you, thank you so much for real."

"You're welcome. And Thomas, you needn't worry; we cast everyone," I say comfortingly.

"Oh, I know, I know," he says for the first time serious. "It's just that I don't do sports or anything, this is really it for me. It means *everything*. I'm committed one hundred percent." He looks so boyish and sincere, peeking through the shock of hair that keeps tumbling down his forehead into his eyes.

"We know you are, Thomas. We look forward to having you on board," Jackson says.

Thomas mimes tipping an invisible hat, gives a final hammy bow then scoots out the door calling impetuously, "Cheerio, I'll be back soon!"

I don't need to write a single note on his audition sheet other than two words: "Callback: Fagin."

### Home, Way Later

Jackson and I sit cross-legged on our living room floor eating Chinese food from their cartons. Spread out on the ratty carpeting before us, are the audition sheets of the kids we want to see tomorrow at callbacks.

"Pass me the noodles," Jackson says between slurps.

The auditions went just about as we imagined. Excited and nervous kids, cracked notes, a few tears. The usual highs and lows of how kids react under pressure when emotions are running high.

But we can easily cast all the parts in this show. We really don't have a *short* Oliver, so we went back and forth about using maybe one of the smaller girls. The part of Oliver should, ideally, be played by a small child, but at the high school level, you choose from what you've got. I think we'll go with this kid Blake. Although he's not short, he's got a slight build and a sweet innocence about him for a ninth grader. Coupled with his blond hair and soft, rounded cheeks– and the fact that I don't think Mr. Testosterone has begun making visits to his physique yet– I think he's our best bet. Casting a show is an art in and of itself– there are so many factors to weigh and figure in. We'll get a better idea tomorrow at callbacks when we see them all together, side-by-side.

Although many of them are involved in other sports and clubs, virtually all of them have scribbled notes across the bottom of their audition sheets, things like: "I'm absolutely committed," and "I'll be at every rehearsal!" But how can they be?

Most of them are already over-scheduled with other after-school activities, and blithely don't see this as a conflict. That may be due to the fact that the parents tried to set our rehearsal schedule last semester during *Arsenic and Old Lace* by asking us to accommodate their children's sports schedules. Here at Samuel P., it is expected that the students do *everything*. We disagree with that "philosophy," but as newbies, we actually tried to do as the parents wished and rehearsed the kids in shifts. But we absolutely can't do that this time. It made for a messy and disjointed rehearsal process, and was too hard on Jackson and me. We'll just have to make it absolutely clear what we expect commitment-wise.

I bring up my biggest question.

"Jackson, what's your take on Delaney?" I ask as I spear a dumpling.

"She's fantastic," he says through a mouthful of lo mien.

"Yeah, she can sing, but did you catch the attitude?"

He chews quietly for a moment, then says slowly, "Yeah; but what's your point? Her talent is undeniable." He leans his head back against the couch and says, "She'd make a perfect Nancy."

"So what do we do?"

"About what?"

"Well, a couple of things: one, she got the lead last year; isn't it unfair to give it to her again?"

Jackson puts down the lo mien and says, "We've had this discussion before Kel. You know we try our best to give the leads to seniors, but if there is someone who *obviously* outshines an upperclassman, I say we cast them. Why can't Delaney get the lead a couple of years in a row if she deserves it? You wouldn't let the best kid qualified to be quarterback sit on the bench. *She's* the quarterback."

"What about giving someone else a chance? This is education," I say reasonably.

"High school sports is education, too. You don't see the coaches dumbing down their sports programs to be equitable, do you? Every time they play, they play to win, so they put their strongest players in the top spots."

I see his point, but I'm feeling leery about casting this girl.

"How do you think this academy got its stellar sports reputation? I'll tell you how: they put their best people out on the front lines," Jackson says as he twirls his lo mein.

"But if there's another girl who could play Nancy, like Jasmine Hart," I persist, "then why not give her a chance? Jasmine's a senior. Delaney still has another year. Plus, Delaney will probably pursue this as a career. It wouldn't hurt her to learn some humility by being in the ensemble with a smaller part. We have to start reminding them, 'There are no small parts, only small actors.' I think she *especially* could learn from that lesson."

Jackson reaches for a plastic packet of soy sauce and tears it open with his teeth.

"But then you're opening another can of worms, Kel," he says. "You leave us open to criticism for *not* casting the most obviously talented kid we've seen. You'll definitely hear from her parents, and you'll probably hear from administration, too. It will make us look like we have bad judgment and are incapable of evaluating talent."

"Well I'm not a bad judge of *character*." I say imperiously. "And that brings me to my number two concern." We switch cartons, and I grab a little bag of duck sauce. "Jackson, I sense a major manipulator in Delaney. She asked to go first to show those other kids who was boss. Did you see their reactions?"

Jackson laughs, "Oh, yeah, it was obvious she was doing what the wolves do: pissing around the borders to mark her territory. But deservedly so, Kelly. You're not asking her to hide her gifts and not shine, are you?"

"No, of course not," I say quickly. "I know what it's like to be the most talented student in a high school theater program; that was me. But I wasn't as..."

"...competitive?" he says.

"No," I say pensively as I try to think of the right word. "*Devious.* She went in there to show the other students, 'Listen: don't even *think* about going out for the part of Nancy.'"

"She went in to win the part, Kelly!" Jackson laughs again. "You've got to applaud that initiative. They'd applaud it out on the AstroTurf! Look, Kel, I see your points, and if I were casting this for a professional company outside of Samuel P., maybe I'd choose someone with a better attitude. But this is high school. You don't *not* cast her because you suspect she's a bitch."

I poke around at the bright colored vegetables in my lo mien. Jackson doused this with too much soy sauce.

"She's really right for the part, Kel," he insists.

"Should I be worried that she may be a handful?"

"Nah," he says with bravado. "We can handle her. Who are the grown-ups in charge here?"

In case I'm unclear of the answer, he points his chopsticks emphatically at me, then directs them back at his chest.

"We'll just have to work a little harder to keep her in line and guide her, that's all." He smiles beguilingly at me as he coaxes, "Come on, Kel-Kel, let's face it; you're the best at that. The ultimate bossy, motherly-nurturing type."

I smile back, "It's the old sod in me. I come from very strong, matriarchal Irish stock."

"Ay, you with your wee little nose, missy," he says with a brogue.

"You making fun of my nose, Mr. Graham?" I counter like De Niro as I squint my eyes to look tough.

"Never," he says, moving in for a kiss.

"Jackson!" I nudge him away. "We have to concentrate. Focus! Now give me your top three students for each of the main characters."

And so we continue throughout the night.

# March 6th
## 3pm
## Samuel P. Chester Academy
## The Little Theater

Callbacks are a different animal than general auditions. Now that we have some specific notions in mind for how we want to cast the show, physically pairing up the kids today will allow us to see how they actually interact.

We're looking for that elusive quality we call chemistry. We're also looking for practical things, like how do they physically look together? For example, Nancy shouldn't be taller than the evil Bill Sykes; he should dominate her in both girth and stature. Even at the high school level, these things are important.

With the piano in the Little Theater now properly tuned, we are meeting here with the twenty students we've called back. Seated in the first two rows, the kids look nervous and itchy to start.

Lillette hasn't shown up yet, but Jackson, Amber and I stand before them, going over instructions.

"Congratulations, everyone, on making it this far," Jackson says as he jams his clipboard under one arm so he can applaud them. "We know you can sing, so today is about acting and dancing. We'll begin in a moment with some scene work, then your choreographer, Miss Brewster, will lead you in a few dance combinations."

I watch the boys give each other uneasy nudges and tense smiles.

Jackson looks down at his clipboard for a moment, then says, "Listen guys, I will give you only one piece of advice: Bring it." He spreads his arms wide and pauses, like he's waiting for someone to toss him a beach ball. "Come up here and command the stage. I'd rather see you play something too big than too small. I know you all have it in you; you're all just a big bunch of hams anyway," he grins.

They all titter and squirm a bit in their seats. I know first-hand how they all feel right now: their mouths are dry, their hearts are pounding– they have the urge to either perform, or run from the room. I don't want to keep them waiting, but feel I have to add this:

"If there is nothing else we teach you about acting, let it be this: acting is what takes place here." I indicate the open space between Jackson and me. "Acting is what takes place *between* actors. So really listen to one another, and react to your scene partner. Don't just be a talking head waiting to say your next line. Got it?"

They all nod solemnly.

"Good. Any questions?"

Silence. I am so proud that they are all taking this so seriously. I also know it's fear that's gluing their mouths shut; they'll never be this attentive and quiet again!

Still no Lillette. I check my watch.

Jackson crosses over to me and whispers, "Where's our girl?"

I shrug and turn to Amber and say, "Can you please call Miss Brewster for me? You can use my cell."

Once we begin, callbacks go smoothly, and we even have some fun as they start to loosen up. The kids from *Arsenic and Old Lace* are used to our ways, and luckily the other kids fall in line and follow their lead.

We do have two resisters, though: a broody-looking kid named Forrest, and our little Miss Delaney. We haven't worked with either of them, and I have my reservations about casting them at all. This will never fly with Jackson, not after our chat last night, but I see both of them leading the others in a bad way. This kid Forrest in particular seems like a loose cannon. He's not a super tall kid, but he's got a beefy, football body-build with arms that look like he pumps iron or something. He looks the most mannish of all the students, but I don't know. The whiff of danger about him unsettles me. I sense a real bully. He'd be perfect for Bill Sykes because he has an actual sinister quality– good for on stage, but scary-creepy in real life. The problem is, he's exhibiting some real talent– in that James Dean rebel sort of way. He gave a really solid audition, but I don't know if we should take the chance.

And Delaney is not mixing in with the group. It's like she sees herself as above everyone else, and only engages when she gets up to perform. Then she flicks on some inner switch and blows us all away. What to do? I'm sure Jackson and I will go over all this tonight when we finalize our cast list; I just hope he'll really listen to me.

Lillette has never surfaced. Amber called her repeatedly, but was put through to voice mail every time.

Just as I'm starting to think something really bad must have happened, and I'm wondering what the consequences will be of not having the dance portion of callbacks take place, she arrives.

Tripping down the aisle, dropping her cell phone, then her scarf, she jabbers, "I'm sorry I'm late, did you start without me? I was up until the early morning hours coming up with the cutest little combination to teach the kiddies, but it turns out I left my headlights on last night, so when I went to start the car today, it was as dead as a corpse."

As she hurriedly leans forward to retrieve her cell, her purse tips and its contents come tumbling out. Standing up abruptly to make a frantic dash to collect various tubes of lipsticks and lotions now scattered and rolling helter-skelter down the aisle, she becomes tangled in her scarf and falls backward onto her butt with a thump. The script and various loose papers she has been holding in her hand fly up in a whoosh, then slowly flutter down around her. She sits in the center of the heap like a strange bird perched in her peculiar nest. Giving us all a surprised look with those huge, bulging blue eyes, she takes a mad swipe at her bangs and says, "Whew!"

The students laugh like this was a planned performance just for them. Who doesn't love a clown? Amber rushes over to assist her, and Lillette looks up at her with gratitude.

Clawing at Amber's tiny frame, she tries to climb her way back onto her feet.

"Thank you, Amber," I say. "Everyone, please give it up for the woman who really knows how to make an entrance– this is Miss Brewster, your choreographer."

The students give her some lively applause, with Erik and Blake whooping it up with some of those two fingered whistles that all the gym teachers know how to do.

Lillette limps down the aisle on Amber's arm, and when she's still a good three rows away from us, stage whispers out of the side of her mouth: "I think I twisted my ankle!"

—◆—

Despite the Lillette fiasco, and despite my concerns about Forrest and Delaney in lead roles, at 1:15am, we finish casting this show.

No, Miss Courtroom Jester did not sprain her ankle, but we appointed Marta to be student dance captain to back her up anyway. Together, they got us through a brief and "good enough" dance audition. Most of the girls can move, having been placed into dance schools practically at birth, so I'm not worried about choreography.

But, I *am* completely worried about what we may face with Forrest and Delaney. We have cast them as two of the leads: Bill Sykes and Nancy.

Are we out of our minds, or what?

## HOW TO
## POST A CAST LIST:

1.) Post it at 2:20pm on Friday, just before dismissal.

2.) Run like crazy to your car.

3.) Do not look back.

4.) Drive safely, but purposefully off school grounds.

5.) Do not go directly home. In fact, go away for the weekend. Take the phone off the hook. If you don't, it will begin to ring incessantly for the next two days, disturbing your neighbors, making all the dogs bark, and giving you your first migraine.

6.) Home computer. Turn it off. Expect a flooded e-mail box filled with irate messages from disgruntled parents come Monday morning.

7.) Brace yourself. Monday morning will come sooner that you think.

### *Oliver!* Cast List:

| | |
|---|---|
| Oliver | Blake Anderson |
| Fagin | Thomas Cannon |

| | |
|---|---|
| Nancy | Delaney Barnes |
| Bill Sykes | Forrest Keller |
| Mr. Bumble | Shane Cooper |
| Widow Corney | Jasmine Hart |
| Artful Dodger | Christian Morrow |
| Charley Bates | Grant Stillwell |
| Mr. Sowerberry | Duncan Greenway |
| Mrs. Sowerberry | Sienna Travers |
| Charlotte Sowerberry | Taffy Dollinger |
| Noah Claypole | Erik Kirkland |
| Bet | Noelle Pratt |
| Mr. Brownlow | Hamilton Conrad 111 |
| Mrs. Bedwin | Liana Stadtlander |
| Dr. Grimwig | Ryan Newman |
| Old Sally | Daisy Brady |

<u>Orphans/Fagin's Boys:</u>
Marta Reynolds, Tiana Aboff, Sawyer Bedell, Misty
Jensen, Julie Eng, Michael Glover, Casey Harrington
<u>Chorus:</u>
Christine Waldner, Shea LeBlanc, Henry Jasper Jones,
Roxy Parsons, Dominique Marks, Chloe Chung, Holly
Kellogg, Kristy Welles, Tristan Henderson, Tucker Oehl
Please initial by your name.
See you next week!
Monday: 3pm to 5:30pm,
The Little Theater: FULL CAST
Congratulations to all!
– Mr. and Mrs. Graham,
Directors of *Oliver!*

# March 10th
## 8am
## Home
## Fallout

"**H**eads up. Just passing these on..." reads the subject line on the headmaster's e-mail.

He has forwarded us the fallout, with instructions not to be concerned, as it happens every year.

The first one, in part, reads:

*"My daughter is always overlooked for a good part. She sings like a bird, and was recently complimented by my entire extended family for singing beautifully at her grandmother's birthday party. She is devastated to be left out of a good role again. Why do the same people get the leads year after year? What criterion is used to determine who has talent and who doesn't? I believe this bears looking in to..."*

And this one:

*"My child was told he cannot participate in any other activities while rehearsing for the school musical. It's been proven that exposing children to many different disciplines can only be beneficial. I want him to play lacrosse and be in the play. Why can't he have it all? Why won't the directors be flexible and work around existing schedules?"*

There's more:

*"We are disappointed with the outcome of the Oliver! casting. We heard a boy recited a poem he wrote for his audition, then wound up*

*getting the lead. How is that fair to allow one child to perform some-*
*thing extra, when the other children didn't get a chance to do the same?*
*Our son said all he was required to do was sing a song from the play.*
*It didn't say anything about..."*

And finally:

*"We reviewed our daughter's part in the play, and it seems she's*
*mostly just in the chorus, with only a couple of lines. She doesn't seem*
*to have much of a role, and we wonder if we will allow her to continue.*
*We were hoping this would be an enriching experience, but think now*
*she is not being properly rewarded..."*

Jackson is annoyed and wants to respond by issuing a statement.

"Why bother?" I ask. "I doubt they'll be receptive. You can't really be reasonable with disgruntled parents. Just let it blow over." I shake a bottle of Magenta Swirl nail polish, my wrist snapping smartly up and down.

"No," he grumbles, as he stares at his screen. "If we don't set the tone and address this now, they'll keep at us. We got a bitter taste of this last semester, Kelly, so I'm not waiting and being Mr. Nice Guy anymore. This time, I'm all over it."

"It's not going to woooork," I singsong as I carefully brush glistening layers of polish onto my toenails.

"If they don't want to teach their kids about sour grapes and learning to be happy with what they get, then I'm glad to do it for them," he says.

"The old 'you get what you get and you don't get upset' mantra from preschool, huh?"

"Correct-o-rama." He begins typing furiously and we're silent for a moment.

I *do* remember, all too well, how demanding the parents were last semester. We were doing a fine job directing the kids but the parents began showing up at rehearsals, trying to dictate how things should be done. Strangely, they tried everything from bossing us around about the costumes, to telling us how their kids should be mic'd. We had to walk that fine line between keeping the peace, yet asserting our positions. It got pretty tense towards the end of *Arsenic and Old Lace,* but the headmaster says he'll run interference for us this time. He had warned us that the parents could get a little carried away, but we're still holding out hope that this time will be different.

"You know Jackson, I've given this a lot of thought. And I think at the heart of it, these parents are just disappointed. They're sad. It's human nature."

Jackson stops and looks over at me. "How can you be so compassionate?" he says irritably. "Compassion is not called for here."

"Because I truly understand what it's like to feel left out. I think that's all it comes down to. They're just blinded by their love for their kids. I'm sure they honestly think they're doing the right thing."

"No they're not, Kelly. They're whining, 'What about *my* kid?' Can't they see the student we chose is *worthy*? And it's our call. Period."

I open my mouth to respond, but Jackson is on a roll.

"Do they go to the *coaches* with their so-called complaints?" he rails.

"I don't know, probably," I say, giving the bottle another shake. I think half the time I re-shake my nail polish just to hear the bright, rhythmic rattle of the little ball inside.

"And how can they expect their child to be fully committed to two extracurricular activities and not compromise one or the other, or *both*?"

He's all worked up, and when he's all worked up, he doesn't listen to anything other than the arguments spinning around in his brain.

I say as breezily as I can muster, "Don't let this stuff ruin it for you, Jackson. It has *nothing* to do with directing the play. Soon enough their kids will be running home, bursting with excitement from all the fun they're having at rehearsal with us."

"I know that," Jackson scowls. "But Kelly, we've always been straightforward: we are an ensemble, period. We give every kid *lots* of opportunities to grow and shine. I'm nipping this in the bud." He goes back to typing, then says distractedly, "Kel, could you please crack a window; that stuff stinks."

### 2pm, Main Office

In the end, Jackson typed up a simple statement and now I'm photocopying it onto the official Samuel P. Chester Academy letterhead.

While I'm making copies, listening to the rhythmic sounds of the copier snapping paper through its system, a thought flutters through my mind: how did some parent know that Thomas read a poem? Did Thomas tell any other students about it when he was waiting to audition?

Then I remember that Tony was with Thomas the night of his audition. Did Thomas mention it to Tony? I would guess he probably did. Maybe he even recited it for Tony.

The copier makes a strangled noise, and I know it's jammed. Choking on a slice of paper, it wheezes to a halt. As I remove the offending piece, I'm lulled back into my musing. I wonder if maybe Tony could be a troublemaker. It's the first time this thought has occurred to me, but what if it was Tony that stirred the pot and let the parents know about Thomas's poem? The implications are sort of creepy to think about.

The copier stops again, without distress this time, and I'm kind of glad the job is done. I don't want to dwell on what it could mean if Tony would do such a thing.

I tap the stack of pages into order and smooth my hand over the top sheet. The words look so organized and official on the academy stationery. Typing always gives words that extra credibility. I feel bolstered by the official-ness of it all.

Jackson's message reads:

"Congratulations to the cast of *Oliver!* It's great to have each and every one of you on board. We look forward to having a wonderful time working with you on this production. Everyone plays an integral part in its success, so let's support each other and remember what we say in the professional theater: 'There are no small parts, only small actors.' To paraphrase Tom Hanks' character in *A League of their Own*: there is no whining in theater! Be grateful for how you were cast, and do your best."

We'll pass these out during our first rehearsal later, and then, as Jackson said, "See how it lands." Hopefully, that's the end of it!

**3pm, The Little Theater**

"Circle up!" Jackson calls from center stage, his cupped hands shaped like parenthesis around his mouth. "We begin promptly at three, so let's get a move on!"

Milling about below him, thirty-four students, some still texting on their cell phones, some lost in idle conversations, gradually make their way to the stairs that flank each side of the stage. The orchestra pit is jammed with metal music stands, but some kids scoot around them and try to heft themselves onto the stage. Jackson sees what's going on and walks to the edge of the apron, shakes his head "no" and points to the stairs.

I sit cross-legged on the apron, fumbling with the ancient Boom Box Lillette is lending us. I'm trying to cue up an original cast recording of *Oliver!* to play during our read-through.

Amber approaches me timidly and kneels down beside me. In a small voice she says, "Mrs. Graham? I don't know a lot of these kids. I don't know who's who, so I can't give out the scripts and flyers like you asked." She indicates the stack of scripts and the photocopied "statement" flyer she's balancing on her knees.

"Oh, okay," I say. "Marta!"

Marta hurries over. Everything about her is ethereal– from her delicate face, framed with thin, ash blonde hair, to her long, slender body, dressed in a gauzy top with yoga pants. She is a person who lives in service of her body's movements.

I ask her to help Amber pass out the scripts. She looks around and asks, "Who's Amber?"

Amber all but curls up by my side with embarrassment as I point to her. But Marta gives Amber a genuine smile and extends a hand to help her to her feet. Amber seems a little surprised, and gives a delighted little smile back as Marta pulls her up. Sweet.

Jackson addresses the sea of faces in the circle with announcements: "Congratulations to all of you. We are so excited to have such a wonderful cast."

Everyone looks around and applauds loudly.

"We start promptly at three o'clock. That's plenty of time after dismissal to get to your locker, change out of your uniform, and get over here by three. If you're going to be late, or absent, you must contact us via e-mail or phone. Contact information is on the flyer Marta and Amber are passing out. When you get here, first thing you do is sign the attendance sheet. The sheet will be set up on a music stand stage right."

A hand shoots up. Duncan.

"Which is stage right, and which is stage left?" he asks.

Some seasoned performers titter, but Jackson says, "Good question, Duncan. For all of you who don't already know, here's how you remember. Christian, would you please stand center stage and look out at the audience?"

Christian smiles and walks to the center of the circle. He's a super nice kid who wears his uniform shirt untucked, and his academy tie loosened from his neck.

"Christian! Christian!" Forrest yells, and the guys sitting next to him join in with hoots and catcalls.

Jackson instructs, "Stage right and stage left are always from the actor's point of view, facing the audience. So where is stage right, Christian?"

Christian points correctly, to his right, then abruptly points to his left and says charmingly, "Ha ha, just kidding," and points back to his right.

Jackson smiles and says, "Weisenheimer. Correct. So where is stage left?"

Christian spins on his heel and points to his left, then takes a stiff and proper bow, like a maitre d'.

"Excellent. Duncan, do you understand now?"

Duncan nods, but his hand is creeping back up again.

"Another question, Duncan?"

"Duuh," I hear Forrest whisper. "It's Duh-Duncan!"

I shoot him a warning look.

"Yeah, but it's related to my first question, Mr. Graham. Where are down stage and up stage?" His eyes are looking up into the rafters above the stage as he rubs the top of his sandy brown hair.

"Duncan, we'll get to stage directions soon enough, but since you brought it up..."

Jasmine jumps up, "I can demonstrate!" she says vivaciously. She skips forward and deftly lands with a hop center stage. "*This* is center stage," she says with a rich, full voice. Dang. She would have made a fine Nancy.

"Duh. We got that one, Jazz," Forrest calls out obnoxiously.

I get up from where I'm sitting and go around to stand behind Forrest. He sees me approaching and flips his hood onto his head.

Jasmine disregards him. As she walks forward towards the audience, she says, "See? As I walk towards the apron, it's called moving *down stage*. That's because the first theaters had raked stages. They were highest at the back of the stage, and curved down towards the front."

She turns quickly, so her back is now to the audience. She does an exaggerated march towards the back wall of the stage. "Now I'm going *upstage*. See, Duncan?" She calls over her shoulder. "Upstage is the part of the stage *farthest* from the audience." She runs back to take her place back in the circle, but sweeps by Forrest first and curls her lip in a snarl at him. He growls back at her, so I place my hand on the top of his head. He stops.

"Thank you, Jasmine. Okay," Jackson continues. "Today we'll be doing a read-through of act one."

Amber and Marta are done handing out the scripts and have joined us back in the circle.

"Let's get to know each other first. We'll go around the circle, beginning with Thomas. Please say your name and what part you are playing."

We begin with Thomas and end with Amber. As all eyes rest on her, though, she freezes up and I can tell she is really uncomfortable. She looks at me desperately, but before I can even open my mouth, Marta has come to her rescue. Throwing a friendly arm around her shoulders, Marta announces, "This is Amber, our stage manager."

Marta looks fondly at Amber and I say, "Thank you, Marta." Amber looks around nervously, but manages to smile a little all the same.

I continue, saying, "Amber is pretty much my right arm. So when she gives you an instruction, please listen to her and be respectful. In the theater, when the stage manager announces a break, they'll say, 'Everyone, take five.' Your response back would be, 'Thank you, five.' It's part of theater etiquette; an acknowledgment you heard the instruction. Everyone got it?"

"Thank you, got it!" pipes up Sienna.

I smile over to her and everyone laughs.

"Okay, are we ready? We're going to read-through the entire play today. Amber will play the songs from the original cast recording. Everyone ready?"

The kids shuffle their scripts and settle in next to each other.

"Okay, then from the top of act one..."

I nod to Amber, who reaches over to press "play."

# March 13th
## 3pm
# The Little Theater

A bunch of kids surround the piano in the pit. The music stands have been cleared, so there's plenty of space down there now. Jackson teaches the kids the songs over there, while I work on the stage itself, blocking the scenes.

They're learning the opening song, "Food, Glorious, Food," and I'm getting ready to call up cast members in Sowerberry's Funeral Parlor. In just the few days we've been rehearsing, we've accomplished a lot. I credit Jackson for this, as he's the one who came up with "the formula."

"The formula" is how he breaks down how much material we need to cover at each rehearsal so we finish on time. It's like a big math problem (shudder): when we first get the script, we work backward from opening night. We know where we need to end up by April 25th, so we break the script down into blocks of time to address staging and rehearsing each part. We have never slid into Tech Week without having the cast well-rehearsed and ready to go. So!

Amber and I kneel on the floor stage left, figuring out where the couch will sit in this next scene, so we can mark out that space with gaffer's tape.

From my vantage point on the stage, I can see Sienna, Duncan, Taffy, Blake and Erik sitting out in the audience– faces illuminated by the blue-gray light of their cell phones. It looks like a scene out of a sci-fi horror movie: innocent kids, jaws hanging slack, industriously, no, *fervently*– pressing on their hand-held devices. It's as though aliens have gained control of their brains through the tiny, lit monitors, and have forced them to sit, hunched like the elderly, furiously tapping out messages of the gravest importance: "lol", "idk", "l8r", "brb". No doubt this complex and mysterious code was created by a tenacious and resourceful race of the sub-world: teenagers!

What they're really doing of course, is keeping in touch *incessantly* with each other by communicating via text messages. They can be sitting right next to each other, but instead of talking, they text. Kind of how we used to pass notes in class, and probably with the same trivial content.

It's so weird. The other day, when I asked Amber to call Delaney on stage, instead of yelling, "Delaney on stage," she pulled out her cell phone and tickety-tap-tapped a quick message to Delaney. Then Delaney, seated maybe twenty yards away at the back of the theater, checked her vibrating cell and rose from her seat. Seconds later, she bounded up the stairs and took her place on stage. Message received, vocal chords undisturbed, human interaction sidestepped.

When I made an announcement after that incident– that we'd just keep doing it the old-fashioned way by *talking* to each other– they looked at me as if *I* were the alien!

Amber and I are almost done marking out the floor when Sienna comes skipping up to the apron of the stage.

"I started memorizing my lines, Mrs. Graham," she reports smartly.

"Come around," I say, pointing to the staircase. Sienna is a cute, chubbyish girl, who religiously wears several rubber bracelets in assorted colors jumbled on her wrist.

I can tell she feels proud of herself, so I smile back as she makes her way up. "That's great, Sienna! You may find that after rehearsal today it's even easier to memorize them. Remember when we did *Arsenic and Old Lace,* how fast you got your lines down after repeating the scene over and over? The same thing will happen here. You may find you have them down cold by dismissal."

"Epic!" she says, "I can't wait! I love to act, Mrs. Graham!"

"I know, Sienna, it really shows. You did such a good job in *Arsenic and Old Lace* I'm so glad you're part of *this* show, too."

She claps her hands rapidly together and asks, "When are we starting?"

I indicate the floor covered in tape and say, "In just a few; as soon as we're done with this."

"Okay!" she says, then turns around and calls out, "Taffy! Hey, Taffeta! We start in, like, five."

Taffy tears her eyes away from her cell screen, looks up at us and nods.

"Taffeta– what a cute nickname for Taffy," I say to Sienna.

She turns back and says, "It's the other way around, Mrs. Graham."

"How do you mean?"

"'Taffy' is a nickname for 'Taffeta.'"

"You mean her real name is Taffeta? Like the fabric?"

"Uh huh. You didn't know that? Her mom used to be a fashion designer until she had kids."

"Kids? Taffy has a sister?"

"Brother."

"Oh," I say. "What's his name?"

And then I wait for it. Almost squeezing my eyes shut in anticipation– what will it be? "Corduroy"– Roy, maybe for short; or "Brody" after "Brocade?"

"Denim. Denim Blue," she answers.

I double over, laughing. Amber stops taping and looks up to join me with a shy smile and then a giggle. But Sienna looks like I've personally insulted her.

Quickly, I try to cover. "What a great name, Sienna. What a clever family. Um, you guys can come on up now. Let's start your scene."

Sienna gives me a brief, tolerant little smile then hops back down from the stage into the orchestra pit.

"Use the stairs!" I call out after her, but she is already down the aisle. My shoulders still shake with the laughter I'm trying to contain. Jackson looks up from the piano, smiles and mouths, "Why are you laughing?" I shake my head and call out, "Tell you later!"

—ɯ—

After an hour, we need a break. I turn to Amber and say, "Amber, give them fifteen, please."

"Take fifteen, everyone," Amber calls out meekly.

"Thank you fifteen," some answer back. I don't think everyone heard.

I shout out, "Your stage manager has called for a fifteen minute break everyone. How do you respond?" I hold my hand to my ear and lean forward, indicating I am awaiting their answer.

"THANK YOU, FIFTEEN," they heartily yell back.

"Excellent." I turn to Amber, who is shrinking by my side. "Nice big voice, next time, Amber. Don't be afraid to take charge." I drop my voice and say, "I'll let you in on a little secret that all actors know– it feels really good to use a booming voice.

It's like having *permission* to let out the really loud part of yourself. I think you have it in you, so I totally give you my permission to let it out." I smile and she ducks her head and smiles back.

"Go take a break," I say warmly.

She puts her ever-present promptbook on the floor and carefully places her pencil on top. She hovers her palm over it for a second to be sure it doesn't roll off, like a magician holding it in some invisible force field. Satisfied, she says, "Be right back," and waves a bashful goodbye.

Jackson comes over and says, "What were you and Amber laughing about earlier?"

"Oh, Jackson, the cutest thing!" I say as I pull him by his arm into the wings. I lead him semi-blindly backstage behind the curtain for a moment of privacy.

It's dark back there, but there's enough light for me to spy a wooden stool. I sit on it as I tell him, "Sienna told me that Taffy's real name is *Taffeta,* you know, like the fabric?"

"Yeah?" he says. "So?"

"So she wasn't named after a *candy,* like we thought. She was named after a *fabric.* The mom is a fashion designer." I pause. "There's a brother." I arch my eyebrows and ask pointedly. "So what's *his* name?"

I see the lightbulb go off in his head. He waves his hands wildly and says, "No, no, no, wait, don't tell me!"

I'm bursting inside, but I wait as he thinks.

"Terry!" he blurts out.

"Terry?"

"For terry cloth?"

"That stinks, Jackson. And it's a 'no.' Try again."

He scratches his ear, something he does on occasion when he's trying to figure something out. "I can only think of girlie sounding fabric names: Gingham, Lace, Velvet."

"Yeah, if she's a porn star!"

"Oooh, wait," he says again. "I don't know if this is right, but, Camouflage?"

"It's not camouflage."

"Man! But wouldn't that make a great name?" he says.

"Not as good as Denim Blue," I say gleefully.

He laughs. "You're kidding. Is it really Denim Blue?"

I nod, and we laugh together. Placing my hands in his I ask, "How's rehearsal going for you today, Mr. Graham?"

He pulls me up from the stool and says, "Good, good, Mrs. Graham; they're picking it up easily." We switch places by doing a quick do-si-do and Jackson settles me onto his lap.

"Jackson, no," I say.

"We're just sharing a seat," he says innocently as he tries to kiss me.

I put my hand over his mouth and say, "Do not get me fired up, Jackson. I think I'm ovulating, so you're all I'm thinking about anyway."

He peels my hand away and gently takes little bites along the side of my palm. "Then I have to have a smooch," he says seductively. "I can tell by your breath when you're ovulating. It gets real sweet when you're tossing out your eggs."

Before I can protest, his warm mouth is on mine and a zing of desire flashes through me. Jackson slips his hands under my sweater and they slide easily up my back. I feel his fingers slowly moving around to my belly and with a sharp intake of breath, I wait for the shivery feeling of anticipation that grips me as he reaches for my breasts.

"PLACES IN FIVE!" Amber's voice booms through the entire theater loud and clear.

I leap off Jackson's lap in a flash and pull my shirt down. We both look at each other and start cracking up nervously.

I push my hair from my face and whisper, "I'm sure they heard that in Poland!"

"THANK YOU, FIVE!" A chorus of voices shouts back.

Jackson smiles as I pull him to his feet and say, "That Amber; I *knew* she had it in her!"

**Later, After rehearsal**

Lillette, Marta, Amber and I are sitting cross-legged on the stage having a meeting about the choreography.

"'Oom Pah Pah' opens act two in the tavern," I say. "It's done in three-quarter time; a waltz rhythm. Are you familiar with the song yet?"

Lillette, who I thought was paying attention, just looks blankly at me.

"Lillette?"

"Yes?"

"Are you familiar with the song yet?"

"Me? No!" She scrunches up her face like she's smelling rotten garbage. "I gave that one to Marta."

Marta looks surprised and says, "Um, Miss Brewster?"

Lillette swings her head over to Marta and plunks her chin into her hand, "Yes, Dearie?"

"You didn't tell me you wanted me to do the choreography for 'Oom Pah Pah.'"

Lillette looks startled. "I didn't?" She narrows her eyes and leans towards Marta like she's swooping in to make a microscopic inspection. "Are you sure?"

Marta looks embarrassed as she nods her head.

"Hmm..." says Lillette, placing her forefinger to her lips. "Now let me think."

She looks like an absent-minded professor, with her fluffy blonde ponytail forming an electrified puff on the very top of her head, and her spacey eyes darting around like she's searching for the answer in thin air.

"Wait!" she cries exuberantly as she throws her arms over her head. "I've got it! My note!"

She reaches down and starts to take off her shoes, explaining as she goes, "I put my dance shoes in color order every night. See? Today is Thursday, so I'm wearing blue."

We all look at her shoes. They are, indeed, blue.

"I leave little notes inside them to remind me what to do the next day. It's all very organized. I made it up!"

We all smile and nod. What else can we do?

"For example," she chatters on, "if it's Sunday, I check inside my *red* shoes for my messages. ROYGBIV, right?" She pronounces it "roy-gee-bihv", just like we learned in kindergarten.

"So Sunday is *red*, Monday is *orange*, Tuesday is *yellow*, etcetera, etcetera, get it?"

We all nod, fascinated.

"But *last* week I went off my schedule and wore my *blue* shoes on Saturday, and my *violet* shoes on Thursday, and it obviously messed me up!"

Obviously!

"But see, here it is!" she cries joyfully.

She pulls a damp looking piece of paper from the bottom of her shoe and unfolds it carefully.

"Give Marta 'Oom Pah Pah,' says it right here!" She gives it a little wave in the air, then goes to hand it to Marta. Marta rears back from its earthy scent and says politely, "Oh, no thank you, Miss Brewster."

It's always an unexpected ride with Lillette. But no matter. I find my voice and say, "Wow, what a quirky little system you've worked out for yourself, Lillette."

She begins to slip her shoes back on and nods sagely, "Oh, I know. I've been doing this for years now. Once I figured out that the seven days of the week matched perfectly with the seven colors of the rainbow, I knew I was on to something."

Marta and Amber look positively dazzled by Lillette's eccentric ways. I have to admit, it *is* a pretty creative system.

The girls ask her some practical questions, like where did she find dance shoes in all the colors of the rainbow? ("Had 'em dyed.") And what made her think of the system in the first place? ("I notice things in sevens: seven years bad luck, seven deadly sins. I think it started with the seven dwarfs. Don't you just love Dopey?")

Wanting to jump on the bandwagon, Marta pipes up, "I have a fashion quirk too, Miss Brewster. I can't wear the same thing two days in a row."

"Oh, yeah, we had that in high school, too," says Lillette with a vague wave. "But that goes away in college."

Marta looks at Amber and asks, "Do you have any funny little fashion habits, Amber?"

Amber smiles shyly, then offers, "I have to triple knot my sneakers in gym." She blushes deeply then adds, "It makes me feel secure."

I put my hand on the top of her head and say, "Amber, I'm sure you're not alone."

Marta asks, "Do you have some fashion idiosyncrasy, Mrs. Graham?"

I declare, "Yes, I do! Amber, mine is all about security, too. I can *only* wear really tight, matching white knee socks."

They look at me, waiting for an explanation.

"When I was a little girl, growing up with four brothers, my mother couldn't keep up with all our socks. So we had one big laundry basket filled with clean socks of various colors and sizes. We had to pick through them to find a match, and very often I couldn't find one. I don't know if it was because the dryer ate them, as my mother claimed, or if my brothers wrecked the balance by grabbing out any old socks because they didn't give a hoot about fashion. In addition, lots of times the socks were flabby with worn-out elastic, so they'd slip down my legs all day. I hated that feeling, so I was constantly tugging them up. I finally started wearing rubber bands to hold them in place, but they dug into my calves and hurt too much."

"Poor thing," Lillette murmurs, and rubs her own legs in sympathy.

"By the time I got to high school, I was spending all my baby-sitting money on socks, and hoarding them in a shoebox in my closet. I loved them so much– so white, so snug, they never 'let me down!'" I say with my fingers creating air quotes in front of me.

They all start laughing. I pull my sweat pants up to reveal my super-white tube socks, tightly clinging to my calves all the way up to my knees. With a sweep of my hand I say, "Exhibit A!"

Suddenly Amber blurts, "My hair has to cover my ears at all times!"

We all look at her and ask why.

"I have ugly ears," she moans.

Timidly, she reaches up for the pencil wedged behind her ear and pulls her hair back so we can take a peek.

Instantly, we all cry at once, *No you don't! They're cute! There's nothing wrong with them!*

Amber claps her hands over her ears and protests, "They stick out too much!"

Marta waves her arm and says, "Ooh, ooh, pick me!" like a six year old.

We look at her and she says, "I have to throw things out in pairs. If I drop a piece of apple on the floor, I have to throw away another piece so the first one won't be lonely."

"I sleep with my baby pacifier under my pillow," Amber confesses. "I don't suck on it or anything," she adds hastily.

We're really on a roll now.

"I can't pee in public bathrooms," says Lillette tensely. "I'm not kidding. I'll have to go really bad, but I don't want anyone to hear me. So I sit there, balanced on a rim of toilet paper ringing the bowl, and the pressure starts to build. It builds and builds so bad that I start to panic, because I know that the other people in there are waiting to hear the sound of me tinkling into the toilet, but I JUST CAN'T GO!"

We are all still.

Uh oh. I think we've crossed an awkward little line there.

Amber's eyes are bugging out, and Marta looks away uncomfortably.

"Well!" I say briskly. "It's good to know we're not alone in our silly little quirks and habits. It means we're all only human, right girls?"

They all nod dumbly.

"Okay. Back to our original discussion: choreography. How will we divide up the big group numbers?"

I see everyone looks relieved to be back on topic. Everyone except Lillette, that is. She's busy scribbling a note on loose-leaf paper and stuffing it into her blue left shoe.

# March 14th
# 8:15am
# Home

Beep!
"Good morning, Mr. and Mrs. Graham. This is Gert Barnes, Delaney's mother. We just want to say we are so pleased and proud that Delaney has won the part of Nancy. We always thought she was a shining star; glad you recognize it, too.

Delaney has some upcoming commitments I need to go over with you. Nothing serious, but it will mean she is a teensy bit late for rehearsal sometimes, or she may have to leave a little earlier, but no mind. Nothing to worry about.

I'll send her schedule through e-mail– so easy to see a schedule when it's right in front of your nose, don't you agree? A talent like Delaney's is always in demand, so in order to... BEEEEEP!"

Beep!
"Seems I got cut off. Gertie Barnes here again. As I was saying, Delaney's voice is wanted at a few other venues, so I'll e-mail you her schedule. Please don't hesitate to contact us via phone or e-mail. We're looking forward to adding this as another important experience for our gifted daughter, in our commitment to provide her with every opportunity possible to grow into her ultimate self."

### 3pm, The Little Theater

Aisle seat. Row L, seat 101. I'm huddled up here, going over my notes. I already talked to the headmaster about having the music stands removed from the pit on a more regular basis, so now I'm just waiting for the kids.

Students start to stream in, various parts of their academy uniforms still intact. They've taken to changing in the bathrooms at dismissal, but sometimes forget to bring a full set of rehearsal clothes to switch into. This means they're forging new territory in the fashion department, with the guys appearing in silky maroon gym shorts, coupled with their proper white button-down shirts. And some girls are making eclectic new statements attired in their pleated, gray skirts paired with a rebellious black tank top. For some reason, they also enjoy rolling their knee socks down to their ankles. It's a weird, roly-poly look that reminds me of those Dr. Seuss characters. Their disheveled appearances could spawn a whole new look: "Academy Trash."

I turn around in my seat to look for Amber, just as Forrest enters. He's wearing a tee shirt that says "Contents Under Pressure" emblazoned on the front. As he sweeps by, I lean my head out into the aisle to see what it says on the back. "Do Not Puncture." I smirk.

Once Lillette and Amber arrive, we're going to tackle "I'd Do Anything." Piece of cake. I'm looking forward to it!

### Later

No Lillette. Not just late, not here at all. We'll work on the staging anyway with Marta, (thank-you-God-for-Marta.)

### A Little Later

No Lillette. Ever. So we'll just work off the CD. At least we can use the one quality we know Lillette has to our advantage: she's so scatterbrained she's fortunately forgotten her

Boom Box once again. The CD is still buried safely inside. Perfect.

## Super Later

I come back after the break to find sleeves of socks discarded and scattered in the pit, like large, empty tubes of spent toothpaste.

On stage, the cast dances barefoot to the latest throbbing hip-hop music blaring from the Boom Box. From the pit, I reach onto the stage and snap the music off. The sudden silence brings them all to a crashing stop.

I break my own rule, and hop onto the stage. Luckily, I don't look too frumpy as I execute the move fairly smoothly.

In my bossy voice I ask, "Why are you all in your bare feet? Everyone get down off the stage and put your shoes and socks on immediately."

The kids run to the edge of the stage en masse and jump down into the pit.

"Use the stairs!" I bellow.

I continue shouting from the stage, "Guys, you know the rules; feet are to be covered at all times. Mr. Glynn and his stage crew work here, too. That means there could be a random staple or rusty nail still about."

I rake my fingers through my hair– as if quelling the curls that dance on my head will still the chaos around me as the kids toss socks through the air.

I notice Amber is watching me closely.

"Did you have a question, Amber?"

"Oh, um, no. It was nothing, Mrs. Graham," she says. She smoothes her hair over her ears, a habit I had unconsciously noticed before, but now understand what's behind it. We must look funny, standing together side-by-side, plastering down our hair.

"Right, then. Let's pick up with the last scene. There's only fifteen minutes left anyway."

"Okay, Mrs. Graham," she says as she stands slightly stoop-shouldered at my side. "But Mrs. Graham?"

I'm looking out over the pit, watching the cast put their shoes and socks back on. Forrest spins a sock in front of him, twirling it like he's in the locker room, then snaps it at Grant's leg.

"Forrest!" I shake my head no, then ask Amber, "What is it?"

"Um, are you upset with them because," but then she stops. "Because, what?"

"Is this about that thing with you and the socks?" she asks with a pained look on her face. She wears a mask of empathy, like she's a little old schoolmarm, fretting over a troubled child.

For a second I don't understand what she's talking about. But then it hits me and I laugh out, "Oh no, Amber, no!"

She smiles with relief and says, "Oh, good. I just thought that maybe the sight of all those socks laying there brought back like, traumatic memories or something."

"No, I'm fine," I say. "I'm not tortured by big mounds of socks anymore." I start laughing again. She's right though, it did look like a sock massacre! I feel a snort coming on.

"Good," she says again. "I'm glad."

Delaney approaches with a piece of paper in her hand. "My mother asked me to give this to you," she says. For someone with a keen talent to emote on stage, Delaney is almost robotic in her monotone when she's not acting.

She deposits the envelope in my hand and walks away. For the first time I notice little bluish-gray bags under her eyes.

I unfold the note and read,
*"Dear Mr. and Mrs. Graham,*

*I left a message on your machine this morning to please check your e-mail today. It contains vital information about Delaney's schedule of commitments. I have not received a response thus far, so in case you did not get my phone message, this is a reminder to check that e-mail soon. I do not have your cell numbers, or I would have tried to reach you that way as well.*

*Regards,*

*Mrs. Gert Barnes"*

Oooh. Push-y.

She's calling us at our home? I guess we're not responding fast enough. Is this what she does to Delaney? I'm not even her child and I feel micromanaged!

Wait a sec. *What* other commitments is she talking about? Didn't we make it clear to everyone that their commitment should be to the *play*? Her child has THE LEAD. In addition to carrying an advanced academic course load, isn't that enough for one student?

And Mrs. Barnes? You will *never* get your hands on our cell phone numbers!

### To Do List For This Weekend:

- Order Backdrop Scrim
- Order Tickets
- Get program bios. to Mrs. Benson and Mrs. Harrington
- Posters to printers: Tuesday
- Costume rental (?)

# March 18th
## 7:50 am
# Home

S itting up, side-by-side in our bed, Jackson flips open the laptop and presses it on. I slide closer to him for a better look at the screen.

"You're hogging my pillow," he snarls playfully as I nestle in closer to him. His body, so taut and warm, feels as solid and reassuring as a tree. I pull the blanket up tighter around us, but the laptop bobbles on his knees. "Kelly!" he warns, as he rights it and keeps typing.

I wonder what Mrs. Barnes has in store for us today? We dealt with her this past weekend via e-mail, but it hasn't stopped her from trying to add more singing engagements to Delaney's already over-scheduled life. This kid's schedule would wear out an Olympic triathlete. We've kept our responses brief, and firm, but like a persistent and annoying child, she keeps trying to get her way through arguing, and re-arguing her position. (Which is, basically, that if Delaney has a minute, it should be filled with something *productive*.)

"Check our e-mail first; let's get it over with," I say into his shoulder. Are his shoulders always this smooth? Does he walk around all day with these smooth shoulders hidden beneath some shirt so I don't get a chance to feel them? I brush my lips back and forth over his skin, inhaling his sweet scent. I'm lost in shoulder-land, so I don't see right away what's caused him to stop typing. He has opened our e-mail account and is staring at seventeen new e-mails in our inbox.

"What the...?" he mutters under his breath as he clicks open the first one. I watch dully with my head drooped on his shoulder as he makes his way down the list. Short notes, long notes; every one of them is from a parent. Mostly mothers. Mothers with rehearsal conflicts, mothers with complaints about how their child is being overlooked, and/or is not being given enough to do, mothers who want us to call them to discuss said concerns. So much for our hopeful little flyer making some impact. It didn't even glance them.

Jackson is giving brief replies to some, deleting others, but is, in general, quite annoyed with some of the nonsense.

"Comes with the territory," I remind him as he clicks on the final message, number seventeen.

"It never used to be like this before, Kelly," he says. "This technology just keeps us at their beck and call 24/7. Nothing is filtered anymore, or shrugged off with common sense. Whatever happened to letting us do our jobs? Can you imagine if we were this involved with *their* jobs? Never happen. They'd never allow it."

"It's because we work with children, Jackson. I have to think they're just a little overzealous. Or else I was neglected. My mother never had the time to manage my every move. Should I feel jealous?" I ask as I doodle small stars on his back with my fingernail.

But he's not listening to me. His eyes have grown wide with disbelief as he scans number seventeen. Oh. I see who it's from. As predicted, it's Delaney's mom. Or perhaps we should crown her with a new title: Mama Diva. Let me put it this way, she's starting to make the ultimate pushy stage mother– Mama Rose from *Gypsy*– look like Mother Teresa.

We both scan it quickly.

She's going on and on again about Delaney's other commitments that, and I quote, "won't interfere with your rehearsal schedule because I'll just have her practice in the car."

Hoooo boy. I thought we took care of this, but this mother is relentless.

Jackson and I exchange bleary-eyed glances. "Go get 'em, Tiger," I say.

I pull away from him and flop my head back onto my own pillow. I feel dazed, but Jackson is already firing back a response.

I wrap a strand of my hair around my finger and begin to absently graze a trail along my lips. It tickles too much, so I grab some of my cherry ChapStick off the nightstand and turn my attention back to Jackson.

As I run a few swipes around my mouth, I notice that being a pianist gives Jackson an air of virtuosity when he types. As he pounds the keys, the sinewy muscles in his arms and fingers contract and expand as if he's playing a Rachmaninoff piece. His back labors in the sexiest way, and as he leans into the laptop, it seems to undulate and tremble under his touch. A symphony of an e-mail is being composed! The way his fingers fly across the keyboard, I can see genius is being created. I can hear it in the rhythm as he strikes the keys, strokes the keys, hammering them into submission.

"Read it back to me, Jackson, read it back to me now; I can't wait!" I cry out.

He stops abruptly, and turns to give me a smile. "Is this turning you on?" he asks.

I grin back. "Yep."

He lets the laptop slide off his knees and pushes me flat onto my back. In one swift move, he raises my arms over my head and pins my wrists together with one hand. He locks eyes with me for a second before he leans down to kiss me deeply.

"But what about..." I gasp.

"They can wait," he growls.

"Play me," I whisper.

And he does.

—⟐—

JACKSON'S E-MAIL RESPONSE TO #17:

*Dear Mrs. Barnes,*

*Can't write right now; too busy ravaging my wife.*

*Best,*

*J. Graham*

(Ha ha. Just kidding!)

### 2:25pm, The Little Theater

The last bell of the day has yet to ring, so I take advantage of the empty hallways and make my way over to the theater in record time. My head is still full of thoughts of Jackson and our hot love encounter this morning. As he left for Melodies, we had trouble letting go of each other. Humming "As Long As He Needs Me," I dance down the aisle only to stop abruptly as I come upon Amber, seated in the front row. Bent studiously over her homework, her hair practically conceals her entire face.

"Math?" I ask, spying numbers and, (gasp!) *letters* in the same equations.

"Yeah. Algebra."

I shudder inwardly. I had to go to summer school for algebra. And even then, I barely squeaked by with a passing grade. I just could not understand it– numbers and letters arranged in long lines, laid out like sentences to be read. And always at the end, the dreaded equal sign, demanding an answer.

Math and I got along fairly well in elementary school, when the numbers stacked up neatly upon each other like square boxes. La, la, la, laaaa, we were carefree friends in those days, math and I. My stubby pencils with their capable erasers were able to tackle any problem with confidence. But that all ended when binomials, trinomials, exponents and probability busted in on us. Once numbers were catapulted away from their meat and potatoes functions, and began buddying up with letters from the alphabet– (predominantly 'x' and 'y'), we had a falling out.

"Why?" I'd ask, like a jilted lover. Followed by, "Why should I care about you?" And many times, with a screech: "It's over. You are useless and incomprehensible!"

"Do you like algebra?" I ask Amber casually.

She continues to work, but says, "Oh, yeah. I'm good at math."

"That's great!" I say. Wow. To be good at math. I watch over her shoulder as she effortlessly slides her pencil across the equations and deposits an answer at the end. Her page is pristine– clear of any signs of distress in their relationship. There's nothing angrily crossed out, no leftover roly-poly eraser dust littering her paper like rubber tears.

"Tiana has plantar warts," she says quietly.

"Oh! Okay," I say, caught off guard. "She probably got them in gym from walking barefoot on the locker room floor."

"No," Amber says as she lifts her head to look at me. "She says she thinks she got them from when everyone was dancing barefoot on the stage."

"No, Amber," I say doubtfully. "I don't think so. That was just last week. But maybe, who knows?" I try to give her a friendly nudge with my shoulder, but she doesn't move. She looks so glum.

"What is it, Amber?" She has too serious a countenance for a teenager. She's starting to resemble Wednesday Addams from *The Addams Family* with her black, pin-straight hair concealing each side of her face like curtains. I think her glasses are the only thing keeping her hair from covering her face entirely.

"This isn't one of the Three Terrible Things, is it?" she asks in a small voice.

"What? No!" I bat at the air like I'm literally batting her question away. "In fact, I've never heard of *anyone* getting plantar warts during one of my shows. It's a first."

"Uh huh," she says morosely.

"Amber, it's not that bad an affliction," I say consolingly. "Tiana's doctor will take care of her and she'll be warts-free in no time."

She nods.

"Amber," I say, taking an educated guess. "Are you worried about getting them, too?"

A torrential outpouring ensues. "Well, it's just that you and I *always* sit on that stage, Mrs. Graham, and what if I get them on my hands? We lean back on our hands a lot, and what if the germs are there– will warts grow? She says they hurt."

I'm so taken by surprise, it takes me a second to gather my thoughts to reassure her.

"You know what, Amber? I honestly don't know. I've never heard of plantar warts growing on hands. But when I get home after rehearsal today, I'll look it up on the internet. In the meantime, let's spread our jackets out on the stage and sit on top of them for extra added protection, okay?"

She smiles the sweetest little smile of relief and nods forlornly.

This kid is breaking my heart. Oh, Amber– one step forward, two steps back.

### 3pm, The Little Theater

Taffy enters the theater leaping down the aisle dressed in shorts, tee shirt and a baseball cap. It's still freezing outside for March, but Sienna rushes up to greet her in a similar get-up. I hear their entire girl chat:

SIENNA: Are you wearing underwear?

TAFFY: WHAT?!

SIENNA: Those are your brother's boxer shorts, right?

TAFFY: Yeah, so?

SIENNA: So are you wearing underwear underneath them?

TAFFY: Do *boys*?

SIENNA: Do boys what?

TAFFY: Do *boys* wear underwear underneath their underwear?

SIENNA: If you're wearing them as *shorts* you should!

They shriek and giggle, flipping and tossing their glossy hair in that teenage dance of exuberance– both unrestrained and self-conscious all at once. A burst of movement, then an accounting of their bodies: hands fly up to pat their hair, pull at a shirt, tug at their shorts.

I can see now the nuanced way they are wearing the boxers: elastic waistband turned down twice, tee shirts secured on the side with a ponytail holder, and baseball caps worn (how else?)– backward. For them, it's another fashion statement. We'll have to have a talk about proper rehearsal clothes again. During *Arsenic and Old Lace* they were showing up in pajama bottoms!

After Amber gathers them into a circle, I say, "Listen up, everyone. We are becoming too lax in what we are wearing to rehearsal. Gym shorts from your lockers are okay, but no pajama bottoms or boys boxers, please."

A flurry of protests erupts, loudest among them from the guys teasing, "But my mother will kill me!" and "No problem for me; I wear tighty-whities!" Before I can clarify that I meant the girls wearing boys' underwear as shorts, Delaney's hand has shot up. Not waiting to be called on, she speaks loudly over the din with self-righteous importance.

"Mrs. Graham, what's the difference? These clothes are all just made from cloth! And just because we label one set as 'underwear' or pajamas, how far apart are they, really, from say, your sweatpants?"

Ouch. A swipe at my Old Navy sweats!

A chorus of "Exactly!" "My point!" and fist bumps follow. Taffy tips her baseball cap back a notch and juts her chin out like an umpire ready for a fight. Spirited discussion breaks out all around the circle.

I hold my hands up for quiet. "I appreciate your argument, Delaney, but then where do we draw the line?"

"Well, my mother says they're fine, so what's the problem? If my mother allows me to dress this way, why should it matter to you?" she asks defensively.

Noelle Pratt says, "We have to wear our uniforms all day, but they don't want us wearing them to after-school activities. All the sports teams get to change into practice clothes. We just wear whatever we want."

"Yeah, Mrs. Graham. We're not trying to make you mad," says Sienna contritely.

More nods of agreement, then Taffy pipes up, "And nobody says anything to Forrest when he comes dressed all gangsta." She crosses her arms in front of her chest, posing in her version of a cool gangsta move. "I can't even see his face when he covers it with that hood."

Forrest looks up from where he has been slumped on the floor next to Grant. His expression reads, *What did I do?*

Grant comes to his defense. "We live in America, people. It's called freedom from expression."

"Of!" shouts Jasmine.

Grant looks puzzled. "What?"

"Freedom *of* expression, Grant," Jasmine informs him smartly.

"That's what I meant, Jazz," he scowls.

"Okay, okay, guys, enough," I intercede. "We're doing a musical. There will be lots of freedom of expression going on here. But sorry, no boxer shorts or p.j. bottoms, and Forrest, while we rehearse, please keep the hood down."

Thomas raises his hand and asks anxiously, "I can still wear my dad's jacket, right? I'm wearing it to get into character and it holds all my scarves. I'm not wearing it to, like, upset anyone."

"The jacket is fine," I say.

"And my top hat, Mrs. Graham?" asks Christian.

I address the whole group: "All hats and props you have been using all along have my stamp of approval."

"I'm approved!" says Thomas as he throws a red handkerchief in the air.

Forrest lunges for it and misses. "Epic fail," he says dejectedly.

"You guys aren't even speaking proper English," scoffs Jasmine.

"We're not prop-uh, now then, are we, love?" Thomas teases her in his Cockney accent.

"You fink yer beh-uh than us, do ya?" jeers Forrest in a pretty damn good Cockney accent, too.

Thomas throws his arm around Forrest and starts to lead him away, saying, "You're givin' me ah 'eadache, you are!"

Forrest shoves Thomas hard, and stalks back over to Jasmine.

"Beh-uh watch yer back, sistuh," he says menacingly.

Jasmine takes a startled step back, and says, "Temper, much? Knock it off, Forrest."

I stand up quickly to indicate we're starting and say, "Settle down, guys. Amber, please call places."

"Places please, act one scene two," Amber calls.

As they drift off to the wings, I catch three things: Delaney rolling her eyes in disgust at me; Thomas looking at Forrest with distrust; and Sienna and Taffy trying to say "underwear underneath underwear" three times fast.

I'll have to watch about that eye rolling.

And the shoving.

# March 19th
# 8am
# Home

*From: Gertie Barnes*
*To: Jackson and Kelly Graham*

*Hello Grahams,*
*I notice you have added another half hour to next Thursday's rehearsal.*
*This will not work for us. Delaney cannot miss her voice lesson at*
*6:15pm. It has already been paid for, and cannot be rescheduled. As I*
*think I have made clear, her schedule is tight enough as it is, and even*
*adding what you may think of as a short amount of time like a half*
*hour, throws us off balance completely.*

*To give you a glimpse of our reality on Thursdays, when Delaney's*
*nanny picks her up from your rehearsal at 5:30pm promptly, she*
*hands her a change of clothes and a slice of pizza. While they drive*
*to her lesson, Delaney changes her clothes, wolfs down her dinner,*
*and is required to drink 8 ounces of water. After a dose of liquid*
*vitamins from our health food store, she warms up her voice by sing-*
*ing scales piped in through her iPod. Her nanny deposits her for her*
*voice lesson at 6:15, and then we're into our evening routine: home-*
*work, piano practice, shower, prayers. Surely you can plainly see*
*that Delaney has no wiggle room and will therefore be unavailable*

*for that portion of rehearsal. Thank you for your understanding.*
*--Gert Barnes*

"Wow," I whisper. "Delaney is like a professional child. Her life is like a *job.*"

"Brutal," agrees Jackson, still staring at the screen. "Why are they pushing her so hard? It's so bizarre. Why can't she develop at her own pace, the way kids naturally do?"

We're in the living room, sitting on the edge of the couch; both of us leaning towards the laptop on the coffee table the way people in the olden days leaned towards the fire. Our mouths agape, we're used to Mrs. Barnes being in contact with us everyday, but we're still shocked about the stuff she says.

Closing my mouth in an effort to remain unfazed, I say, "That's a really good question, Jackson. Why *can't* Delaney just develop at a more natural pace? I don't know. Competition, maybe? It's like they don't trust her to grow up okay without all their maneuvering. But at what cost, you know?"

"We're not going to raise our kids this way, are we?" Jackson asks.

"Heck, no!" I say. "Cob is going to be a free child; a real boy, like Peter Pan!"

Jackson turns his face to me and grins. "You know Peter Pan isn't real, right Kelly?"

"Of *course* he's real," I cry. "He's full of vim and vigor– fights pirates and smokes a peace pipe!" I put my hand on his arm and ask seriously, "But do you know why you should you never fly with Peter Pan?"

Jackson smiles and says, "I'm sure I'll regret this, but: why?"

"Because you'll never, never land." I smile sweetly and bat my eyes.

He grabs me by the waist and tosses me back onto the couch. I laugh and push his hands away as he tries to tickle me. "You're too weird for me, Kel. Why did I marry you again?"

I spit out a curl that has landed in my mouth with a "ptooey" and answer from my prone position, "Because I'm hot."

He crawls on top of me and starts kissing my neck with smooches that are a cross between a nibble and a tender bite.

"Oh, yes," he breathes. "Now I remember."

### 2:30pm, Samuel P. Chester Academy

Angelo, the sweetest, roundest guy on the custodial staff, pushes his rolling garbage cart down the hallway of the main building. As I see him from a distance, all I can think is, *Weebles wobble but they don't fall down.* I'm here hoping to ask him for another set of keys to open the theater; mine have stubbornly stopped cooperating. He's the go-to guy for keys, so I'm glad I've spotted him.

I fall in step beside him and greet him warmly. He's in the academy signature gray custodial jumpsuit, with his name embroidered in black thread on his pocket. It goes perfectly with the silver bandana he wears wrapped around his head. Where he got a bandana in *silver*, I have no clue. Those flashy disco days from the 70's?

He waves back a hello and asks after the musical. We chat amiably for a bit. As we talk, I notice whenever he smiles, his plump cheeks puff out, pushing his glasses up until they rise above his eyebrows. He looks like Botero himself created him, right down to his big, soulful eyes.

"Whatcha need, Mrs. Graham?" he asks.

I explain, and he says, "No problem-o. But they're up on two. Care to take a walk?"

Although I said I'd never take the back stairway again, it may be easier for Angelo. It is a faster way to go, and I'll bet he doesn't share my mice fears.

"Do you want to take the back stairway?" I offer. "It's closer."

He abruptly stops pushing the cart and his face falls, his glasses slipping down to their rightful position. His eyes are wide and filled with warning.

He says, "No, no, no, Mrs. Graham. Not that way. Don't you know the story?"

I wrinkle up my nose and ask, "About the mice?"

Angelo shakes his head and says, "Nuh, nuh, nuh." Through clenched teeth he whispers, "About the girl."

"What girl?" I ask.

He looks quickly up and down the hallway. "There's a rumor that a girl died back in that stairway."

"Oh no," I say. "When?"

He closes his eyes and says, "Um, umm," while he thinks. They pop open again and he exclaims, "The thirties!"

"The *nineteen* thirties?" I ask, kind of crestfallen.

"Yeah, yeah, that's it. 'Course I wasn't here yet," he chuckles. "But that's what the fellas told me."

"Oh. Well, that was a long time ago, Angelo, so it doesn't really bother me. Honestly, if you think it's faster, I don't mind going that way."

"Nuh, nuh, nuh," he says again, this time wagging his finger admonishingly at me. "Some say it's haunted."

"How do you know?" I ask, playing along.

"Sometimes, the fellas tell me, they've heard noises."

"What kind of noises?" I ask. I'm still trying not to smile.

"Like a girl crying."

Oh.

That's so sad. I didn't expect that. I thought he was going to say the usual spooky stuff, like noisy chains rattling, or banshees wailing woooo, wooooo!

"Yeah. Chilling stuff," he says solemnly. He takes me firmly by the elbow and begins to steer me away. "So if it's all the same to you, I don't mind the longer route."

"Oh, no, that's fine. I don't mind at all."

We lumber along and I say, "I thought everyone avoided that stairway because a colony of mice lived there."

He laughs a little and his cheeks and glasses rise up again. "Mice, you say? How about *rats?*"

EWWW! RATS?!

"No, Angelo, don't tell me that! That's much worse!" I cry.

"Worse than a haunting by a dead girl?" he asks with an arched eyebrow.

"Haven't they exterminated?"

"Yeah, sure, sure, sure. But this is a very old building, with more nooks and crannies than an English Muffin." He holds back the door to an ancient open elevator.

I try to smile, but now I'm skeeved out. I go back to the rumor about the girl. "Did you ever hear anything suspicious, Angelo?"

The cart rumbles like thunder as we enter the creaky lift. He looks pensive and says, "Yes, Kelly, I think one time I did. I know you won't think I'm a kook if I tell you, but it was pretty recently."

The lift grinds and we rise slowly.

"What did you hear?"

"It sounded just like what they said: a girl crying."

"But couldn't it have been a student? Teenage girls cry all the time, right?"

"Well, I thought so, too. But it was after school, and I had already locked up the building. I went to check, but no one was there," he says ominously. He looks at me dolefully with those big eyes and the hair on my arms starts to prickle.

Come on! There has to be a logical explanation.

He pulls the greasy slats of the lift open, and we walk out onto the second floor. As we continue down the hall he says, "But who knows? It could just be me, Mrs. Graham. Heaven knows, when I'm under stress, my mind can play tricks on me. Maybe my mind was just playing tricks on me."

He starts nodding as if trying to convince himself.

I smile and nod along, too.

Yeah. Probably.

# March 20th
## 10am
# Samuel P. Chester Academy
## Main Building

At Chester Academy, the school building itself is all about the wood. It may be built with bricks for its exterior, but inside it smells like a church. Rich, brown wainscoting lines every hallway, and the highly polished wood floors appear brand new and glossy every day of the year. This was not the case in my public high school, where we only had a wood floor in one room– the gym. And even then, it only appeared this glossy on the first day of school. After that, a thousand dirty, sweaty sneakers dulled the shine right out of it.

As I walk down the corridors, I marvel at the aristocratic setting– it makes me feel like I've been transported to another, more elegant time. The kids passing by in their proper gray and maroon uniforms look like they've been dropped into an old English film. It makes them seem more well-bred and refined, hiding their true crazy teenage impulses behind, well... costumes. Isn't that what the uniforms really are, after all?

I even feel a deep urge from time to time, to drag out my upper British accent and inquire if anyone would care for a spot of tea and crumpets? Yes, I dare say, old chap, it's simply a smashingly splendid place!

I've stopped by the main office (yes, wood, wood and more wood), to make copies before rehearsal this afternoon. I was hoping to inconspicuously breeze in, so I could get back home quickly to go over the music with Jackson. But just as I'm about to leave, this parent we know– Mrs. Claudine Kirkland– comes charging down the hallway, dressed impeccably in tennis whites. She stands out garishly against the dark wood– her modern clothes clashing incongruously with the old-world polish of the formal surroundings. It makes her look like a crude interloper. I find myself thinking: *The students have a dress code of fancy uniforms– maybe the parents should have one, too!*

Her perky sneakers slap at the floor, bearing not a single smudge of dirt. Her highlighted blonde hair is pulled back into a sleek ponytail; her gelled bangs jut out from her forehead like an awning. Nothing jiggles. Her skin is as taut and tight as the plastic smile she has attached to her perfectly made-up face. I always feel a bit diminished as a female in her presence, like I'm the sloppy, threadbare version of what a woman should look like.

As she approaches, I fumble with my batch of copies, trying to quickly open the outside door to make my escape.

"Kelly!" she cries as she spots me. "Did you hear the latest?"

Caught. Dang.

"The latest?" I say. "Er, um, no, I haven't."

Mrs. Kirkland stops short in front of me and claps her hands together excitedly. "Oh. Well! Then let me be the first to tell you: I won!"

I look at her uncomprehendingly.

"You won? Oh, good. That's good." Smiling tentatively, I ask, "What did you win?"

She throws her head back like she just stepped on a tack and is in excruciating pain, and shrieks, "I can't believe no one told you! At the last parents meeting, I got funding approved for updated sound equipment in the Little Theater!"

This actually is good news. But why did she say she *won*? Was there a fight? Who would be *against* a new sound system?

"That's great," I smile. "The students will be so happy. No more worries about the sound cutting out, or..."

She interrupts and boasts, "I know, I know. It was such a close vote, but I haven't lost the touch. I still know how to negotiate a deal."

"Congratulations," I say, trying to keep up with her. "And thank you, on behalf of both myself and the students..."

She doesn't appear to be listening, so I stop. With her eyes lowered demurely, she clears her throat and says, "I hear the play is going really well."

Before I can respond with some heartfelt gushing, her hand darts forward to grab my wrist. "Just be careful," she whispers conspiratorially, her eyes flicking from side to side like we're in a dangerous, dark alley.

Trapped in her web, like the little insect I feel, I try to pull my arm away but she tightens her grip. Geez, it's like "the claw."

"Careful about what?" I ask warily, my hand still caught in her grasp.

She leans in so close to me, I can see where her tan line ends around her face. Sprayed on. I might have figured.

She whispers, "Be careful not to make it *too* good."

"What, what do you mean?" I stammer.

"Well," she releases me to adjust her crisply turned up collar. "You did a respectable job with *Arsenic and Old Lace* last semester– my son Erik just *loved* that experience– but that was low profile. This is a popular musical, sure to attract a lot of attention. You don't want to shine too brightly around here. Jealousy. You know how people are." She wrinkles her nose and nods knowingly.

I echo her bobbing head and we stand there nodding idiotically at each other.

"Um, what people, Mrs. Kirkland? Who are we talking about?" I venture.

She goes in for the wrist grip again, but I feint to the left and shift my bag to my other shoulder. She then steps in close to the space most cultures reserve for lovers and surgeons, and spits, "The staff."

She nods once again for emphasis, and takes a tiny step backward.

I look at her blankly.

"You're too new here to understand," she says evenly. "But consider this a warning: don't take away the spotlight from our sports department. You don't want to upset the coaches. The coaches are king here, that's just the way it is. Our teams are the competitive best and we're known for it all over the country." She holds my gaze, staring me down meaningfully.

Beyond bewildered I start, "But how would a good show interfere with..." but she cuts me off.

"Oops! Look at the time!" She grabs her wrist to squint at her exquisite little Cartier watch and says pointedly, "Just think about what I've said. I have to dash."

She lingers for a moment, and looks at me expectantly. What is she waiting for? I'm so tongue-tied, I don't know what else to say. With a sweep of my hand I indicate her outfit and ask, "Tennis?"

"No," she responds, looking at me strangely. "Errands."

Right. Silly me. The tennis whites are her *costume*. She stays dressed in them all day.

### 10:45am, Home

I come home to find Jackson practicing the music from *Oliver!* on his keyboard. I recognize the song immediately: "That's Your Funeral."

"I just saw Mrs. Kirkland," I say over his playing.

"Uh huh."

"Brace yourself for this one: she told me not to make the play too good."

"Delete," says Jackson immediately.

"Jackson, I'm serious! She said we shouldn't steal the spotlight from the sports department."

"Or what?" he says as his hands move over the keyboard.

"I don't know. Or, or, we'll piss them off, and, and, then they'll be jealous."

"So?"

"So then, maybe, I don't know; I think she was implying we may lose our jobs."

"Delete!"

"Jackson!"

"Delete, Kelly. Disregard! Erase! What do you want me to say? Don't listen to her!" he shouts.

I fold my arms over my chest in frustration. He knows I clam up when he yells at me.

He stops playing and maneuvers me over to the couch. I flop down in a huff and hang my head. I feel him reach for the curls that have settled on my shoulder and he says softly, "I'm just saying you can't take anything she says to heart. You remember what a nuisance she was with Dr. Waldner on *Arsenic and Old Lace?* These people just want to boss us around. Ignore her. Just forget it!"

"But what if it's true?" I wail. "This stuff worries me, Jackson. It was kind of *menacing* the way she told me."

"Kelly, we're doing a great job. The kids are having fun. Administration is happy. Do you think Headmaster Hank wants us to do less than we're capable of for his students? This is education. This is a *musical*, remember? Pretty much the most fun you can have, so don't let her spoil it with her neurotic little warnings. Besides, I'll take on the big, fat sports department if they mess with us." He pumps his arms and flexes his muscles for me. "Lemme at 'em!"

He leaps to his feet and spars at the air. Little ringlets of his hair spring upward like Slinkey's as he bounces up and down on his toes.

I laugh and fall back against the cushions. He leans over to lift my chin for a quick smooch then sits back at his piano.

As I listen to him practice, I call out from the couch, "Okay, but I'm going to call Headmaster Hank if she ever says anything like that again."

Jackson plays on, lost again in the notes.

"That's Your Funeral. " Ha ha. Better not be.

### 3pm, The Little Theater

I arrive at the Little Theater to find Sienna and Taffy sitting on the apron of the stage swinging their legs back and forth with abandon, the way small children do.

"Hey, Mrs. Graham, are you proud of us?"

"For what?" I ask.

They link arms and recite together, "If you're early, you're on time. If you're on time, you're late. If you're late, you're fired!"

I laugh and say, "Very good. Yes, I *am* proud of you both for being early *and* 'on time,' and for memorizing that old theater adage!" I give them a thumbs-up, then cross backstage to set up for rehearsal.

### Overheard Girl-Chat While Setting Up:

SIENNA: I heard the back stairway in the main building is haunted.

TAFFY: I heard that, too! They say a girl died back there in 1931.

SIENNA: I know. But she didn't just die. I heard she was murdered.

TAFFY: Murdered?! I never heard she was *murdered!* I heard she fell down a flight of stairs and hit her head.

SIENNA: Exactly. Someone *pushed* her down the stairs. She didn't just fall.

TAFFY: Who pushed her?

SIENNA: I heard it was her boyfriend.

(*There's silence for a moment.*)

TAFFY: I don't think so.

SIENNA: What do you mean? Why not?

TAFFY: I don't think they were allowed to date back then.

SIENNA: It wasn't the dark ages, Taffeta! They had love back then. You can't stop love. Look at Romeo and Juliet. They fell in love before 1931!

TAFFY: I know they had love back then, Sienna! I just mean they had rules and curfews and stuff. The parents back then were really strict.

SIENNA: I have a curfew.

TAFFY: Yeah, so?

SIENNA: So having a curfew doesn't stop love!

TAFFY: Oh my God, Sienna, are you in love? Is it Duncan? When you guys were singing "That's Your Funeral" I could just see you liked him!

SIENNA: WHAT?!

TAFFY: You just said...

SIENNA: No, Taffy I am not in love! Duncan's my friend! We were *acting!*

TAFFY: Oh. Sorry. I'm lost.

SIENNA: Yeah, me too.

(*Silence again. Then suddenly:*)

TAFFY: OhmyGod, what a coincidence– Juliet died, too!

SIENNA: She wasn't murdered, Taffeta. She took her own life.

TAFFY: Oh. Right.

SIENNA: For love. Romeo would never murder her. They were trying to live, to *express* their forbidden love for each other.
TAFFY: Right! Oh, yeah, right. (*Silence.*)
SIENNA: The point is, I would never use that stairway. Whether I had a boyfriend or not.
TAFFY: Oh, no, me neither.
SIENNA: Because I don't want to hear her crying.
TAFFY: Who?
SIENNA: The dead girl.
TAFFY: She *cries?!*
SIENNA: Yeah. Some kids said they heard her crying.
TAFFY: How?
SIENNA: What do you mean *"how?"*
TAFFY: *How* can they hear her crying if she's dead?
SIENNA: Because she's a ghost now, Taffy! A really, really sad ghost. Wouldn't you cry too if you were murdered?

I have to stop the madness, so I call over to them, "Girls, can you please help me set up for your scene?"

While the three of us drag the coffin that the stage crew kids built for the funeral parlor scene, I wonder about this rumor. Angelo never said anything about murder. That's seriously creepy. And horrifying, if it's true. And what's with the crying? I think I've heard enough speculation; I'll have to go straight to Headmaster Hank and ask him myself.

As we push the ratty looking furniture into place, I steal a glance at my watch. Where are Erik and Blake?

"Did you girls see Erik and Blake in school today?"

Before they can answer, Erik and Blake come tumbling through the doors, laughing and texting at the same time.

"Come on up, guys," I call. "You're late. Did you happen to see Amber out there?"

"Yep," says Erik as he skips down the aisle. "I'll text her."

With their cell phones ever at the ready, Erik stops at the end of aisle B and begins pressing away. It's like they have these invisible umbilical cords to each other, linking them all together. Do they really want to be this accessible all the time?

In the moments it takes me to think this, Erik thrusts his arms into the air and holds his cell phone high. "We have contact!" he cries proudly. Blake pumps his arms and cheers as Erik deposits his backpack on the edge of the stage and says, "She's in the lobby."

"Erik!" I exclaim. "This is so silly. Can't you please just go get her...?" But before I can finish, Amber walks in, weighted down as much by the ton of books on her back as by her melancholy personality.

"Hi, Amber. Come on in," I say. As she plods down the aisle, I turn to address the other kids. "What is the problem with getting here on time?"

Erik and Blake look at each other.

"Main building logistics," Erik says.

"What do you mean, Erik?" I ask. We form a comfortable little circle center stage and sit down cross-legged while Amber collects the attendance sheet.

"Um, well, we have to take the long way to avoid the death stairway, so it makes us late."

Oh Lord, do the students really come right out and call it "the death stairway?"

"What death stairway?" I ask, trying to sound casual.

Blake looks to Erik again to do all the talking. Erik tosses his head back and says, "The back stairway in the main building. *I'm* man enough to face my fears, but *some* freshman I know are little babies." He leans over and stares directly at Blake.

"Not true, not true, Mrs. Graham!" Blake says earnestly. "I'm not afraid of the stairway because of the dead girl. I'm afraid because it's always deserted and dark."

Sienna pipes up, "That's because everyone avoids it; even the custodians. They're spooked by it, too, and won't fix it up back there."

"Yeah," Taffy says as she rolls and unrolls her script. "My mother has been back there, and she complained to the headmaster that it's not bright enough."

"Who died back there?" I ask.

They all start talking at once, so I put my hands up and say, "One at a time, one at a time."

Sienna stands up and announces, "It was a girl, like, about our age. She was murdered by her boyfriend, and now she cries all the time." She sits back down and crosses her arms in front of her like she knows she's going to be challenged.

Erik wastes no time and pounces. "She wasn't *murdered,* you dick. She slipped and hit her head against the wall. Get the facts, Sienna. Brick is hard, in case you didn't know."

Taffy sits up indignantly to defend Sienna and says contemptuously, "She knows brick is hard, Erik! What a stupid, obvious statement! And don't call her a dick! She's a *girl!"*

"Don't call her names," I say, turning to Erik.

Blake has been watching the exchange tensely and says, "Do you think it was maybe too dark back then, too?"

"None of us were there, Blake. How should *we* know?" Sienna taunts.

"Yeah, who's the real dick *now?*" Taffy tosses in.

"Taffy! Guys! Do not talk to each other like that. I don't allow potty language at my rehearsals."

They all look down. "Sorry," they mutter.

"Okay, guys, listen," I say. "I'll call the headmaster and see what can be done about getting some lights put back there. But in the meanwhile, please try to do your best to get here on time."

Erik puts his head on Blake's shoulder and teases, "I can hold Blakey's hand if he's afraid of the dark."

Blake gives Erik a good-natured shove and says, "Knock it off, Erik."

Something occurs to me then.

"Blake," I say. "You know Erik's character, Noah, has to put you into a coffin in this scene, don't you?"

Blake glances over at the coffin and drops his head into his hands. Mumbling miserably he says, "Yeah, I know."

I walk over to the coffin and open the lid.

"But Blake," I say, indicting the coffin, "if you're afraid of the dark, we can arrange to have a flashlight in here, so you can snap it right on when the coffin lid closes."

As Blake looks up gratefully, Erik pulls a flashlight out of his hoodie pocket and holds it aloft.

"Done!" Erik cries jubilantly, with a big grin on his face. He hands it to Blake, who looks down at it like someone just handed him the keys to a Porsche. Blake gives Erik a crooked little smile and I almost say, awww, but catch myself before I embarrass them. You know, Erik is really nothing like his strident monster, I mean, mother– Mrs. Claudine Kirkland.

I smile and say, "Nice. Erik to the rescue! That was sort of magical, Erik. Did you plan that?"

Erik shrugs nonchalantly and says, "Yeah, I knew he was afraid of the dark, so I borrowed the flashlight from Mr. Glynn's collection. I had the same idea, Mrs. Graham. I was going to slip it into the coffin to surprise him, too!"

"Very thoughtful, Erik," I say approvingly. "Maybe you two can use it on the back stairway so you'll get here on time."

"I'll try, Mrs. Graham," says Erik. "But the second I hear the dead girl bawling, I'm history."

# March 21st
## 10am
## Home


"**G**ood morning, Headmaster Hank, this is Kelly Graham. How are you?"

"Fine, fine," he says in his rich, velvety voice. "Yourself?"

"I'm fine, thank you. Jackson and I will be in later this afternoon for our three o'clock rehearsal, but I have a rather awkward question to ask you first."

He doesn't skip a beat, and asks neutrally, "And what is that?"

"I feel, um, a bit foolish asking you this," I say as I begin to blush. I'm glad I'm asking him this question over the phone.

"That's fine, Kelly; what is it?"

I bite the bullet and say, "Apparently, there's a rumor going around that a female student died in the back stairway in the main building, and I was wondering if it was true or not?"

There's a split second of silence that my hyper-vigilant self takes the wrong way and assumes it means the headmaster has pegged me as a gossip for repeating rumors.

But he clears his throat and says matter-of-factly, "It is, unfortunately, true."

"Oh," I say. "I'm so sorry. When did this happen?"

I can hear his chair creak and groan as I imagine him leaning back to think about it.

"That was, I believe, in the spring of 1931."

I'm quiet for a moment, uncertain if I should ask for more specific details. He must take my silence as shock or grief, because he begins comforting me.

"It was many decades ago, Kelly; before even I was born. There's no need to worry yourself."

"Oh, no, I was just asking because I overheard the students talking about it, and you know how rumors can get exaggerated."

"I do, indeed," he agrees. "These things can take on a life of their own, like those urban legends."

"Right," I say. "But to, uh, set the record straight, what exactly happened?"

"It was apparently just an unfortunate accident," he says regretfully. "The young lady fell down the stairs and hit her head against the brick wall in such a way that she fell unconscious and never woke up."

"How awful," I say. And then timidly, "There wasn't a boyfriend involved or anything, was there?"

He chuckles a bit and says, "That's the urban legend I was alluding to; is that one still circulating?"

"Some of my students repeated that, yes."

"No, no," he says mildly. "It was nothing like that."

I exhale. So it was just one of those freaky things. I hate that life can suddenly turn on a dime like that. It makes us all so vulnerable.

"Was that all, Kelly?" Headmaster Hank interrupts my musings.

Part of me wants to ask him about the dead-girl-crying rumors, but I'm afraid of his reaction. Because, if I ask him point blank, "Is it true that the dead girl's ghost haunts that stairwell and can, on occasion, be heard crying?" He'll have no choice but to respond, "Well, dear, now what does an educated person such as yourself think?"

Then I'll have to feel my face burn with shame for asking such a stupid question.

"Oh, yes, that was it, Headmaster Hank," I say quickly. "Thanks for clearing up that mystery for me."

"No trouble at all. I'll see you and Jackson soon."

I hang up the phone and sit perfectly still. Now I have to try not to recreate the scene if I have to use that stairway again. But I know myself. My imagination will torment me. I know I may even try to visualize the whole sad scene to life. As I stand in the stairwell, I may try to actually picture her lying there. And I may get caught up in trying to imagine that spring day, when people shouted and screamed for help as they knelt by her side and tried to rouse her.

I'm obviously not the only one to taunt herself with these thoughts. If her story is still told often enough that it's turned into a ghostly urban legend, I have to wonder: why?

How did this story get its mythical status? Why doesn't everyone at the academy talk about the great football pass that clinched some important title for the school instead?

Well, let's face it. It's *death*.

And I'm in theater, right? Death is *huge* in dramas. From the Greeks, to Shakespeare, to *The Sopranos*, there's every kind of death you can imagine. Death fascinates us. Death *sells*.

The very symbols that represent the human condition are the comedy/tragedy masks that have been around for centuries. These icons tell you everything right there about our lives. When we watch a play, we can work out some of our complicated reactions to the inevitable realities in our lives: sometimes we're happy, sometimes we're sad.

But a tragic death will trump just about anything else in life, and endure, I think.

How else to explain her persistent death?

That stairway is just a plain, blank backdrop again. All that commotion is almost eighty years gone. But at one time, it held heavy grief, and the body of a young girl, dead too soon.

That's just so disturbing.

I prefer all my drama to take place in the designated, safe arms of a theater– on a proper, useful stage. There, I can manipulate interactions and call forth fabricated emotions. Where comedy and tragedy are pretend.

A dead girl in a stairway is too true and too heartbreaking.

I can't help but think that the ongoing intrigue is about something bigger. It's so ridiculous that in some form of mass hysteria, people here at the academy say they hear her crying. In this day and age!

Because there's no such thing as ghosts, right?

I suddenly sit bolt upright.

Oh snap! I forgot to ask about the lights!

**5:45pm, The Little Theater**

It's the end of rehearsal, and we're all tired but happy. I put aside what I learned from the headmaster this morning, and none of the kids brought it up again, so I'm not going to dwell on it. Luckily, I wasn't even in the main building today, so I wasn't tempted to torture myself!

The last of the Fagin caps have been tossed into a box, and the kids have left the theater in a boisterous clamor out the back doors. We had a great rehearsal; things are moving along exactly according to our schedule. But just as a sweet silence descends over the theater, the back door bangs open.

I raise my head like a gazelle at a watering hole, sensing in my gut that a pack of lions has arrived looking for dinner. I'm not far off. It's two parents, Mr. Kane and Mr. Longo, fathers to sullen stage crew teenagers Chip and Allen. I can see by their grim expressions that they have come with an ax to grind. Chip and Allen shuffle in behind them and stand to the side awkwardly.

"Mr. Kane and Mr. Longo," I whisper to Jackson as we walk up the aisle to greet them.

"Got it. Good cop, bad cop," he instructs back, and I nod.

Jackson extends his hand and says, "Good evening, gentlemen. Nice to see you; won't you have a seat?"

There's a table set up at the back of the theater with a few metal folding chairs, so we all noisily take our seats while the chairs rasp and squeak into place. Once seated, I suddenly feel as though I've been transported to the set of *The Apprentice.* From the fathers' grave faces to the corporate boardroom feel of the table, it's like we're about to discuss some life or death legal issue instead of a play.

Turns out they heard about the new sound system. How can this be bad news?

Jackson says in a neutral tone, "Yes, the parents committee has raised the funds; we're very excited."

Mr. Kane, father of sullen child number one, rests his elbows on the table and steeples his fingers in front of him. "We don't see it that way," he says. "The old system was run by the students, but my boy won't get a chance to learn on this new equipment."

Jackson frowns and says, "Sure he will, Mr. Kane. This is just an upgrade to the system that..."

But before he can finish, Mr. Kane points an accusing finger at Jackson and says curtly, "Untrue. You are disastrously uninformed."

Jackson catches his hostile tone and sits up a little straighter. Even I feel the low rumble of a testosterone fight brewing. I'm a gazelle; I want to run for the hills.

And then I remember my stilted conversation with Mrs. Kirkland. Is this what she meant by her victorious "I won!"?

Mr. Kane leans forward and says, "The new system is being implemented on the condition that only PowerTech employees run it. If you're not a technician from PowerTech, they won't let you touch it."

"That's ridiculous," Jackson says.

"Oh, really?" booms Mr. Longo from the other side of the table. "Ask Charlie Barnes, PowerTech CEO and father of Delaney Barnes." Mr. Longo cuts his eyes over to Mr. Kane and sneers, "Just providing for his little star, I guess." Mr. Kane snickers back, but Chip and Allen just sit there, stiff and blank as cardboard.

"Ask Claudey Kirkland– she doesn't care about the big picture," says Mr. Kane scornfully. "She's so competitive, she'd sell her grandmother's heart to get what she wants."

Wow. What a show. So they don't just play cutthroat with us, they treat their own kind this way, too. What the heck kind of a community is this?

"I don't care if the kids aren't heard perfectly," continues Mr. Kane as he rubs at a little spot on the table with his thumb. "It's more important that they're learning the ropes."

"Oh, I agree," says Jackson earnestly. "But, see, that's where the problem lies. We've got parents, such as yourselves, with stage crew students who want to learn, but on the other hand, we have parents of performers who want their kids' every note heard unblemished. We thought this upgrade would benefit everyone."

Mr. Kane says belligerently, "Disastrously uninformed. These students are not included." He doesn't even blink. Maybe he's not a lion; maybe he's a snake.

Jackson *does* blink. Several times. I know he's struggling to keep his cool. Luckily, his eyes come to rest on the cowering

Chip and Allen, and he asks them, "What's your take on this, guys?"

In unison the boys shrug. Good cop to the rescue. I know my cue when it comes up. "Do you guys want to be a part of this production?" I ask.

Allen looks at me and mumbles, "Sure."

"Yeah, sure," echoes Chip faintly.

"Good," I smile encouragingly. "Because we could use your help. You guys were good workers on *Arsenic and Old Lace*, and we could sure use your help on this musical, too. There's lots to do: set construction, lighting..."

"What about the sound?" demands Mr. Longo, glowering. "These boys want to do *sound*. Are you going to cater to Charlie Barnes and Claudey Kirkland?" He pounds his fist on the table, and we all jump. He is barking directly at Jackson, and has not looked my way once. Just as well. I'm a gazelle, remember?

Jackson can take no more, and stands up abruptly. "I'll have to check out what you've told me, sirs," he says curtly.

Mr. Kane pushes his chair back with an ear-shattering scrape. "If this isn't rectified to my satisfaction, I'm going to the board," he says darkly. "I'm sure they'd like to be informed that three of my kids are being denied hands-on learning on your watch, Mr. Graham."

Jackson ducks his head and then nods. "That's a fine idea, Mr. Kane. The board is the perfect place to air your concerns." He starts to leave, but Mr. Kane goes in for the kill.

"This tech guy, Tony, seems to have a firm grip on how to run things around here," Mr. Kane says easily. "Maybe he'd be better suited to take on the entire job."

How come the lethal words are always delivered quietly? Jackson's cheeks are aflame. The curls on his head seem to be rising up like steam. "Perhaps, Mr. Kane," he replies tersely. "Perhaps."

And with that, Jackson nods a short goodbye and starts back down the aisle to the front of the theater.

"On your watch, Mr. Graham," Mr. Longo roars after him.

I stand at the table looking at the boys in distress. For one tiny millisecond something passes between our eyes, and I realize we're feeling the same thing. And in a flash I know what it's called, too: mutual chagrin. Chip and Allen, sadly, are gazelles, too.

I feel suddenly protective of the boys, but without looking at me, they turn away and trail out behind their lions, I mean, their fathers. The door closes behind them with a shudder.

Depleted, I make my way over to Jackson by the piano.

"Well, that went well," I say sarcastically. "Are you all right?"

He shrugs.

I tilt my head and ask, "Have you noticed we're on the wrong side of the stage here, Jackson?"

He says nothing as he gathers his music into a pile. I can tell he's really stirred up by our encounter with the leader of the pack by the angry way he's stuffing his music into his backpack.

"Jackson?"

"What?" he asks distractedly.

"They're crazy, honey. They're all the hateful words you can be: arrogant, pompous, condescending..."

"Patronizing."

"Yeah, patronizing. Supercilious," I think the word may bring a smile to his face, but he's still all shut down.

He finally grunts, "I didn't know you knew that word."

"Yeah, sure," I say. "Supercilious describes us perfectly: super-silly-us!"

Now I got him. I'm rewarded with a tiny crooked smile.

"Don't let them get to you, Jackson," I implore. "I said we're on the wrong side of the stage because all the real drama is taking place in these cheesy little encounters *off* stage. Arthur

Miller himself couldn't have written better lines, 'Disastrously uninformed!'" I imitate Mr. Kane by slamming my fist on the piano.

"You insult Arthur Miller," Jackson scoffs. "Their tacky lines are straight out of a soap opera."

He clicks off his piano light and pauses before he looks at me and asks, "You ready to go home now?"

I smile and take a step back.

"Actually, no," I say as I climb onto the apron of the stage. Walking to center stage I turn to face him, arms stretched out like Eva Peron. "I want to act!"

"Kelly..."

"Wait, Jackson, just watch a second." I pull out a crumpled piece of paper from my pocket, and smooth it on the front of my shirt.

"I know these parents are demanding, but that's not why we signed on for this. I wrote this a long time ago, but I fished it out last night from my journal."

Jackson's shoulders slump, and he lets his backpack slip to the ground. With a resolute sigh, he takes a seat in the front row.

I tilt my chin up and address my audience of one.

"Why I Do This. A poem, by Kelly Graham," I read. I let the paper flutter down to the floor of the stage, and begin:

"Actors one,
Actors all,
At some time
Receive a call:
'Go embrace
The sturdy stage,
It's your birthplace
At any age.'

Actors, with all our vanity,
Illuminate humanity.
We see ourselves reflected here,
We laugh, we cry, we shed a tear.

It gives me hope
To self-express
My inner joy,
And theater-ness!
Without this high,
I'd cry and rage,
For I would die
Without the stage."

And with that, I crumble to the floor, flat on my back, dead.

There's a dreaded moment of silence, but then I hear Jackson applauding. As I roll back over on my side to face him, I see he's standing, too. Standing ovation! Woo hoo!

I scramble to my feet to take a bow, then flip my hair off my face to look at him. He has hoisted his knapsack back over his shoulder, and is smiling and shaking his head at me. There's still an air of dejection about him, but he looks a bit better. We hold each other's gaze and then he does my favorite thing in the universe: he extends his arm, beckoning me to join him under the comfort of his wing. I don't know why this gesture always gets to me, but it does. Something about it being noble and gallant, I guess. Jackson *is* noble. And *tolerant.* And although he's been bandied back and forth like a mouse between the perilous paws of Messrs. Kane and Longo, he still stands. My heart actually flip-flops.

I hop down off the stage and fly to him. Tucking myself under his arm, we stand quietly like this for a few moments. It's only then that I feel a wave of exhaustion come over me. We're both beat.

He finally looks down at me, tucked under his shoulder and says, "Let's go the frig home."

**7pm, Home**

We drive in silence back to the apartment.

I pop two Swanson Chicken Frozen Delights into the microwave and rip open a bag of pre-washed salad as soon as we walk in the door. The ridiculous ease of my modern life.

I can tell Jackson doesn't want to talk any further about our encounter with those parents, so I set us up to eat in front of the TV. I snap it on just in time to watch Judge Jenny.

As usual, Judge Jenny is not accepting any nonsense in her court, and is deftly putting people in their place with her acid tongue.

"You go, Judge Jenny," Jackson says as he raises a forkful of salad to her in solidarity. "Judge Jenny would have a field day over at Samuel P."

I smile sardonically just imagining it.

# March 24th
## 3pm
## The Little Theater

The kids are on stage warming up with Amber for today's rehearsal when the back door of the theater screeches open. In walks another parent– the bossy psychologist known as Dr. Gail Waldner. Evil chord: dunt-dunt-duuuh. She looks eerily like Catherine Zeta Jones in the film version of *Chicago*. Same silky black hair cut in that Cleopatra bowler style, blood-red lipstick glistening like she just devoured someone. I can almost hear steamy jazz music curling around her as she tightens the belt of her leather jacket.

Her daughter, Christine, exhibits none of her mother's seductive charisma. In fact, she's a rather plain girl who perpetually wears a pinched, worried look on her face. In contrast to her mother's throbbing dominatrix persona, I can understand why.

Dr. Waldner slinks her way down the long, side aisle, clutching a tiny notebook and pen to her chest. Seeing as she's a psychologist, maybe she brought along the notebook from a recent therapy session. I can just imagine the secrets and feelings of her unassuming patient now being strangled literally in the clutch of her bony fingers.

I wonder what she's doing here. Does it have something to do with Mr. Kane and Mr. Longo's visit the other day?

We keep repeating the "no-parents-please" rule as respectfully as possible, but they keep popping by anyway. Oh, that's right. I forgot; it's *Dr. Waldner*– she doesn't think the rules apply to her. This is what got us into trouble with her during *Arsenic and Old Lace* last semester. She and Mrs. Kirkland were the lead players in an off-stage power-struggle for control of the show. It's a very competitive town, but there's support and then there's interference. Guess which category they fell into?

I walk over to meet her, but she looks past me, eyes darting back and forth as she searches for...who? Christine, maybe? I look up onto the stage, but Christine seems completely involved in the warm-up exercise.

Dr. Waldner and I meet in the orchestra pit, surrounded by a black forest of metal music stands. They stand at attention like a military brigade. For once, I'm glad Angelo forgot to remove them. I stand among them, bolstered by their stalwart presence. I even feel the urge to salute. Or maybe duck and cover. Dr. Waldner has that kind of effect on me. Although she is clearly several inches shorter than me, I feel unnaturally intimidated.

"Hello, Dr. Waldner, may I help you?" Her eyes still don't meet mine as her head jerks in tiny birdlike motions to avoid my gaze.

"No," she replies. "Is Jackson here?" She adds a dismissive sniff as she continues to look around.

"Sorry, no," I say. "Jackson won't be at rehearsal today. Can I give him a message?"

"Well," she sniffs again– (OK, coke addiction or just really rude?) "If I'm going to be Head Parent Chaperone, I need a cast list so I can form a parent contact list ASAP. We're already behind in getting that information out. I'll need to speak to him right now."

I bite the inside of my cheek. Didn't she just hear what I said? Perhaps she's too tired from listening to her patients and has lost her capacity for hearing anyone else. Maybe her ears are so full that she can't fit anymore language in there. I can feel my animosity being whipped up as I'm reminded all too clearly about the way she always treats us.

I must be crazy for allowing her to be Head Chaperone again for *Oliver!* I should have my head examined. Ha, ha– but obviously not by Dr. Waldner, because, ironically, she's a psychologist with a listening problem!

"Dr. Waldner, as you can see, Jackson is not here, and I have a rehearsal to start, but I'll have him call you later this afternoon, all right?"

She narrows her cat eyes at me, and grabs hold of the nearest music stand around its neck. With a sharp intake of breath, she hisses, "No. It's not all right. I don't have all the time in the world. I have patients to see this afternoon. I've come here to take care of this *now*."

She jabs her index finger on the back of the music stand for emphasis and it yelps out a dull ping. She continues tapping her finger impatiently while awaiting my response, but I freeze up. Her imperious tone has stopped me cold. I am utterly speechless.

Luckily, Amber calls from the stage, "They're all warmed up, Mrs. Graham. Should I start act one, scene four?"

Relieved for the save, I call back a strangled "Sure" to her, then turn to address Dr. Waldner. Deep breath.

"I'm sorry, but this will have to wait. I have to go now, but I'll have Jackson e-mail you the list later this afternoon." Flustered, I turn away abruptly and stumble into one of the music stands. The stand shudders and then topples onto the one next to it, and a chain reaction is started. As they all clatter and crash to the ground, I immediately stoop to try and right them. This is useless, as I become caught up in the tangle and fall on my butt. I feel my cheeks flush red, but when I look up, Dr. Waldner is already stalking back up the aisle in a huff.

Thomas jumps into the pit and says gallantly, "I'll save you, Mrs. Graham!"

He starts to pull apart the stack of stands like I'm stuck under a life-sized game of Pick-Up Sticks. I sit still for a demoralized moment among my fallen comrades and mutter, "I can't believe this woman *helps* people."

Thomas reaches me at last, and I smile awkwardly. I feel embarrassed being rescued by a student. But Thomas just smiles and then springs back up onto the stage from the pit.

"Use the stairs!" I cry without much conviction. "Thanks, Thomas," I add as I dust myself off.

I climb the side stairs slowly and join Amber and the cast on stage. As I focus on their faces, I begin to relax. Rehearsing kids, I know how to do. Talking to demanding parents, not so much. These close encounters of the parental kind don't always go well for me. I look over to Amber to see what page she's on and smile at her. She tilts her script towards me and points a finger at page thirty-four. I nod thanks, then search for my pencil in my jacket pocket.

Amber calls out, "Places for act one, scene four, please." There is general chatter and goofing around as they find their spots. A cell phone skitters across the stage and I call out, "Loose cell phone; please put it away." Amber and I spread out a blanket, (a concession to avail her fears about plantar warts or any free-range germs), and take our places sitting cross-legged on the floor. She lathers a gooey blob of Purell onto her hands and sits back with a satisfied sigh. Side by side we face the kids and begin.

As the cast settles into places, I steal a sidelong glance at Amber to watch her in action. With new authority she is pointing to Shane and reminding him that according to the blocking she wrote down at the last rehearsal, he is on the chair, not the couch. "Everyone else should be backstage," she calls out. "Widow Corney, get ready for your entrance."

This is the part about my job I love most; watching kids like Amber who were once kind of invisible, suddenly take shape through a job they're given. Already, in just this teeny amount of time, she seems a bit more confident, and the kids seem to really respect her. Yippee for Amber. And yippee for teaching the same stuff that sports does! Take that, Mr. and Mrs. Superior Sports Department!

As the kids start running their lines, I lean back onto my hands to regard them. But I'm suddenly aware of someone talking out in the audience. I turn to face what should be empty seats, only to spy Dr. Waldner and Christian about halfway up in row H.

The tableau is unmistakable: Christian, hands clasped behind his head, leans back slightly while he talks straight up to the ceiling. Dr. Waldner's head is bent as she scribbles away on that tiny pad she brought with her. Quickie therapy session for Christian? Doubtful. I know what she's doing. Dr. Gail Waldner is doing what she always does: she's disregarding what I have said and is doing what she wants anyway. I suddenly think of Judge Jenny. I'm certain *she* would side with me. But what more can I do? I can't even state the obvious: Dr. Waldner can't wait for Jackson to e-mail her, so she is pumping Christian for the information now, literally behind my back.

This has to stop. But how?

Judge Jenny!

MY JUDGE JENNY FANTASY:

Judge Jenny comes sweeping down the aisle, black robes flying in a tornado of violent authority. She stops short at row H, and beams her eyes down on Dr. Waldner. Dr. Waldner shrinks back in horror, terrified she will be unable to handle JJ's wrath. Judge Jenny raises her arms like Moses and let's loose.

"These young professionals are trying to rehearse the students for a play. So far, right?"

Dr. Waldner whispers a papery, "Yes."

"And it's my understanding that parents are permitted, even *welcomed* to assist them in a supportive capacity. Also right?"

Dr. Waldner can only nod.

"Then what is it about the rules they have asked you to follow that you can't understand?" she thunders, her voice rising with each word.

"Um...well, they, they..."

"Spit it out! Mumbles mean lies!" There it is! JJ's most famous sentence. *Mumbles mean lies.* The best intimidating line in the biz! (And so true!)

Dr. Waldner suddenly remembers herself, and with self-righteous indignation says, "I have every right to do things as I see fit. They work for *us,* and the customer is always right," she concludes smugly.

"Really," drawls Judge Jenny. "Does it work that way in your profession, as well?"

"Well, no, of course not. I am responsible for treating the mental illnesses of my patients, so of course *I* guide them with what's best."

"Well it's the same here!" JJ bellows. "Stay out of it unless you are asked, and then comply with their wishes. Anything else is undermining and unwelcome. Got it?"

Dr. Waldner nods primly, her pale face struggling for composure.

Judge Jenny turns away, and with a theatrical sweep of her robe, disappears up the aisle.

Dr. Waldner rises and steadies herself on the back of the chair. But before she departs, she tears a slip of paper from her notepad and leaves it on chair 102, row H. When I open it, in teeny-weeny letters are two words: I'm sorry.

Yeah, right. Back to reality. If that ever happened, I'll bet the two words would be: Fuck you!

**6:15pm, Melodies Music Shop**

"Why are they there, again?" Larry asks with a frown.

I've stopped by to meet Jackson at Melodies to tell him about my run-in with Dr. Waldner. We're standing around the front counter, and Lisa and Larry have overheard the whole thing.

Larry's bushy red eyebrows bunch together, giving him the look of a Norse God. In fact, if you saw him, you'd think: *This guy's name has got to be 'Thor.'*

"They're there," Jackson explains for the millionth time, "to support the theater program."

Larry rubs his hand along the underside of his beard, taking this in.

Lisa watches from the far end of the counter, where she's busy wiping down the music cases. As burly as Larry is, Lisa is the opposite: diminutive and petite, her elfin pixie face makes her look like she's about twelve years old. Not that we go to bars a lot, but when we do, Lisa always gets carded, and they look at me suspiciously.

We all love to watch Larry think. You can actually see the wheels spinning in his head as he tries to make sense of what we tell him. He wants to truly understand the motivating forces behind behavior, so his observations, while slow to come at first, are often then spot on.

He recaps. "From what you tell me, these parents have everything a human can hope for in this life: tons of money, beautiful homes, servants to tend to the crap, healthy kids, the finest of schools."

Jackson shrugs, "Yup; that about sums it up."

Larry leans forward on the counter and asks, "Then why do they still act so deprived?"

We all burst out laughing. Why indeed? Larry has done it again! He distills the truth out of all the information; cuts right to the heart of it. I think he would have made a great judge. Not along the Judge Jenny line of judges, more like the kindly grandfatherly type.

I point out, "Money can't buy happiness, so maybe they feel deprived because they can't be happy inside."

Jackson jumps on top of my answer and says, "But money *can* buy you power. I don't think this is about them feeling happy or not. Power and control is what they seek; *that's* what they want."

Larry's brows have not unknit since we first began this discussion. "Why?" he asks. "*Why* do they want control over how you do your job? That's like a parent coming in here, thinking they can teach trombone lessons to their own kid without any knowledge of the instrument."

Jackson and I smile the same dopey smile. "Logic does not apply here," Jackson says simply. "Kelly and I have been all around this a million times. It's not going to make sense; we no longer even try to get into their mindset."

"It's true, Larry," I say. "We keep asking ourselves, 'why are we being treated this way?' and our only conclusion is that they see us like their hired help."

Lisa throws her hands up in disgust and says, "Ugh! Forget these people! Why do you even bother to put up with all this garbage?" She throws her dust rag on the counter, and puts her hands on her hips, "Isn't there somewhere else you guys can do this?"

I sigh and shake my head. "No. Well, maybe. But we're in a funny position. We're not teachers in the school; we're hired as professionals from the outside. In these schools they have to offer the positions to the teachers who actually teach in the school first. If the position doesn't get filled, that's when they seek people from the outside. These jobs are just not that easy to come by."

"Well, it just makes me mad," Lisa says loyally. "They're lucky to have you guys."

She reaches for me and gives me a hug. Over my shoulder I see Larry smile at Jackson and say, "Do you need a hug, man? I'm in touch with my feminine side; I'll grab you right across the counter."

Jackson laughs and picks up a drumstick from a display on the wall and leaps backward into a fencing pose, "Back! Back, I say! Or I shall banish you to Bogey Land!"

This is an ancient reference to the Laurel and Hardy version of "March of the Wooden Soldiers." In addition to being music-types, Lisa and Larry are serious old film aficionados. They like to fire up their antique VCR player and have us over to their apartment for wine and old movie nights. They'll keep us sane through this whole thing, one vintage movie at a time. I hope that's all it takes!

# March 26th
## 2:45pm
## The Little Theater

I'm backstage behind the closed curtains, locking up the pen when I hear the muffled voices of some of the girls from the cast. I recognize their voices right away: Delaney, Noelle and Marta. I'm smugly congratulating myself that I must be a *wonderful* director to have influenced them to show up early, when I suddenly focus on what they're saying. Although the curtain is drawn, their voices easily pierce through the heavy fabric.

DELANEY: I think Miss Brewster is incompetent. Don't you think so? I mean, why did the Grahams choose her?

I freeze backstage. Uh oh. Are they going to trash Lillette? I don't think I want to hear this. Should I announce myself? Too late. Noelle starts talking in a really bitchy tone.

NOELLE: I have no idea why they would pick someone like her. She totally can't dance. And excuse me, but she's sort of fat for a dancer.
DELANEY: I know. It's like they don't care about the show.

MARTA: I think the Grahams care about the show.

DELANEY: Then why are they letting Miss Brewster do the choreography?

MARTA: Why don't you like Miss Brewster? I think she's fun.

DELANEY: Her work is too...loose.

MARTA: (*Laughing*) I like her *because* she's loose. I've been through so many rigid, strict teachers, I forgot dancing could be so much fun.

NOELLE: You're just being nice, Marta, because Mrs. Graham made you work with her.

MARTA: (*Firmly*) She didn't force me; I *wanted* to do this.

DELANEY: Uh huh. Yeah, sure, Marta, right. You're a good dancer– and Miss Brewster's like a...a... gawky freakazoid. She looks like a giant, spastic Tweety Bird next to you.

NOELLE: Oh my God, yes! She does! We're not kidding, Marta. It's, like, *exactly*!

(*Delaney and Noelle start cackling cruelly.*)

MARTA: You are both so immature.

DELANEY: The show's going to fail and you're worried about my maturity?

NOELLE: Yeah, Marta. Delaney, I think it's mature of you to speak up!

DELANEY: Thanks, Noelle. At least you recognize that I know what I'm talking about. I've had more training before I was eight than the Grahams have had in their entire lives put together.

NOELLE: Oh, I know it! Everyone knows how professional you are, Delaney. (*Giggling*) Tony was even talking about it.

MARTA: Who's Tony?

NOELLE: You know, you know– uh, Mr. Glynn.

MARTA: Oh. You call him Tony? Why do...

NOELLE: (*Interrupting*) Delaney, he was telling me he thought you can maybe really make it in show business!

DELANEY: Yeah, I know. He told me.

NOELLE: Really? When?

DELANEY: Last year. When he helped me out on *Kiss Me Kate*.

NOELLE: What do you mean "helped you out?"

MARTA: Yeah, how did he help you out, Delaney?

DELANEY: We'd meet before rehearsals so he could explain some stuff to me about my character.

NOELLE: Oh.

DELANEY: He said he'd give me some direction about Nancy, too. He used to be an actor and he says actors always help each other out. He's *very* talented, and *very* helpful.

NOELLE: I know. Oh, *I know*. He's helpful to me, too.

DELANEY: What are you talking about, Noelle? You've never had a big part before.

NOELLE: Well, he just talks to me. About my feelings, you know, and, and...stuff.

They are suddenly interrupted by the loud burst of new voices—more of the cast has arrived. The riotous jumble of sounds masks the girls' voices, and cuts me off from my eavesdropping. I strain to hear what Noelle is saying, but it's just a garbled mess. I slide the combination lock back into place and notice that my hands are shaking.

So Tony has been a helpful guy in the past, has he? Coaching the kids with his "helpful" acting direction? He'd better not have his sights set on being "helpful" again.

Not on this show. He was warned not to cross that line. I'll be all over him.

Yeah, tough talk from a girl whose hands are still shaking.

**4pm, On stage**

"Blake, why are you saying the line that way? Did you forget how you said it at our last rehearsal?" I ask.

"Delaney told me I should say it like that." He shoots a wide-eyed look over to Delaney for confirmation and says, "She said that's how Oliver says it in the movie."

I, too, look over at Delaney, who, seeing the frown on my face, says defensively, "Well, he *does*."

I'm not sure what to address first, so I simply say to Blake, "There's lots of ways to say that line, and it will be right if the actor's intention is clear. The new choice doesn't make it clear, so please go back to the way we worked on it last time." I look over at Amber and punch it up by adding, "Because we thought that way worked really well." Amber nods back eagerly in agreement. I think she has a little crush on Blake.

"But I don't *feel* anything," Blake complains as he slaps his script against his leg. His hair looks even blonder when his cheeks turn pink.

I smile. "That's okay, Blake. You don't have to feel anything. Just play the action. You'll exhaust yourself if you try to really feel everything. Because ultimately it doesn't matter what *you* feel; it only matters what the audience feels."

"Huh?" says Blake.

But for the first time I see Delaney stop and fix a hard look at me. That's right, kid; I have the drug you want.

"There's a famous passage that the great actor, George C. Scott said...oh, where is it?" I grab my purse and hurriedly search for it in my side pouch. I have Delaney's fickle attention at last, and I know if I don't hurry, it will skitter away in a flash.

"Here!" I shout a little too jubilantly as I unfold the paper. "Listen up everyone: 'The only measure of fine acting is what the *character* feels. He can feel nothing or suffer the agonies of the damned, but unless that is communicated to the guy who paid to see it, then he has failed. The question is, did the guy in the tenth row or the lady in the blue dress feel it? If *they* do, then you've been a success.'"

I look up, straight into the open, receptive face of Delaney. She looks startling young and innocent, all traces of smug superiority erased. Our eyes lock, but then she quickly looks away and the hard, closed look snaps back into place. That's fine. Message received. I feel a victorious flip in my heart and turn to Blake.

"You're *pretending*. It's as simple as that. Do you see my point, Blake?"

Blake, hearing the rest of the cast murmuring, "Wow," "Deep!" and "I so get it now," reluctantly says, "Yeah."

I know he doesn't, but that's okay. We'll work on it. That little gem of acting advice was for Delaney. I can't be direct with her. Her guard is too firmly in place. Instead, I have to go down back alleys with the goods and slip them under her barricaded door.

We finish the scene and when Amber calls for a break, I catch her mooning after Blake, and Delaney eying me warily.

—⁓—

Thomas sits on top of a junky looking table stage right. He's telling us how hard he's been trying to grow a beard for the show. "I'm eating red meat and hot peppers. Those are macho foods, aren't they?" he asks sincerely.

Amber and I exchange amused glances. Amber bites down on her lip to try to hold her laughter in, but I see her shoulders start to shake softly. I try to control myself and say as seriously as I can muster, "Yes, those are very manly foods, Thomas. You're sure to see something sprout soon."

He's been trying desperately to grow something, anything.

"I'll settle for stubble!" he says now. "One of those five o'clock shadows like Fred Flintstone has. I don't need much."

"His friend Barney has some whiskers, too," Amber calls out boldly.

"Right!" Thomas says, pointing at her. "You're right, Amber. Even side-kick Barney Rubble has a five o'clock shadow!"

Amber nods wisely. "He has Barney Rubble stubble."

No way! I am so caught off guard by Amber's joke, that I cough out a shocked laugh, my eyes wide with surprise.

Thomas leaps off the table and kneels before Amber. "Amber!" he says. "There's a funny girl in there! I love that you let her out to play!"

Amber flushes with delight and covers her face with her promptbook. Thomas whirls around and dramatically raises his fist to the heavens.

He cries defiantly, "Why do you torment this young thespian, oh God of facial hair? Why do you give a five o'clock shadow so generously to cartoon characters Barney and Fred, but leave me smooth as a baby's bottom? Why do you doom me to slathering on spirit gum and a fake itchy beard? Is it too much to ask for a little manly face-fuzz so that I may be spared the humiliation of a beard that falls off mid-song, and the agony of spirit gum removal?!"

As Amber and I start cracking up, Thomas dips into one of his famous sweeping bows, and we clap and clap until our hands are raw.

"I'm just saying," he says casually as he wriggles his eyebrows at us.

I'm so proud of Thomas. He's doing a fantastic job finding Fagin's character. He camps it up and has been having a great time. But he's hit a bump in this scene, and that's why he's stalling with all these entertaining shenanigans.

I collect myself and we all settle down. Clearing my throat, I ask Thomas directly, "Thomas, what's really going on here?"

Thomas squints his eyes at me and strokes his nonexistent whiskers thoughtfully.

"I don't quite know how to play this," he admits.

"Let's do a quick theater game," I suggest. "This may help." I turn and ask the kids who are sitting out in the audience waiting for their scenes to come up on stage. "Gather around Thomas, and sit in a semi circle," I tell them. "We're going to play a game to teach us about subtext."

"What's subtext?" asks Duncan as he finds a seat next to Grant.

"I know!" Jasmine's arm shoots up and she announces, "Subtext is the meaning underneath the words." She gives a confident nod of her head as if she's both teacher and student, confirming her response is correct.

Well, she *is* correct, and I applaud her certainty.

"Excellent, Jasmine. Did you remember that from *Arsenic and Old Lace*?"

She nods. "I'm impressed," I say.

Jasmine beams and sits up a little straighter.

"Okay, Thomas, this exercise is simple. Say 'Don't go.'"

Thomas looks baffled but repeats, without emotion, "Don't go."

"Good. Now say, 'Don't go,' like 'I command you to stay.'"

Thomas points to an imaginary person to his left and barks, "DON'T GO!"

"Good. Now say 'Don't go' like, 'Please stay if you care anything about me.'"

He falls to his knees and begs, "Dooon't gooo!"

"Okay, now say it like 'It's not safe for you to go out there.'"

Throwing his body against an imaginary door, Thomas blocks it and implores, "Don't go!"

"Say it like 'I love you.'"

He drops his arms to his sides, hangs his head, then lifts it and says softly, "Don't go."

"Say it like 'I'm about to throw up.'"

Clutching his stomach, he waves his right arm in front of him, his face contorted with nausea, "Don't...don't go."

Everyone laughs.

"Excellent. Okay, break," I say. Thomas bounds back to his place in the circle and accepts high fives and fist bumps from all the guys.

"Thomas, *that's* subtext: same line, different meaning. Do you get it, now?"

Thomas grins happily and nods. "I'll just make a choice then, right?"

"Right."

The kids' imaginations have been whipped up by the exercise and they start calling out, "Let's do more! That was fun!"

I laugh along with them and say, "Okay, we'll try one more. This is a different theater game that teaches physical action. I need a volunteer."

Several hands shoot up, Delaney, I note, not among them. My eyes settle on Erik Kirkland, fluttering his fingers and smiling shyly.

"Okay, Erik. Come to the center."

Erik smiles tentatively and says, "Play nice with me, Mrs. Graham. I have a fragile little ego."

"No problem, Erik. Go get a chair. Sometimes it makes actors feel more secure to have a prop on stage. Go ahead, scoot, but listen while I explain to the whole group."

Erik runs awkwardly backstage to get a chair. Like the Scarecrow in *The Wizard of Oz*, he looks like he may fall down splat any second.

"In this next exercise, Erik is going to tell us about his day in his normal voice."

"He is *not* normal," Forrest stage whispers as he nudges Blake. Blake frowns but says nothing.

"While he speaks," I continue, ignoring Forrest. "I will call out some actions for him to do. 'To act' is a verb; acting is from the same root as 'action.' So acting requires not just the words we say, but the physicality of them as well. This exercise will give Erik an activity– an *action*. Actions are what make each of you different playing the character than someone else."

Erik is back with the chair, just in time, too; their eyes are starting to get the glaze!

"I know I'm talking too much again. Let's just do the exercise, you'll see; it will make everything clear."

Erik sits obediently in the chair, and I instruct: "Tell us about your day."

Erik wriggles a little at first, but then says, "Well, I got up really early because I had to take a shower. I usually take a shower at night, but last night I didn't finish my homework until 11:30 and I was just too tired."

I interrupt to say, "You get something in your eye."

Erik slaps his hand to his eye and starts rubbing it as he continues, "So I set my alarm for 5:45 so I could hit the showers then."

I interrupt again, "You get a sudden itch."

He stops rubbing his eye and begins scratching at his arm while continuing, "That's what my mother calls it, 'hit the showers,' I guess from her jock days..."

"You begin to grow old," I interject.

Erik laughs, but doesn't break his concentration and instantly adopts a shaky old man's voice, "After my shower, I went downstairs to get some cereal."

"Use your body, Erik," I side coach. "Show me you're old in your body."

He carefully tries to get out of the chair, using the back to brace himself. In his creaky voice he says, "My mother believes in a good hearty breakfast every day."

"You feel really sleepy."

Erik collapses onto the floor and says in a tired voice from his prone position, "She says with a hearty breakfast I can kick-start my day." He yawns and stretches.

"Okay, break. Thank you Erik."

Erik rises sheepishly from the floor and blushes as everyone applauds for him. Even Forrest makes some noise by pounding his fist against the stage floor.

"Look how interesting Erik's story became when he brought it to life with a physical action." My eyes sweep the circle, but they keep flashing back to Delaney. I notice she has been watching attentively. Noelle sits beside her, braiding her hair.

"Delaney," I ask casually. "Do you want to give it a try?"

She tugs at the bottom of her jeans, then pulls them over her jazz shoes. "No," she says. "That's all right; let someone else go." She tries to brush me off, but I persist.

"It's a lot of fun," I wheedle.

Noelle finishes tying the end of Delaney's braid with a hair-band and coaxes, "Go on, Delaney; show them how it's done!"

Delaney pulls away gruffly from Noelle and says, "No. I'd rather not."

Noelle looks puzzled, but I think I know what's going on. Delaney hugs her tiny half sweater to her, then busies herself retying the bow at the bottom.

I ask, "Delaney, have you ever done theater games before?"

She squirms a bit, then says, "Yeah. But I'm not very good at them. They're not my thing."

Just as I suspected. Delaney only wants to do what she's good at. She's got a bag of tricks that work for her, but she won't step outside her comfort zone to learn something new. Behind her haughty mask, lies a fearful heart, heavy with insecurity.

"Delaney, you don't have to go today. But I'd like you to someday feel brave enough to try these games with us."

"I'm *brave*," she says hotly, fire leaping into her eyes.

I smile. "Yes. You are. Undoubtedly. You are an excellent young actress, but these theater games will help make you even better. They'll loosen you up a bit, though, and that may make you feel vulnerable."

She's on her feet now. She yells, "You can't *make* me do anything I don't want to. I'm not going to be vulnerable with you! That's *so* inappropriate!"

With that, she rips the ponytail from the end of her braid and her hair springs to life like Medusa's snakes. Flouncing off the stage, in true prima donna fashion with her chin held high, she snaps her fingers impatiently behind her at Noelle. Noelle scampers to her feet and rushes after Delaney in her wake– like a faithful dog.

I face the cast, who all look subdued by the outburst. Even Forrest is looking at the floor.

I sigh and say, "Okay guys; let's stop for today. Good job." I rub at my forehead and continue automatically, "I'll see you all tomorrow; check with Amber if you're uncertain about your times."

They all disperse quietly, carefully avoiding Delaney as she roughly grabs up her things while Noelle scurries by her side trying to placate her.

As I watch them go, and the theater empties, Amber stands beside me, like a loyal first mate on a ship. She chews thoughtfully on the tip of her eraser then says, "Our little drama queen cracks at last."

I'm so surprised, I say, "Amber!" and laugh and laugh.

**7pm, Home**

From: Mrs. Marjorie Henderson
To: Kelly and Jackson Graham

Dear Mr. and Mrs. Graham,
I don't know if my son, Tristan, mentioned this or not, but he is allergic to wool. I am writing to inform you that his costume CANNOT contain any wool fibers, or he'll develop a rash. I cannot have him miss school time for an unplanned rash because you failed to make note of this. Please save this e-mail correspondence as proof I informed you of his condition. Thank you, Mrs. Marjorie Henderson

From: Dr. Gail Waldner
To: K and J Graham

Quick one, Grahams: Please tell each cast member to send in $75 towards the cast party. It will be held at Cafe L'Artiste, at 5pm after the Sunday matinee performance. I know you had the cast stay and strike the set after the last performance of Arsenic and Old Lace, but is it really necessary this time? Surely they've worked hard enough already, haven't they? In my professional opinion, I think they're entitled to a break. Isn't this the domain of the stage crew anyway? –Dr. Gail Waldner
Beeeeeep!
"Hi Sugarpies, it's me, Lillette. Sorry I've been missing some rehearsals. I have one more dance class tomorrow, but then I'm all yours. What happens is, my dance classes are so exhausting, I fall dead asleep. Sometimes in the car. Not driving, of course, but in the parking lot! Or sometimes on a little side road. I promise I'll shake the cobwebs out of my pea brain and see you at my next scheduled rehearsal. For sure!"

—ɯ—

I walk into the kitchen where Jackson is making dinner. "She's doing it again, Jackson."

"Lillette? I know," he says. "I just heard her message."

I pull out the little bistro chair to our dinette set and sit down dejectedly.

"Oh, forget the Lillette stuff," I wave dismissively. "I mean Dr. Waldner. Did you read her e-mail?"

Jackson shakes his head no as he stirs the Ragu.

"She *knows* the kids have to stay to strike the set on Sunday. And here she's gone ahead and booked a restaurant for the cast party at a time that's too early! Plus, she thinks they should be excused from striking the set. Since when does she get to call the shots?" I rest my chin in the palms of my hand and feel that stiffness in my shoulders again.

Jackson sighs as he dips his finger into the pot for a taste. "We'll just have to tell her to change the time, Kel."

"Oh, yeah, that'll be an easy conversation to have," I say, stifling a yawn.

"Hey, we're the directors," he says as he pours a box of cooks-in-seven-minutes pasta into a boiling vat of water. "We'll have to make it clear that no one leaves until the stage is completely struck and Tony dismisses them." He says this so adamantly, I believe he can make it happen– because I want to believe it will be that simple. But an uneasy feeling is starting to bubble up inside me, as agitated as the turbulent water Jackson is stirring. Something tells me Dr. Waldner won't take this in stride. Something tells me, in fact, she'll fight us on this.

"Jackson, when will this be ready? I'm falling asleep."

*I'm* sleepy– *Lillette's* sleepy. Isn't sleepiness a symptom of mono? Dang. I hope we're not coming down with *that*. I told Amber that was one of the Three Terrible Things that can happen, but not one of them has ever actually happened to me.

Jackson grabs up a box of Ronzoni and flashes a winning smile. "Cooks in just seven minutes," he says as he runs his hand under the box as if on display. "Six-minutes-if-you-like-it-al-dente," he finishes in a super-fast funny voice. Look at my charming Jackson. I manage a wan smile and say, "Okay."

I'm pooped. I try to distract myself from my lethargy by running various possible dialogues between Dr. Waldner and myself:

"Yes, um, hi, Dr. Waldner. We got your message about the cast party, but unfortunately the time will have to be changed."

"WHAT?!" I imagine her shrieking like a banshee. "Impossible! This isn't a fast food restaurant! I cannot get my refund returned nor change the time at this point. I signed a *contract!*"

Or...

"Hello, Dr. Waldner. Who the FONDUE do you think you are to go ahead and set a time for the cast party without consulting with us first? And it's not your place to excuse the cast, YOU COW!"

Oops. Have to maintain civility. I must be more exhausted than I thought, if I'm thinking like this.

"Jackson," I say, "I'm sorry to be such a pill, but I can't wait even one more minute for dinner. I'm zapped, I'm going to sleep." I lay my head down on my folded arms and prepare to fall asleep right here at the kitchen table.

Jackson abandons the wooden spoon in the pot and wraps his arms around me. I lean against him and he shuffles me down the hall, guiding my every move like I'm a sick child.

I crawl into bed, and feel Jackson deposit a forgiving kiss on my forehead. As I drift off to sleep, I see Dr. Waldner's red lips mouthing, "*You* strike the set. *You're* the help."

# March 27th
## 1:45pm
## On my way to rehearsal

I t is such a bad idea to go to bed on an empty stomach when your last conscious thought was of some parent's lips. It spawned the freakiest dream:

Two gigantic, blood red lips were screaming at me. That's right. Just a pair of lips; no face, no body. Like the ones in *The Rocky Horror Picture Show*– suspended before me, complete with icky strings of saliva.

I knew this was not the best breakfast conversation, so as I described them to Jackson this morning, he rolled his eyes in revulsion and said, "Eating here, Kel."

"I know, but you're so good at figuring out what it all means," I begged.

Ever since college, Jackson has been analyzing my dreams. He seems to have a knack for it.

He sighed and hung his head. "Continue," he said with a resigned wave of his spoon.

"The voice was Dr. Waldner's," I explained. "And she was yelling at me about the show. Screaming things like, 'Get me that cast list now!' and, '*I'm* the director, you inconsequential pip!'"

"Pip?"

"Yes, Jackson. The lips called me a pip. I guess like 'pip-squeak.'"

Jackson dropped his spoon into his Raisin Bran and tipped his chair back to let out a big old belly laugh.

"Why are you laughing?" I asked, kind of hurt. He'd never laughed at my dreams before.

"Oh, Kel, I'm not laughing at you. I'm laughing at the thought of anyone calling you a pip-squeak! You're a solid *woman*, woman!"

I was kind of taken aback by Jackson's "solid woman" view of me. I always thought he saw me as someone who needed protecting. And I *like* that. I know I can take care of myself, but I like the part of Jackson that's, well, my hero.

Anyway, he was laughing too hard to give me any real insight as to what it meant other than the obvious: Dr. Waldner loves to boss me around, and I guess I let her.

These aren't the most positive thoughts to be having as I drive to Samuel P. Chester today. We're still in the grip of a really cold March, and the steely gray skies match my sour mood perfectly.

I hated that dream. It's made me feel sluggish and peeved since this morning. As I drive along, the sweeping pines that crowd the road seem to close in on me. The weight of their ominous presence bears down on my dinky car and for the first time in my life, I wish I didn't have to go to rehearsal. Everywhere I look, all I see is gray and green– the colors of decay.

This is not at all like me.

To say I feel off is an understatement. I guess it's Delaney, the parents. The BIG LIPS! I think I'm letting them get to me too much. Maybe it's the limbo of March, too: no snow, no spring.

I'm on my own today– again. Lillette has that dance class, and Jackson is scheduled to work at the music store.

When I get to the Little Theater, the door is unlocked. Which means someone is already here. I cross through the lobby and tug open one of the double doors that leads to the theater itself. The lights are on, but the theater is empty. I hear voices. The lighting booth?

I look to my left to see the lighting booth door ajar, held open at its base by a stubby piece of wood. I slip just inside the door and listen. The booth itself is on the second floor, but standing in the stairwell, Tony and Delaney's voices float down crystal clear.

"Nancy loves Bill Sykes, despite how horribly he treats her," I hear Tony say.

"I would *never* stay with a guy who treated me that badly," says Delaney with disgust. "He's a total abuser."

"That's why you're having trouble with this scene. You need to find the part of you that *would* put up with his shit," Tony says.

Delaney laughs, "I know!"

"You sing the song perfectly, though; just like I taught you. Try the scene again. I know you can do it," he says.

I gasp involuntarily. He's directing her!

And he said "shit"!!!

Delaney starts reciting her lines and I am flummoxed. What the hell do I do? Adrenaline answers for me, and I take the steps two at a time.

Their heads swivel towards me in unison, but neither of them looks surprised.

"What are you doing?" I ask, my heart pounding ridiculously loudly in my ears.

Tony looks at Delaney, then back at me and answers matter-of-factly, "Rehearsing."

"I see that," I say. "And *why* are you rehearsing?"

Tony stands up and puts himself between Delaney and me like he's her bodyguard and I pose some sort of threat to her. He says smoothly, "Delaney asked me for some help." He rests his hand on her shoulder and says to her directly, "Delbar, will you please wait downstairs? I'll be down in a minute."

Delaney grabs her script and her jacket and without even a glance in my direction, ducks past me.

I still don't know what to say.

Tony indicates the stool Delaney has just vacated and I cross to sit down. I don't like it up here. The lighting booth has become Tony's office, slash, lair. The far wall is lined with a massive amount of ancient looking tools. The threatening teeth on the rusty old saws he's hammered onto the walls give the place the sinister atmosphere of a torture chamber. Sweeney Todd had nothing on this guy.

Tony remains standing and says, "Kelly, I know how this looks." He reaches into his pocket and tips a Tic Tac into his palm. "Want one?" I shake my head no.

"The thing is," he continues as he lobs the Tic Tac into his mouth, "Delbar has come to me for help before. It has nothing to do with you and Jack, I hope you understand that." He smiles easily, coaxing me with the Tony charm. "She's a great kid, isn't she?" he smiles fondly. I nod. What are we doing?

"I've known the family for years," he continues. "She comes from a long line of feisty. Have you noticed the feisty?"

"I guess so, Tony. But Tony..."

"Oh, I know she can be a handful. The talented ones usually are. I'll bet that was you in high school; am I right?" He tilts his head down at me, like a concerned therapist, really interested in the inner me. His eyes boldly hold my gaze, but I look away.

I've seen him in action before, seducing lots of other people with his wily ways, but he's never used it on me. The problem is, he's really persuasive. Kind of mesmerizing. Like a magician directing the whole phony trick, he holds me, stupid me, in the palm of his hand.

"Listen, Tony," I say, trying to snap out of it. "Jackson and I have told you before that directing the students is not part of your job. I thought we made that clear."

"Oh, you did, you did," he says earnestly. "But the thing is, I have a personal history with Delbar, so when she texted me last night and told me you had some kind of run-in with her, she said she needed my help. As a member of this team, I was trying to do just that. I didn't want to bother you with this; I thought I'd just take care of it with Delbar directly."

His Tic Tac breath must be acting as some sort of anesthesia, because I think I see his point. Derailed, I ask, "Why do you call her 'Delbar?'"

He laughs and throws his head back. I spot the disappearing Tic Tac in his mouth. It looks like a tiny, lost tooth.

"Oh, that! Yeah, yeah, it's something I just call her. A combination of her first and last names: *Del*aney *Bar*-nes? Delbar. See?" He shrugs and smiles sheepishly.

There's something wrong with me. I just thought he looked cute.

I stand up abruptly to break the spell and try to regain my businesslike manner.

"Okay, Tony, so, yes; Delaney had a little hissy fit yesterday, but I still don't want her running to you when she has trouble with us. It sets up an 'us versus them' mentality that won't be good for the show. Characterizations and how something should be played are up to the directors only," I say adamantly. "Anything else undermines what we do, and is confusing for Delaney. If we give her conflicting pieces of business, who will she listen to? Ultimately that has to be us, her directors. You take care of the tech stuff, got it?"

Tony's eyes dance with amusement, like he thinks I'm kind of funny. And not funny in a good way. Funny like I'm an idiot. He was making a big production of sucking on that Tic Tac the entire time I was talking– like he was making out with the damn thing. It's completely infuriating that he's taking this like a big joke.

I want to go. I start for the stairs.

"You got it, KellsBells," he calls after me cheerfully.

I stop in my tracks so abruptly I can feel my curls still swirling in motion around my head.

"No, Tony." I turn to face him. "Please do not call me that. 'Kelly' is just fine."

"Got it, Chief; aw! I mean, Kelly." He's standing now, one hip jutting forward, running his hand through his hair like he's posing for an underwear ad.

I flee.

—␜—

When I get downstairs, most of the cast has assembled and is lined up by the attendance music stand, signing in. I spot Delaney and Noelle down in the pit, backs against the stage, talking intensely.

As I approach, they both look up, expressionless.

"Hi girls. Delaney, can I talk to you for a sec please?"

Delaney exchanges an uneasy glance with Noelle. Noelle gives her a subtle nod of support, and Delaney rises to her feet.

"Step into my office," I try to joke as I walk over to the stairs. "Delaney, I'm sorry I put you on the spot yesterday. I shouldn't have done that."

I see a flicker of surprise cross her face, but she says nothing. Her arms remain tightly folded across her chest.

"I think pushing you is really kind of dumb. Am I right in guessing that in addition to you pushing yourself, you have a whole entourage of grown-ups pushing you?"

Her eyes grow wide and she says immediately, "Yes."

I nod. "Well, from now on, let's try to keep rehearsals simply fun for you, okay? No pressure. You have my permission to enjoy yourself here and just have fun."

Although she's still guarded, her fingers loosen their grip on her elbows and her arms unfold. I take this as a good sign and say, "One more thing, Delaney. I'd like you to try and trust Mr. Graham and me. We only have your best interests in mind. This means taking direction from us only, and not going to Mr. Glynn."

Her lips squish into a tight line, but she mutters, "Okay." I nod to dismiss her, and she walks away stiffly. She falls into Noelle's waiting arms, like she's just returned from war. Noelle squeezes her tight, and pats and fusses over her like a little lost kitten and I walk away.

I really don't know what Delaney's life is like, with so much pressure to succeed. I guess I'd be guarded and pissed off, too, if the grown-ups in my life were expecting so much from me.

At least it's nice she's found an ally in Noelle. Originally, I thought Delaney was using Noelle, but maybe they really fill a need in each other.

As to the way Delaney treats me? I'm probably the safest target for her to lash out at. I'm not her parent or even a teacher who grades her at this school. I'm totally disposable in her life.

Maybe I am an inconsequential pip.

—⁓—

At the end of rehearsal, the kids all rise in high spirits and run for the stairs. Clumping up at the top, they start purposefully bumping into each other with their bellies. What is this, preschool?

"Stop that, guys! Careful. Slow down! One at a time!" I call from center stage.

I could have used Jackson here today. "And remember, it's tomorrow at three for all of you again."

I'm still looking right at them, so I see the whole thing happen: Casey Harrington trips and grabs for Michael Glover. Michael has nowhere to go but forward, and knocks into tiny Misty Jensen, who stumbles and misses the last three steps entirely.

I watch in horror as Misty's arms fly upward like a rag doll, as if she's reaching for something high on a shelf. But a split second later, she crashes to the floor, landing on her side with a dull thud.

Misty screams and everyone suddenly freezes. Amber and I leap to our feet and push by the clot of kids jammed up on the steps to get to her. Thomas jumps into the pit and arrives at the same time. I see Sienna and Jasmine pulling their cell phones from their pockets as I bend over Misty and ask if she can sit up. She's pale and shaking, crying, "No, no, ow, it hurts, it hurts!"

"What hurts, Misty?" I feel a wave of pure dread and nausea sweep over me. Tiny black speckles dance before my eyes. I feel like my insides are turning to liquid; I'm terrible at anything medical.

"My arm, my arm," she cries.

I can see from where I am crouched by her side that her arm doesn't look right.

"Sienna, call 911," I say sharply.

Sienna is still frozen on the steps, phone clutched in her hand. When she doesn't respond, I bark, "Jasmine, someone, call 911!"

Delaney yells, "I got it."

The next thing I know, I'm instructing the dispatchers to the Academy. Thomas and Christian are laying a jacket on Misty, and Amber is handing me her cell, saying, "It's Misty's mom."

—⟋⟍—

Everything happens in a blur after that. The ambulance arrives, Misty's mom arrives. The attendants work quickly, saying words like, "shock," and "broken ulna," and "it's okay, she'll be fine." Hordes of parents and nannies arrive and disappear with their children, Jackson arrives and Misty is whisked away.

Alone in the profound, heavy silence that seems to follow tragedy, Jackson, Amber and I sit on the floor of the pit in shocked silence. The adrenaline that had been sustaining me is suddenly gone and I begin to weep. Jackson puts his arm around me and Amber moves quietly about the theater, collecting her things.

"Amber, are you okay?" I ask as I wipe my tears on Jackson's shoulder.

She nods as she wraps her scarf around her neck.

"You were great, Amber. You were a real help today," Jackson says. "Thank you."

She nods again.

"Amber, tell your mom I'm going to call her later to explain about what happened, okay?"

She nods again and turns to leave.

"Amber!" I call out. "Are you sure you're okay?"

Expressionless, she pulls a white crocheted hat down over her head– it stops just above her glasses. Peering out, she nods slowly, as if in a trance, then says, "Yes, I'm fine." She raises a finger in the air, like she's about to make a point and says, "A broken ulna is a broken bone. The curse has begun."

And then she leaves.

"That was a little freaky," Jackson says. "She must still be in shock."

But I've grabbed hold of each side of my head and I'm groaning, "Oh no, no, no, no."

"What's the matter?" Jackson asks as he pulls away.

I shake my head and say, "I'm such an idiot. I told Amber my Three Terrible Things theory."

"Your what?"

I push my damn curls from my face and repeat tersely, "My Three Terrible Things theory."

I don't want to explain any further. I'm furious with myself and feel too shaky to go on. I bury my face in my hands.

"What is that?" I hear Jackson ask, as I keep my head down. Can't he see I'm hiding? Can't he see I'm a coward?

I raise my head abruptly, but close my eyes and say impatiently, "I just mentioned that three terrible things always seem to happen when I work on a play." I drop my head back into my hands.

Jackson asks, "They do? Really? What are they?"

"Oh, someone will break a bone, someone will get, like, really sick, and someone will, you know– die," I say in a dismissive huff.

Jackson is quiet for a moment. Then I hear him snort as he adds it all up and confirms, "Yeah. That's actually true."

He collects my purse and slides my coat over my shoulders. Oh, oh, Jackson is being so nice to me. No one should be this nice to me. Terrible things happen when children are in my care. And look at how I upset poor Amber. I start to cry again.

"Shh, Shh," Jackson whispers.

My feet float away from the floor. I press my wet face into Jackson's coat and wrap my arms around his neck as he carries me away.

And then I'm in the car. And then I'm home. And then I'm asleep.

# March 28th
## 11am
# Home

After a deep and completely dreamless sleep, I feel better. Jackson indulged me a long lie-in where I just lounged in our bed, replaying what happened yesterday. He even contacted Misty's parents already, and luckily, she's doing fine. She's home, they said, with a hot pink cast that stops short at her fingers and doesn't, thank the Lord, impede her ability to text.

Jackson told her parents that when Misty's feeling up to it, she can rejoin us back at rehearsals. He also reported Headmaster Hank was terrific. H.H. said it seems like the sports department has some broken bone or concussion issue weekly, so it comes as no surprise to him that students can get hurt in a theater, too. He'll walk us through filing a report and all the legal stuff, but he reassured Jackson that the academy is plenty insured, and not to worry.

When Jackson brought me some o.j. earlier, I asked him if it seemed like this was *too many* problems, but he just shrugged and said, "Par for the course." Men with their sports metaphors– gets them through everything.

It's not that I'm bad at solving problems; when you rehearse a play that involves fifty people, you spend a good deal of your time addressing lots of them. But most of these issues feel, I don't know, "man-made;" like a lot of them could be avoided if everyone just did what was expected of them.

When I was in bed this morning, I remembered something that happened when I was a teenager that had a huge impact on me. An eight-year-old boy in our neighborhood got cancer. I'd known him since he was three– I used to babysit for him and his six-year-old sister. His name was Scott, and he was the cutest thing.

When my mother first told us he was sick and had to go through chemotherapy treatments, I was so shocked. He was so young! How could this happen to a little kid? I felt bad for him and his whole family. The whole neighborhood banded together, though, taking turns making dinner for them and having fundraisers to help out with their medical bills.

Once I got past the fear I felt when I saw his perfectly round, perfectly bald head, I saw he was still the same– like any other kid. Only sick. He still played, and begged to watch "Rug Rats," but he did lay down a lot. So when I visited him, we played multiple rounds of his favorite card game: "Uno." The point of the game is to get rid of all your cards; that's how you're declared the winner. But "Uno" is one of those exasperating card games where it can look like you're just one discard away from winning, and then, BAM!– you're scooping up card after card until you're swamped and losing again.

Scott *always* won. And not because I let him win, either. Well, in the beginning I admit I did, but then I really tried to win with all my might, and couldn't. So I studied how he played. He didn't seem to have an obvious strategy– not at first, anyway. I began to notice that when he didn't have a match, and he had to start picking up cards, he *laughed*. I don't mean like a nervous giggle– I mean full bust-out laughing, like when they say "peals of childish laughter." That joyful ringing sound that comes from gleeful happiness.

*Picking up a batch of cards makes this kid happy?* I thought incredulously. So I asked him, "Scott, how come you start laughing when you pick up all those cards? Because I feel mad when I get a handful like that."

He'd laughed and rolled on his bed like I'd said the most hilarious thing.

"Come on, tell me, Scott!" I begged. "Because I hate picking up all those cards. It seems like a big problem to me, you know, having so many cards in my hand. Can you tell me why it makes you so happy?"

He smiled and said simply, "I'm gonna need those cards."

His answer struck me like a thunderbolt. He didn't see it as a problem; he saw it as an opportunity!

Of course he was going to need those cards. Lots of cards gave him more *opportunity* to control the game in his favor because it increased his chances of picking up cards that would send *me* back to the pickup pile.

What I saw as a negative, he turned into a positive. And he won every time.

I had forgotten this lesson until this morning. I've got to try to apply this philosophy to all the extra problems we're experiencing on this show. I have to look at things from another angle. Here comes a problem? Okay, how can I look at it differently instead? It can't hurt to try.

I'll also have to check in on Scott's progress. I heard he's fine– studying science at Columbia. Probably solving the mysteries of the universe with laughter.

## 2pm

We're on our way to the theater. Once we arrive, Jackson and I will go our separate ways until rehearsal. Jackson will meet H.H. in the main office to get the purchase orders for the tickets and the backdrop, and I'll go straight to the theater to set up for today's rehearsal at three o'clock. I told Jackson not to fret; I really need the quiet time alone. I want to return to "the scene of the crime" by myself before everyone arrives.

I unlock the doors of the Little Theater, and let myself in. I feel a little chill as I cross to the theater doors because I swear I think I hear voices.

Not Tony again!

I unlock the box office door with a warning jangle of my keys and call out, "Hellooo..."

Nothing.

Ever since Headmaster Hank confirmed that a girl *did* die in the back stairway, I've been kind of teasing myself– listening extra hard to see if I hear anything unusual. This wasn't crying, though. It was voices.

I think.

Now I'm second-guessing myself; did I really hear something from *inside* the theater? It was locked. So maybe it was just some kids outside by the sports arena. Or maybe I'm still kind of fragile and set myself up to be spooked.

I cross the expanse of the stage and flip on the backstage lights. The fluorescents hum to life in a high-pitched buzz, and cast stark, flat shadows on the scenery jammed against the walls.

Still nothing. But I have this strange vibe; it feels like someone was just here. Like they just left, in fact, but couldn't help leaving some stray atoms of themselves still whirring in the air. I know it's weird, and it's not rational, but I can absolutely feel the leftover presence of someone. I do *not* believe in ghosts, but...

Oh, snap. Now I'm catching that stupid mass hysteria myself! I do *not* believe a dead girl is haunting this academy– I'm probably just being paranoid. Angelo's right; your mind can play tricks on you at any time, but especially when you're under stress. If that's true, then I definitely qualify.

I pace around the stage, picking at it: Could it have been one of the custodial staff? But then why don't I see them? What if it was Tony or Lillette? They have the other sets of keys, but why would they relock the outside door once they were inside? It's sort of an unwritten rule that if you open up the theater, it's now open for everyone to gather. Unless they relocked it because they were up to no good and didn't want to get caught doing...well, I don't know what.

And why would they arrive early and then *hide*? I shiver a bit and sit down on the stage. "Think!" I command myself. "How would Scott view this?"

My eyes come to rest on a lone Tic Tac. Oh, this is too easy. I pinch it between my thumb and forefinger like a captured bug.

I smile to myself. I get it. It *is* Tony. Has to be. And he's probably not alone. I'll bet he's rehearsing up in his primitive lair with Delaney again. He knows I'll go absolutely-positively ballistic if I catch him in the act again. I hop down off the stage and walk briskly back up the aisle to get to the lighting booth. If they're up there rehearsing again...

As I walk, I start working up a full head of steam as I put it all together. Over the past two weeks, I have noticed that it's not only Delaney who idolizes him. The stage crew kids trail behind him like he's their own personal messiah. Chip and Allen lead the pack as his top disciples. I've heard Tony call them by the oddest nicknames: "Lifegazer" and "Woodstroke." Nicknames I'm sure their fathers didn't dub them. Nicknames that don't even make sense. "Delbar" for Delaney. And I'll bet there are others. Oh, now I'm *so* going to listen for more.

I reach for the door to the lighting booth and am not even fazed when it springs open in my hand, unlocked. I mount the steps, taking my sweet time.

These are the little red flags that have been waving in my peripheral vision all this time. I've just been so distracted by so many extra problems, I haven't been paying close enough attention. I have felt this undercurrent of doubt and uncertainty about Tony since last semester. But it's just been a funny feeling.

Oh my God, this is just like the play *Doubt*! In that play, a head nun suspects a priest of doing unseemly things with a student, and decides to keep a look out for clues. I have no *proof* that anything inappropriate is going on, but my gut tells me I'd better pay attention.

So I will. Just like Sister Aloysius Beauvier (played by Meryl Streep in the movie version), I'm going to cultivate a scary, searing look, and send out the stink eye as a warning for Tony to behave properly.

In case he's not.

Of which I have no proof of at this time.

I reach the top of the stairs. Intuition rewarded. Sitting on the small desk next to the lighting board are Tony's cell phone and jacket. And a cup of coffee– piping hot.

But where is he? And if he's not here– how did he get out?

**3pm, The Little Theater**

We have a brief discussion with the cast about yesterday's events, including an important safety lesson about getting on and off the stage.

Jackson says, "I know you guys think it's overkill about the way we talk about this safety issue, but look what happened to Misty. We don't want a repeat of that again. You guys know how important this is; you've been on stage for concerts and graduation ceremonies. Did you know that the number one fear people talk about when it comes to the stage isn't stage fright, it's that they'll trip and fall?"

They all stare at us solemnly. Thomas raises a tentative hand.

"Yes, Thomas?" Jackson points to him.

"It makes sense what you're saying, Mr. Graham. My mother fell off the bleachers in high school during a choral concert and chipped her tooth."

Jackson and I nod soberly.

"It does happen a lot," adds Jasmine. "Look at all those *America's Funniest Home Video* segments that show people falling off the stage."

"Oh, I love those!" laughs Forrest. "Wham! They just nose-dive right off the stage, it's so funny!"

"It's not funny if it's you, Forrest. Just ask Misty about that," Jackson says.

Forrest sobers up, but still has to give Christian a little shove to dispel his embarrassment. Christian scowls at him and rubs his arm.

We go so far as to make them go up and down the stairs in different groups, to practice stair etiquette. While Jackson runs that, I sit in the pit with Amber and ask how she's doing.

"I'm fine," she says, expressionless.

I'm surprised to see Tony swagger by, flipping his hair out of his eyes like a surfer dude emerging from the ocean. Where did he come from? I never saw him reenter the theater. Maybe there isn't a ghost girl after all– maybe it's a ghost *guy*, and it's Tony wafting through the walls! I've just got to pay stricter attention.

"Yesterday was a pretty traumatic day," I say, tearing my eyes away from Tony. "I was really upset by everything that happened." I think maybe sharing my feelings will help Amber open up, but she just pulls out her sharpener from her gum wrapper purse and searches for a pencil.

"Mm hmm," she says as she lays a piece of paper on the floor.

"And you were a big help, keeping a cool head."

"Uh huh."

"Did you want to talk about it or anything?"

"No," she says shortly.

Amber grips the red pencil sharpener and carefully gives it a spin. The curled shavings drop down neatly onto the sheet of paper. As she whittles away at the pencil, the skritching and scratching sound is oddly comforting. It sounds like grade school, where the focus on one simple task, like sharpening your pencil, made for an easy and controlled little elementary school life.

"It was a pretty scary thing that happened, Amber..."

"No," she cuts me off. "It was just a broken bone. I was prepared. You told me it was going to happen."

I cringe. "I know I did, Amber, but still. I'm sure it rattled you a bit, and I just wanted to check in with you to see if you're okay."

She says nothing as she fastidiously folds the paper into a little pouch, careful not to let any pencil shavings spill onto the floor.

I don't know what else to say. When I called her mother earlier, she didn't have much to say, either. Maybe they're just a reticent family about speaking about their feelings.

A wave of exhaustion rolls over me, and I may actually be out of words. I definitely feel out of steam, and we haven't even started rehearsing yet.

I'll leave it. Amber carefully slides her pencil back behind her ear, then conscientiously walks backstage with her perfectly bound up little pouch to find a trash can.

# March 29th
## Saturday Rehearsal
### Noon

As if there isn't already enough draaama going on off stage to keep me in a perpetually drained state, I had my eyes on Tony all day yesterday at rehearsal, looking for clues.

I am scrutinizing apparently innocent moments with a cynical eye, but Jackson is not happy with my silent sleuthing. As our car exits onto Northern Highway, he reiterates that he thinks I'm just looking for trouble.

"I don't know what you're searching for, Kelly. Trouble usually announces itself loud and clear. If Tony's up to no good, believe me, you'll know."

I disagree. And when I ask him why he's suddenly coming to Tony's defense on this issue, he explains that as a man working with kids, he's sensitive to the subject. He insists anything can be taken the wrong way, even truly innocent things, like asking a student to stay late, or praising them for a job well done.

"Remember that mother from Northingham Middle School, who asked the principal there why a young guy like me was putting on plays with the kids?" he asks. "Like I was a dirty old man hanging out with the kids in the school yard! Men have taught children for centuries, but with all the mess from the priest sex scandals and all the newspaper press about educator sex abuse, male teachers are in the hot seat and I'm feeling downright paranoid."

I gaze out the window at a frozen pond, deserted except for one lone duck. I hear him, but still. So he's bonded on some level with Tony because they're men who work with kids in the theater? Well, that's nice, but I'm going to keep watching out anyway.

I shift in my seat and turn my face towards him. I go over it again. "How can you explain Tony's stuff being in the booth when I got there early yesterday?" I challenge.

"So he came in early. *You* got there early, too. So what?"

"He *disappeared*, Jackson. The outside door was *locked*. He was there when I first arrived, but then somehow he slipped out because he didn't want to get caught."

"Get caught doing *what*? Kelly, please stop this. It's too wacky– even for you."

But it's too late. In my vow to pay closer attention to Tony, here's what I've picked up so far:

1.) He pops Tic Tacs like an addict. The sound of the box being pulled from his front pocket is starting to produce a Pavlovian response in me; I begin to salivate for them too. (But I refuse to ask him for one. Started carrying around Mentos.)

2.) When he wants help from his stage crew students, he *whistles* for them, like dogs.

And 3.), When he praises the kids, he does it quietly. A compliment delivered in a low voice, entre nous. What's with the hush-hush voice, huh? Seems too intimate to me.

I tell Jackson all this, but he disagrees with my analysis, and says this is *exactly* what he means when he talks about perception.

"Look, I'm not a big fan of the guy, but if he whistles like a coach and likes to munch on Tic Tacs, so what?"

I guess so. Not much of an indictment there when you put it that way. But Tony's hanging lights with Chip today, so I'm going to watch thcm work up in the catwalk.

We pass the discreet little sign that says "Harding Cove" in blue and white, and I know we're just minutes from arrival. I feel around in my jacket pocket for my ChapStick and get ready to put on my Sister Aloysius scowl.

—∿—

Jackson and Lillette are on stage with most of the cast, so I start for the doors that lead up to the catwalk to check on Tony and Chip.

Just then, Mrs. Kirkland enters the theater and makes a beeline for where I'm standing.

Did I ever mention she doesn't actually walk? She marches. Not like parade marching– measured steps heavy and steady– more like brigadier general marching, with "destroy!" blazing in her eyes. Long, purposeful strides, arms pumping up and down aggressively. All I can do is brace myself. And try not to call her "sir."

"Yeah, listen, Mrs. Graham," (yes, that's her greeting.) "What's happening with next Saturday's rehearsal? I heard you scheduled it at the same time we have the big game against Cloister West." She thrusts a piece of paper into my hands and raps on it with her finger, causing it to bounce up and down so I can't read it. "See? It's been on the calendar since the beginning of the year."

I try to redirect. "Hello, Mrs. Kirkland, how are you?"

"I'd be better if I didn't have parents calling me at all hours demanding to know what the heck is going on over here," she says belligerently.

I am never, ever, ever ready for what she says, or how she says it.

"Uh huh. What seems to be the problem?"

"Saturday," she says through clenched teeth. I'm positive her teeth are clenched to prevent her from adding, "You idiot."

"Your Saturday rehearsal will interfere with our game against Cloister West," she says with an "I-just-told-you-that" grimace.

I say carefully, "Um, none of the cast members are on the team, so how exactly would this interfere?"

She closes her eyes and places her fingers to her temple, as if warding off a pending migraine. Happy to pounce while I still have an opening, I continue, "The students have known about this rehearsal for three weeks, Mrs. Kirkland. Not one of them has come forward to say there is a conflict, so there shouldn't be a problem." I smile a small smudge of a smile, and hope she won't notice the strain underneath it.

"Well, there *is* a problem," she says sternly. She begins to grind her jaw like she's warming up to bite someone. Hopefully not me.

"You don't understand," she says. "I tried to explain this to you as clearly as I could weeks ago. This school *revolves* around our championship teams. It's all well and good we have a little acting program going on now, but your work here is inconsequential compared to our sports teams."

I'm so shocked my mouth drops open. There's the "inconsequential pip" reference from my dream! Am I clairvoyant, or did my unconscious just speak the truth before I knew what the words were? And holy snap, did she just *sneer* when she said, "little acting program?" Her own *son* is a part of this "little acting program!"

"Just because a child isn't *playing* the sport doesn't mean their whole family doesn't support it!" she says– (sneering, absolutely.) "Although my son, Erik, isn't sports-minded, he still has to be there to root for his older brothers. The coaches expect this kind of loyalty and participation from the team-mates' families– that's just the way it is."

With this woman's combativeness, she could have been a coach herself. Or a gladiator. Or a Doberman.

I am nervously sliding my fingers along the edge of the paper when I suddenly feel the sharp sting of a paper cut. Wounded in the line of duty!

She grabs for the paper and says, "Look. It's right here. See?"

She recoils as she notices my blood trailing down the page. This momentarily derails her and she looks at me in surprise. I raise my finger in silent explanation, but instead of acknowl-edging she sees I'm hurt, she thrusts the paper back at me and says gruffly, "I have another copy at home."

I pop my finger in my mouth mostly as an excuse not to scream, but the tinny taste of blood can only pacify me for so long.

I say, "Mrs. Kirkland, the students have rehearsal Saturday. If even one of them is missing, we can't progress."

And then an idea strikes me and I enthuse, "We're a team here, too, Mrs. Kirkland– just like in sports. We call it an 'ensemble' in the theater– you call it a 'team,' but it's the exact same thing. We need the whole team committed and on board so that when opening night comes– that's *our* 'big game'– everyone is prepared."

I'm so proud of my sports talk I am now genuinely beaming at her. She's got to love this; I just spoke her language!

Mrs. Kirkland has been smoothing nonexistent stray hairs on her head back into place and regards me with a squint in her eyes. "This is a family function," she says staunchly. "It is causing our families stress. In light of the popular consensus, I am going to have to ask you to reschedule this rehearsal."

Now I'm angry. She doesn't tell us what to do! Headmaster Hank flashes instantly into my head and I blurt his name out like a steel shield.

"We'll have to go to the headmaster with this conflict, Mrs. Kirkland. We are not changing this rehearsal."

She looks at me evenly as if she's apprising me anew. I think she's surprised I stood up to her and said no.

"Fine," she snips. "Let's call him. But I'll win." Oh great, now I'm back in sixth grade. Why didn't she just stick her tongue out at me and say "Nah-nuh-nah-nuh-naaaah-nah!" too?

She pulls out a complicated looking cell phone, slides it open and presses a button.

She's going to call him *now?* But it's Saturday. Can't this wait until Monday?

"I have him on speed dial," she says smugly.

Poor Headmaster Hank.

"Headmaster, Claudine Kirkland here with a problem about next Saturday. Seems the Grahams have scheduled a rehearsal for *Oliver!* at the same time as our Chester versus Cloister West big game. No, no, it's been on the calendar for months, I guess they didn't see it. We all know how much is riding on this for our school, and we need the entire community to support us. I know *you* understand this, but the Grahams are new to our family here. They don't understand about the outstanding caliber of our sports programs, so it's just a matter of making this clear," she purrs. "I don't think they really grasp how tight knit a family we are here at the academy. I know you and I speak the same language, headmaster, so I'm sure we can easily convey this to the Grahams..."

We're a *family?* What is she, like, buttering him up with this phony intimacy by pretending they're old pals? *This* is how she negotiates what she wants? Will he really fall for it?

She's nodding her head and looking over at me. Big smug smile plastered across her face. Holy snap, she *is* winning!

"Thank you, Headmaster. I'll be sure to pass along your message." She slides the cell phone shut with a triumphant flourish and says, "You're going to have to eat crow."

She did not just say that. Is she really this petty and mean? I didn't even argue with my brothers like this, and they *are* my family!

I think I hate her.

"You'll need to change the rehearsal, and if you have a problem with that, he said to see him in person." She tosses her phone back into her Coach bag and crosses her arms expectantly.

"Right," I say crisply. "You win, Mrs. Kirkland. I'll make a change to the rehearsal schedule."

This seems to satisfy her as much as if I'd just given her an orgasm. She nods victoriously, then turns on her heel and placidly walks back up the aisle.

"You win, but the kids lose." I say after her as the door slips shut. I'm not brave enough to say it to her face.

Okay, so I was wrong about that appraisal. I am no match for her.

4.) Tony smokes.

### 9pm, Home

*From: Dr. Gail Waldner*
*To: K & J Graham*

*Dear Grahams,*

*Have you collected any money yet for the cast party? Christine reports you have not made an announcement.*

*Please remind all cast and crew to send in their money ASAP in an envelope marked "Cast Party." Please also mention, in keeping with the theme, attire is to be formal to contrast with the impoverished nature of the play. –Dr. G. Waldner*

**4am**

I wake up with a start. My heart racing, I feel a little dizzy. I sit up for a moment and snap on my bedside lamp to get my bearings.

"It was just a dream, it was just a dream," I insist to myself. Wow. This was worse than the big lips.

I slide back down between the covers and curve my body along Jackson's curled back. I cling to him for awhile, absorbing his heat and the still heaviness of his body in sleep. My breathing finally slows in time to his.

"Jackson?" I whisper.

"Mmph."

"Are you awake?"

"Mmmphh no."

"I had a bad dream."

He groans and rolls over to face me, his eyes still shut.

"Wha hapnd?" he slurs.

I ball my fists up and tuck them under my chin. "I was in a little town," I say. "In the middle of it, like, the *heart* of the town. When suddenly this huge...force...starts pushing aside buildings until I'm revealed there, exposed behind the rubble."

"You were the town," he mumbles with his eyes still shut.

I pause. "Okay. I was the town." I continue, "I scramble to find a chair, like when I was in kindergarten and the teacher asked us to find our seats; I used to obediently scamper to get to my chair first so I would be seen as a good girl."

"Mmm hmm," he grunts.

"So I find a chair and sit up straight, my hands folded in my lap. Then I look up and see that this force is really a huge *giant*, standing in the shadows holding clumps of the buildings in her hands. The light shifts and I see the giant's angry face beaming down at me. It's Mrs. Kirkland."

"Really," Jackson murmurs.

"I take a piece of chalk and write in the air between us: 'She could part buildings with her gaze, and find me sitting there, innocent as breakfast.'"

Jackson opens his eyes. "Whoa," he says. He swallows, and then says, "Wow, Kel. Profound."

"You think?" We are laying perfectly still, our faces perched on our pillows, inches apart. The silence envelops us like a physical presence.

He stares at me and replies, "Yeah. You dream in poetry. The town was really you, Kelly. Like your soul." The "s" sound in "soul" blows across my face and I close my eyes. The comforting clicks and moist noises his mouth make when he whispers lull and calm me.

"And Mrs. Kirkland represents the outside world of the parents who have been straying past any decent boundaries you've put up, just destroying your selfhood– your soul. And you're struggling to still be the good girl. This dream is telling you to screw that."

He's brilliant. It's all true. What a guy; he can still analyze even when he's still half asleep!

I open my eyes and look at him in contemplative wonder. He gives his pillow a punch, then passes out.

I lie still for a moment longer, the lush silence enfolding me in its embrace.

*Silence could maybe save humanity,* I think. More silence in our everyday lives: whispers only in line at the bank; whispers in school, supermarkets, war zones. Maybe we'd all fall under the spell of the sibilant, soft sounds and lead placid, stress-free lives.

Is this why they send people to a nice, quiet psychiatric ward when they're falling apart? I can see how it would be effective therapy to soothe jumpy nerves.

Oh, snap. I hope I'm not cracking up.

Why do I have to feel things so much?

# March 31st
## 3pm
## The Little Theater

I'm hidden deep in the back of the pen, scrounging around for umbrellas to use for "I'd Do Anything" when I overhear Delaney talking to Noelle. Grrr. I'm caught in the same position as last week. What to do?

"If she gives you a direction and you don't like it, just don't do it," I overhear Delaney say.

"But how do I pull that off?" Noelle asks.

"Just act like you don't get it. Pretend you're just not capable, you know, act stupid. There's lots of ways to get around it. You don't *have* to do what they say."

Is she talking about us? Or is she referring to their mothers? I sit down on a faded old armchair and try not to breathe.

"They think they're these great actors, but if they are so great, wouldn't they already have careers in the theater?"

Oh snap. She *is* talking about us!

"I guess so," says Noelle.

"Did you ever hear of the saying, 'Those who can, do; those who can't, teach?' That describes the gag-me-Grahams exactly."

Well, that settles it. No room for doubt there. Damn! And I thought Delaney and I were doing a bit better after our talk. Spit!

I can't let this continue.

I make my way down the narrow, jammed aisle of the pen and emerge backstage, paces away from where Delaney and Noelle stand by the closed curtain.

Under the harsh glare of the fluorescent lights, Noelle spots me and instantly looks stricken. But two-faced Delaney calls out a sunny, "Hi, Mrs. Graham," to cover any hint of what they were just talking about.

"Hi girls," I greet them, like I don't have poison dripping from my ears. Noelle looks paler than usual, and has the decency to look frightened, but Delaney shows no sign of discomfort.

"Noelle, can you please leave us alone for a minute? I'd like to talk to Delaney privately."

Noelle shoots Delaney a terrified look, then begins patting the curtains, looking for the opening. She slips out and I turn to Delaney.

"I heard what you said."

She says nothing, but crosses her arms and looks down.

"Delaney, turning cast members against Mr. Graham and me won't make you the new leader. That kind of leadership actually has the opposite effect. The play will suffer if you rally your castmates to defy us. That's called sabotage. Do you know what that means?"

She looks bored and rolls her eyes. "Uh huh, I *am* in AP Lit.," she says.

"Don't try to divide and conquer, Delaney. 'Us versus Them' is the worst way for a group of people to get anything done. I'd better not hear you ever coaching cast members to defy us again. The consequence will be you'll lose your part. Do you understand?"

Her face looks frozen, like she's used to enduring lengthy lectures and just numbs herself to get through it.

We stare at each other until she finally nods. She moves to leave, but I add, "And Delaney? Something to think about: if there weren't any teachers, how would you learn?"

As she shrugs and breaks through the curtain, I realize I don't feel angry. My main feeling is a queasy disappointment. I thought I'd made some headway with this kid, and I'm bummed to learn she's been harboring all this nasty hatred towards us.

I go back to close the pen with a pinch to the lock and spin the little dial of numbers. I feel like the biggest jerk. One sour kid can ruin your whole day.

—✺—

As if to seal my crummy mood, I emerge from backstage to find Tony holding court in the pit. The cast bunches up around him like a crowd of adoring fans at a rock concert. They're not just attentive, they're fired up. Their rapt expressions make them look like devoted followers of some cult guru. He stands before them, one leg up on a chair, leaning towards them the way rock stars dangle themselves tantalizingly in front of their audience.

Amber spots me and leaves the group to hand me the attendance sheet. Keeping her eyes on Tony, she whispers, "Miss Brewster called; she's going to be late." Amber's glassy eyes are locked on the back of Tony's head. Dang– what's this? I look at Amber closely. Is she falling for his act, too?

"And Dr. Waldner stopped by, but I couldn't find you. She wanted to give you this note." She holds it out for me to take, never making eye contact with me.

I take it from her and say, "Thanks, Amber. You can call places in five; it seems Mr. Glynn is holding them spellbound for the moment."

"Yeah, I know," she squeals. "He's the best!" She skips back to the group with her eyes filled with Tony-worship.

"Et tu, Amber?" I whisper to myself.

I know I'm being a big baby. I'm just feeling sorry for myself. And I'm probably jealous, too. I may as well acknowledge the whole shebang now before Jackson points it out. I *get* that Tony exudes this natural charisma with kids, and that in comparison I don't have it. Maybe I don't have the right rapport to work with kids after all. But what's his secret? How does he do it?

Tony's back is to me, so I watch a little longer, unbeknownst to him. The thing that strikes me this time is how he relates to them. Like he's one *of* them– not a grown-up registered with the grown-up tribe. He spars back and forth with them, using their words, ("Epic fail, Thomas!"), and their mannerisms, (running his hands excessively through his hair like he's doing a shampoo commercial.) He's definitely a leader, but wasn't the Pied Piper, too?

Bottom line: they adore him. And as Amber calls places, they collectively groan and reach towards him for one last fist bump of solidarity.

I unfold the note:

*Dear Grahams,*

*I still have not received any money for the cast party.*

*In addition, I must inform you I have worked exceedingly hard getting a number of parents lined up and ready to sit in on rehearsals as parental chaperones.*

*However, I have heard through the grapevine that you prefer not to have parents in attendance during the final few weeks of rehearsals. I must tell you the parental chaperones will be annoyed. Exclusionary ways are rankling to the parents who pay good money for this school and need to be sure to monitor the teachers involved with their children. I know you are new here, but surely, even as amateurs, you can understand that in these times, it is in the best interests of everyone to have as many eyes on the students as possible. It's for your protection as well as theirs.*

*Our culture is finally embracing the notion of complete transparency in all areas of community life: finance, politics, education, et al. Transparency is of the utmost importance to this program in particular, as it has floundered in the past. Therefore, we need to be sure all available eyes are watching to be certain the program is soundly progressing, especially since there are two novices at the helm.*

*We will abide by your wishes, for now, not to be present at rehearsals, but many parents are already upset by your stance and are seeking ways to have the headmaster respond. We will leave the final decision in his hands, but pledge to be in constant contact to remain vigilant.*

*–Dr. Gail Waldner*

You. Have. Got. To. Be. Kidding.

What will it be next for these parents– bodyguards to escort their child's every move?

The kids swarm around me, but I feel completely alone and separate.

When we chanted "sticks and stones may break my bones, but names can never harm me," in childhood, we used it as a buffer to bolster ourselves from the mean kids calling us Fatso, or Four-eyes. But even as adults, the subtle grown-up words really *can* harm you. So now we're "amateurs" and "novices"? Her words are knocking me out. I feel so crappy, I want to lie right down on this stage and disappear into the floor.

Tony is sauntering back up the aisle, and for a flicker of an instant I consider calling out to him. Maybe I should show him this note and ask what he would do? But the impulse dies as quickly as it comes, as I watch Chip and Allen scamper after him. Tony turns as he hears them approach, crouches into a ninja pose, and starts sparring with them. The boys' faces light up as they try to land their karate chops on him.

I am feeling small and uncertain. Maybe it's me. Maybe I need a thicker skin, because maybe these parents have a point. Although their arguments strike *me* as over-the-top, maybe I'm blind. Or come from another planet. Yeah, that's it; I come from planet middle class, where our values and perceptions are different, I guess.

The local customs here– of browbeating with supercilious arguments– are an accepted way to get what you want. I just have to get with the program.

I feel so wobbly, but I have to put this aside. I shove the note into my pocket, take a deep breath and yell, "Top of scene six, please!"

**Home, 7pm**

*From: Gertie Barnes*
*To: Grahams*

*Dear Mr. and Mrs. Graham,*
*We would appreciate it, if in the future, you refrained from threatening our daughter with the removal of her part.*

*According to Delaney, she caught Mrs. Graham eavesdropping on a private conversation she was having with her dear friend Noelle. As if this wasn't a tawdry enough violation, Mrs. Graham then went on to censure Delaney in a most unfair matter.*

*We feel the infraction is on Mrs. Graham's part, as Delaney insists she was speaking privately to a friend, and as I am sure you are aware, the tenets of free speech and the right to privacy are guaranteed in the constitution.*

*We will not take this to the headmaster if we have your assurance you will not breech Delaney's right to privacy again. Regards, G. and K. Barnes*

"Jackson, consider me now incapable of not having a reaction when this woman communicates with us! Delaney 'caught *me?*' She's twisting what happened! I'm allowed to discipline a cast member as I see fit! I'm just doing my job! That's why they hired us!"

I rant on, pacing back and forth in our tiny bedroom, while Jackson looks on from our bed. Every now and then he reaches out to try and grab me, but I push him away. I finally stop shrugging him off and let him tackle me into a bear hug. He flips me onto the bed and holds me tightly until I start to calm down. I roll over onto my belly as he strokes my arms. Within seconds, he straddles my back and begins massaging my shoulders. I allow it because, with a groan of pleasure, I release all this stupid parent-tension.

"*Is* there a right to privacy in the constitution?" I mumble into the pillow.

"Yeah," Jackson says. "I think there is. I don't think it's stated outright or anything. I think it falls under all that inalienable rights stuff."

This sets me off again. "So, so, *what?* In her eyes I've committed some federal offense because I disciplined her daughter?" I lift my head up off the pillow, but Jackson gently presses me back down.

My head pops right back up like a Pop Tart. "When did parents become so aggressive, Jackson? Would your parents have ever gone to the teacher in such a self-righteous manner?"

"Never," he soothes.

"Would your mother have ever, ever, EVER called a teacher *at home?!*"

"No. Never. Shh, shh, stop."

I feel him reach over and fumble with the laptop. I roll over on to my side as he says, "Look– look, Kelly."

I watch him as he raises a long, slender finger tantalizingly over the delete button.

"Do it," I whisper.

"Now?" he teases.

"Yes, now," I say.

"You mean *right* now?"

"Yes! Now! *Now!*" I scream.

His finger hovers there a torturous second longer. Then he brings it down quickly and deftly presses "delete."

I moan with relief, then sink back into the pillows, spent.

# April 2nd
## 10am
## Home

I'm calling The Prof. Or should I say, "The Preeminent Prof." Professor Bennett Jeffries is retired now, but he is one of our favorite teachers from college. Before he taught us, he was a high school theater teacher. I'm calling him because I need his guidance, or, let me drop the "edu-speak" and say simply: because the parents are driving us crazy!

I couldn't sleep last night, and I felt Jackson tossing and turning, too. Maybe The Prof can assure me outright that all the crap we're encountering is not because of anything we are/aren't doing.

He greets me so warmly, I instantly feel tears leap to my eyes. Yikes, I'm like some needy abuse victim who collapses when someone shows the smallest kindness. I don't want to blubber out all my stress-fueled feelings in one gush, but his friendly voice is so welcoming, I just might.

I try to overcome the waver that's suddenly gripped my voice, and tell him, briefly, of the top scenarios that have occurred. I want to read him some of the e-mails and letters, but there are just too many. I blab out what I can, then finish up by asking if parents had ever treated him this way.

He chuckles softly and says, "Oh, so many painful memories." In my mind, I can see him shaking his wise old head, and squeezing his crinkly eyes shut against the images.

"My specific stories aren't the same, and remember, I was teaching in public high schools with the protection of tenure. But sure, there were always parents trying to manipulate things to their child's advantage."

"*My* parents didn't!" I cry.

"You were raised in another time," he explains. "But the problem, as I see it in your case, is that the parents have been allowed too far in."

"Exactly!" I blurt.

"Parental assistance and support only works when you have boundaries everyone respects. It sounds like with these parents, their overzealous behavior has made it hard for you and Jackson to hold back the tide."

I grip the phone tightly in my hand, hanging on to every word. He understands completely! He could teach a class in this: *Basic Understanding of Out-of-Control Parenting Ways 101.*

I should be recording this! Transcribed and put into a handy, helpful little pamphlet, it would be a lifesaver for newbie teachers.

"And it sounds like it's not just one or two parents putting the squeeze to you..."

"Oh, you're right," I exhale. "There are so many of them. I feel like I'm on a tennis court batting away fifty balls careening towards me at once."

"I know, I understand," he murmurs.

"And Prof, without sounding like I'm profiling these people, their common denominator is their demanding demeanors."

I hear him take a surprised intake of breath. "Did you just use a math phrase, Miss Theater Girl?"

"Ah! Yes I did, Prof! Bet you didn't know I had it in me!" We share a little laugh that does me the world of good. Wiping my eyes, I draw my knees up to my chest.

"The *equation*," I smile into the phone, "goes something like this: if we say 'no' to something– *anything*, it is met with first, hostility, then backstabbing, then retaliation. It all *equals* a vindictive campaign to get what they want through any avenue. But Prof," I implore. "We are not talking about a cure for cancer here, we're talking about what, in the grand scheme of things, are the pettiest of problems."

"They just want what they want," he says. "And it sounds like they want to be in charge. I saw this at the high school level, but it virtually disappeared when I taught college. And honestly, Kelly, I never saw as much of this as you're seeing. This may also have to do with a sense of entitlement brought on by their wealthy status."

I sigh. Maybe. Probably. "Do you think they get together at these parents' meetings to discuss using these tactics?" I ask anxiously.

The Prof laughs loud and hearty, "No, Kelly; I don't think so." He takes a breath and sings, "Paranoia will destroy-ya."

"Okay, okay; I get it Prof!"

"Remember this," he harrumphs back into his best gravelly lecture voice. "When people are acting really improperly and poorly, it is not *you*; it's *them*. I will say it again so you really hear it: it's not you. It's them."

The Prof still knows how to drive a point home!

He continues, "And the root of the bad behavior comes from fear. Every single time. If you can just understand that *this* is their motivating force, then you can detach yourself. All good leaders have to learn this skill."

I am silent. So I guess he's saying it's their problem.

"What are they afraid of?" I ask eventually.

"Not feeling in control, not feeling a part of things."

"It's not my job to make them feel included! I'm directing their children in a play," I huff.

"I know," he says. "But think about it."

"Well," I waver. "I remember reading Vonnegut in high school, and he sort of said the same thing; that people want to feel like they're *participating*."

"Yes, yes," he says.

"But they don't play nice, Prof! They throw tantrums to get what they want. I don't want them around under the guise of 'supporting the production,' when, really they're only out for themselves."

"I know it's complex, Kelly, but you and Jackson have to work on not having such a personal response to everything. You'll both burn out before you're thirty."

"I'm almost thirty now, Prof."

"Wow. Really? Where did the time go?"

I laugh and say, "I don't know. It feels like I'm right back in your class again, like no time has passed at all."

He chuckles warmly and says, "If only that were true. Because Kelly, bottom line is, as cliché as it sounds, life is just too short. Stand up to these people as best you can. You are the professionals hired to do the job. Be your own best advocate. Detach."

"And what about the students? It's really just this one girl, Delaney, and this other boy, Forrest– but they take so much of my energy."

"Same thing. Show them who is boss by implementing boundaries and consequences."

"The parents won't *allow* us to use consequences."

"Too bad. Use them anyway. Maybe the parents will get the message then, too."

I tend to doubt it. Look how Gert Barnes reacted to my use of consequences with her daughter.

"I tried that already with that Delaney kid, but her mother freaked out."

"Too bad. Carry on. *You're* in charge. *You're* driving the bus," he says emphatically.

I exhale and say, "Prof, you're the best. This has really been helpful. Thank you so much. I'm going to send you a batch of my chocolate chip cookies."

"What?" he gasps. "No comp tickets to the show?" I can feel the twinkle in his eyes right in my heart. I love the Prof!

"Not for this one Prof. Not unless you want to visit our little fire pit of fried hell."

"Okay, okay; then the cookies sound fine. Does Jackson still peel the chocolate chips out before he eats them?"

I laugh with surprise. "You remember that? Yeah, he does. Still makes a big crumbly mess!"

"A metaphor for life," says the Prof. "A big crumbly mess!"

—⟋⟍⟍—

*From: Amber*
*To: Mr. + Mrs. Graham*

*Hi Mr. + Mrs. Graham, it's me, Amber. Holly Kellogg got a text from Dominique Marks during Global History that Julie Eng was out sick with a virus. Holly texted Tristan Henderson, who texted Sawyer Bedell, that he heard it wasn't just a plain virus, it was mono. Daisy Brady just texted me in Honors Chem to confirm: It's mono.*
*sent via my blackberry*

# April 4th
## 3pm
## The Little Theater

The kids gather in clumps at the beginning of rehearsal. Clustered backstage I see stage crew students lifting the wood that will be the bridge where Nancy gets murdered. It's a really scary scene, gritty and violent, so we are going to have the actual murder part take place off stage with a bloodcurdling scream. Bill Sykes and Nancy have to at least meet on the bridge, though. And with my two fave students– Forrest and Delaney– cast in these roles, I am *not* looking forward to staging that.

With only three weeks left, everything starts to heat up at this point. This sometimes includes my temper. I'm focused on the many details that still need addressing, so I tend to have a shorter fuse with the nonsense.

I'm kneeling onstage, rummaging through a box of fabric that will be sewn into some of the costumes, when Allen tentatively approaches me.

"Mrs. Graham?"

"Yes, Allen, what it is?" I say, head still in the box.

"I found this today," he says, and opens his palm to reveal a tiny pink iPod.

I take a quick look, then all business, say, "Thanks, Allen. I'll have Amber make an announcement so the owner can claim it." I go to reach for it, but he closes his fingers purposefully back around it and pulls his hand away.

"No," he says. "I know whose it is."

"Oh," I say, and sit back on my heels. "Okay, then why don't you give it to them?" I'm instantly irritated. If he knows who the owner is, why hasn't he just given it back? No time for nonsense!

He hesitates a moment, then shuffles from one foot to the next. He looks embarrassed for some reason. Finally, with his head down as he gazes at the iPod in what I can only describe as a mournful yearning, he says, "Okay," then turns away.

Sheesh. What did he want me to say– he can keep it because he found it?

I put my head back into the box and hear a little voice inside telling me I was a little harsh. I pop my head back up and call, "Hey, Allen!" to his retreating back.

"Yes, Mrs. Graham?"

Adopting a sweeter tone, I ask, "Is everything okay?"

He begins a slow nod, then shrugs and says, "Yeah. Sure."

I'm obviously not getting the whole story, but okay. I asked. I never know how much to really push with teens. Something may be bothering him, but I'm not sure. Could be big, probably is small. With teens it all reads the same!

"Okay, good."

Back to the fabric, I begin sorting it into color combinations: black, navy, dark green and lots of brown. Excellent. This will all do fine. Maybe I can enlist Taffy's mother, the-former-fashion-designer, to sew a few skirts. We're going to rent Nancy's red costume, and the Artful Dodger's blue jacket, too. Everything else we'll cobble together from thrift shops or from stuff we already have. Note to self: do they have thrift shops in wealthy communities?

I'm looking down when I see a pair of familiar sneakers appear again. Allen.

I stop what I'm doing, look up, and give him a concerted warm smile. "Back so soon?"

He stands awkwardly and nods a shy "yes."

"What?" I tease. "Found another one?"

He smiles a little, then opens his palm. The same pink iPod is still nestled there, only this time I notice it's glistening in a pool of his sweat.

"Can *you* give it to her?" he asks.

"Sure," I say as I reach for it. "Who does it belong to?"

I am not kidding when I say a blush explodes over his face like someone threw red paint on him.

"It's Noelle's," he stammers.

Oh. Dopey me– now I get it: sweaty palms plus raging blush equals teenage crush. I'm always so slow with the math! Arrrgh! How could I have missed this one? Poor kid.

I pry it gently out of his hand and say, "No worries, Allen. I'll be sure she gets it back anonymously."

He turns away quickly and wipes his hands along the thighs of his jeans. "Okay, thanks," he says as he lopes away.

Aww. Poor Allen. Noelle probably hasn't even given him a second glance. Sadly, and in general, I've noticed stage crew kids and cast members really don't hook up together. Probably some status thing.

I search discreetly for a tissue in my sweatshirt pocket and give the iPod a quick towel off. An inscription catches my eye: "To N., Love, Tiger."

Wow. I didn't know Noelle had a boyfriend. I've never seen her with anyone. Huh. Maybe a past sweetheart. With no further time to dwell on it, I stash the iPod in the front pouch of my sweatshirt and call out for Amber.

Amber scurries to my side, heaving her promptbook to her chest. She announces breathlessly, "Mrs. Graham, Sienna won't be here today; she has an emergency doctor's appointment."

She pauses, then looks at me meaningfully. "They think she has mono."

I pull a face and say, "Okay. Thanks for telling me, Amber."

As we settle into our usual spots, I take a deep breath and lean forward. Amber looks to me for the cue, and I nod. "Places please, act two, scene four," she shouts.

And so we begin again, as we always do in the theater, trying to make what is familiar sound brand new.

Three short weeks to go.

**5:30pm**

"Sanford Meisner said, 'Acting is living truthfully under the given imaginary circumstances.'"

I face the kids, still in their staggered positions at the end of the scene.

"I am proud to report that you are all doing a fine job in this department," I say.

They all smile. I ask them to have a seat where they are so I can give some brief notes.

As they sink to the floor, I say, "Good job, everyone. You're really incorporating all the stuff we've been talking about: being alert and alive on stage, and really reacting back and forth like a tennis match. But please memorize those lines! You were supposed be off-book as of yesterday. You see how this slows us down? Repetition, repetition, repetition. It's not magic. You have to physically say the words in your mouth. It's just like learning a dance– put it into your body, and your body won't forget."

Although they're looking at me, I can see they're starting to glaze over.

"Okay, that's it for today," I say, releasing them. "Please see Amber for call time tomorrow if you're unsure." They make a break for it and race to get their jackets and backpacks. Erik stays on stage, flings his arm over Blake's shoulder and sings, "I'd do anything, for you, Blake, anything, for you mean everything to meee!"

Blake sings back, "Would you do my homework?"

"Anything," sings Erik.

"Get me a new cell phone?"

"Anything!"

"Let me borrow that shirt?"

"Anything?" Erik stops singing and says, "You like this shirt? I took it from my butch brother's closet. He'll kill me with his meaty man-hands if he ever finds out."

Blake's face falls and he says soberly, "Then don't give it to me, Erik. I don't want to end up like the dead girl."

"Which one?" Erik asks.

"There's more than one dead girl?" Blake blanches.

"Yeah, dopewad. There's the dead girl from the back hallway– where you refuse to walk– and then there's Nancy, Bill Sykes' girlfriend in the play."

Blake lets out a huge gust of air and says tersely, "Re-al-i-ty, Erik. Try to keep up with me in reality, okay? Delaney won't *really* die as Nancy. It's *fake*."

Erik crosses his arms and harrumphs, "Well, with Forrest playing Bill Sykes, anything is possible!"

I interrupt them and say, "Guys, don't even joke about that. And please get a move on; don't keep your parents waiting."

Blake looks up from zippering his jacket and says, "You mean my driver."

"Okay, your driver then," I say. "And don't forget to check your e-mail!" I holler out to the whole cast still gathering up their stuff.

I hang my head for a second. That was kind of disturbing what Erik said about Forrest. It means even the kids sense Forrest is a loose cannon.

As I look back up to watch them trickle out through the back doors, I suddenly remember about the iPod.

"Noelle! Wait!" I call out. I've caught her just in time, halfway up the aisle kick-sliding her backpack with her right foot.

She turns and says, "Yeah?"

With her satiny white jacket, big green eyes and blonde hair cascading around her shoulders, she is the spitting image of a young Haley Mills. When I told her that once she said, "Who?"

I said, "Haley Mills. The first *Parent Trap?*"

"You mean Lindsay Lohan?" she asked.

"No, that was the second one. Haley Mills was in the original."

"Oh," she said. And then obnoxiously, "Thanks, maybe?"

Grrrr.

She abandons the backpack and makes her way up the stage right stairs to meet me center stage.

I pull the iPod from my pouch in a jumbled mess, the ear buds unraveled and tangled.

Noelle gasps, and her hands fly to cover her mouth. "My iPod!" she squeaks.

"Yes," I say. "It was found backstage by a gallant hero."

"It was?" she looks startled by the news.

"Yes." I give it a little shake for her to take it, but she doesn't move.

"Really? Who found it?" Her eyes dart back and forth and she gives a furtive little glance over her shoulder.

"That's not important. He wishes to remain anonymous."
I'm still holding the iPod out in front of me. The earbud wires
dangle between us like limp spaghetti, but she doesn't reach
for it.

"It is *yours*, right?" I ask.

"Um... yes, I think so," she says nervously. The child is turning as pink as the iPod, and it looks as though she's about to
hyperventilate.

"It has an inscription on the back," I say as I flip it over. I
read aloud, "'To N., Love, Tiger.' Sound familiar?"

I look back up at her expectantly, but she is just staring at it
like it's a bomb. Why is she behaving so peculiarly? First Allen,
now Noelle.

Nervously, she licks her lips and says, "Yeah, yeah, yeah,
that's mine," then she finally makes a jerky lunge for it.

I haven't been in theater my whole life not to know that she
is exhibiting classic paranoid behavior. That's one of the things
we do here in the theater: find characterizations by dissecting
human emotions and behavior. I don't need to be a psychologist like Dr. Waldner to read the signs. Why is she so freaked
out? Is this her iPod or not? Did she steal it? Is Allen covering
for her? Is it really, maybe, Delaney's? Delaney plays Nancy in
the play, so maybe she's the "N" and not Noelle. Her reaction
is screaming that something does not add up.

Before I can ask anything else, she unravels the earbuds
and pokes them into her ears. Beating a hasty retreat, she
begins backing away while saying, "Yeah, great. So, thanks, Mrs.
Graham."

"I guess your mother will be relieved, right?"

She stops abruptly on the stairs and holds onto the wall to
steady herself. She turns back to me and pleads, "Please don't
tell my Mom about this."

She looks so stricken, I say, "Well, just be more careful next time, Noelle."

She unfreezes and gushes, "Oh, I will, Mrs. Graham, I really will."

And then she rushes up the aisle, stopping only to stoop and drag her backpack alongside her. Seconds later she is out the door with a crash and a bang and all falls silent.

What was *that*?!

Kids!


5.) Tony *is* married.

5a.) Has two little kids.

# April 7th
## 3pm
## The Little Theater

*Dear Jasmine,*

*You are doing an excellent job playing Widow Corney. We think you are a wonderful actress!*

*Your Fans,*

*Mrs. Graham and Miss Brewster*

Lillette and I giggle down front in row C. We're deep into writing our ninth fan letter. We've been scribbling words of praise to every cast member while they rehearse on stage. This idea just came to us when Lillette was writing up her reminder note to stick in her shoe for the night.

We always give notes at the end of rehearsal, but they're mostly corrections and constructive criticisms; so we thought we'd switch it up a little and compliment them on what a great job they're doing. This has turned out to be a nice change from regular notes, and a lot of fun, too.

I fold Jasmine's note in half and write her name in my neatest script. Amber smiles as I pass it to her and whisper, "You know what to do."

She nods and scurries to the end of the aisle. Looking both ways, like she's checking for traffic, she crosses through the pit, tiptoes up the stairs and disappears behind the curtain.

Although we told the cast to stay backstage while we run the musical numbers from act two, they keep slipping out as they receive their fan mail. They sidle over to Lillette and me, and blush and stammer out the sweetest thank you's I've ever heard. This is great– a real morale booster for everyone. Why didn't we think of it sooner?

I glance over at Lillette and ask, "Okay, who's next?"

Lillette's face lights up. "Delaney!"

She grabs the legal pad from me and begins dashing off our next missive.

I grit my teeth. "Let me hear it," I say as I see her signing our names in her loopy cursive.

She holds it out in front of her stiffly, the way children in elementary school do when reading a report to the class.

"Dear Delaney," she says.

"A shining star about to burst,

Who worked so hard when we rehearsed.

You gave your all, you're so well versed,

But you gotta love yourself first."

"Lillette!" I nudge her with my elbow. "I didn't know you wrote poetry!"

Lillette blushes and busies herself doodling stars and hearts all over the page. "Yeah, yeah, on occasion I do."

"So do I!" I laugh. "Just goofy little ditties, really, but this one to Delaney is so good. Really *accurate*," I stress.

"Actually, I wrote that awhile ago. When I saw the way she was being pushed around by everyone, it got me right here." She pounds her fist into her chest with such force she breaks into a jagged little coughing spasm. As I rub her back, she wheezes out, "It's no good to break people. She's just a young girl."

"Yes," I agree, my face clouding over. "A very talented, tightly managed young girl."

Ever since her mother's last e-mail, I have been giving Delaney a wide berth. And remarkably, her mother's everyday updates have finally slowed to a trickle. Maybe Mama Diva is finally running out of steam.

Amber pokes her face out from behind the side curtain. She gives a sly look around, then, like she's a spy in danger of being spotted, she crouches down low by the stairs. Half rising, she bolts from her position and I swear I can almost hear the music from "Mission Impossible" underscoring her moves. Like she's starring in her own action movie, she makes a break for it, then dashes to the end of row C. With her head popping up and down behind each seat like a whack-a-mole, she looks furtively to her right and left to be sure the coast is clear, then springs back into her chair. Flipping her hair behind her ears she whispers, "Mission accomplished!"

This gives Lillette and me a fit of giggles, and Jackson shoots us the mean schoolmaster look. We shrug helplessly, so he shakes his head in defeat and yells up to the booth, "Tony, we're gonna need fifteen!"

Amber leaps to her feet and hollers out, "TAKE FIFTEEN, EVERYONE!"

And everyone; from the cast hidden backstage behind the curtain, to Lillette and me holding our ears in exaggerated pain, chorus back, "Thank you fifteen!"

Amber sits back down, grinning from ear to ear– extremely pleased with herself.

During the break, Sienna, Taffy and Jasmine sit along the side stairs passing around gum. Jackson plays "Where is Love" softly at the piano, stopping every few measures to transpose the notes to a lower key for Blake. I sit center stage with Amber, going over the props list.

We hear...

SIENNA: I can't figure out if I like Forrest or not.

JASMINE: You mean *like* like?

SIENNA: No– just plain like.

JASMINE: Yeah, he's hard to like.

TAFFY: But you don't mean it's hard to *like* him like him, right?

JASMINE: Right. I definitely don't *like* him like him. Do you?

TAFFY: Like him like him?

JASMINE: Yeah.

TAFFY: Yecch, no!

SIENNA: I guess I like him.

JASMINE: Plain like him?

SIENNA: Yeah. I feel sorry for him. His eyes are sad behind all that anger.

JASMINE: He asked me out in tenth grade.

SIENNA: Really? Did you like him like him then?

JASMINE: No. So I told him no.

SIENNA: Was he crushed?

JASMINE: Yeah. He told me to watch my back. But he always says that to me– he's all talk.

*(There is a pause.)*

TAFFY: Did you ever try to "*watch* your back?"

I look over to see Taffy twisting and turning her neck in an effort to literally "watch her back."

The girls double over laughing at Taffy's literal joke, and I smile.

I feel Amber's eyes on me. When I look at her, she's giving me this weird death stare.

"What?" I say.

"It's not funny, Mrs. Graham. Forrest is mean." Her chin starts to quiver and I stare at her for a startled moment. When realization hits, I always feel like a complete dummy. Does Amber actually "*like* like" Forrest? He's been nothing but horrible to her!

"Sorry, Amber," I say. "I wasn't laughing about what they were saying about Forrest..."

"I know. It's just, he's a really troubled person."

Okay. Where do we go from here? But before I can continue to probe, Amber looks at her watch and stands up.

"Break is over!" She shouts. "Everyone back onstage!"

Amber is becoming a complete enigma to me.

**5:45 pm, Samuel P. Chester Parking Lot**

Jackson and I emerge, blinking out into the balmy arms of April. A sweet-smelling wind blows and my hair flies crazily around my head. I feel ready to lift my arms and fly away.

"Thank you, April," I say up to the sky.

Jackson nudges me, but I've closed my eyes and say, "Not now, Jackson; I'm getting a wind massage."

But he pokes me again and I open my eyes, about to protest.

"Look," he says. I follow his gaze across the parking lot to see Tony getting into his car with Chip, Allen, Noelle and Delaney.

We exchange glances and I ask, "Should I say something to him?"

Jackson throws an arm over my shoulders. "What's to say?" he shrugs.

We start to walk towards our car, but I keep my head turned in their direction. Tony must say something funny, because all four kids fold forward in unison, laughing. That is such a *weird* combination of kids. Allen couldn't even face Noelle to return her iPod last week, and now he's in Tony's car acting like they're old pals.

"Shouldn't I ask them where they're going?"

"Why?"

I feel myself tense up. How come the things that I see as red alerts, Jackson dismisses as nothing? I feel the itchy presence of Sister Aloysius crawl under my skin and take up residence.

"Well, is he supposed to drive students in his car? Is he *allowed?*" I ask. I'm positive my face must be pinched into the exact scowl Meryl Streep used in the movie.

"It's a school, Kelly, not a jail."

That stings. I break away and trot over to the car ahead of him.

When he arrives, I'm standing with my arms crossed over my chest, leaning against the passenger side door.

He comes around to unlock my door, but stops in front of me and says, "Sorry."

My hair whirls and waves around my head, like it's still carrying on the argument with him independent of my mouth.

Tony swings his car around and it crunches noisily over the gravel. As his car passes us, Noelle catches my eye and waves. I give her one of those fake smiles, where you pull your lips into the shape of a smile, but your eyes stay dead. You may as well not smile at all.

"I'm sorry, Kel," Jackson says again. "I know you've got your eye on Tony, but he's probably just taking them home. He knows their families and they know him. They wouldn't let him take their kids if they didn't trust him."

"Fine," I concede. Who wants to fight over something I have no control over anyway? I let it go.

"Consider it dropped," I say lightly. Sister Aloysius recedes.

Jackson's right. Tony wants to take their kids to McDonald's, Montana, the moon, who am I to interfere?

To show Jackson there are no hard feelings, I smile, a *real* smile, and pull him close to me by his scarf.

"Kiss me, Mr. Graham."

"Kelly, Kelly, Kelly," he exhales. "You blow hot and cold, just like this damn wind."

He looks around at the mostly empty parking lot, then puts his hands on either side of my face and smushes it a little. It doesn't hurt, but I jerk away, only to have him pull me back and kiss me deeply for real.

"No P.D.A.'s!" A familiar deep voice calls from a distance.

We pull apart abruptly, only to see the portly figure of Headmaster Hank cutting his way across the parking lot towards us. He's smiling as he swings his briefcase and says, "It does my heart good to see a couple of young people in love—just so long as they're not my *students* carrying on in public," he chuckles.

Jackson sticks his hand out and gives the headmaster an enthusiastic shake. I do the same, my heart still ricocheting around my ribs from being "caught."

"How's the play coming?" he asks.

Jackson smiles and says, "Good, good. Have you been getting my e-mail updates?"

"Oh, sure, sure. Thank you for keeping me in the loop. Lillette is also a fine source, keeping me posted about the progress."

We all smile at one another, and it's on the tip of my tongue to say *Tony Glynn has just left the premises with four students, and is there a school policy about that?*– but I don't. I don't because the headmaster is staring at us with a twinkle in his eye, rocking back and forth on his feet. A big grin spreads across his face and something tells me to stay very still.

Sure enough, the headmaster starts swinging his briefcase up and down, catching it in his left hand like he's demonstrating some cool ninja move.

He suddenly raises the suitcase over his head and yells, "Hah! Hah! Hah!" Wielding it like a machete, he appears to be fending off his invisible archenemies. He proceeds to bend his knees in the most embarrassing position I've ever seen him in, and scuffles energetically in front of us like a little boy with a plastic sword. Jackson takes a funny little hop backward and my mouth drops open.

As the headmaster dodges the imaginary bad guys, he bobs and weaves– Jackson flinching and grimacing every time the headmaster gets thisclose to actually hitting him.

What's with the sudden play that's gripped everyone? First Amber with her spy moves, now the headmaster busting out his super hero stuff. It's in the wind, I tell ya. It's the blowsy, bloomin' wind!

Headmaster Hank stops as abruptly as he started and pats his tie back into place. "Off to a meeting," he says, catching his breath.

Gripping his suitcase in a more dignified fashion, he tells us, "I've got to dash now; but it was a pleasure to see you both." He raises his fingers to his forehead and gives us a small salute as he wanders away, whistling.

Jackson and I stay frozen where we are. When Headmaster Hank is a safe distance away, we start laughing uncontrollably. Jackson laughs so hard he's completely disabled and has to lie over the front hood of the car until he can stand up again.

"That," he gasps, with his arm raised into the air, "is the power of spring fever!"

**7pm, Home**

*From: Me, Amber*
*To: Mr. + Mrs. Graham*

*Hi Mr. + Mrs. Graham,*
*It's me, Amber. Sienna just texted me. She DOES NOT have mono. We are safe. Love, Amber.*

"What does she mean, 'We are safe?'" Jackson asks from over my shoulder.

I press "delete" and say nonchalantly, "No clue. You know how sensitive she is. Maybe she thought we'd all get mono or something."

I switch the subject quickly. "I never saw that side of the headmaster, did you, Jackson?"

Judge Jenny is on mute as we wait for the commercials to end. We're checking e-mails and devouring huge amounts of Dulce de Leche ice cream. It's amazing what the combination of Judge Jenny and a dish of Haagen-Daz can do to make everything all right in our world.

"I didn't know that side *existed* in the man!" Jackson laughs. "That was wild, Kelly."

I see there's an e-mail from Dr. Waldner, but I close the laptop like I'm kicking my dirty clothes under my bed to hide them.

"I know," I say. "He was *so* funny! Maybe I should bring in a big towel for him tomorrow. I could pin it around his neck so he can be the cool caped-crusader of Samuel P. Chester Academy!"

Jackson laughs and says, "Oh, yeah, perfect. That'll go down great with the parents. He must have to hide this playful side of himself from everyone. Do you remember what he was like when we first interviewed?"

"Oh, yeah, he was great. A total gentleman. I thought he was so charming and courtly; remember how he gave us a tiny bow as he opened the doors to the Little Theater to give us a tour?"

"Yeah, I do. And I remember him telling us about how they hadn't had much success building a theater program. I remember how I felt a surge of pride, because I knew you and I could make it happen." He gives my leg a little squeeze.

"Then you don't remember what the reason was for them not having much success, do you?"

Jackson's face grows still. Judge Jenny is back, but neither of us touch the remote to unmute her.

"Actually, now I do," he says slowly. "He said something about it having to do with parental influence at the academy being so strong."

"Yep. And you were nodding your head, saying, 'Uh huh, uh huh,' but I didn't understand what 'parental influence' meant. Now I do. It's code for 'parental *interference.*'"

Judge Jenny is looking at some poor sap with disgust. Even without the sound on, you can see the sparks crackling in her eyes. I can only imagine the dressing-down she's giving the guy.

I say, "I was ready for parental involvement of some sort, but I was idealistic about it. I thought the parents would be so dazzled by the wonderful job we'd be doing with their kids that they'd be happy to take their place in this background supportive way. I thought they'd appear only when we needed them to help."

"Ha! How dopey and naive were we?"

I nod. "But the thing I was *totally* unprepared for was the crazy gangbusters way they go about making their wishes known, you know? I mean, who comes out with pistols drawn and a chip on their shoulder the size of Texas at the first hint of a conflict?"

"Bullies."

"Yeah, you're right. It's like living in Toddler Town here—where they learn to get their way by screaming and throwing a tantrum."

Jackson licks a blob of ice cream off the corner of his mouth. "Headmaster Hank was probably trying to warn us in the nicest way possible. But what can he do, really? He has to deal with them everyday."

"I'd bust a few moves as a super hero, too, if it kept me from going crazy!"

"Hey, why don't you do that, Kel? Next time one of them is pulling their entitlement 'tude on you, stand up tall like Wonder Woman and look at your watch. Grab your head and say, 'Holy Cannoli, Mrs. Crazy Parent– look at the time! It's time for me to vaporize you into a thousand proton particles. Stay perfectly still; you won't feel a thing!' That ought to at least knock them off balance for a sec."

"I don't know, Jackson. I think you mixed up your super powers. I'm trying not to have such a personal response to their behavior, like the Prof suggested," I say.

I put my dish on top of the coffee table. "Isn't it weird, Jackson, to act so entitled just because you're rich? I mean, we're all still just plain old people first."

We both look back at the muted Judge Jenny. She's chewing up another guy now, her mouth moving a mile a minute, fire shooting out of her ears. I've got to admire her command. I'll never have her authority. Not at this school. It's hard for us to just be treated respectfully.

I glance anxiously at the laptop.

I know inside lies another reminder from Dr. Waldner about the cast party money.

It's wrong of me not to bite the bullet and contact her about the time change, but I just can't face her.

# April 8th
## 1pm
## The Little Theater

Walking through the lobby towards the theater doors, I stop. I hear someone crying. It's funny; I never noticed it before, but it sounds like the exact words boo hoo hoo hoo.

There is no way this is a dead girl. If it is her, she's got a very healthy set of alive lungs to be sobbing so loudly.

To my left, the box office door is closed, but as I get closer, I confirm it's definitely coming from inside there. I knock softly, and the crying stops.

"Everything all right in there?" I ask.

I hear a huge intake of breath, and then a high-pitched, "Nooooo," wobbles back out at me.

"Lillette Brewster, is that you?"

"Yeeesss," comes the shaky reply.

"Can I come in?"

"Ooooh-kaay."

Cracking the door ajar, I peer inside to see Lillette's swollen, red face– her blue eyes rimmed in red.

"What's the matter?" I ask.

Instead of an answer, she starts wailing again. She cries just like a toddler does: with abandon and gusto. Her mouth opens wide, her eyes squeeze shut, and an ocean of tears streak down her face. The wall of sound actually causes the door to vibrate and makes me squint.

I gently push on the door to let myself in. I maneuver her over to the box office swivel chair and she slumps into it as if she's made of Jell-O.

I kneel by her side and ask, "What happened, Lillette? Are you hurt?"

"Yeees."

"Where?"

"Not like *that,*" her voice quavers. "My pride. My *pride* is hurt."

"What hurt your pride?"

"Not *what; who.*"

"Okay, who?" I wait patiently. After lots of blowing and wiping and mopping, she takes a stuttering intake of air and says, "Tony."

"Tony *Glynn?*"

Through the slits in her swollen eyes she regards me as if I'm insane. "Of course Tony *Glynn.* Is there any other Tony?"

"Do you want to tell me what happened?" I stand up and lean my back against the brown file cabinet. This may take awhile.

Her left hand searches to find her ponytail, relocated in all the fuss to just above her left ear, and she begins to loop it around her forefinger.

"I feel like a moron loser," she says bitterly as she twirls the blonde strands.

"What happened?" I persist.

"It's so stupid!" She grabs her face and squeezes her flushed cheeks.

"Lillette, stop that." I pull her hands gently off her face and say, "It's okay, just tell me."

"Well, all this time I thought I had something, something, *special* with Tony. We were always laughing when we were together. He'd tell me funny little jokes all the time..." she trails off.

I nod.

"It's the *way* he told me, though. He always whispered them into my ear, like it was just for us– him and me. And sometimes, he'd come up behind me and tug on my ponytail and say 'ding dong,' like he was ringing my doorbell."

Oh no. I'm beginning to get the picture.

"So, so, when I asked him if he maybe wanted to get together sometime, I thought he'd say yes." Her eyes start to fill up again, and her chin starts to quiver. "But instead he said I deserve someone better. He thinks we should just be friends." She starts crying again, inconsolably.

I rub her back and say, "Lillette, you're too sweet. You wear your heart on your sleeve."

Startled out of her crying for a moment, she actually looks down at her sleeve, checking for evidence that it's laying there, pulsating.

"It's an expression," I say gently. "For people like you, who are big old softies when it comes to love."

"But I thought he felt the same way," she whimpers. "He *acted* like he did."

That Tony! How dare he? Doesn't he realize how he hurts people by toying with them, using his manipulative and charming ways? Lillette is so trusting. If we were living in another time, Tony would be called a cad.

"He's married, Lillette," I say softly. "You didn't know that?"

She pulls the tissue from her nose and, looking perplexed asks, "He is?"

I nod my head.

"Then where is his ring?" she challenges, lifting her left hand and wiggling her fingers.

"I guess he doesn't wear it," I sigh. Cad. Rascal. Scoundrel! Why don't we use these words anymore? They describe Tony perfectly.

"I just thought he was brushing me off because I'm fat."

Whoa. There's that word. So raw and charged with meaning: fat. This is a delicate subject for us girls; we measure so much of who we are by our appearance. And unfortunately, whether skinny or chubby or anywhere in-between, few of us feel we measure up.

"You're not fat, Lillette, you're curvy and luscious!" I say firmly.

That's right! I'm starting right here and now to make new inroads for womanhood. I'll trot out more accurate descriptions than the soul-destroying "fat."

She looks at me dubiously, but I stand my ground. I nod and say adamantly, "It's absolutely true."

"But all my life I wanted to be skinny," she says. "Everyone always made fun of how I looked. Do you know what the kids at school used to call me?"

I shake my head no.

"There was this sitcom on TV that I *loved* called *Punky Brewster*, but they wrecked it for me." She looks away. "They called me '*Chunky* Brewster.'"

I look down and shake my head. "That was so mean," I say. I remember that show. I loved it, too.

"And do you have any idea the pressure I feel because I'm a Little?"

"A little what?" I ask.

"I'm a Little. A Little." She looks at me as if I have suddenly stopped speaking English.

"You can tell me, Lillette; you're a little what?" I coax.

She smacks the palm of her hand against her forehead, then grabs my wrists. "That's our family *name.* My ancestors name is 'Little.' The *Little* Theater?"

It sinks in slowly, but then I laugh out loud as I put it all together. "Oh! Right! I get it now! I thought it was called 'The Little Theater' because the building was cute and, well, little."

She shakes her head, her ponytail spinning and whirling wildly.

"The theater was named after my great-great-gram, Elsie Mary Little. She was an actress and loved the stage." She smiles ever so shyly. "I think that's where I get it from."

"I'll bet you're right," I say with a confirming nod.

"And that's how I got my name, too. Lillette is an anagram for 'Le Little.'"

She shakes her head like she's trying to shake away a bad memory. "But I couldn't live up to my own name. I'm big. But I always *wished* I was little," she sighs glumly.

A new thought seems to wash over her, because she slumps forward and says softly, "Tony called me 'Lissome Lill.' He gave me the nickname of my dreams. I looked it up. It means 'lithe.' No one has ever thought of me as lithe." She looks up at me. "I *loved* that," she says plaintively.

I purse my lips angrily. Who does Tony think he is, making up these nicknames like he's God naming his creations? All my vigilance hasn't led to much, but this is just not right. Pinning down the name of his offense just slips through the legal cracks. What crime can I seriously accuse Tony of committing? Being a serial nicknamer to emotionally needy people?

I don't know what to say. Lillette sits quietly for a moment, recovering. Other than an occasional hiccup, I think the storm has passed.

"Why don't you throw some cold water on your face, Lillette? We have rehearsal in an hour and a half; we're going to run all the major numbers in act one, okay?"

She nods and leans down to tap her yellow shoe. "I know. I got my own message."

I smile and put my hand on her sweaty head.

"Let me fix your pony, first," I say. I swivel the chair around and use my fingers as a substitute comb to gather her fluffy hair into a new ponytail at the back.

"I have horrible hair," she says.

"No you don't! Look at mine!" I swing the chair back around and shake my tangled, crazy curls at her.

She laughs at last and says, "I *wish* I had your curls."

"I know, I know," I sigh. "We always want what we don't have. Believe me, if you had my ringlets for a day, you'd long for your hair back again. We girls have to start being nicer to ourselves. Do you think *guys* obsess over all this stuff?"

"I think maybe Tony does," she says. "He's always asking me if I think he looks good."

Egomaniacal blowhard!

"Listen, Lillette; here's some unsolicited advice: stay away from Tony, okay? We have less than three weeks to go before opening night. Let's just keep focused on the show."

She nods as she walks to the door. She starts to slip out, but then pokes her head back in and smiles sadly, "Thanks, Kelly."

When she is gone, I look down at the floor. My feet are covered in wet tissues, piled high as sodden snowdrifts.

**1:30pm**

As I throw the last of Lillette's tissues into the bin in the lobby, Amber rushes through the door, promptbook cradled in her arms.

"Mrs. Graham," she blurts. "Grant has mono."

With a sigh I say, "Yes, Amber, thank you, I already know. His mom e-mailed me." I gather up my jacket and pile it on top of my books.

Amber hasn't moved.

"What?" I ask.

"But that makes two, Mrs. Graham. *Two* people with mono. Not one."

She purposefully starts rifling through her promptbook as I say, "Oh, yes. You're right."

I'm about to walk into the theater, when I notice she has stopped at a page that features a line drawing of boxes. Three columns are labeled across the top: "Mono," "Broken Bone," and "Death."

Oh my God. A chart. She's drawn a chart and placed tiny black check marks under "Mono" and "Broken Bone."

"What's this?" I ask with a sudden stab of anxiety.

"It's my 'Three Terrible Things' chart. I use it to keep track of the three terrible things you told me were going to happen."

My throat feels like it's closing up. "Oh, I see," I manage.

OHMIGOD– A CHART!

She pulls her pencil from behind her ear, and as the tips of her hair brush the page, she draws another tiny, perfect check mark in the "Mono" box. When she is done, she looks back up at me and slides the pencil behind her ear.

"There's only one category left," she reports calmly, like a doctor who is gravely announcing the news that there's nothing more that can be done.

"Yes, yes," I croak. My mouth has turned to sawdust, and I feel a little faint. She may be checking off that last box sooner than she thinks.

This has obviously gone too far. I made such a mistake in presenting my moronic theory to her. I'll bet hundreds, no, *thousands* of high schools across the country have never had *any* of these things happen when they did a show. I am an imbecile.

I lick my dry lips and pull her by the crook of her arm to a cushy old-fashioned bench by the box office.

"Amber, sit down a sec," I say as I pull her down beside me. OHMIGODACHART.

"You know, Amber, when I told you that story, I really should have made it clearer that it was just a funny little theory. There's a logical explanation. You see, it's really common for teenagers to get mono. And with their rambunctious ways and all the sports they play, it's also a common occurrence for teenagers to break a bone." I smile and bat my eyes encouragingly, like I'm Claire Huxtable.

"See? That's all there is to it. Do you understand now?" I almost call her "dear."

She bites the corner of her lip and says, "But what about the death part? How can you explain that?"

I say slowly, "Unfortunately in life, sometimes people we love die."

What the *hell* am I saying? I'm suddenly Miss Bradley, my pre-school teacher, with a splash of Mr. Rogers and his sweater thrown in.

She pulls the pencil out from behind her ear and taps it on the empty "death" box. She raises her eyebrows, continues tapping on the box, and says calmly, "Seventeen days to go. Maybe we'll cheat it this time."

I give her a cheesy smile and say, "Yes. Right. I'm sure we will."

I stand and say in an unfamiliar high-pitched voice, "Can you please go inside now? I'll be right back."

I've got to find some water.

And maybe a bottle of wine. Do they sell wine in the cafeteria?

They should.

I can split it with Lillette.

**2:30pm, The Little Theater**

I check my watch. Jackson must be running late at Melodies. Well, he's still got half an hour. After a stiff drink of water and a bunch of yoga breaths, I feel calmer.

I enter the theater to find Delaney and Thomas on stage. Amber is all squashed up in the front row, doing her math again. Delaney and Thomas appear to be running through a scene in Fagin's den.

"Hi guys," I call out. "What's up?"

Thomas runs to the edge of the apron and says excitedly, "We get it, Mrs. Graham. We're doing it!"

"Doing what?" I ask as I climb the steps to meet them.

Thomas just can't contain himself, and races around in tight little circles like a puppy on the loose. "We understand about intentions and objectives! And the scene is fantastic now! It's just like you said: figure out what your character wants, and then play an intention to get it. Let's hear it for an actor's best friend: the verbs! It's making the scene so *interesting*, Mrs. Graham. Watch this, watch this!"

He darts back over to Delaney and says, "Let's do it from the top."

Delaney gives me a thin smile as she walks into place, and looks, as always, kind of forlorn. When she's not acting and "on," she almost appears neglected. The grayish grooves beneath her eyes seem to have deepened, and the fact that she's wearing a huge, oversized red sweatshirt just contributes to her ragamuffin look.

They begin their scene, and as it unfolds, sure enough, it's full of new life. More dynamic, more dramatic. When they finish, they look to me for approval. Even Delaney. But I'm already up on my feet, applauding. "Yes, yes! That's it!" I cry. "Good job!"

They give each other high fives, and then an awkward little spontaneous hug.

"Guys, I know this sound corny, but all I did was give you the key; you unlocked the door yourselves. You've experienced firsthand what I meant when I told you that even in real life, people mostly hear the *way* things are said– the *subtext,* versus *what* is being said. We hear the subtext because that speaks straight to our hearts. And, in fact, I think as feeling human beings, that's probably how most of our communication is received. Good job."

The one distraction I had with the scene was that I couldn't keep my eyes off of the words on Delaney's sweatshirt. "The Ultimate Me" fairly screams out in huge white, block letters across both the front and the back.

"What's 'The Ultimate Me?'" I ask.

Delaney pulls the sweatshirt away from her body as if to read the words upside down, then looks at me and says tonelessly, "It's my mother's company."

"Oh," I say. "What kind of company is that?"

Delaney sighs the sigh of a desperately world-weary soul. As if even talking about it is too exhausting, she sinks down to the floor and explains, "She has this website. She wrote a book and sells apparel with 'The Ultimate Me' on everything. Even on baby onesies. It's, like, her philosophy for how to raise children."

I'm so curious to ask more, but I'm not sure I should.

"Pop a squat," Thomas says jovially to me as he sits next to Delaney. He pats the spot next to him, shifting happily on his butt like he's settling in for a good chat.

"What does 'The Ultimate Me' mean?" Thomas asks, reading my mind.

"Well," Delaney begins slowly. "According to my mother, everyone has this unlimited capacity to be much more than they already are. They just have to tap into it. She says if people demand the best from themselves by trying to fill their time with stuff to enrich them, then they can be at the top of their game in life and become their ultimate selves."

"Is she pushing you to be 'The Ultimate Me,' too?" I ask cautiously.

"Oh, yeah," she says, rolling her eyes. "Big time. I'm, like, her biggest project. I have to be the proof that it works. She said that when she gave birth to me, I was her prototype."

"How does she suggest people do this?" I ask quietly, knowing I could spook Delaney back into her shell at any moment.

"There's lots of ways. But mostly you have to start when you conceive your baby. Then you do all the usual stuff: Baby Mozart, reading textbooks to the baby growing inside, speaking other languages, stuff like that. Then when the baby's born, you sign 'em up for every class available. 'Input to enrich,' that's her main catch phrase, 'input to enrich.'"

Thomas clarifies, "You mean like a computer? So she sees kids like computers, right? Input/output; I get it. Put something in, something will come back out! Genius!" He shakes his head like he just can't believe what a wonderful concept it is. "You know they say we only use a tiny portion of our brain power, so I think your mom is on to something!"

Thomas beams at Delaney, and she rewards him with a half-hearted, cheesy smile.

"So have you arrived yet? Are you the ultimate you, yet?" I ask.

Delaney draws her knees up to her chest and slides her sweatshirt over her legs. She's all tucked inside the bright red sweatshirt like she's back in the Ultimate Womb. Hugging her arms around her legs, she leans her head on her knees.

"I don't think it's working for me. I give it my all, but my mother says she thinks there's more I'm holding back." She closes her eyes forlornly and says, "I don't know who 'The Ultimate Me' is. And I don't know where to find her."

Thomas pipes up, "I think I'm 'The Ultimate Me' right now, Delaney. I gotta get me one of those sweatshirts pronto!"

Delaney looks at him sharply and says vehemently, "No. You're not there yet, Thomas. You do *not* qualify as 'The Ultimate Me' right now. You haven't pushed yourself hard enough yet."

Thomas looks confused. "So it's not a state of mind? I push myself to take all Honors and AP classes all the time. And I push myself to be the best me, like, every single day!" He leans closer to Delaney and says, "I may be the first senior at the academy to *will* my facial hair to grow. If that's not in 'The Ultimate Me' spirit, then I don't know what is."

She looks away miserably and says, "That's not it, either, Thomas. You won't be the ultimate you until, until," her voice falters and her eyes fill with tears. "You won't be the ultimate you until you're broken."

Thomas and I both visibly soften and I ask, "Why do you have to push so hard?"

"Because, because, it's important to compete to be the best. You have to strive for perfection, so you can't miss out on anything. You have to input to enrich, and you can never let an opportunity pass you by."

"What would happen if you did?" I ask, playing devil's advocate.

"No, no! You can't. You shouldn't! Then you'll never catch up," she says with real alarm.

"To what?" I ask softly.

Delaney looks momentarily dazed. Like she was busy running a marathon but then suddenly smacked into a wall.

She says wearily, "I'm not really explaining it right. You should ask my mother; she'll tell you all about it. Believe me, she can be *very* persuasive."

"Yes, I know that about your mother," I say. I meant to say that as neutrally as possible, but Delaney detects the whiff of criticism in my tone and is instantly roused from her musing.

"She means well," she says defensively, as her legs bolt out from under the sweatshirt.

"Yeah, yeah, we know," says Thomas earnestly. "She's a great lady. She's 'The Ultimate Mom,' Delaney!" He smiles winningly at her and she backs down.

But I can feel her barricade going back up. Her face clouds over and I can tell she's sealing her heart back up into a small box she hides away from the world that keeps trying to take it from her.

"Well, guys, you're 'The Ultimate Actors' today. I'm really proud of both of you."

Thomas scrambles to his feet and starts singing, "I'll be back soooooon" at the top of his lungs. He suddenly lowers his voice and whispers conspiratorially, "I'm going to the bathroom!"

He resumes his raucous singing and Delaney lies down on her side to watch him. With a freedom Delaney seems to yearn for, Thomas camps it up in high style as he dances down the stairs and up the aisle. Delaney doesn't look at me, but I am completely astounded she's been so vulnerable with us. And she took my acting instruction and applied it!

"Delaney?"

"What?" she says, sitting up.

"Thanks for telling us about your mom's company."

Distrust swims back into her eyes. "Well," she says curtly. "You asked."

We rise to our feet as we hear the doors open and the cast, (and Jackson!), start flooding in. There's a swell of boisterous greetings followed by the usual rowdy hubbub, but I manage to ask Delaney softly, "We start in five, but do you want to go freshen up first? I could give you ten if you want."

"I'm fine," she says with a frown; then, spotting Noelle, she screeches, "NOELLE! Where have you been?" She rushes to the stairs while screaming, "Why didn't you meet me at my locker fourth period?!"

Jackson holds his hands over his ears, like that guy in the painting "The Scream," and strides down the aisle.

But I feel like I've just evaporated from view. What did my mother used to say? The tough ones were the most rewarding? Funk that!

### 7pm, Home

What a day. Broody. Brooding?

Jackson is in the kitchen whistling, but I'm holed up in our bedroom, feeling moody. As I peel off my socks and rub my feet, I think about Delaney.

Each encounter with Delaney leaves me feeling uncertain. Uncertain about my abilities to teach this kid, and uncertain about who I was (am?) as an actress.

The frustrating thing is, Delaney doesn't respect me as a director or as an actress. It's bugging me that she'd rather be directed by Tony, a guy who, it's becoming clearer to me, just loves to be worshipped.

Why am I feeling so thin-skinned these days? I decide, in a very wimpy, defeated state, to call the Prof again.

I plump up my pillows and reach for the phone.

"Prof," I ask in a small voice, "am I still an actress if I don't act anymore?" I know I sound needy, but my self-confidence has taken such a nosedive that I don't care.

The heavy silence that ensues tells me he's weighing his words carefully.

"Did you train to be an actress?"

"Yes," I say.

"Did you perform in plays?"

"Yeah."

"Then you're an actress."

"No, Prof– doesn't that make me a *former* actress?"

He counters again with another question. "When Grace Kelly stopped acting, did she become the former actress Grace Kelly?"

"I guess not, but isn't she considered an actress in the first place because she produced a known body of work? You know, she established herself as an actress first?"

"She had to start somewhere. Are you saying that before she was cast in her first role she wasn't an actress? That the contract only legitimized it?"

"Ummm...well, yeah?"

"So you think being paid a lot for your art is the qualifying criterion?"

"Well..."

"If I go with that argument, then how much money does an artist, dancer, actress, musician, or painter have to make to be able to claim the title? And if they make millions, does that mean they're better artists? Because if *that* were true, Van Gogh would never have called himself an artist during his penniless lifetime, and Adam Sandler could be dubbed the premier actor of your generation."

"Ew, no! But, but Prof," I sputter. "Then anyone who feels they can act can call themselves an actor. Just because they think it, doesn't make it true, right? Don't they actually have to *do* it?"

The Prof pauses.

"I hear your anguish, Kelly. Now I understand what you're asking, and the answer is, yes, you're an actress."

I *am?*

"But how do you know?"

"Because I said so."

The pity tears that were collecting tremulously in the corners of my eyes now release themselves and splash down my cheeks as I laugh out loud.

"Because you *said so?*" I repeat incredulously. "What are you– my mother?"

The Prof laughs back, then says, "I was your *teacher*, Kelly. They paid me good money, and lots of it, to train young students in the craft of acting. The university had enough faith in my abilities to consider me an arbiter and judge, and I say, yes, you are an actress."

I laugh and laugh. Mostly from relief, but with a huge touch of love for my old Prof, too.

"Okay, Prof. How can I argue? You laid it out like one of those math problems that used to confound me. But your logic *is* sound. If you say I'm still an actress, then I'm an actress."

"And always will be, my dear," he adds.

"I don't know about that, Prof, but I appreciate the confidence booster."

"Kelly?"

Uh oh, I can feel one of his Yoda proclamations coming down the pike. I ready myself. "Yeah, Prof?"

"You knew the answer to this one. You were born an actress, dear. As Michelangelo said, 'The sculpture is in the marble; I just set it free.'"

I am too humbled to speak. I can only dream of being half the teacher the Prof is.

—ᴍ—

I hang up the phone and sit quietly in my chair.

The thing is, what happens if you can't pursue your art? Where does all that talent go? And what if you're the vessel holding the talent?

I know I was only set free by the glory of the opportunities that allowed me to showcase my craft. Unfortunately, staying focused on that goal became harder and harder as I struggled to make a living while I slung another plate of Pasta Primavera at the customer at table eight. Lots of our friends gave up in disillusioned frustration, too. Their talents unused, yearning unrequited– slogging through life in despair, because there is this *thing* in them.

When I have the opportunity to work in the theater, I am at my shining best.

Why was I given such an impossible gift? And how can I share it with someone like Delaney, who just turns her nose up at it?

# April 10th
## 10am
## Home

Biting the bullet:
*From: Jackson and Kelly Graham*
*To: Dr. Gail Waldner*

*Dear Dr. Waldner,*
*Thank you for taking the time to set up a cast party for the cast and crew of* Oliver! *However, both the cast and crew are required to stay to strike the set after the Sunday performance. This means everyone should be ready for dismissal at approximately 7pm. The entire cast and crew looks forward to celebrating a wonderful run at Cafe L'Artiste at that time. Thank you, Jackson and Kelly*

Now we hold our breath...
### 2pm, Samuel P. Chester Academy
I pull past the black iron gates at the entrance to the academy. It's not quite early spring yet, but the trees have definite buds, and the grass is already perking up to a deeper shade of green.

I think there's only one more scheduled rehearsal that I have to work solo. Jackson is working two shifts at Melodies, but has promised me dinner again when I get home.

I can totally handle this, because it's going to be a short day for me anyway. We're giving stage crew a huge hunk of time this afternoon to finish building and painting the set without the whole cast underfoot. I'm just meeting briefly with the cast involved with "Who Will Buy," then stage crew will take over from there. I'll be feasting on frozen pseudo-browned chicken pot pie before you know it.

I'm glad Forrest isn't in this number. I don't like dealing with him one-on-one; he drains all my energy. It's arduous having to focus so much attention on just keeping him in line. In addition to the aforementioned dinner, Jackson has also promised me he'll work with Forrest and Delaney on the scene where Nancy is murdered during rehearsal tomorrow. Forrest has been semi-okay lately under Jackson's direction, but is still snarky and disrespectful under mine. No matter– that's why we're a team. Forrest needs an alpha male to keep him in check, so I just send in Jackson. Ha ha, it's still crazy to think of Jackson, my mild-mannered, skinny, music man as an alpha-guy, but if Forrest perceives him that way, good for us. And I think I've done all I can with Delaney at this point.

I pull into my usual spot and climb out of the car.

It's funny how nice weather can affect your mood. I love April. I feel happy with the breeze in my hair. They say it's the cruelest month, but I don't think so. I love the sudden soft winds, the hint of true spring teasing in the air. Maybe they say it's the cruelest month because it's mercurial. Tomorrow may be dreary and rainy again, but for now the sun warms my face as I head towards the Little Theater with more *Oliver!* posters. Our colorful posters dot the campus and look so professional. Mrs. Benson and Mrs. Harrington (two nice, normal mothers of two nice, normal students) did a fine job designing them, and promised to hang more of them in town.

Hope rises in me, and despite the morning lethargy I've been experiencing, I feel great. I swing the lobby door open to find Angelo with his cart. He looks like he's finishing up as he pulls the trash can behind him.

"Hello, Mrs. Graham, how are you today?" he greets me with his shiny apple cheeks pushed up to their highest.

"I'm fine, Angelo, and won't you please call me Kelly?"

He adjusts his silver bandana and says, "Oh no, I couldn't possibly. This is the way the big guy said I should address you."

How cute. But I really can't imagine the headmaster caring one way or another. Whatever. "Fair enough," I say.

"The set looks great," he says.

"Yes, it's really coming along," I smile as I move to enter the theater.

Angelo looks a little uncomfortable, so I pause. "Was there something else?"

Angelo looks down at his feet and does a little shuffle, the dance of a child who's done something he's ashamed of.

"What is it, Angelo?"

He peers up over his glasses, his eyes as soulful as a baby seal's. "I don't want you to think I'm bonkers, but I have something to tell you. You know– about the dead girl."

I roll my lips together so I won't smile. "What about the, uh, dead girl?"

He looks down again at his feet and mumbles, "I heard her."

"You *heard* the dead girl?" I blurt– maybe a little too loudly.

He nods his head seriously. "The other day."

The other day. The other day. Oh! The other day! I laugh a little and say, "Oh, no Angelo, I know what that was."

He blinks rapidly, waiting nervously for the relief of an explanation.

"I'm fairly certain what you heard was our choreographer, Lillette. That was her crying here in the box office."

He looks doubtful. "But how could I hear her all the way over in the main building? Isn't there too much brick?"

"She has a fairly vociferous cry," I say.

"Vociferous?"

"Loud. Blaring. Piercing." (I did great on my English SAT's. Despite the perception, actors are very intelligent. Don't ask about the Math part.)

"Oh, oh, yeah," he nods. He adjusts his glasses a bit, then looks appealingly at me. "But this sounded like it came from the haunted stairway. It was soft. Like weeping. Like when you try to hold it in."

I nod. I can see he wants me to believe him so badly, so I say, "Angelo, I'm glad you told me. And I believe you. But, I'm just curious– was it around one, one thirty-ish in the afternoon when you heard it?"

He tips his head back to think for a moment, then nods, "Yes."

"Listen, don't worry about it," I say sweetly. "Okay?"

It had to be Lillette. It was *obviously* Lillette, but this creepy legend is taking on a life of its own and is making everyone nervous.

Angelo gives me a tiny smile, barely enough to move his glasses up at all, and says bashfully, "So you don't think I'm a kook?"

I just have to give him a squeeze. I wrap my right arm around his wide shoulders and say, "Never. I believe you heard what you heard."

Satisfied, he nods and says, "Okay, okay. Thanks, Mrs. Graham." He readjusts his sparkly bandana, poking it higher up onto his forehead. Then he trundles over to the door and pushes it open. A gust of fresh air blows in as he smiles good-bye. I watch him cross to the main building, his cart bumbling along behind him.

I linger a moment longer to watch the wind sweep riotously through the trees. A lonely grove of maple trees sways in the wind. The long, bare branches of their arms wave at me, as if trying to get my attention.

Absurdly, I almost wave back.

**After my rehearsal**

I'm free! I'm free! Amber and the cast have gone home, so now all that's left to do is go over the last details about the set with Tony.

It's dark when I re-enter the theater. The house lights are off, but some of the red and yellow stage lights are on. Was Tony working on lighting cues?

At the front of the theater, down in the orchestra pit, I see the silhouetted outline of a bunch of boys standing with their backs to me. They form a circle and are cheering and egging someone on, like they're at a boxing match. I can't see who it is, so I stuff my hat into my sleeve and deposit my jacket distractedly on a chair in row M and go investigate. I hear grunts and assorted other guy guttural sounds as I approach, and although something compels me to go forward, a part of me doesn't want to.

I come up behind the group and look over the shoulders of Chip and Sammy. At the center of the circle, in a sweaty heap like two slimy pigs, wrestle Tony and Allen. Tony's arm is wrapped completely around Allen's waist, and he is grappling and pawing at him in an effort to keep him in his grip. Allen's face is hidden to me, but his shirt rides halfway up his back, revealing his naked, muscular torso, slippery with sweat.

I feel the color drain from my face. I almost scream out, "What the FUCK?!" but instead I raise my voice and say, "Hey, Tony, what's going on?"

Tony instantly releases Allen from the bear hug and sits back on his heels, panting. Allen jumps to his feet and quickly pulls his shirt back down to face me. But I am looking directly at Tony with a pinched face that clearly says *I am waiting for an answer.*

"What?" Tony shrugs. "Just wrestling with the guys during our break. Right, boys?"

The boys shuffle uncomfortably in place and give half-hearted nods. My eyes make a quick sweep of the group. I can tell by their disheveled and red-faced appearances that they've all been taking turns in the match.

"Break it up, boys," I say briskly. "And in fact, get ready for dismissal. Stage Crew work is done for the day."

Tony looks at me incredulously. "Wait a minute. You can't do that. We haven't even started. We have to finish building the stairs today."

The boys remain frozen where they are, eyes darting back and forth between Tony and me.

"Tony, they're done for the day. Boys, do as I ask. Tony, let's go speak privately."

It's subtle, but before they move, they shoot a collective look at Tony first. He nods a curt consent and they all wipe their brows with the hems of their shirts and flip open their cell phones.

—◊—

It's either the lighting booth or the box office to talk privately, and I refuse to stand on Tony's turf– the booth. I sweep past the lighting booth door and motion him into the box office, then close the door behind me.

Maybe I'm just fired up because of how Tony's been messing with Lillette, or maybe I've just had it with all his frustrating boundary-hopping, but whatever the reason, I come straight to the point.

"Tony, I don't think it's appropriate for you to do whatever it was you were just doing with those boys."

"Wrestling."

"Yes."

He's not looking at me. He stares out the box office window, and focuses on something in the distance.

"You didn't like it," he says flatly.

"That's right."

He finally turns to face me. "But *they* liked it, and they're *my* crew. We're tight. We were tight before you got here. Frankly, Kelly, I think you're interfering."

I feel my cheeks grow hot, and my eyes narrow.

"Be careful, Kelly," he croons smoothly. "You're causing a rift between my stage crew kids and you and Jack. If they don't like how you're treating them, they'll walk."

"I don't think so, Tony," I say sharply. My voice sounds like acid compared to his cool tones. "This is a school function. They don't get to decide if they can leave or not. They're not the adults in charge calling the shots. It's off-base for you to even suggest such a thing. You have to corral their bad attitude and put a stop to it."

Tony's mouth twists and he openly glowers at me. His eyes dance maliciously and a violent tension crackles between us.

For the first time I think he looks incredibly ugly.

He takes a predatory step forward, his body looming over me– so close I feel his heat and see his chest rising. The expanse of his chest seems as large as a mattress. For a split second I think he's going to reach for me, but his arm shoots past and he grasps the doorknob.

"I'll see what I can do," he says gruffly as he steps past me and walks out.

## Home

"Jackson, I walked in on a scene today that was really disturbing and inappropriate. We have to call the Headmaster for guidance."

Jackson closes the laptop and pats the seat next to him on the couch. I throw myself down next to him and he says, "Tell me what happened."

It's so good to see his reassuring face. I feel comforted by his genial presence– my ally, my friend. Although Jackson has been very tolerant about working with a peacock like Tony, I know he's still not his favorite person. This will finally, *definitely*, wake him up to Tony's inappropriate ways.

I take a deep breath and explain the whole sordid thing. I get upset recounting it all over again, and I expect Jackson to ride the turbulent waves with me, but he is reacting very strangely. He doesn't look upset at all, and in fact, he almost *smiles* a couple of times.

"Jackson, what is so amusing? Aren't you alarmed?"

"Kel," he says with his arm casually thrown across the back of the couch. "You're not going to like hearing this, but I think you overreacted."

"What?!" I am off that couch in an instant, like someone just jabbed a needle into my stomach.

"I'm just saying, guys play like this." He turns his palms up and shrugs, like this explains everything.

"Jackson! They weren't playing with each other; they were being led by Tony!"

"Kelly, calm down, just listen..."

"It was like *Lord of the Flies!*"

"Listen," he says as he pulls me back down onto the couch. "It sounds like it was just all in good fun. Those boys are all raised by nannies with invisible fathers, right? I'll bet they've never even thrown so much as a *football* around with their dads on their mega front lawns." He shrugs again. "Tony kind of provides that."

"It's not his job to provide that, Jackson. In addition, did you know that they have rules in some public schools now that the teachers are not allowed to touch the students at all– not even a friendly hug or 'good job' pat on the head?"

"Yeah," says Jackson contemptuously. "And how overblown a reaction is that? I also hear in some public schools the kids aren't allowed to bring in cupcakes to celebrate their birthdays anymore."

"Jackson, stick to the subject! What on earth does that have to do with this?"

"I think these new policies are over-controlling and interfere with the way teachers teach. It takes a village, Kel. I don't see anything wrong with what they were doing. Guys clown around," he concludes with absolute conviction.

I pull my curls back into a messy ponytail and busy myself cinching it with a clip. I can feel Xena, Warrior Princess rising up in me and I'm ready to do battle. "I can't believe you're not on my side about this," I say roughly.

"Kelly, you're going to detest me for saying this, but you'd understand if you were born male. It's a guy thing, that's all. Wrestling is a sport. I promise you, this is no big thing."

That's all he can say? He's going to side with Tony just because they're *guys?* What is this, some kind of macho guy conspiracy?

I feel completely alone. Must call someone. The Prof? No– guy. Headmaster Hank? No– guy. My brothers? No– guys. Larry? No– guy. I'll bet *Lisa* would see my point. Is Jackson really telling me all guys would see it his way?

"Kel, you're just mad because you can't be Meryl Streep."

I look at him incredulously and sputter, "What?! Jackson, what are you talking about?"

"You told me you were going to keep an eye on Tony like Meryl Streep did in *Doubt*, right?"

I can't even answer.

"Well," he continues stridently, "I think you've been looking for problems, so now you're creating one where it doesn't exist. You *wanted* to be on some kind of crusade. And I don't know why, because haven't we had enough *real* problems thrown at us every day on this production?"

I find my Xena voice: "First of all, I don't want to *be* Meryl Streep. When I told you that, I said I was going to keep an eye on everything like her *character* did. And that's because although I couldn't put my finger on what it was exactly, something about Tony felt *off*. And second, I don't have to be a guy to find Tony's behavior out of bounds. None of the teachers in *my* high school ever wrestled with students between classes! And finally, if you don't think this is a real problem, then this conversation has deteriorated and I can't talk to you anymore!" I end up shouting the last sentence in a crescendo that ends in a shriek.

I bolt from the room and slam the bedroom door behind me.

Jackson screams after me, "Yeah, well, now we're a day behind with stage crew, Kelly! Where did your high-minded interference get us? Who gets hurt here, huh? Huh?!"

I throw myself on our bed, too outraged to do anything but scream ferociously into my pillow. Then I grab Jackson's pillow and hurl it at the door.

We have never had a fight like this.

Not hungry for stupid pot pie.


6.) I heard the distinct jingling myself. The stage crew kids are packing Tic Tacs, too.

# April 11th
## 8am
## Home

*From: Dr. Gail Waldner*
*To: K & J Graham*
*I will make the time change with the restaurant.*
*Thank you,*
*G. Waldner*

Deceptively congenial. I am on high alert.

That's the trouble with e-mail. No subtext to feel a person's true intent. Whatever. I've got bigger things to worry about.

Jackson didn't sleep with me in our bed last night. He never even came in for his pillow. It still lies squashed beside the door like a deflated marshmallow.

**11 am, Melodies Music Shop**

Larry and Lisa have been tiptoeing around Jackson and me all morning. I've caught their glances zipping back and forth to each other; the universal eye code for "What's up with *them?*"

But I cannot speak. My mouth is set in a straight line as I busy myself restocking the classical music section. The shop is still empty when Lisa finally approaches me and asks, "What happened?"

"We had a fight," I say shortly.

"About something personal?" she asks tentatively.

I look at her, expressionless, then say, "Aren't *all* fights about something personal?"

She smiles gently and says, "I mean versus something work-related."

That perks me up. "Oh, it started out work-related all right, but it ended up being personal in the end."

Lisa nods with understanding, sympathy shining from her green eyes. "Believe me, Kelly, I understand what it's like to work with your husband. We do it everyday, too. But you can't let the work get between the two of you."

I reach for a stack of Beethoven sonatas and say, "I don't know how to separate it. Rehearsing a play becomes too all-encompassing."

She says, "We learned a long time ago that it was better to lock the door to the shop each night and leave the business here. Otherwise, it was like we were working all the time."

"But doesn't it sometimes leak back in?"

"Yes, but we have a code word we say if one of us feels we're dragging work home with us."

"Really?" My curiosity is piqued. I love creative solutions; it kind of makes the problem fun. "What's the code word?"

"Rest."

I smile, getting its double entendre meaning instantly. "Rest" is a musical term that means "stop" between notes, and of course it also means, literally, *rest.*

I sigh witheringly. It is a good idea. But I don't know if it would work for Jackson and me. We're too steeped in the process; putting on a show permeates everything we do. But the way it's been going lately...maybe we *could* try to separate from it a little.

"Won't you go talk to him?" she asks.

I look over to Larry and Jackson, talking together on the other side of the shop. My heart lifts. Larry has his hefty arm around Jackson's shoulders and is talking to him quietly. Tag team– Lisa is working on me, while Larry works on Jackson. I'm touched. We have the sweetest friends.

I don't know what I'll say, but I allow Lisa to push me towards the guys. They turn together as they hear us approach. With Lisa and Larry resting their hands on our shoulders, we square off like we're a pair of errant schoolchildren forced to face each other on the playground to offer an apology.

Jackson looks at me warily and says formally, "I'm sorry, Kelly."

He thrusts his hand forward to shake. What's this? Suddenly so corporate with each other?

I place my hand in his and say leerily, "I'm sorry, too." We pump a stiff little handshake and drop our hands.

"What else do you have to say to each other?" Larry coaxes.

Jackson says, "I'm sorry I said you were looking for problems. I know you wouldn't do that. You were legitimately concerned about Tony wrestling with the kids."

Lisa gasps, "That tech director guy was wrestling with the students?"

Larry puts his hand up and growls, "Lisa, stay out of it."

Lisa makes a face and purses her lips. She gives me a nudge and I say, "I'm sorry I flew off the handle. I just felt alone and kind of desperate. Let's just drop the whole thing."

Jackson smiles his goofiest smile, reaches for my waist and pulls me close. "Works for me!" he says.

I put my arms around his neck and murmur into his ear, "Sorry, sorry, sorry." He pulls back a bit, but keeps his face close to mine.

"Not the whispering in the ear thing, Kel; you know what that does to me." He kisses me and I kiss him back, relieved.

Lisa and Larry retreat, but I notice they give each other a high five as they walk to the back of the store.

When I return to the back to finish restocking, I whisper over to Lisa. "Psst, Lisa. What do you really think about Tony wrestling with the boys?"

She rolls her eyes and slaps her hands on her thighs in disgust. "That guy is a creeper!"

### 2:30pm, The Little Theater

Jackson and I are still a little bruised from our disagreement, but we hold hands in the car during our drive over to Samuel P. all the same.

We decided to postpone working on the Bill Sykes/Nancy murder scene; we need to focus on other things. It's just as well.

We prattle on about the show and what still needs to be done, but discussing Tony any further is off limits. I privately don't feel done with Tony yet, and notice I feel a little nervous about seeing him again today. I don't confess this to Jackson– I'm trying to give it a "rest" like Lisa and Larry do.

We sweep by the open lighting booth door and go straight into the theater. I know Tony's up there, but I don't want to see him yet. I spot Lillette (on time!) center stage, and head off to speak with her. Maybe she can give me some insight into Tony. I know that's asking a lot, but sometimes Lillette surprises me with her take on things. And maybe she's tipped Headmaster Hank off about Tony's behavior already.

As Jackson busies himself at the piano, I pull Lillette stage right to talk to her quietly.

"Lillette, did you ever tell your uncle about Tony toying with you?" I ask.

She pulls her arm away and recoils with dismay. "No!" she says. "Why would I do that? He lives in Cincinnati!"

We look at each other for a moment in utter confusion.

I raise my voice, "Your uncle– the headmaster of *this* academy, lives in *Cincinnati*?!"

"What?! No! Oh, you mean *that* uncle! No, he lives right here in Harding Cove with my Auntie Bess!"

"Right. Good," I say as I press my hands down onto her shoulders. "*That's* the uncle I'm talking about."

Her face is still comically aghast. "Then why were you asking about my uncle who lives in Cincinnati?"

I shake my head in exasperation. With my hands still gripping her shoulders, I shout, "Lillette! Focus. Look at me. I was talking about your Uncle Hank, the headmaster over there!" I point in the direction of the main building, stabbing my finger repeatedly in the air for emphasis.

"Okay, okay," she huffs. "Don't get so excited!" She smoothes and pats her tee shirt back into place indignantly, as if the force of my words has actually wrinkled her clothes.

I guess I'm still really on edge. I draw in a huge yoga breath and exhale slowly. Barreling on I ask, "Did you ever report how Tony was treating you to your Uncle Hank?"

She crosses her arms and looks up towards the lighting booth. "No," she says reluctantly. "I was too embarrassed."

We can both see Tony's silhouette, outlined like a cardboard cut-out as he stands, immobile, at the booth's open window. Framed in the giant rectangular opening, his face appears in shadow, but I can just feel him peering down at us.

I turn my back to him and ask, "How does he treat you now?"

"Ignores me," Lillette says uncomfortably as she raises her chin. "Pals around with the kids more than me. No more 'ding dong' with my ponytail." Her lip starts to tremble. "But I don't care. It's his loss," she says with as much dignity as she can muster.

Does Tony really think it was a good idea to mess with the headmaster's niece? Surely he knows that could cost him his job. The arrogance!

Just then Lillette turns her back on Tony, and cupping her hand directly over my ear, whispers, "He's probably watching our every move. Act natural."

She abruptly drops to the floor and spreads her legs open into a "v" shape. Stretching with an exaggerated gusto like one of those manic aerobics instructors she barks, "ONE, TWO, THREE, FOUR..."

I kneel down beside her and smile tolerantly. "Lillette, please stop. He can't hear us."

She continues bouncing as she stretches, "SEVEN, EIGHT! I know," she lowers her voice. "But just in case. Maybe he's planted a microphone down here. He was helping those PowerTech sound guys all week, so maybe he slipped a weensy super-tech mic into my ponytail when I wasn't looking. Maybe that's why Tony was always pulling on it!"

Her face lights up with sudden understanding.

"Eureka!" she says. "I'll bet that's it!"

I pull a face and say, "Come on, Lillette, I doubt it. I mean, practically speaking, wouldn't you have washed it out by now?"

"Oh, yeah, yeah; you're right," she says nodding her addled head.

She suddenly grabs her ponytail and pulls the tip of it around to the corner of her mouth. Talking into it like an actual little microphone, she sputters, "If you can hear me now, Tony Glynn, get this through your thick, golden locks: you can't hurt me anymore. You, you, why, you're nothing but a sleaze tease!"

We both spin around to look back up at the booth. No reaction from Tony. He hasn't moved a muscle. Even reduced to the simple, rugged outlines that comprise his physique, you can tell he's the epitome of the word *hunk*. He's got a predator's stillness about him, though, that's giving me the creeps.

Leaning towards Lillette, I gingerly take hold of the tip of her ponytail and say into it: "Yeah, Mr. Hot Stuff, just because you're a beefcake, and made Lillette all moany and groany, you're nothing but a *phony*, Tony!"

We flip back around again, but he's disappeared. We gasp in surprise, then grab each other and burst into nervous giggles.

Jackson calls out from the piano, "Can you two possibly get it together? We go up in fourteen days!"

**3pm, Rehearsal**

Excellent. Other than Forrest and Delaney's murder scene, the entire show is blocked. Now we're just polishing up the scenes that need shoring up.

"Christian, try it again," I say from the apron.

Christian is standing with Blake and Grant stage right, getting ready to go into the next number.

Christian looks at me uncertainly. "I just made it bigger. It's still not coming across?"

"It's reading too big now, like you're mugging for comic effect."

Jackson stands by the piano in the pit and calls up, "Remember what we told you? The cornerstone of acting is believability."

Christian spins his Live Strong bracelet around his wrist nervously. He jams his hands into his pockets and says, "Okay, I'll try it again."

By the slump of his shoulders I can see that he's getting upset. Blake pats him on the back and I say, "Christian, don't take this criticism too hard. Your Artful Dodger is terrific. We're just tweaking it now."

He nods, but I can see his confidence is sinking. This is pretty much the time we see kids start to slip a bit. They're at the point where they've memorized their lines, they know their blocking, we've talked about their characters and how to play them, but it's normal for some of them to feel the strain of keeping it all going.

"Christian!" Jackson calls from the piano. "Mrs. Graham is right. You're doing a good, solid job!"

While Jackson talks, I spot Amber on the floor next to me writing, "The cornerstone of acting is..."

"Believability is a funny word," Jackson says. "The great actor Sir Laurence Olivier said that basically, acting is just really good lying. And *seeming* real is an important word we can add to that. Because it can't *really* be real or we'll all be in a lot of trouble. When we practice the craft of acting, we have to remember this. At all times we must be aware we are pretending..."

Christian begins to fidget. He pulls his Live Strong bracelet off his wrist and twists it like a rope of worry beads.

But Jackson lectures on. "Actors have to portray the emotion. Do you understand what that means?"

They all stare back, blank-faced.

I jump in. "It means you have to represent the emotion–enact it. Just like you did in preschool when your whole day was spent pretending and acting out stuff. As Viola Spolin, the mother of theater games said, 'At the heart of all acting is play.'"

Tipped to his limit, Christian grabs his Artful Dodger top hat and pulls it down over his face. From inside he pleads, "Enough! TMI! Please stop already with the quotes!"

The cast cracks up, as do Jackson and I. Grant peeks under Christian's hat and says into his hidden face, "Our savior! You speak for many!"

Blake starts to chant, "No more quotes! No more quotes!"

"Okay, sorry," I smile.

I know we're always spitting out too many words at them. I sometimes forget we're just in a high school, and that these kids are not here to become actors when they graduate. Heaven forbid! Samuel P. Chester Academy churns out tomorrows' doctors, lawyers and sports stars, not starving actors. Most of the time, this is just another extracurricular activity on their checklists– between Crew and Newspaper Club. Something to put on their college apps to show they're "well-rounded." That's not to say that Jackson and I would ever dumb down what we do, but because it's theater education at the high school level, there's only so far we can go.

Christian tries his line again, but fumbles over the words.

"Line!" he calls helplessly.

Amber, clutching her promptbook in her lap, yells out the correct line. Christian smacks his hand on the side of his head and says, "Right, right. I *know* that line!"

Amber smiles encouragingly, and once again I'm struck by the growth in this girl. She told me yesterday that she loves following along "on book," as we say, and is fairly certain she has the entire play memorized. She also confided she was a little worried because she's been hearing the lines running through her head when she goes to bed at night. She thought it maybe indicated she had a neurological disorder or something.

"Yes," I told her gravely. "You do have a very rare condition, found only in the best and brightest of all teenagers."

"What is it?" she asked, her eyes wide.

"It's called E.M.R. Excellent Memory Recall!"

She had given me a proud smile then, and I think she grew an inch taller right there in my presence.

Christian is still flustered about his lines, and says plaintively, "What's happening to me Mr. Graham?"

Blake throws a protective arm around him. Jackson abandons his position at the piano and starts walking up the stairs to the stage. He says over his shoulder, "Amber, please call ten."

I love my Jackson. I know what he's going to do. He's going to talk to Christian and bolster his confidence until his pride is restored.

The true art of an acting teacher, to me, is to provide a net. To give students a safe place to try and to fail. To provide a place where they feel secure enough to freely explore all the worlds inside them. A place where they can use their imaginations with abandon, knowing there's this net.

It's okay. Try it again. Try this.

Jackson is going to coach Christian to feel free and safe again. He's going to be his net.

**7:30pm, Home**

Great. Just how I like to slip into my evening after work: with a cup of tea and an inflammatory e-mail forwarded to us by our boss.

*FYI. Keeping you in the loop. Wanted you to know this is circulating. We will deal with this post-show when we meet to discuss. Try not to let this bother you. As I have mentioned before, we see this every year.*

*–H.H. Prescott*

And the e-mail reads:

*To all parents/guardians of Oliver! students,*

*It has come to our attention that in the recent weeks the Grahams have been in charge of the spring musical, several problems have arisen and been handled poorly.*

*We hope to expose our children to the best experiences possible, but sometimes the people we choose to guide them fall short of our expectations.*

*In moving to correct this situation, we are hoping you will sign the attached petition to have Mr. Tony Glynn take over the acting program.*

*Mr. Glynn, a seasoned actor and technical director, is far more suited to the job. He has engaged our children in all aspects of theater, and goes the creative extra mile to build strong bodies and character as well. He incorporates physical education in the form of wrestling, has put in endless extra hours learning the new sound system to teach the stage crew students, and is always readily available to address any concerns we have. Unfortunately, as I'm sure you are aware, the Grahams have disappointed us in all these avenues. Student injuries, non-inclusion of parents, and argumentative ways with our children have forced this decision.*

*Our goal is to implement this change as soon as the current production is completed.*

*If you are in favor, please sign and return ASAP. Thank you.*

*– Parents Committee for 'Oliver!'*

Man, this is a fickle town! You're only as good as your last interaction. They are relentless and their aggression knows no bounds.

Is this how Dr. Waldner "retaliates" when she doesn't get her way?

What is with these people?

I feel slightly nauseous. How am I going to tell Jackson? We were so happy after today's rehearsal, he just popped out for Carvel to celebrate. I don't feel like eating anything now. And how do we get through our huge Saturday rehearsal tomorrow, *knowing* this is out there? And Tony's scheduled to be there in the morning to work on the set, so he'll be there too– gloating, I'm sure. I'll bet the headmaster sent this to him, too.

How can we face him?

I lie down on the couch and prop my feet up on the armrest. I gaze up at the ceiling and wrap my fingers in the swirls of my ringlets. This smells like it's being pushed by Dr. Waldner. And maybe Mr. Kane and Mr. Longo. And probably Mrs. Kirkland. And toss in Mrs. Barnes, too, for all I know.

I study the fine cracks sending spidery lines along the ceiling. Maybe, like those Rorschach blobs, they'll reveal some insight into my unconscious state of mind. Hell, yeah, they do– obviously! The cracks mean I'm *cracking up* under all this friggin' pressure. How much more of a sign do I need? And how much more of this will we be able to stand?

I think about how I'm supposed to assemble our pre-made dinners into some arrangement on the coffee table, but I can't move right now. Good-bye dinner. Good-bye Carvel.

I turn on my side and quickly fall asleep.

# April 12th
## 8am
## Home

I found a gray hair in my right eyebrow. I have hair the color of copper tubing, so it leapt right out at me this morning. Now I'm mooning over whether I should pluck it or not. To pluck, or not to pluck; that is the question. What would Hamlet do?

I know this is small potatoes compared to all we've been going through, but it's still affected me. The reminder that time is marching on and all that.

There's a part of me that thinks it was born directly from our *Oliver!* stresses, but on the other hand, maybe it snaked out through my pores as a visual reminder that I'm just plain aging. A silver flag, waving, "Yoo hoo! Time is not on your side! Us body parts are getting on in here!"

Maybe it was caused by reading the Parents Committee e-mail last night. Jackson woke me up when he got back from Carvel, but I could only point mutely at the laptop. After reading it through, he was just as numb as I was. We nibbled at our dinners, but bailed on the ice cream. Jackson shoved it into the freezer where it will stay until one of has the heart to throw it out.

It's this thing with us; we hate freezing soft-serve ice cream. It hardens into a rock, and then neither of us can face eating it. The whole point of buying Carvel in the first place is for its creamy, soft-tempered loveliness. Once it's stashed in the freezer, it's unsalvageable really. Even a nice long thaw on the kitchen counter can't revive it to its former scoopable state. Grrrr. I know this is so trivial and stupid. Do all stresses, even the stupid, everyday petty ones, contribute to gray eyebrows?

The thing is, I don't mind gray eyebrows or growing older; that's not my fear. My fear is dying before I get to do everything I need to do.

I have always felt as if I'm in this mad dash against time–like I have to hurry up and squeeze out all my creativity before it's too late. I'm terrified of dying young with all this stuff still inside me. Death is the ultimate defeat to me– the complete loss of power. It's so passive! I just know if I died, I'd be so outraged that I'd pop right back up in that coffin, and scream, "How dare you dismiss me, world! I can't be dead– I've got stuff to do!"

I recognize that this scenario would scare the bejeezus out of all my relatives in the funeral parlor, and might even induce a few heart attacks, but maybe the benefit of having me un-dead would help them overlook their trauma.

I don't want to die because I have too much yet to accomplish.

I know– silly narcissistic me. All this brought on by one gray hair. Who's the drama queen now?

That settles it. I'm leaving it. I'll wear it like a badge.

And as for the lethal letter? Jackson and I have decided to take Headmaster Hank's advice and take their e-mail with a grain of salt. We'll meet with the headmaster, as he mentioned, after the show has closed and give our side of the story.

Maybe my eyebrows will be totally gray by then, and I'll look remarkably wise.

### 10am, Main Building, Samuel P. Chester Academy

Do not tell me. It's broad daylight and I swear I'm losing my mind, because I think I hear it: the sound of a girl weeping. Absolutely *not* Lillette.

Oh snap. So of course I finally hear this on a Saturday, when the building is all but deserted. Am I catching the hysteria too, or what? Although the corridor is empty, I plan on grabbing the first person who saunters by to ask, "Listen? Do you hear that?"

I lean against the wall that leads to the back stairway and wait. Empty. Where is Angelo? If only he'd appear– then we could be spooked by this together.

Well, fine. I'll just go down and check this out for myself. I take a few tentative steps.

I still hear it, faint and far off– muffled. Maybe it's the wind? Maybe those nooks and crannies Angelo told me about fill the drafty spaces between the walls to produce that thin, flat wail.

It's definitely real. Halfway down the hall, though, it stops. I do a quick little run/skip to the end, but now all is silent. From the base of the stairs, I look up. The dizzying pattern of four flights up looks like an M.C. Escher puzzle, but it's quiet as a tomb.

And then I do it– the Kelly mind-fuck torture. I stand perfectly still and sic my imagination on the innocent walls. I try to see that spring day, almost eighty years ago: these are the stairs, these are the rough bricks, this is the mortar that witnessed her descent. This is where she fell. This is the floor that cradled her crumpled body. This is the air where she gasped her last breath. This is where she died.

This space is exactly the same. But she is gone. Who was the girl who died too soon?

And why is her presence so strongly held onto by all of us?

My gaze settles on the plain, empty space of the floor. She is completely gone. There isn't even a vibe that she existed. Are we really this gone when we're gone?

Why am I trying to imagine her death? Maybe it's not her death I'm trying to imagine. Maybe it's my own.

Without warning, I suddenly feel faint. My knees start to buckle and I reach shakily for the bannister to steady myself. This is ridiculous. I am ridiculous.

I take a deep breath and run back out into the hallway, into the light.

—ᙍᙍ—

"Chip! Don't bring that extra wood backstage, there's no room," I call from row B, seat 108.

Chip stops mid-step on his way up to the stage. I motion with my hand, "Just put it out in the lobby for now."

Chip says, "Tony told me to put it backstage."

"Tony?!" I exclaim as I rise to my feet.

"Yeah. He told me to put all the extra wood backstage, so..."

"Chip," I interrupt. "Why are you calling Mr. Glynn *Tony*?"

His face clouds over and he says defensively, "He said I could."

I recognize I'm about to throw down a gauntlet, but I don't care. "Please go back to calling him Mr. Glynn, Chip." My Sister Aloysius alarm just went off like a siren. I know she would not approve. Her pinched, disapproving look takes over my face like a rubber Halloween mask.

Although Chip has been standing perfectly still, something in him tightens further, and I see a flicker of hatred cross his face. With his arms straining under the weight of the wood, he begins to step backward, away from me.

"Fine," he mutters.

I watch him retreat back down the stairs, his tee shirt flecked along the back with dust and specks of lumber.

Amber unceremoniously dumps her backpack in the aisle and slumps down into seat 107, next to me.

"Hi Amber, what's up?"

Her trusting brown eyes look at me and she says, "I heard that, Mrs. Graham."

"You heard what, Amber?" I say airily, trying to erase the sour pickle scrunch on my face.

"I heard you tell Chip not to call Mr. Glynn 'Tony.'"

"Oh. That's right. He should call him Mr. Glynn like all the students do."

She chews her bottom lip for a few seconds, and then says, "Chip's not the only one, Mrs. Graham."

I turn in my seat and ask, "What do you mean?"

"I'm just saying a lot of us kids are calling him, um, 'Tony' now." She sees my disapproval, but as I open my mouth to speak, she shakes her head and says firmly, "It just makes us feel more grown up, Mrs. Graham, that's all. It's not a big thing."

I think I'm more surprised by the fact that Amber is asserting herself than anything else. I close my mouth so abruptly it makes a little popping sound.

"You see," she goes on, "he's the first grown-up at the academy that we can really relate to. He understands us, and all the pressures we're under. He's better than a teacher– he's like our friend."

Oh my God. They all love him. Is this her way of telling me the kids want Tony to run the program, too? Have they seen the petition being sent around-- or overheard their parents talking? The Prof was right: "Paranoia will destroy ya!"

I don't believe I can articulate just how completely fucked I feel.

My voice thick, I say, "Thanks for telling me this, Amber. Mr. Graham will be here shortly, and then we'll start with a rough run of act one. Probably in about forty five minutes."

"Okay," she says, with this new air of authority about her. She looks so self-confident, like she's a new world leader who just aced her first summit talk.

She hops up from her seat and yells with the force of a fog horn, "Places in forty-five!" Looking down at me she says, "I can get that box of props in the main office, too, if you want, Mrs. Graham."

I shake my head and say, "No, that's okay. I'll get them."

She turns to exit back up the aisle and says briskly, "Then I'll alert Tony up in the booth as to the start time."

I nod mutely after her.

Snapshot of Amber, seven weeks ago: Charlie Brown-ish. Today? Lucy all the way.

—ഡ—

Erik and Blake, hunkered down in a dispirited slump with their backs against the stage, look like leftovers from the cast of *Les Misérables*. Deflated as rag dolls, the only way I know they're alive and breathing is by the industrious way they're working on some lollipops. Erik spins his frenetically around his mouth, while Blake stores it passively in his cheek, giving him the uneven appearance of a lopsided hamster.

"What's happening, guys?" I ask as I drop the box of props on the floor.

"Nada," says Erik, removing the lollipop from his mouth. Orange.

"You both look zapped. Is the schedule becoming too much?"

Erik answers, "Nah. We're just weighted down by what society expects from us, right Blake?" He gives Blake a nudge, and Blake grunts, "Mmph."

"If you mean that your teachers expect you to do your homework, then you could be using this time to take a bite out of it," I say. "We're not starting for another thirty-five minutes."

"It's not the homework, Mrs. Graham. It's not the play; it's trying to make it through these exhausting teenage years in general. Haven't you heard about our generation? We're plagued by major, epic problems. That's what's getting to us."

I look to Blake. "What problems? Blake, what is he talking about?"

Blake pulls the lollipop from his mouth and says, "His mom is filling his head with weird stuff. Like about how terrible it is being a teenager today. He thinks he has to live up to the press.

"What?" I ask. "I'm totally lost."

Erik raises his hands, and clutches at the air dramatically. He says, "We are the juvenile delinquents of today, Mrs. Graham, didn't you know?"

I shake my head no. Erik is a juvenile delinquent? Impossible. I'm positive his mother would never allow it!

"According to my mother, we're all nothing but trouble. She says we're all adolescent heroin addicts, having oral sex in the bathroom stalls at our schools, while we cut our classes so we can cut our bodies."

Blake and I exchange glances and grimace in unison.

"She quotes from *Dr. Phil*, and she reads aloud from the newspaper to me and my brothers over breakfast every morning. She lectures us about everything from teenage pregnancy to depression and teenage suicide. Over breakfast!" Erik exclaims. "She reads this stuff to us while we're trying to choke down our Cheerios!"

Blake pops his lollipop out of his mouth and asks Erik, "How do we cut ourselves?"

"*We* don't cut ourselves, you noob; other kids do. It's called being a cutter."

Blake holds his green lollipop to the side of his face as he contemplates this bit of information. I begin pulling scarves and a treasure chest filled with plastic jewels from my box, and place them onto the floor next to me.

"How do cutters cut themselves?" Blake asks.

Erik shrugs. "I don't know. With a knife or something, I guess. They make these little cuts because they feel so bad inside."

Blake frowns and asks, "But doesn't the wound make them feel bad *outside?*"

"Nah," says Erik. "It releases the pain or something." He looks back at me. "So you see Mrs. Graham, we are plagued by pressures and expectations to mess up. And according to my mother, sports are our only savior, keeping us off the streets."

Does Mrs. Kirkland mean the streets of *Harding Cove?* The bucolic byways I travel everyday without ever passing a single person? *Harding Cove,* voted one of the top ten wealthiest places to live in the nation? She wants to keep them off *these* troubled streets?!

"We're weighted down by the gloom of our tawdry teenage behaviors. We're slipping deeper into the bottomless ennui, Mrs. Graham. So in short, it's giving us the blues," Erik says, his voice full of despair.

Blake nods, "Yep, I'm down with that."

I bite the inside of my cheek to keep from laughing.

"Do the lollipops help?" I smile.

"Somewhat," acknowledges Erik.

"But you guys don't actually *do* any of these things, right? I mean, you're not heroin addicts, are you?" I don't want to ask about what's going on in the bathrooms.

Erik regards me with a condescending look, remarkably like the one his mother has used on me.

"Of course not, Mrs. Graham. It just makes me feel gloomy sometimes that this is how my mother sees us."

"I've not only got the blues– I've got the reds, greens and yellows, too!" Blake says glumly.

Erik shakes his head fondly at Blake then rests it on his shoulder. "What about the purples and periwinkles? The chartreuses and magentas?" he asks sweetly.

Blake says with certainty, "I have all the shades of despair. My blues include all the weirdo colors, too."

"Well," I say. "I hope you guys can shake them before we start, because we're going to have a really good rehearsal today."

This piques their interest, and Erik lifts his head from Blake's shoulder. "We are? How can you tell?" he asks.

"Because every rehearsal has the potential to be amazing. Think of it, guys; look what we get to do: we get to play, and emote, and create! How lucky are *we?*"

Their eyes brighten, and Erik gives a loud chomp on his lollipop and begins grinding it to pieces.

"Awake ye lads! There's work to be done!" I shout with theatrical gusto.

The boys look startled, but their ears perk up like puppies and they lean forward.

"We're awake, Mrs. Graham. Get up, Erik!"

Blake swallows the rest of his lollipop and says "Okay, I'm psyched, Mrs. Graham! We won't let you down, will we Erik?" He pulls Erik up by his hands and they begin to spar with their little white lollipop sticks.

"Avast ye, me hearty! Take that!" Blake grabs one of the scarves and ties it around his waist. Erik gets into the spirit and ties another around his head, blocking one of his eyes.

"Shiver me timbers," I suddenly yell, pointing over their shoulders. "Pirates! Starboard side!"

"Pirates!" they both scream back, readying their lollipop swords to do battle with the enemies.

"Back! Back, ye scallywags!" Erik cries.

"Help!" I shriek, as I knot a scarf around my wrists and clasp them behind my back. "It's Cap'n Jack Silver, making me walk the plank!" I teeter on a wobbly plank, screwing my face up in anguish.

"No worries, me beauty! We'll save you!" Blake brandishes his sword and springs into action, fending off the imaginary pirates. "Be ye not afeared, me beauty, for they are dead as a scurvy mongrel dog."

"That be a good one!" says Erik to Blake with a gigantic smile on his face.

"Thank you lad, now swap that deck!" Blake points imperiously at the floor.

Erik lifts the scarf away from his eye for a second and says, "It's 'swab the deck,' matey."

"Swab?" says Blake as he cocks his head to the side.

"Yeah, like 'swab the poop deck.'"

Blake stage whispers out of the side of his mouth, "I'm not saying 'poop' in front of Mrs. Graham!"

"Then just say 'swab the deck' without the poop part!" Erik shouts impatiently.

"Okay fine, don't scream at me! It's me that's the Cap'n of this here vessel!"

"Hey!" I yell. "Over here! Help me with these shackles!"

The boys race to my side and frantically untie the scarf. I pretend to rub my wrists back to life and say, "My heroes! Yo ho ho, and arrg, and all that stuff!"

Erik drops his lollipop sword for a second and says in his regular voice, "You're very silly, Mrs. Graham. I think we love you for it."

Blake blushes straight up to the blond roots of his hair and stammers, "Yeah, it's true, Mrs. Graham. We love you for it."

My turn to blush. I feel a surge of affection for these guys and say, "Aw, shucks. You guys are making me blush."

"Me beauty blushes!" declares Blake with a rise of his sword. "Avenge her honor! Attack the landlubbers!"

While they resume fighting off the imaginary foes again, I slip happily backstage to bring the props to the pen.

—⁋—

"He'll *kill* me! Don't tell him, please," I hear someone begging.

From my vantage point inside the pen, I can just make out Chip and Allen hovering over Noelle, as they escort her backstage and help her sit on a stool.

"Don't worry, Noelle; I won't tell him," says Allen.

"No, me neither," murmurs Chip comfortingly. "I promise we won't."

Noelle makes little kitten sniffle noises that sound fabricated to me– the mark of a bad actress.

Lately Noelle has become this little drama queen in training. She can't command the big attention Delaney gets by virtue of her talent, but she's discovered she can get the boys to notice her by fake crying. This is not the first time I've seen her pull this. I have the sense she has the boys just where she wants them: eating out of the palm of her delicate white hand. But this is the first time I've overheard what she says to them.

Allen says, "Maybe we'll find it again. That's what happened last time."

Are they talking about her damn iPod again? What is wrong with this girl? Why doesn't she just leave the thing home if she keeps misplacing it?

I remember when I was in high school, I wanted to wear this beautiful birthstone necklace to school. My grandmother had given it to me, and my mother absolutely forbade it. She said it was too precious and expensive to wear to school, but I wanted to show it off on my birthday.

It almost goes without saying that my mother was right. No, I didn't lose it, but I kept my hand clasped over it all day in a fearful paranoid haze. I knew I'd catch hell from my mother if I lost it, and I knew I would hate myself for losing something that meant so much to me. What I'm trying to say is that the value of the thing had been so impressed upon me, I knew to respect the necklace. No one really saw it that day, and I really couldn't relax to enjoy it, but at least I still have it! At the rate Noelle is going, I doubt she'll still have her iPod a week from now.

"But what if he asks to see it?" Noelle whines.

"Just tell him you left it home," Allen reasons.

"Oh. Yeah. That's a good idea, Allen. Thanks a lot." She gives him a phony brave smile and wipes at her dry eyes with a tissue.

This is starting to read like she's "losing" it on purpose just to get them to play "go fetch" for the poor damsel in distress. Ah well. The dramatic life of the teenager. Maybe *she's* the one faking the weeping dead-girl noises to drive us all to distraction.

### Rough Run of Act 1

"Quiet backstage!" Jackson bellows from the pit.

We've finally settled the cast backstage, but the closed curtain does little to muffle their titters and giggles of excitement.

In the final moments before we run act one, I grab a pencil from my jacket pocket and motion for Amber to follow me.

All in all, I'm feeling pretty good about the shape the show is in. That's not to say I don't expect today to be a disaster, I do. But it's to be expected.

We explained to everyone earlier that we'd be doing a rough run without stopping, so they were to keep going, no matter what. This, of course, brought a flurry of objections:

"Even if my pants rip?"

"Yes, Duncan."

"Even if I have to go to the bathroom?"

"Yes, Shane. Please go now if you have to go."

"Even if I have to shave?"

"Forrest," I warned. "Stop."

"We'll be like the post office," Taffy said. "Neither rain, nor snow, not heat nor gloom..."

Jasmine interrupted, "What? No we're not. Where's the correlation between the weather and our show?"

"It's right there in front of you, Jazz." Taffy said.

"The show and the postal people keep going no matter what!"

"Oh, right, right. I get it, now. Epic win, Taff!" Jasmine smiled.

Etcetera.

We'd told them it's completely normal for it to feel odd and off– like putting on your costume when it's two sizes too big. Adjustments will be made, we assured them, and eventually everything will fit comfortably. For now, we explained, the purpose of the rough run is to get an idea of the timing and to feel how everything flows.

So now we're at five minutes till curtain. Jackson, pacing in the pit, takes his place at the piano and fusses with his sheet music. Tony's in the booth with a couple of stage crew kids, and

Lillette? AWOL. Again. Oh snap. I know she'll show up eventually, even if it's only to take a nap.

Amber and I settle into two seats in row J to watch the run and take notes. I scrunch down, trusty writing pad leaning against my knees, pencil tapping lightly on my teeth. I slowly roll my head from side to side against the back of the seat and arch my back like a cat stretching on a scratch post. I let out a deep breath and we sit quietly, waiting for Jackson to give the thumbs-up cue for Tony to call curtain.

Suddenly, Amber pipes up, "Mrs. Graham, can we get lice if we rest our heads like this?"

Startled, I turn my face towards her and say, "What?"

"Can we get lice from sitting like this? I was just wondering, because if you think about it, these are fabric-covered seats, so if someone happened to have lice, and they put their head on it, couldn't, like, the lice crawl in and reproduce?"

I raise my eyes to the ceiling and cover my face.

Amber continues to prattle, "Then if we come along and rest our heads in the same spot, couldn't the lice, theoretically, crawl onto our heads and then we'd get lice, too? Statistically speaking, it must happen." She pauses a moment to ponder, with her pencil resting on her lips. "If hundreds of people use these seats, then maybe it happens more often than we know."

I begin to massage my face. I rub it so hard I half expect to see I've rubbed it off into my hands. I picture looking down into my hands and seeing my face there, looking back at me in fixed horror.

"And think of all the seats we share in other public places, Mrs. Graham: movie theaters, playhouses, auditoriums. We're told not to share combs or hats, but isn't this just like sharing a hat? We used to share smocks in Art, but then some kids got lice, so we had to stop."

I sit up abruptly and scratch my scalp.

I say, "Shh, shh, Amber, listen. I honestly don't know, but I've never heard about lice being transmitted in that way. Let's just concentrate on the run-through for now, okay?" I face forward again, back to feeling jittery and strained.

"Okay," she says. But I notice she discreetly scratches at the back of her head with her pencil.

Oh dear God, please don't let Amber and me get lice from sitting here innocently in row J. And please God, don't let her add a "Lice" box to The Chart.

And then it hits me:

OHMIGOD THEY SHARE THE FAGIN'S CAPS!

In a rush of adrenaline-fueled panic, I hop to my feet, clamber over Amber, and run like a madwoman towards the piano. Seeing my frantic and wild-eyed state, Jackson rears back in shock, then leaps to his feet, knocking back the piano bench. "What?!" he cries.

"Jackson! The kids shouldn't be sharing the Fagin's caps; they can get lice." I'm breathing so hard my nostrils flare in and out in time like they're doing calisthenics.

Jackson stands for a stunned moment longer, then bangs his baton on top of the piano so hard it breaks.

In thin-lipped fury he hisses, "Kelly, have you lost your mind? You almost gave me a heart attack. I thought someone was hurt!"

"Jackson, you're not listening." I'm trying not to raise my voice and spook everyone, so I over-enunciate, like he's hard of hearing. "They can get LICE. We have to stop this NOW. Don't start the run, yet. I'm going backstage to collect caps."

I start for the stairs, but he grabs me roughly by the arm.

"Kelly! What the ef is the matter with you?" he hisses. "Nobody has lice! They've been rehearsing with those friggin' caps for weeks now! Knock it off and go sit back down."

He's squeezing my arm so hard it hurts. I open my mouth to protest, but instead I jerk my arm away emphatically and adjust my skewered sleeve. Tears flood my eyes, and I notice the whole theater around us has fallen silent.

Amber appears next to me and holds out a tissue. I snatch it from her, but use it to wave at Jackson. Jutting my chin defiantly in his face I say, "Don't *ever* grab my arm that way again."

As I propel myself out the side door, I hear Amber, bless her heart, call out: "Take five, everyone." I assume everyone calls back, "Thank you, five," but I don't know for sure because I'm already gone.

—m—

Jackson pounds on the box office door. "Kelly? Kelly, let me in."

Blinded by hot, meaty tears, I cover my face and sob into my hands. The tissue Amber gave me is totally soaked; I use my sleeve as backup.

"Kelly? Kel, I'm sorry, please. We are just so over-stressed. That's all this is. We're like tinderboxes, you and I. Let me in."

I cough out a thick, "No," and go back to crying. I sit backward in the box office swivel chair with my head on its back. All is silent for a moment, and then I hear a light tapping at the box office window. I swing around in the chair to see Jackson standing outside, hands on the glass.

My eyes feel all puffy and swollen, but even through the blur of my tears, I can see how stricken he looks.

"Please?" he mouths silently and points to the inside door.

"I can hear you through the opening Jackson," I say aloud.

"I'm sorry," he mouths again.

I look at him and draw in a shaky breath. "I'm too upset."

He speaks out loud, "Kelly, we're both upset. Times have been upsetting. Our nerves are in shreds; we both just exploded when we should have stayed calm."

I dab at my eyes. Hanging my head, I say begrudgingly, "It just struck me about the lice. I freaked out because I got terrified thinking of one more problem to take on. I just wanted to stop it before it happened."

"It's okay," he nods. He's looking at me intently as he tries to slide his hand through the opening in the window. Only his fingers fit.

I lean forward and grip the tips of his fingers and say tearfully through the glass, "I'm so frazzled. I've never been this frazzled before, Jackson."

"Me, too," he says tiredly. "Me, too. But we're almost there, Kelly. Let's just try to keep it together for thirteen more days, okay?"

As he talks, each puff of his breath leaves a little circle of condensation on the window. Mesmerizing. Why can't I just stay here and watch the little circles all night? Suddenly, that's all I want to be in life: a condensation circle watcher.

Jackson pulls his hand back and reaches into his pocket. He pulls out a little scrap of paper and scribbles something on it. He rolls it into a little tube and slips it through the opening.

I reach out to take it. He watches me as I unfurl it and read: *You are an actor's director, everything a good director should be: inspiring, encouraging, supportive and fun. Love, Your Biggest Fan, The Music Guy.*

Tears spring to my eyes again; he wrote me my own fan mail! I shake my head in wonder and point to the inside door. He disappears from view in a flash, and appears at the box office door just as I unlatch it. We clutch at each other and he holds me so tightly, for a moment I can't breathe. Our embrace feels desperate, like we're two shipwrecked castaways, clinging alone onto the same lifeboat for survival.

But we are not alone. I look up at him.

"We left the kids!"

—ⁿⁿ—

We dash back inside, but stop short when we see Tony and Amber standing center stage with their backs to us. Tony's body is half engulfed in the still closed curtain while Amber stands to his side. The lower part of his body sticks out: legs, butt and tool belt, but I can hear his muffled voice saying, "I'm sure they'll be right back. Just keep it together for the sake of the show, okay mis amigos? Here!"

Jackson and I stop at the end of the apron and hear the kids laughing and play-fighting behind the curtain. "That's mine! I got it first! Tony, here! Throw *me* one; I'm open!"

Tony laughs and says, "Try again! Oh! Epic fail, you just missed, Duncan-my-Dude!"

Amber gives a quick tug at Tony's tool belt, and he emerges from the curtain, little Tic Tac box in hand. He looks directly at Amber, unaware that we are watching, and says, "You want some, too, AmberGlow?"

Before she can say anything, he reaches out and takes her hand. "AmberGlow, AmberGlow, face so pretty, but filled with woe," he singsongs. Cupping his hand under hers, he begins shaking some Tic Tacs into her palm, but she tries to pull away and points mutely to us. Tony turns.

"Oh, hey," he says with surprise, dropping her hand like it was on fire. Tic Tacs rain down onto the floor and bounce like hail across the stage. As Amber drops to her knees to corral them, Tony re-tucks his shirt and adjusts his tool belt.

"Just keeping the peace," he says easily. "They love these." He flashes the Tic Tac box with a huge phony smile like he's doing a commercial to sell the damn things.

Jackson nods curtly. "Yeah, thanks. We're going to start now." He hops onto the stage and brushes roughly past Tony.

He disappears as he parts the curtains and says to the cast, "Sorry for the delay, guys. Places, please."

Tony trains his eyes on me still standing down in the pit. In a low voice he taunts, "Heat getting to you?"

I'm too wrung out to spar with him, so I just say dismissively, "Yeah. You know how it is."

"Yeah," he says. "And you know what they say: 'Can't take the heat? Get out of the kitchen.'"

He vaults down into the pit with the tiger-like grace of an Olympic athlete and passes me with a sneer that he hides from Jackson. I take an unsteady step back.

I want to scream out, "You just can't wait to take over, can you? Well, I'm not leaving the ef-ing kitchen yet! We're still in charge here, you a-hole!"

But of course, I don't.

Amber looks around helplessly with the palm full of Tic Tacs nesting in her hand and I say, "Just hand them down to me, Amber. I'll throw them out."

"No, wait," she says quickly, as she folds them over her heart. "I want to save them."

Too weary to respond, I shrug and walk away.

It was only a short while ago that I got Erik and Blake all excited for this rehearsal, and now look at me. I'm a puffy-eyed, teed off, Tony-hating harpy. In short, I'm a bitch.

Seconds later, as Amber and I settle into our potentially lice infested seats, Lillette bustles in and says, "Sorry I'm late; what did I miss?"

# April 14th
## 11:30am
## Home

The e-mail's are constant.
In among requests for tickets...

*We need eight tickets for the Friday night performance for Oliver!*
*Can you please seat us on the side of the audience where our daughter*
*mostly performs? To clarify, if she appears primarily on the left side of*
*the stage, then that is where we want to be seated.*

...and complaints about moving to evening hours for Tech
Week...

*Why are you changing the routine at this late hour? We are all*
*used to the afternoon schedule, and find this disruptive to our family.*
*Can you please consider going back to the afternoon hours?*

...is the winning e-mail of the morning! It comes to us from
Dr. Waldner, Mrs. Kirkland and Mrs. Barnes:

*Hello, Mr. and Mrs. Graham,*
*Please be advised that Gertie Barnes, Claudine Kirkland and I will be*
*available to dress the children for the show. As our assistance has been*
*greatly appreciated by the directors in the past, we hope to continue our*
*work in the same capacity on this current production.*
*Regards,*
*Dr. Gail Waldner, Mrs. Claudine Kirkland and Mrs. G. Barnes*

It's the three amigos! Or more like the three furies, depending on how you look at it.

After reading through it again, it's sort of reasonable and even respectful how they're semi-asking to help out, but when I first read it, all I saw was the phrase "dress the children." Dress. The. Children. *Dress* the *children?* Why? Can't they dress themselves? Some of these kids already drive cars. And some of them are already eligible to fight in a war– but these mothers think their kids are incapable of putting on their costume for their school play? It's too funny. I can just picture it, too: these three bossy women commanding, "Hands up. Turn around. Don't pick at the collar," like they're dressing toddlers.

I have to be careful here. This is where everything unraveled last semester. The parents appeared during Tech Week and began openly criticizing everything they saw– from the colors of the costumes, to the way the students personally looked in them. The cast got flustered and morale dropped. Who can blame the kids? They were doing fine without their mommies' input, but these women just couldn't take a backseat position.

Unfortunately, we're already on shaky ground with these parents, so I really don't know how to respond to this e-mail.

Jackson is pissed enough for the both of us and is busy abusing his laptop on the coffee table. He reads me his response before he hits send and propels it out into cyberland. I'm in the bedroom finishing dressing, so he reads loudly from his spot on the living room couch.

"Dear Dr. Waldner, Mrs. Barnes and Mrs. Kirkland,

Thank you for offering to assist the cast in getting into costumes, but it isn't necessary; the students will do this for themselves.

As with all backstage preparations before a show goes up, (make-up, vocal warm up, costumes), these tasks are best performed by the cast themselves. The reasons for this are many–

1.) This is a time of focus and concentration,

2.) It's important they learn the rhythm and the timing of what they need to do backstage to prepare,

3.) It's important for them to accomplish these tasks on their own, with their peers in both the cast and stage crew assisting them when need be. This fosters the teamwork ethic we work so hard to build, another important aspect of a show's run. The pride and independence they feel from doing things on their own is an invaluable part of this process, and is the whole point of education, really."

He's silent for a second, then calls out, "What do you think?"

I call back out from the bedroom, where I'm pulling my crisp, tight socks into place, "Why are you bothering, Jackson? Too much detail. It's too much talk. They don't want a reasonable, well-thought-out response."

I poke my head back into the living room. "They just want you to say yes, because honey, they're gonna show up anyway, just like they did with *Arsenic and Old Lace.*" I lean against the entryway and give my knee socks a firm tug.

Jackson looks up at me, lost.

"Jackson, I speak their language now," I say. "So let me translate for you. The purpose of that e-mail was to inform us that this is what they *intend* to do. Period. They aren't asking for permission." I walk into the kitchen in search of my sneaks.

Jackson calls out in anguish, "I'm just so frustrated with these parents, Kel! What the hell! Why do we have to fight them every step of the way?"

"I don't know, Jackson," I shout back. "Why are we *bothering* to fight them every step of the way? They push, we resist. I have a great idea, let's stop resisting! Let's give up!"

I come back into the living room, really into it now. I flail my arms around and pace back and forth in front of the TV.

"Let's let them take over and direct the show. They think they can do it better? I say we let them, and just show up on opening night to collect our checks!"

"They don't want to direct the *show*," Jackson says as he runs his fingers through his hair in exasperation. "They want to direct *us*!"

"Well, then, we're the idiots, Jackson. We have never been able to set up proper boundaries to corral them. That's our fault!" I look at the time. "I have to get to rehearsal early and you're going to be late for Melodies."

"Should I send it?" he asks, his knee bouncing up and down like it's ready to take off on its own.

I tuck my laces into my sneakers and say rashly, "Sure. Why not? Because ultimately, it doesn't matter what we say or do. They're like this inevitable tidal wave rushing towards the shore, and we're these teeny little specks on the beach, obliviously lathering suntan lotion onto our backs. We look up as a giant shadow looms and BAM! We're toast. We can't fight something this huge and powerful anymore, Jackson."

Jackson stares down at the laptop like it's an oracle and he's waiting for it to speak.

"Maybe I should just say something like, 'Thanks, but no thanks, we've got this covered. But we could use your help elsewhere.'"

"Yeah, like in Alaska, or off the Amalfi Coast," I joke.

Jackson doesn't laugh. His knee is bouncing, he's rubbing his thumbnail against his lips, and he's intermittently scratching at his ear. My husband is becoming a neurotic bunch of nervous tics.

He abruptly slaps the laptop closed and says, "I'll deal with this later. I'm out of here."

"Wait a minute!" I'm suddenly struck with inspiration. I pounce on the couch and say, "I've got it!"

Jackson grabs his jacket and searches for his keys while I babble, "I'll take this to the cast. I'll ask them what *they* want. I doubt they want all their mommies around backstage bossing them into place, right? And while their mommies may go against *our* wishes, I can't see them denying what their *kids* wishes are. How's that?" I sit back, quite pleased with myself.

Jackson plants a distracted smooch on my cheek and says, "Yeah, sure, that's fine, Kel."

Impulsively, I throw my arms around his neck and squeeze him tight. When I release him, I look into his eyes and ask, "Do you love me, Jackson Graham?"

He focuses on me and smiles. "With all my heart." Then he gives me a quick peck and says, "I gotta go."

**3pm, The Little Theater**

"Circle up, cast!" Amber calls from center stage.

Forrest rushes towards the stage, falls to his knees in the pit, and calls up to her, "Amber! I love you! I'm yours! Just say when and where!"

He slides his hand under his shirt and starts rubbing his chest. A bunch of the kids snicker and nudge each other as they watch his antics on their way up the side stairs.

Oh brother. Just great. No Jackson today to keep Forrest in line.

"C'mon, Forrest," I say as I stand in front of a blushing Amber. "Knock it off."

Forrest swings his body up onto the stage and I snap, "*Stairs,* Forrest, *stairs.* You know better."

He lopes over to us and smiles easily as he says, "Yeah, but I wanted to get right over to Amber here as quick as possible to say I'm sorry."

Amber shrinks back next to me as he sticks his face into hers and says, "Sorry, Amber, baby. Forgive me?"

Amber stutters, "It's, it's all right."

"Forrest, go sit down," I say in my most fed up big sister voice. I pull Amber by her elbow to the safety of stage left. While the cast settles down, I ask, "You okay?"

She says, "Yeah. He's just an intimidating beast, Mrs. Graham. He'll never get a girlfriend that way."

"Very true, Amber. But I'll still have Mr. Graham talk with him about his behavior."

I look over to the other side of the stage, where Forrest is showing off by walking on his hands.

"In the meanwhile," I continue. "I've added something new to announcements."

"Okay," she says, already pulling the pencil out from behind her ear. "Should I take notes?"

"Sure," I reply. "But I'm really letting you know because it may throw today's schedule off a little."

"A big discussion then?" she guesses, and I nod. She purses her lips and says primly, "Then I may need *two* pencils."

"Guys," I address the circle of faces. "We're getting close to tech week. You all have the schedule, so you should know by now that on that Wednesday and Thursday, we have dress rehearsal. That means we run the entire show with lights, sound, costumes and make-up."

They're with me so far, so I barrel ahead. "It's come to my attention that in years past, some of the parent chaperones have done more backstage than just chaperone; they have assisted by getting you into your costumes and putting on your make-up, too. Is that right?"

There are some confirming nods around the circle, but I still can't gauge their reaction yet.

"For this show," I continue. "Mr. Graham and I think you can manage these tasks for yourselves."

Still no reaction. "But maybe you like it this way, so I want to take a vote: raise your hand if you'd like parents backstage to help out."

At first I think they don't understand, because they gaze back at me and not one hand goes up. "Guys? Did you hear me?"

Amber, like a good little court stenographer, reads back from her notes: "You said, 'I want to take a vote. Raise your hand if you'd like parents backstage to help out.'"

"Thank you, Amber. Everyone, do you understand? I'm asking if you want your parents backstage to help you out."

This seems to rouse them. Jasmine says, "We love our parents, but we never wanted them backstage."

"Yeah," says Duncan. "It's too embarrassing to have my mother there. She still calls me Dunkie Duck!"

Delaney calls out, "They never used to do all that stuff, Mrs. Graham." She casts her eyes down to the floor and says reluctantly, "It may be my fault. I think it started with my mother coming backstage to do my hair. She thinks she's the only one who can do it right."

She stops to roll her eyes, then explains, "Once the other mothers saw what was going on, they said, 'what about us?' and jumped on the band wagon. Now they're all back there and I, for one, can't stand the hovering."

"I second that!" Noelle says, nodding her head vigorously. "I can't stand my mother acting like I can't even tie my shoelaces right. She just won't let me go!"

She blushes suddenly as she hears the vehemence in her voice.

Amber's arm is racing across the page as she hurries to write down every word.

Christian says, "Noelle, they mean well. They're not doing it to make us feel bad; they're doing it to make us feel good."

"I feel *smothered!*" Noelle cries.

"*My* mother still picks out my clothes," says Taffy with disgust.

"Yeah, but she's a designer, Taffy. She knows good clothes," Marta consoles.

"But how will *I* ever know?" Taffy asks mournfully.

"*My* mother makes my nanny brush my hair every night. It's humiliating," says Sienna bleakly.

"But maybe that's why your hair always looks so pretty," Thomas says.

Sienna smiles at him, then quickly flicks her hair in front of her face flirtatiously.

"Yeah, well, does *your* nanny still put toothpaste on your toothbrush?" That's Blake, two crimson spots appearing on his cherub little cheeks.

"Just tell her to cut it out," councils Erik dryly from his spot next to Blake. "Lock the door so she can't get in."

Oh geez; we're moving into group therapy here. I didn't know they'd feel this strongly about it. I even sort of expected some opposition to our idea, so this is an interesting turn of events.

Delaney raises her hand and asks, "Mrs. Graham, do you want them there?" She looks at me evenly, so I can't tell if this is a challenge or not.

I say slowly, "We think you'd learn more from doing these things yourselves, but I'm trying to figure out if *you* want them there or not."

Delaney keeps her eyes locked on mine and says purposefully, "If you don't want them there, Mrs. Graham, then neither do we." She hops to her feet like Joan of Arc and says valiantly, "We've had it with our parents taking over everything we do. They treat us like we're babies, or handicapped, like we can't do anything on our own. And I'm sick of my mother telling me how and when to breathe, and I AM NEVER LETTING MY NANNY STICK ANOTHER DROPPER FULL OF REPULSIVE VITAMINS DOWN MY THROAT EVER AGAIN!"

She thrusts a raised fist boldly into the air and pandemonium breaks out as the kids erupt with cheers and high fives. Noelle tackle-hugs Delaney; several boys jump onto each other's backs and gallop around the stage. Amber drops her promptbook and pencils on the floor and gives up, massaging her hand. I stand and pat at the air, calling out loudly, "Settle down, settle down."

Over Noelle's shoulder, Delaney looks at me square in the eye and gives me her first genuine smile.

As their euphoria subsides, I say, "I read you all loud and clear. No parents backstage. I'll let Mr. Graham know."

Now it's just a matter of how to let the parents know.

Mass e-mail?

**8:30pm, Home**

Beeep!

"Hi Mr. and Mrs. Graham, it's Erik Kirkland, your favorite wicked Noah Claypole. I just wanted to tell you my mother is on the warpath. I overheard her talking to some other mother— Dr. Waldner, I think, and they are not happy campers. Please check your e-mail for the whole scoop. Sorry if this wrecks your night, but I thought you should know about it before the stuff hits the fan! Byeee!"

*From: Erik Kirkland*

*To: Kelly and Jackson Graham*

*Hi Mr./Mrs. Graham, it's me, Erik. I feel like a spy living in enemy camp. If they find out I am communicating with you, will you adopt me? jk jk!*

*My mother and Dr. Waldner are spitting nails you e-mailed to tell them we don't need them backstage. See, they take that personally, and it just makes them fight harder to get what they want. And if they want to dress us, they're gonna to find a way to dress us no matter what you say. It's just how they are.*

*My mother said you were getting too big for your britches and didn't know your place. Don't take it personally. She says the same thing about Carlos and Amelia, the nicest, most subservient people on our staff.*

*I overheard my father laugh one time and say that since my mother is no longer the bully of the boardroom, she had to become the bully of the academy. Get it? When it comes to my mother, she sees everything in terms of winning. It's all about competition for her. Thank God my brothers fulfill her thirst for dominance, because I could care less.*

*When she makes me sit on those bleachers to watch my brothers play their idiotic sports, I can't stand it. What's the point? Can you explain sports and the whole winning thing to me? My brothers run around clutching little balls in various shapes and try to transport them to other places. Why, I ask you? If I had that football in my arms, and a bunch of beefy boys were barreling towards me, I'd just step gingerly to the side and let them pass. Or I'd just hand it to them politely– maybe offer them a cool drink. I'd say, "Boys, boys, calm down. If this ball means so much to you, then, here, take it. No need to get all grabby and aggressive about it. Now let's all disband and channel all this energy into something constructive, like baking a pie, or heading up a new chapter of SADD!"*

*To my mind, I think if aliens were to come from another planet, and trained their eyes on the fans at a sporting event, I believe they would conclude that the sole purpose for gathering to watch groups of people hurl themselves at each other over a circular object was to yell "Woo Hoo!" at random intervals. There is nothing intelligent about it. It caters to our base need to vent aggression in a communal roar. That's why I'm pursuing a higher calling and going into the arts.*

*Thank you for trying for us, but don't fight them, Mr. and Mrs. Graham. Just give in. That's what I do. It's the only way to survive. See you tomorrow! I love the play!*

*Love, your spy,*
*Erik Kirkland*

*From: Claudine Kirkland*
*To: Grahams*
*Yeah, Kelly and Jackson, this is a fine way to hear about your decision— from a mass e-mail. I was on the committee that approved your hire. I tried to warn you about the way we do things here, but you obviously are having trouble adhering to my advice. What is given can easily be rescinded. I don't appreciate you not cooperating with us on this matter. Word to the wise: alienating the parents is not in your best interests. If you haven't heard already, there is a petition circulating, seeking the dismissal of you in favor of Tony Glynn. I have my doubts about Mr. Glynn's ability to head the program, and up until this point I have continued to back the two of you, but in light of recent events, I'll have to rethink my position.*
*–Mrs. Claudine Kirkland*

I can feel fresh gray eyebrows being manufactured in my body as I read this. I'll bet if I look in the mirror right now, several new ones will have crawled out onto my face.

My life has dissolved into one big Trauma Drama.

All I want to do is sleep.

# April 15th
## 10am
## Home

Jackson is at Melodies, so I'm taking this moment to phone the Prof from the kitchen– the most clinical room in our apartment. I'm hoping the efficient order of the room will bolster me into keeping it together. I've brought along a few tissues, just in case. I'm awfully leaky these days. I sit up as straight as I can muster at the kitchen table and dial his number.

"Hi, Prof, it's Kelly. How's everything there?"

I am trying to maintain my normal tone, like I'm just having an everyday, breezy chat from my tidy little kitchen. But like a mother with an automatic pain antenna, the Prof calls me on it and says, "Hi, Kelly, everything's fine here; what's wrong?"

"Well," I begin, my voice quavering. "It's still kind of crazy here, and I know we just spoke recently, but I was wondering if I could ask for a little more guidance?"

The Prof says, "Of course, Kelly. You always like me best in my 'Yoda' mode."

(He knows!)

I bark out a sharp little laugh and wipe the tears that have started collecting at the corners of my eyes with a tissue.

"Oh, Prof, you're on to me now. I hope you take it as a compliment."

"Sure I do," says the Prof. "Now what's up?"

I tell him about everything: the out of control parents, the fights between Jackson and me, Forrest issues, Tony worries. Good thing I brought the tissues. As it turns out, I need the whole blop to get me through the saga.

The Prof listens attentively, then says, "Kelly, it does no good to get upset that the world isn't set up to your standards. Or that it doesn't fall in line behind what you want. There are all kinds of people, with all kinds of needs and wants on this planet."

He's laying down the worldview for me. Good. This is just what I need. Global perspective.

"A school is just a microcosm of the world; the big playground where all of life's scenarios get played out. What you're describing is what we see on the actual playground: the struggle for dominance."

"Dominance," I echo, letting the word sink in. "I can definitely see that Prof, but how come I never knew about any of this? This was never covered in any class I ever took." I pick at my crumpled tissues and begin pulling tiny pieces from them.

"That's because this is Life 101, Kelly."

I roll the little balls between my fingers and begin lining them up in a row.

"So what are you saying, Prof?"

"I'm saying that all these people, with all their egos, are jockeying for position and dominance."

"Well, I don't want them to do that. I'm the director!" I cry.

"So you're jockeying, too."

I am silent. That shut me right up. "Touché, Prof. I get it. But as the director, I still don't know how to *manage* it all."

"That's right, Kelly; now you've said the million dollar word: management. Learning to manage people can be a challenge. Can you enlist the help of the headmaster there?"

I sign. "Oh, Prof, he's a kindly, sweet guy, but he's just a big, yummy cream puff. He takes the parents' side with any issue because he just doesn't want any waves."

"That's unfortunate," says the Prof. "No wonder you and Jackson are overwhelmed. You're pretty much on your own then."

"Tell me about it! We do our best, but it's too much at times. Oh! And that detaching thing, Prof? Let's just say that I've failed at that, too. What's left for us to do?"

"I hate to say it, Kelly, but maybe this isn't the right place for you and Jackson."

I'm silent.

"Kelly?"

"I'm here, Prof, I was just thinking."

Because that very thought has recently crossed my mind, but I would never dare to say it out loud. Instead I say simply, "We're not quitters, Prof."

"It's not a matter of being a quitter, Kelly. I moved on to the university level for some of the reasons you've been citing to me through our talks. This environment may clash with your style, that's all."

I roll a tissue back and forth between my fingers. "I don't know, Prof; it would feel like we failed."

"I don't think failure would be involved here. I didn't mean to imply you should quit mid-production. But certainly once the show closes, you may want to look at the benefits versus the downsides."

Hmm. Maybe.

"Okay, Prof. Good point. I'll keep it in the back of my mind."

Maybe we do have to consider that option. But I can't focus on it now. I wait a beat, then ask, "Hey, Prof, do you believe in the destiny of a name?"

"How do you mean, my dear?"

"Well, I've taken an interest in people's names, and wonder if we live up or down to the definition of them."

When he doesn't respond, I continue, "I was just curious, you know, because I looked up the meanings of the names of various people I know, and they really seem to apply."

"Or maybe you're just reading things into it. Like horoscopes– those traits and predictions are general enough that they can apply to anyone."

"Maybe," I concede.

"I'm curious, though, what do your names mean?" he asks.

"Well, Jackson is simple: 'Jack's son.'"

"And yours?"

"Brave warrior."

He's silent for a moment while I continue to form my squishy tissue balls.

"Kelly, you are brave. I've directed you in *Major Barbara* and *The Miracle Worker*, and your work in both those pieces took bravery and stamina. Your Annie Sullivan in particular, was full of grit and moxie."

I blush past red into violet. "Thanks, Prof, but I was *acting.*"

He laughs big and loud, "You know as well as I do, Kelly, that getting up on that stage and creating believable, compelling characters takes all kinds of courage that most people in this world know nothing about."

"That's what I tell my students!" I exclaim. "I always praise them for their bravery– for getting up in front of everyone with no place to hide."

"See?"

I wipe my eyes and rest my head in my hand.

"And Kelly?"

"Yes, Prof?"

"You're stronger than you think. You come to me for answers, but the answers are already inside you."

I look blankly at my kitchen wall. They are?

The Prof says, "Yes indeed. I'll prove it to you. Allow me to demonstrate with a Zen story. Listen carefully."

I slump back in my chair, close my eyes, and let his voice wash over me.

"A Zen Master tells his student, 'I have a stick in one hand, and cup of tea in the other. If you drink this tea, I will hit you with this stick. If you do not drink this tea, I will hit you with the stick.' What do you do?"

My eyes fly open. Uh oh. I'm really bad at these kinds of things. Let's see. What do I do? Either way I'm going to get hit with the damn stick, right?

I think a moment longer, then blurt out, "Run away! I'd run away so I wouldn't get hurt!"

"Wrong, my little grasshopper."

I groan and say, "So what was I supposed to do?"

I can hear his smile through the phone. He pauses, then says, "Take away the stick."

Ah Ha! Enlightenment!

"Prof, Prof," I say as I shake my head. "You *are* my personal little Yoda. I wish I could carry you around in my back pocket for emergencies. Wouldn't it be great if the mini-you could pop out when these people are driving me crazy? You could wave your miniature arms and scream at them: 'Knock it off! Stop living through your children and leave Kelly alone!'"

"You don't need me–you know what to do, Kelly," he insists. "And besides, what if you accidentally sat on me?" he adds with mock alarm.

I laugh at the image. He laughs, too, but then puts on his stern voice. "Kelly, listen to me: don't go down their path to begin with. Take away the stick. Do you hear me?"

"Loud and clear. I do, I do. Thanks, Prof," I smile back gratefully through the phone as I flick each tear soaked tissue ball off the table.

**11am, Still Home**

*From: Kelly Graham*
*To: Professor Bennett Jeffries*
*Hi Prof,*
*Good news! I googled the meaning of your name. Now you can't tell me you don't think destiny isn't in a name because "Bennett" means "Little Blessed One." See? Your Yoda destiny was preordained! And bad news. "Delaney" means "Enemy's Child." Kind of creepy, right? Anyway, thanks again for always listening to my sagas! I know my troubles stretch on and on, like "The Grapes of Wrath." Okay, maybe not like the hardships endured in "The Grapes of Wrath," I'm capable of perspective, but it sure feels like it sometimes!*
*Warmly,*
*Kelly (the-as-yet-untested-brave-warrior!)*

**3pm, The Little Theater**

I take Zen Master Bennett's lessons to heart and carry them with me as Jackson and I drive over to Samuel P.

I vow to myself that I will not go down anyone's crazy path today. I'm sick of being upset. I'm tired of allowing everyone to walk all over me and knuckling down on us to get their way. I will stay centered in my state of grace, and let the rest roll off my back. Ooooommm.

I told Jackson what the Prof said, and he's fired up and ready, too. We'll be confidently grabbing away enough metaphysical sticks today to build a small cabin. Plus, despite all this side-drama, we actually do have a play to rehearse!

**8pm, Home**

After the Prof's pep talk, the day looked so fresh and promising. I remembered what was important. I was breathing. I was smiling. I was filled with the wonder that I get to be alive– that I get to teach children the joy of theater. My dial was adjusted to Super Zen. I was prepared for the usual nonsense, and was ready to bat it away. I would do just as the Prof instructed, and kick illusional concepts like dominance and ego out on their butts into the eternal cosmos. And I did it. Rehearsal was filled with the usual craziness, but there were no big bombs dropped. Numbers were rehearsed, children sang and danced, and I'm still breathing. Well, lookee here; what do you know. Despite everything, this show is coming together just fine.

We dismissed the cast early so Jackson could finally work with Forrest and Delaney on the infamous London Bridge murder scene.

Amber, Lillette and I watched from a safe distance in the front row, rather than our usual spots on the apron. I guess we were all feeling a collective wariness about how Forrest may handle acting out such an intense scene. But Forrest seemed almost manageable in Jackson's hands. He still had his moments– when his face clouded over menacingly, and he looked like he was ready to really kill Delaney, but Jackson stayed right on top of him. Delaney just turned a blasé face and didn't seem bothered by his bullying ways at all. (She's probably used to it from her mother!)

Lillette whispered to me at one point, "That boy is like a can of Coke shaken up by a sugared-shocked kid at a birthday party. He looks like he's ready to explode any minute."

Amber had adjusted her glasses and said confidently, "He'd benefit from some deep breathing exercises. Maybe I could show him."

I looked at her sharply and said, "I don't think so, Amber."

I guess my tone was a little too harsh because Lillette interceded with a conciliatory, "What Mrs. Graham means,

Honeypie, is that sometimes bottled up kids need a professional can opener."

I looked at Lillette and grinned. "Did you just say, 'A professional can opener?'"

Lillette nodded, her eyebrows raised high in defense.

I took my time. "And where would I, uh, *find* a 'professional can opener,' Lillette? Maybe the Yellow Pages?"

Amber started to laugh and said, "No, I've seen them listed on the internet with the other screw-top psychologists!"

"You mean *screwy* psychologists, like Dr. Waldner," Lillette giggled.

We all started snorting and laughing so hard that Jackson shot us a nasty glance over his shoulder and shouted, "Ladies! Outside!"

In the end, we were banished from the theater, so I can't report exactly how the whole rehearsal went down– but it is finally, finally staged.

Now it's eight o'clock, and as my hands glide over the last of our dishes soaking in soapy water, I feel something akin to true tranquility.

Jackson comes up behind me and slides his hands around my waist. He must feel it too; he hasn't touched me like this in a long time. His lips brush my hair, and his warm breath on my ear sends a cascade of tingles down my spine. For a moment, I let the sponge slip from my fingers and melt completely against his sturdy body. We start to sway a bit, and I'm so relaxed I'm afraid I may actually start to drool.

I abandon the dishes and turn to face him, leaning my head against his shoulder as he runs his hands up and down my back.

"Hey," he murmurs into my ear. "No grenade today."

I pull my head back to look up into his face. My lips curl slowly into a weak smile of victory. "Shh. You'll curse it," I whisper. "The day isn't over yet."

He leans down to place his warm mouth on mine as I bring my arms up around his neck. We kiss deeply, remembering each other, remembering us. His hands slide up over my breasts and I press into him.

And then the phone rings.

We both stiffen, and all my Zen calm shatters and crashes into shards onto the floor. Jackson reaches for the phone, but I pull his arm firmly back to my waist and say, "No. Don't."

With my arms still around his shoulders, I begin to take tiny steps forward. With every step I take, Jackson backs up reluctantly, while the phone shrieks and screams for attention on the counter.

"Just let me check the caller ID..." he says.

"No," I insist. Then I step onto the ends of his feet like I did when I was a little girl and I wanted to dance with my father. Placing my hands on either side of his chiseled face I begin to chant, "Take away the stick, take away the stick."

As we clump down the hall to our bedroom, the phone cries itself out and is silent. I know that if it's one of our top ten favorite parents, even if they leave a message, they'll call back again shortly. It's the age of stalker-calling. These people expect instant access, and when they don't get it, they continue to call/e-mail/text until connection is made. They can't stop themselves. They're relentless. We just have to stop responding. Either that, or get a new unlisted number. Or get a new job. Or become hermits. All excellent sounding options at this point.

**9:30pm**

Beeeeep!

"Dr. Gail Waldner here, calling to inform you that due to the academy's adult chaperone/child ratio rule requiring one adult per every twelve students to be present during extracurricular evening activities, four parental chaperones will be backstage beginning dress rehearsal night. We will see you, therefore, on Wednesday evening at six o'clock. Thank you and good night."

Jackson hits the stop button and we both stare at the machine, like Dr. Waldner herself has personally appeared in our bedroom and is sitting primly atop our nightstand. Suddenly feeling even more naked than I already am, I gather the sheets up around us protectively. Hearing Dr. Waldner's clinical voice floating over our bodies makes me shiver with revulsion.

Jackson grabs my shoulders playfully and says, "The parents are coming! The parents are coming!"

I tuck the sheet under my chin and say, "That's not funny, Jackson. Do you think she's maybe pulling our leg?"

Jackson scoffs and says, "Dr. Waldner does not pull anybody's leg. I can guarantee you that. If she says that the parents are coming, then they're coming!"

"No, I mean what she said about some adult to child ratio as her reason they're coming. Even Mrs. Kirkland didn't throw that one at us. I never heard of that rule. Do you think they're making it up?"

Jackson rests his warm cheek next to mine and says,

"Yeah. They probably held an emergency meeting, and made up this new rule on the spot. You know how driven they are to get what they want." He begins to nibble on my neck.

I snort, "Yeah, you're probably right. Every time they want to get their way, and their normal bullying tactics don't work, I'll bet they make up new rules to fit the situation."

"Exactly!" Jackson says, getting into it. "I picture this dusty old rule book, right? Crackled paper, faded writing. It probably started out in the early 1900's with all these regulation rules, about, like, attendance, and homework requirements. But then, as the turn of the new millennium rolled around, I'll bet weird-o rules began appearing, handwritten in by specific families to conform to their demands. Like, 'We, the members of the Pratt family, hereby do state, that from this day forward, all grades that were originally given as B+, shall be turned into A's, because in our family, we don't get B plusses!'"

"Right!" I laugh. "Or, 'From this day forth, all students with the last name of Wiltshire, shall be granted immunity from standing in the lunch line, and can go straight to the front!'"

Jackson's eyes widen. "They already have that rule, Kelly."

I swat his arm. "They do *not*. I just made that up!"

He breaks from his phony incredulous look and laughs, "Okay, yeah, you're right. I was just trying to freak you out."

I sit up and wave my arms histrionically. "Like all this other stuff isn't enough to freak out about?"

I grab a pillow and launch it at his shoulder. But he's too quick for me. He grabs it up and hits me on my side with a whump.

We tussle for a bit, but this time I give up and shout, "Stop! Stop; you win! You win!"

Jackson looks down at me with that look in his eyes that says he's ready for round two. Oh, fine. But he has to quit playing with my boobies so much; they're getting too sore!

# April 17th
## 9am
## Home

In my quest to stay steeped in the power of positive Zen thinking, I share this:

*From: Lydia Welles*
*To: Mr. and Mrs. Graham*
*Hello. I would like to take a commemorative group photo of the cast of* Oliver! *We will sell copies of this photo in the lobby during intermission to raise funds to support the acting program. Please advise, at your earliest convenience, as to when the best time for you would be. We are looking forward to the opening of* Oliver! *It is all our daughter, Kristy, talks about. We hear such wonderful things!*
*Warm regards,*
*Mrs. L. Welles*

How lovely! Hope bobs to the surface and makes me feel all warm and gooey inside.

(I am not dwelling on the six other black-hearted e-mails, filled with criticisms and complaints. They have already been flushed away by the handy-dandy delete tab! Oooooooommmmmmmm.)

### 3:30pm, The Little Theater

Jackson is down in the pit, seated at the piano, and I'm on stage with fourteen kids running "Oom-Pah-Pah." Lillette sits with Amber to the side on the apron, taking notes. We were hoping to do a rough run of act two, but it may have to wait until tomorrow while we continue to polish the big numbers.

Delaney is belting it out with the chorus behind her, and they sound gloriously big and strong. There's nothing like the sound of things pulling together. The cast feels it, too– I can tell by the smiles on their faces and the joy expressed in their bodies as they move confidently to the music.

Me? I'm happy for the kids, but I feel kind of bent– not quite *broken*, but definitely bent. Maybe battered is the better word.

Lillette is clapping her hands in time to the music, so I join in too, in an effort to boost my sagging spirits. Amber sits up straight, bobbing her head up and down, and with a smile at me, she also starts clapping along. It never fails to amaze me that it's the simplest of things, like communal clapping, that forge the happiest connections. A sweet cheeriness seems to seize us all, and I begin to feel revived.

Without warning, there's a sudden crash from the wings.

Jackson leaps up onto the stage in a flash, while I run across the apron, hopping over Lillette and Amber. We arrive at the dimly lit backstage area at the same moment, bodies tense with anticipation.

Forrest has his back to us, but I can see by his silhouette that he's breathing heavily. Chip, Allen, Freddy and Marcus are all clumped to one side; a chair lays broken by their feet.

"What happened?" asks Jackson in a steely voice.

The stage crew boys say nothing, but real fear is etched onto each of their faces.

"Forrest Keller!" Jackson shouts.

Forrest turns around slowly, breathing through his open mouth. "What?" he pants, dead-eyed.

"What happened? What was that crash?"

Forrest says slowly, "It was just a chair."

I walk over to the stage crew kids and motion for them to go out onto the stage. "Amber, please call ten," I yell to her.

Lillette walks over and asks, "What can I do?"

I see her regarding Forrest cautiously, like a parent genuinely worried and baffled by their child's unruly behavior.

I tell her, "Take these guys out front, please."

Lillette immediately grabs two boys by the wrists and begins to shepherd them out. As the boys pass by me, I ask, "You all okay?" They nod and shuffle past.

I flick on the backstage fluorescents and Forrest blinks, like a bear emerging from its cave.

"Why is this chair broken, Forrest?" Jackson demands as he stands with his hands on his hips.

"I don't know," Forrest says. "I was getting ready to go on; just getting myself in to character."

"Did you *throw* the chair, Forrest?"

"Yeah," he says testily. "Is there a problem?"

I can see Jackson is a hairs breath away from losing it. "Yes, there is a problem, Forrest. The chair is broken. You're out of control."

"No I'm not," Forrest says venomously. "I *said* I was getting into character."

Jackson says, "You absolutely cannot hurt other people or things, Forrest. That's not acting, that's *real* and completely unacceptable."

Forrest looks at us incredulously. "But I have to make it look real, don't I? I play a bad guy, so I have to, like, get enraged don't I?"

Jackson says emphatically, "You have to *play* enraged. You have to pretend. You can't really be angry– we've said this all along. See what happens when you really are?" He indicates the broken chair.

My heart sinks. We let this go on for too long. This is so out of hand. Forrest got carried away and doesn't even recognize it.

"Yeah, well how else am I supposed to do that? How can I be angry and not feel it?" Forrest asks.

Whoa. A glimmer. A teachable moment! Jackson feels it too, and takes a step towards Forrest. There's still a good eight feet between them.

"I'll show you how. Make a mad face, Forrest," Jackson instructs.

Forrest just looks at him.

"Go ahead, humor me. Pull an angry face for me."

Forrest reluctantly mugs a clown-like scowl for about a second, then drops it and says, "That's not acting; that feels so phony!"

Jackson says, "Well, if you won't give this a chance, Forrest..."

Forrest stalks up to Jackson, and within inches of his face shouts, "It's stupid! I know what I'm doing when I act! And I'm good at it– you know I'm good. That's why you cast me; I make it look *real.*" His face is contorted and is turning an ugly reddish purple as he jabs his index finger under Jackson's nose.

Jackson takes a step back and says quietly, "Forrest, I want you to go sit out in the audience to cool down for a while."

Forrest slaps his right fist into his left palm,

lunges across the stage and jumps from the apron into the pit. "Use the stairs," dies in my throat before I even get to utter the first syllable.

Jackson and I stare at each other, our faces identical grim masks. I break the silence. "He has to go Jackson–before someone really gets hurt."

Jackson's head drops and he stares at the floor.

"We let this go on for too long, we have to fix it," I say soberly.

He closes his eyes and rubs them hard, like he's trying to erase what he's seen. When he opens them, he says, "We open in eight days."

I nod, "I know. But there has to be a consequence for this Jackson. That chair just missed the crew. What if it hit one of them? We may not be so lucky next time. Because Jackson, this is Forrest during *rehearsal*. Can you imagine him hyped-up on performance nights?" I don't say it out loud, but in addition, Forrest's behavior has now crossed the line into certifiably dangerous. He could have killed someone.

He nods, "Okay. I'll go dismiss him. Scrap the rest of act two. Can you take over rehearsal? I'll call his parents and wait with him out in the lobby."

I nod, "Sure. We'll talk about recasting later."

He starts for the stage. I call after him, "Jackson, this is absolutely the right decision."

He turns back and nods briefly. I watch him descend the side steps into the darkened theater where Forrest sits glowering in the first row.

### After rehearsal

My car.

"So what happened with Mr. and Mrs. Keller?" I ask.

I'm driving; Jackson sits in the passenger seat with his eyes shut.

"They never showed," he says flatly.

"Then who took Forrest home?"

"They sent a driver."

I steal a glance at him. "You mean like a chauffeur in a limo or something?"

He says in a clipped voice, "It was a Mercedes. Small man in a cap– with a ridge of gray whiskers over his lip, hopped out and held the door open. Forrest bolted from the lobby, ran to the car and was whisked away."

"Oh. Then did you speak with his parents over the phone about what happened?"

He sighs. "Not yet, Kel. I left a message with the house-keeper asking them to call us. I'll e-mail Headmaster Hank when we get home and let him know we need to replace Forrest immediately."

"Okay, good. Good plan, honey," I pat his thigh and he gives me a flimsy smile. I know this is knocking him out. How many more grenades can we diffuse?

"So who should we give the part of Bill Sykes to?"

Jackson puts up his hand. "Kel, if you don't mind, I'm just going to crash right now. We'll talk about it later."

The green and red sign of a 7-Eleven bursts into view, sig-naling our arrival back to civilization. "Want a coffee for later?" I ask.

"Nah," he says as he crosses his arms over his chest and closes his eyes. He's asleep by the time we pull into our complex.

**8pm, E-mails**

"Kelly, take a look at this," Jackson calls from the living room.

I slide next to him on the couch to peer down at the lap-top, open to our e-mail page. I start reading. They're all from parents:

*We heard the part of Bill Sykes was given to Hamilton Conrad. We understand he already has a part and would like to know why you're not using someone from the chorus, like our hard working son, Tucker.*

I look at Jackson uncomprehendingly. "What? How could they hear the part went to *anyone* when we haven't even *decided* yet!"

"Keep reading," he says.

*There has been more turmoil under your direction of this play than anything my child has ever experienced. We understand you are bar-ring any help from willing parents who can watch out for these kinds of things, so our daughter, Roxy Parsons, will not be continuing. She is heartbroken, but we cannot have her in harms way.*

And...

*We heard Forrest Keller broke a chair and grabbed Chris Kane by the throat...*

"What?! Where are these people getting this stuff from?" I say with dismay.

"Read the one from the Keller's," he says, stone-faced.

I hesitate for a second. "No, Jackson, I don't want to. Just tell me the gist and tell me what we have to do. I'm done."

"They're furious and want us to reinstate his part," he says flatly.

"Not happening," I say before he can go any further. "The headmaster will absolutely side with us on this one." I reach across the table for my phone. I've never called that dear man at home, but I think tonight I have no choice.

"I don't know about that one, Kel." Jackson reaches down and clicks on a new e-mail and reads aloud, "What is happening with Forrest Keller and his part in the play? I heard from the Keller's; they are very upset. Can something please be worked out? His parents are on our board." Jackson flips the laptop down. "Signed, Headmaster Hank Prescott."

I gasp like an actress in an old-fashioned melodrama, jamming my knuckle into my mouth to keep from screaming.

"Turn that thing off!" I point my finger at the offensive laptop. It's a despicable machine. "No– better yet, throw it out the window!"

Jackson sinks down onto the couch, arms crossed in despair. I flop down next to him and rest my eyes on the familiar, cracked ceiling.

"We're doomed," Jackson says.

Yep, yep, it certainly feels that way. Reese's Pieces! Who do I grab the stick from now? Where the hell *is* the friggin' stick?

Wait a minute.

Wake up, Kelly. What would Scott do? Isn't this the moment I'm supposed to see as an opportunity? Yeah, well, I'm limited. My brain feels like it's filled with rocks. Not a thing comes to mind.

But Scott laughed. He *laughed* at his problem.

Okay, what the heck. I'll literally try it out.

Like I'm doing an acting exercise in class, where I don't actually feel the emotion I'm playing, I start to laugh softly. I push my belly and force it to jiggle up and down a bit as I say, "Hahaha."

Jackson turns to stare at me. But I don't mind; I'm used to being watched while I go through the paces of learning a technique.

The laugh begins to grow and sound more believable. Jackson laughs involuntarily and says, "What? Kelly, what's so funny?"

But now I've caught it myself, and I'm really bent over laughing so hard that Jackson has caught it for real, too. I grip my belly, edging towards hysteria.

I wheeze out, "What the fuck, Jackson! We're not doomed. It's a play. A stinking *play!* We have eight days to go, and then we walk away. It's just not worth it!"

Jackson wipes his eyes as we settle down and says, "Are you sure? Are you saying what I think you're saying?"

"I have absolutely had enough, Jackson. I'm out." I smile at him.

"Me, too," he smiles back. "I'm out, too. Out! Out! What a great word!"

He pulls me up onto the couch and we do a freaky little happy dance a la Tom Cruise on *Oprah.*

Jackson holds my hands like we're making a pledge to each other and says, "Let's get through the run, then give notice, yes?"

I beam back, "Yes!"

We grab each other in a huge hug– emancipated, exuberant. All that laughter brought tons of fresh oxygen to my whole body and I feel great. In fact, I feel positively ebullient. This explains why I've been so tired– not enough life-affirming laughter!

We had the power to get out all along. It just took a little laughing in the face of adversity to remind us. Thank you, Scott McIntyre. I don't know if this is what he meant, but it helped us reach a sane decision!

I free-fall down onto the couch and grab the phone. With relief in my heart, I call Headmaster Hank.

**10pm**

After getting our side of the story, Headmaster Hank *did* side with us, and Forrest is out.

Forrest's parents, of course, painted a very different picture, telling the headmaster that Forrest was dismissed because we were jealous of his talent! (I know– I can't even go there.)

Once we explained what really happened, the headmaster was completely supportive. We are so relieved.

And we have, in fact, awarded the part of Bill Sykes to a member of our chorus, Henry Jasper Jones. He's already familiar with the entire play, so all that's left for us to do is put him through his paces with the blocking. He'll work with his script in hand for now, obviously, but we've assured him that if he still needs the script on opening night, he can carry it around with him on stage.

Because these things happen. But we deal– and then we go on. It's the theater. The show *must* go on! Problems? Ha! I scoff! I *laugh*. Lemme at 'em.

All that's left to do is sidestep the rest of the incoming grenades. Let the whole place blow up for all I care. We are *so* done. Besides, we've seen it all. What could possibly happen now that we can't handle?

# April 18th
## 10am
## Melodies Music Shop

We share our news with Lisa and Larry as soon as we get to "Melodies." They actually reach for each other first, and embrace like parents who are relieved their crazy children have come to their senses at last. Then they gather us into a crushing group hug, and we start jumping up and down like we belong to some crazy primitive tribe. Or a football team.

Larry breaks away and plays a rousing fanfare on the display keyboard and we all applaud in high spirits.

"Now," Larry breathes. "It's just a matter of time."

"Three quarter time!" Jackson yells, and swings me into a polka. Larry picks up the beat and we swirl around the room. Lisa claps and sways in place, and I have to say, as I spin around in Jackson's arms, I have not felt this simply happy in a very long time.

The truth is, we don't belong at the academy. It wasn't a good "fit," as they say in education. Now that the decision has been made, all we have to do is complete the job, which is oh my God only days away. Gotta go!

# April 23rd
## 6pm
## Tech Week: Dress Rehearsal
## The Little Theater

The set looms– raw and rustic looking. For all the emotional garbage we had to deal with from Tony, there's no denying it– he built us a mighty fine set. Two stories tall, with multi-level platforms and stairs, it's evocative of a gritty London, circa 1850. The backdrop was hung yesterday, and with the lighting Tony threw on it, we have one professional-looking set.

I've stopped watching Tony personally for clues, because I have com-plete-ly let go of all the crap– *his* crap included in the pile. I am in the Zen-zone, dropping days behind me like dirty tissues.

And it's funny how this change of attitude has freed me. Everything has been fine since we decided to leave; isn't that weird? Makes me think it was my problem all along– that I was just wound too tight or something. Or maybe I'm just so bossy I really can't get along with people. I don't know. Suffice it to say, tech week is going just as planned, with Tony actually in sync with us.

Hell, he probably *will* run the whole program when they need to replace us. Then he'll go totally unwatched. Oh, well. Not my problem anymore. I. Do. Not. Care.

Wait a minute. Holy snap– what the heck is Tony doing with these stage crew kids now? They've been running back and forth between the lighting booth and backstage for about an hour, and they're getting dirtier and dirtier. Chip and Sammy emerge from backstage covered in dust and cobwebs. How did they get so grubby?

Jasmine fans her face by her nose and yells, "Dudes! I'm allergic to dust! Get out of here!"

A bunch of girls sitting along the front of the apron rush to Jasmine's rescue and start fanning her with their long skirts.

Chip and Sammy give the girls a cocky look, like being filthy is a badge of male honor. Allen emerges next, carrying an old-fashioned awl. I recognize it instantly– it's pointy and dangerous looking.

"Where did you get that?" I ask him. He looks startled for a second, but then stammers, "Back, um, back there."

"Where? Do you mean the pen?"

A blush begins to creep up his neck and he says quickly, "Yeah. I found it in the pen."

"Really?" I say, going to reach for it. "I never saw anything like this back there. But that doesn't mean much; it's so crammed with stuff, Jimmy Hoffa himself could be buried back there." I smile at him, but he looks back at me blankly.

"Who's Jimmy Hoffa?"

Jasmine snorts, "The *sausage guy*, dweeb!"

All the girls laugh meanly at Allen for being *so stupid*, but I totally let it go.

"Never mind, Allen. What are you doing with that thing?" I ask.

"Oh. I'm bringing it to Tony." He catches himself and says, "Uh, I mean Mr. Glynn. It's for his collection."

Ew. Right. The wall of torture instruments in the lighting booth. The personification of Mr. Wonderful's dark side, I'm sure. Have the parents ever seen that wall? Oooh—wait! I'm doing it again. I don't care anymore, remember?

"Carry on, Allen. But please be careful with that."

He nods, but then walks purposely by Jasmine and the girls and says loudly, "Jimmy *Dean* is the sausage guy, Jazz!"

The girls all squeal and giggle as Allen flips the awl high into the air in a perfect spin. It lands in the palm of his hand with a plop as he expertly catches it with ease.

I'm ready to faint.

"Amber!" I call out. "Where are you?"

Dress rehearsal is like this. Some kids are already in costume and make-up, while others are still getting it together in the tiny costume/make-up room backstage. The tech crew scurries around, putting last minute details into order, lights wink on and off, and Jackson and I wait, and guide, and hold it all together.

Jackson is backstage with the cast and the parental chaperones. There was little more we could do to keep the parents at bay, but that doesn't mean I have to be near them. We had already demonstrated to the cast how to apply their make-up, so at least we were able to teach them that skill. After that, I surrendered.

Jackson had a little talk with Taffy's mom, Mrs. Dollinger, earlier, and found out that there is no formal rule about an adult/child chaperone ratio. Jackson started to get pissed off, but I didn't bat an eye. Typical. They can't reach me anymore.

Armed with that little tidbit, Jackson spoke diplomatically with the parents and explained that as we didn't want to ruin the surprise of opening night for them, once their kids were in costume and make-up, they were free to leave. Remarkably, stupendously, each one of them agreed, so they should be leaving any minute. They got what they wanted out of it, anyway: they wanted to have control over how their kids looked. So okay. Fine. "Whatev," as the kids say.

Amber comes running up the side stairs completely empty-handed for the first time in eight weeks.

"No promptbook?" I smile.

"Backstage, already on a music stand."

"No pencils?"

"Same stand."

"Ponytail?"

"Wrist." She lifts her left arm and I see the red elastic hidden just underneath her sleeve.

"Excellent. How's everyone doing backstage?"

Before Amber can answer, Jasmine calls out from the apron, "They're doing really good, Mrs. Graham! Did I do my foundation right?"

I look at her and at the bunch of chorus girls surrounding her and say, "Yes, girls, you all look fantastic." Then I cup my hands around my mouth and stage whisper, "Psst, Jasmine! Jimmy *Hoffa* was the president of the Teamsters. He disappeared under shady circumstances, and his body has never been found."

Jasmine and the girls look horrified. "But Mrs. Graham, you don't really think he's around here, do you?" Jasmine asks apprehensively. The girls look around in a panic at each other.

What is with me and my big mouth? "No, no, of course not! I just said that because his name is used as sort of a joke..."

Amber puts her hand on my arm and whispers urgently, "Does he qualify if we find him, Mrs. Graham? You know, as the dead person in the Terrible Three?"

I hop up from my chair and say, "Okay, guys, time to drop all chatter and focus. There are no dead people in this theater! We're going to start in about thirty five minutes, so please stay in here or in the lobby."

I lurch for the steps.

"Mrs. Graham?"

"Yes, Amber?"

"Are we really running the show straight through and not stopping no matter what?"

"No matter what."

She begins gathering her hair into a high ponytail at the back of her head, pearly little ears happily on display.

"The cast knows not to call for a line," I say. "If they forget a line, they've been told they have to figure out what to do by themselves. I'll remind them again, but don't call out the line if they flub up, okay?"

"Got it," she says with a thumbs up.

"And Amber, I just want to mention, your hair looks so pretty like that."

"Thanks!" she says brightly. Smiling happily, she skips backstage.

Forty minutes later, the entire cast is finally assembled on stage. Sitting before us, on various levels of the set, they listen as we give them their final instructions for tonight's dress rehearsal. Lillette arrived late, and in the ensuing wait, has fallen asleep in the front row, her head lolling to the side, mouth wide open.

Jackson and I exchange glances, and I whisper, "Let her sleep. She'll wake up instantly when you hit the first chords of the overture."

He nods, but makes his way down the stairs anyway to slip his jacket over her passed out body. As he sits back down at the piano in the pit, I start my pep talk.

"Guys, you all look terrific! You should be very proud of all your hard work; you have a wonderful show. We're going to start in just a few and then it's all up to you. I'll be sitting in the audience cheering you on, Mr. Graham will be playing your music, and you're in the strong, capable hands of Mr. Glynn and our fantastic stage crew to support you for all the tech stuff."

The cast breaks into applause at the mention of Tony's name and they all start chanting, "Tony! Tony!" while looking up at the lighting booth. Tony blinks the onstage lights in recognition and waves from the booth. They go wild– jumping up and down like he was Eminem or something.

The cheering dies down and I continue. "Any problems you encounter on stage are up to you to fix."

They look around a little uneasily. "Just keep going," I encourage. "And remember, you are a team up here. You're not alone. Rely on each other, and for heavens sake, have fun!"

They start clapping again and triple fist-bump each other as Amber calls, "Please stand for mic check."

They all rise and form a long line across the stage.

Tony yells down from the booth, "Say something in your natural voice when I call your number. And keep it clean, peeps! Microphone one!"

Delaney starts talking, her voice loud and clear through the new speakers. But for some reason, the cast stage left begins giggling and whispering.

"Quiet!" Jackson yells from the pit.

But it keeps happening. As mic check continues, random pockets of the cast suddenly erupt into gasps and cover their mouths. What the...?

Are they laughing at Lillette? I turn to look to see if she's drooling disgracefully or something.

And then my gut knows.

Jackson spots him first, but then I catch a fleeting glimpse of him, too.

Forrest is in the house.

A split second later, slipping behind the row where Lillette is sleeping, Forrest pops up next to her seat, drops his pants and brazenly moons the entire cast.

"Forrest Keller!" Jackson bellows as he springs up from the piano bench.

Amid all the shrieking and laughing, Lillette startles awake and looks around in a daze. When her bleary eyes rest on Forrest's butt, shaking back and forth just inches from her face, she lets out a scream and falls out of the chair.

Forrest yanks up his pants in one swift move, and makes a break for the back of the theater. The cast howls and whistles, and over all the commotion I hear some girls scream out, "Run, Forrest, run!"

Lillette recovers in an instant and bolts up the aisle after him. I break my own golden rule and jump into the pit to join the chase– stopping short for a quick second to yell over my shoulder, "Stay with them, Jackson, I'll go."

Jackson shakes his head in absolute final defeat and shouts in a strangled voice at the cast, "Settle down this instant, or I'm canceling the show!"

I burst through the lobby doors and run smack into Tony, coming out of the booth. My head hits his shoulder, and reflexively I put my hands up to steady myself. They land on his hard chest and I feel his breath cross my face.

Tic Tacs.

I look up; his lips close enough to kiss, our arms accidentally tangled– and catch him sneering down at me with a twisted kind of revulsion. Pushing away, I say unsteadily, "I've got it; go back inside."

My adrenaline-soaked state makes me hyperaware, and the deadly look in his eyes is not lost on me.

"You the man, Mrs. Graham," he snarls, eyes locked on mine. He backs away slowly, staring me down.

Resentment, much? My eyes narrow right back at him– their intention crystal clear. *Fuck you, Tony*, they scream without me even having to open my mouth.

I turn away quickly as he retreats, and scan the lobby. No Lillette, no Forrest.

It's then that I see the looney scene unfolding directly outside the glass doors to the parking lot. Lillette is pathetically galloping after Forrest, waving her arms ineffectively in an effort to make him stop. Forrest, like a sheep dog, runs past her, then circles back to taunt her in a game of you-can't-catch-me. Even from where I stand, I can see Lillette's face– bright red from exertion. In direct contrast, Forrest's is lit up with naughty delight from tormenting her. They start yelling animatedly at each other.

Just as I push the door open, Forrest stops in his tracks and sits down. Lillette stumbles over to him, squeezing her sides, panting with her mouth wide open. I stand, braced at the door, unsure whether to stay or go.

The scene continues to unfold like a staccato old silent movie. Lillette's mouth moves a mile a minute, and they begin another rapid back and forth exchange. Forrest snatches a bunch of twigs from the ground and begins disassembling them, hurling piece after piece at an imaginary target.

Lillette flops down next to him, her face aggressively jammed up next to his, yammering, yammering. While she yells at him, Forrest begins to lean away from her, like he's a tree she's chopping down. What the heck is she saying? She appears to be bludgeoning him with her words!

I think that actually happens in a Sam Shepherd play. One character keels right over onto the floor from the force of the other character's words. Maybe Lillette read that play? Or maybe, more likely, she's had just about enough of Forrest's garbage, and is giving him a piece of her mind.

My fear starts to dissipate a bit as I see him grow still for a second, but I keep standing guard nonetheless. I don't want him to suddenly hurt her– like Lennie in *Of Mice and Men,* and I'm stuck with an "Oops-I-killed-her-George" tragedy on my hands.

After several minutes, Forrest's mouth moves again. While repeatedly stabbing a stick into the ground with enough force that clumps of dirt spray onto Lillette's knee, he talks and talks and talks. I never saw him talk so much.

A couple *more* minutes pass, and Lillette gets busy pulling off her shoe. Forrest seems completely engaged, and watches as Lillette pulls a piece of paper from the bottom and hands it to him. Without flinching or making a repugnant "eww" face, he proceeds to unfold the note. His face at first appears solemn, pinched in quiet concentration while he reads. Then suddenly, his face brightens and he begins to laugh. I'm not kidding, I can even see his teeth from here.

He laughs so hard he tips onto his back and kicks his legs in the air. Lillette laughs along, and when he bounces back up to a sitting position, she suddenly reaches out and hugs him. And he *lets* her. She's actually hugging him! Like a sedated bull, he docilely puts his gigantic head on her shoulder and closes his eyes.

No way.

They break from their embrace, and Forrest chivalrously offers her his hand and helps her to her feet. They dust themselves off, Lillette waves a small good bye, and Forrest trudges over to the main building crunching his way across the gravel-filled parking lot. She watches him go with a wistful smile on her face, then she heads towards the doors where I await.

—ᘯ—

I drag Lillette into the box office.

She falls into the swivel chair, then gives herself a few playful spins.

"Lillette?"

"Yeah?"

"What happened?"

She pushes several flyaway wisps of hair from her sweaty face and says, "Well! I was running and running and running after Forrest, and I was yelling, 'How dare you do that to me, you're just a big baby!' And he yelled back, 'I am not!' and I said, 'You are, too!' and he said, 'Am not!' 'Are, too!' 'Am not!'..."

"Lillette?" I interrupt. "Maybe skip the blow by blow and just give me the highlights, okay?"

"Yeah, sure, Kelly, no problem." She pushes her sleeves up and says importantly, "I told him what he did was immature and a big cry for help. Then I said..."

She stops abruptly and stares into space. Her lips barely move, but she seems to be mouthing something to herself.

"Lillette?" I frown.

Silence. Is she having a brain seizure or something? I wave my hand in front of her eyes.

"What?" she asks as she turns her head towards me.

"Why did you stop?"

"I'm sparing you the blow by blow. You told me to just give you the highlights, but I have to play it back in my mind exactly as I remember it happening."

I sigh. I feel a teensy headache beginning over my eye.

"Fine," I say. "I take it back. Give me the blow by blow."

She's reanimated and begins reenacting another shouting match with Forrest, full volume. "I said, 'When you hurt other people, you end up hurting yourself!' And he yelled back, 'No, I don't!' and I said, 'Yes, you do!' 'Do not!' 'Do, too!' 'Do not!' 'Do, too!'"

AHHHHHHHHHHHHH!

"Finally, he settles down and starts talking to me for real. He said everyone treats him like he's this bad person, but he's not." She grabs onto my arm. "Listen, Kelly, it was so sad; he told me he feels like a misfit and he's so lonely," she says mournfully. "I told him I get it because I know firsthand what it feels like to be an outsider, when no one understands you."

"Wait a minute, Lillette. Forrest said he felt like a misfit?" I stare at her in disbelief. "He was playing you Lillette. He isn't some misunderstood outsider– he *chose* to behave as he did."

"No, no, you're so wrong, Kelly. He told me he's lonely because his parents leave him home with the staff all the time. They got rid of his nanny two years ago, and he didn't even get a chance to say good-bye to her. They don't care about him at all. I mean, that is *so* cruel and damaging. And they're never home. They even told him he was a mistake– that they didn't want kids. All they want to do is travel the world on their jet. So he roams around their cold, marble mansion, searching for warmth, searching for love."

"Spare me the psychobabble, Lillette," I say crossly. "I can't believe you fell for this. It's hard for me to feel sorry for a boy who has been so disrespectful to all of us, and who has been nothing but trouble the whole way through."

"It's not psychobabble, Kelly. He opened up to me. He has *issues,*" she argues. "He's telling the truth. I knew about some of this already because I've seen him curled up on the cot in the nurse's office a few times. When I asked the nurse about it, she said he was a frequent flyer."

"Yeah, to get out of school, probably."

"Wrong again, Kelly. He has a real problem. She told me he has so much acid reflux from stress, he burned his esopho-whatcha-ma-callit." Her hands flutter by her throat.

"Esophagus?"

"Yeah. It's legit, Kelly. That's a *real* problem, not made up," she says with conviction.

"Fine, Lillette, whatever. I no longer care." And then I remember. "What was in your shoe?"

"Well, after he choked out his sad, sad, tale, I remembered that I'd been carrying around a poem I wrote for him the day I heard he got the ax. Do you want to hear it?"

"Oh, sure," I say wearily, with a futile wave of my hand.

She closes her eyes and tilts her face to the ceiling. Tiny blue veins cross over her translucent eyelids, like a newborn baby's. She looks so innocent. He really could have eaten her alive.

She begins to recite in a breathy little Marilyn Monroe voice:

"You hide behind an angry mask,
And never do just what we ask.
You hurt your friends, you hurt the chair,
Is your bad life beyond repair?
I think deep inside of you,
You'd like to start brand spanking new.
Come out from hiding, 'cause geez Louise,
We can't see the Forrest for the trees."

I start to laugh and look at her with admiration. She's a walking advertisement for *you can't judge a book by its cover.*

"That was very deep, Lillette. With just the right amount of 'funny' to break through to him," I say, still laughing.

She unrolls her sleeves and wraps her hands up inside them like a little child. With her mittened hands tucked under her chin, she asks with a hopeful smile, "Do you think so? It really seemed to work. I think he just had to know someone truly cared about him, you know?"

Hmm. I don't know about that.

She nods her head and says with assurance, "I told him I'd listen to him anytime he felt gloomy and lonesome again. We're going to keep in touch. You'll see, Kelly– you won't see him running around here causing trouble anymore. Really, you'll see."

Uh huh. Yeah, we'll just see about that, all right. I'm waaaay too jaded at this point to believe Forrest can have a happy ending.

# April 25th
## Opening Night
## The Little Theater

Just like the sports coaches in their glass mega-monument next door, we theater directors give a pep talk before the "big game," too. We pump 'em up just like those hefty guys with the big bellies and screechy whistles.

Fifteen minutes before the curtain "goes up," (technically, our curtain opens horizontally, but it's one of those theater expressions), our cast stands in a circle, crammed into the green room. (No, it's not actually painted green; it's the room backstage where actors wait before they go on stage.)

Taffy and Sienna hold hands as they warm up singing, "Me, may, mah, mo, moo." Jasmine, Shane and Christian sound like motorboats as they trill their lips and blubber out, "Brrrrrrr, brrrr, brrrr!"

Blake is laughing and carrying on with Erik, and looks completely unfazed. Good for him, my little ninth-grader carrying the show! Delaney is humming softly to herself while she smoothes the blush on Noelle's cheeks, and Henry Jasper Jones, our last minute Bill Sykes, stands stoically still. He looks positively ashen-faced, like he's concentrating on not throwing up. Poor kid. Hopefully our pep talk will help him release some of his nervous tension.

Jackson says, "Hey guys; this is our final circle-up before you open."

This pronouncement sends stifled eeks and squeals shivering around the circle.

"You *should* be excited," he says. "You're about to blow this audience away!"

More suppressed yelps and hand squeezing.

"We're going to make an energy circle now. Everyone please hold hands and close your eyes."

I love when the cast holds hands like this. It reminds me of all those happy little Who's in Whoville, holding hands and singing joyously in the face of adversity. As I grab Jackson's right hand tightly in my left, I feel the warm palm of Marta slip into my right. I turn to give her a smile. She gracefully smiles back and bends her head.

"Thomas, will you please start passing the pulse? When you feel someone squeeze your left hand, squeeze your right to keep the pulse going."

I peek through my eyelashes to watch the pulse make its way around the circle. Directly across from me, I see Duncan squinting, too, as he watches the pulse leap from hand to hand. It's a pretty cool thing to watch, this powerful current passed along on a wave of enthusiasm.

When it arrives back to Thomas, he lights up and says, "I got it!"

Jackson suddenly drops down to the floor into a crouch and says, "Follow what I do, and repeat after me."

Like the whole cast is playing "Simon Says," they all crouch down in unison, their eyes glued on Jackson.

Jackson begins, in a soft whisper, "Ooh, I feel so good, ooh, I feel so good." He snaps his fingers to the beat of a hot, jazzy rhythm, and the kids echo back, "Ooh, I feel so good, ooh, I feel so good."

"A little bit louder now," Jackson calls out softly as he rises a couple of inches, bouncing low.

They follow suit, a tiny bit louder, "Ooh, I feel so good, ooh I feel so good..."

"A little bit louder now," Jackson encourages.

Pulled along by the rhythm, they bounce and begin to clap their hands and say, "Ooh, I feel so good, oooh, I feel so good..."

"A little bit LOUDER NOW," he shouts.

"Ooh, I feel so good, ooooooh I feel so GOOD..."

"A little bit louder now!"

The kids are up on their feet now, swaying and stomping like they're at a Gospel revival. Their voices build to a frenzy, and when they shout out the last word, the room explodes with a euphoric outburst of pure, joyous sound.

"Ooh, I feel so good, OOOOOOOOH, I FEEL SO GOOD!"

They're pumped. They're ready. Go team! Jackson starts slapping high five's onto their open palms and yells over the din, "Have a good show everyone!"

"Have fun!" I yell.

Jackson grabs my hand and we scurry out together into the awaiting theater– absolutely sold out and overrun with people.

**Minutes Later**

"Just take the short cut, Kelly." Jackson says with an impatient wave of his hand.

"Jackson," I exclaim, "I am not taking the back stairway. You know how I hate going that way."

He grabs my hands and begs, "Please, Kel, hurry up. Just go."

I literally put my foot down with a defiant stamp and say, "No!"

"Then don't use the short cut, honey, but please, just go. Curtain goes up in ten!"

I pull my hands away and narrow my eyes at him. I know when the curtain goes up. Why make it such a friggin' emergency? It's not *my* fault he misplaced a piece of music.

Raising a pointed finger at him I hiss, "Fine, Jackson, but you owe me." And without waiting for a reply, I take off in a gallop to retrieve his music.

Going against the tide of people streaming in all but stops me in my tracks. Parents clutching programs, students jockeying for seats together– it's impossible to pass. Grrrr. Smiling stiffly, I give up and head back up the aisle towards the stage only to get another beseeching look tossed my way by Jackson from the piano.

I mouth, "I'm going, I'm going," as I jog by, a thin film of sweat forming over my lip. Then I'm out like a shot through the theater's side door, crossing through the packed parking lot to the main building. Night has fallen, and the sound of my feet crunching on the gravel sounds magnified in the gathering gloom. As I yank open the door, the weight of empty silence lands on me like a heavy blanket. I hate deserted buildings. I comfort myself with the knowledge that someone on the custodial staff has to be in here somewhere, so I run towards the stupid corridor from hell.

As I dash around to the back hallway, I pause at the entrance to catch my breath. No lights! The end of the hallway disappears completely into an inky abyss. I feel around on the wall for a light switch. Nothing. A prickle of gooseflesh tingles up from the back of my neck and spreads down my arms.

"Shit, shit, shit," I chant. "C'mon, Kelly," I mutter to myself, "Four flights. Four flights and you're done."

I start inching down the hallway when I notice I actually can see. *So pitch black isn't really pitch black*, I think. I guess this is how the rats get around. No– don't think about the rats!

As I creep along, I remember that the back stairway has those old-fashioned high windows on every landing. The lights from the parking lot must be seeping in to cast a weak glow. I'll take it! My senses on hyper-vigilant, there are absolutely no sounds coming from the stairway. No boohoos from the ghost of dead girl past. No nibble-nibble from rancid rats. Phew, well, that's good.

At the bottom of the dimly lit steps, I steel myself for the climb, then pounce on them, two at a time.

It's only when I'm paused halfway up the second flight with my arms around my waist, panting for breath, that I see something glinting in the darkness. I lean closer and let my eyes adjust further for a moment. I recognize the outline immediately: a small iPod.

I quickly snap it up and turn it over. Drat. It's too dark to see if there's an inscription, but I run my fingers over the smooth surface anyway. I feel the lacy thin indentations there and I know, without seeing, what they spell out: "To N., Love Tiger."

Shaking my head, and now running the rest of the way with it clutched in my hand like a racers baton, I clear the landing, cut down the hallway and grab the music out of room 404.

Fleeing back down the dark stairway, I am working up a full head of steam. My inner arguments rage and rail inside my head: How is it that a little girly-girl like Noelle can face down the macabre images of a dead girl and use this creepy stairway when I can't? *I'm* unnerved, but the teenager remains unfazed?

By the time I land safely on the ground floor with a thump, I am fully furious. I'm so mad I've decided not to return the iPod to Noelle tonight. It's opening night– the day we all worked so hard for and I can't be bothered. Plus, what? I have to worry about giving this student the "this-is-the-second-time-you-lost-the-iPod-now-I-have-no-choice-but-to-phone-your-parents" lecture? Not tonight. Way too pissed.

In fact, right after the show, I'm going to put it right back where I found it.

Merde!

—〰—

Jackson rewards me with a relieved smile and then a smothering hug as he whispers, "Break a leg, my love," into my ear. He lays it on thick and says, "I worship you, I love you," as he kisses my cheeks. I roll my eyes and give him a reluctant smile that finally forgives everything, chalking it all up to pre-show jitters. I almost impulsively pull Noelle's iPod from my pocket to show him, but then decide just as quickly not to– there's just no time.

The audience is still milling in, so after all that, we'll hold for another five. I take off for a quick backstage check. It's dark back there, with just enough light for the cast to find their places.

Thomas prances over to me, his jacket stuffed with scarves, and gives me a huge grin. I beam back.

"Excited?"

He nods vigorously, his floppy Fagin's hat bouncing along in rhythm. "Have fun, Thomas," I say. "Break a leg!"

He raises a partially gloved finger. "Uh, Mrs. Graham?"

"Yes, Thomas?"

"Quick one: where does that expression come from? Saying 'break a leg' is kind of a cruel thing to say to someone under any circumstances, so actors don't *really* mean to literally break a leg, right?"

I nod, while simultaneously giving high five's and fist bumps to passing cast members shuffling into place.

"The origin is kind of sketchy, Thomas, but there are a few theories."

Jasmine gives me a quick hug as she sweeps by.

"Do we say something bad like 'break a leg' for superstitious reasons? You know, so then maybe the opposite will happen?" he asks.

"Maybe. There's also the theory that it means to make it out onto the stage safely. Those side curtains over there are called 'legs,'" I point to the side curtains flanking the stage. "So to 'break a leg' means to part the curtain successfully so you get out onto the stage."

"Oh! I didn't know that."

"Yeah, and then there's some speculation that it means to get lots of applause, because when you bow, or 'break at the leg,' you get applause. And isn't that, in the end, what all of us thirsty little thespians crave most?"

Thomas smiles so brightly it seems his freckles twinkle through his make-up.

"Oh, yeah, yeah, I love applause! It's like the music of the gods!"

"Well, *break a leg*, Thomas. You're the best!"

Thomas presses at his fake beard again and dances in place. "I'm so excited!" he says.

Amber appears next to me in the official stage crew color of black from head to toe. Her face peers out luminously against the darkness; her silver headset with it's thin microphone curving against her cheek, winks in the dull light.

"Mr. Glynn just told me places in five, Mrs. Graham."

"Thank you five, Amber," I say affectionately.

She smiles back and says shyly, "I think we're going to make it, Mrs. Graham." She opens her promptbook to THE CHART and points at the conspicuous blank spot under the "death" column.

"See?" she chatters on, "No death. Maybe because the dead girl from 1931 qualifies in that category. Or maybe Delaney's character dying will satisfy the prophecy. Even though Delaney dies a theatrical, pretend death as Nancy, this is a theatrical ancient curse, right? So maybe we're safe."

Ay yi yi! Only two minutes to places, so I just say, "Right, Amber."

We *did* make it to opening night without my goofy "Three Terrible Things" theory coming to fruition, thank God. I'm so relieved, I swear to never speak of it again.

I squeeze her shoulder and say, "Break a leg, Amber."

Her face falls.

"Oh, Amber, for pity's sake, not literally. It's just a saying– it means 'good luck!'"

"Oh good," she says, relieved. "We don't need any more broken bones on the chart!"

Now I grab her and give her a full out hug. "I'm so proud of you, Amber. Look at you," I step back and take her in. "You have grown so much. And I truly could not have done this without you." She glows, and my heart swells with pride.

She freezes suddenly and grasps her headset. "Places in two!"

"Thank you two!" everyone backstage calls back.

The effect of those words is electric. Everyone lines up into place as I hear the audience behind the curtain buzzing with anticipation. Then Delaney stands before me, clutching her shawl tightly around her shoulders. Her eyes shine, and she has the air of a thoroughbred about her.

"Your hair looks great," I say, admiring the little tendrils framing her face.

She beams and says, "I did it myself."

"But what about your mother...?" I start.

She puts her hand up as if she's stopping traffic and says, "I said she could be with me backstage if she didn't say a word."

"Reeeally," I drawl. "Delaney, of all the growth you've shown on this show, that piece of news is the one I'm most proud about."

She reaches her arms around my neck, like a child reaching up for a hug, and I hold her tight. Categorically, I can tell you now, the tough kids *are* the most rewarding. When I release her I say, "You are one heck of an actress, Miss Barnes. Go knock 'em dead!"

I slap my hand over my mouth. Lord, I hope Amber didn't overhear *that* expression. I dash away and reenter the theater from a side doorway. There's nothing more to be done. The show is now in their hands.

—⟋⟋—

I slip into the last row and spot a seat next to Lillette, all dolled up in make-up of the loudest order; a white feather boa swaddled around her neck. She looks part angel, part trollop.

As I scoot in to take my seat, I freeze. Sitting nonchalantly next to Lillette, is Forrest, flipping nervously through the glossy program. Lillette nudges him. He clears his throat and says gruffly, "Hey, Mrs. Graham."

"Hello, Forrest," I say back neutrally.

His eyes shift back and forth, like he's not sure where to look.

"Sit! Sit!" Lillette cries as she pulls me down next to her.

The lights suddenly flicker, then dim, and the music starts. Lillette grabs my hand and squeezes it tightly as she squeals, "OhmiGosh! OhmiGosh!"

I smile benevolently at her and give her an impulsive kiss on her cheek. "Thanks for everything, Lillette," I whisper. "It's been fun working with you."

I face the stage with a hopeful smile. The overture ends, and the curtain opens...

**11pm, After the show**

The performance runs without a hitch. Everyone is elated. It *always* comes together opening night, but still; I'm relieved.

"You had any doubts?" Jackson says as he folds me into a post-show embrace. His neck is wet against my face and I notice his jacket feels squishy beneath my arms– soaked through from his sweat. I pull away to look at him.

He looks completely spent. I get a flash of how he'll look when he's older and time beats up on him a bit. Before I can ask if he's okay, we are descended upon by several audience members offering thanks and congratulations. We shake tons of parent's hands, all beaming and proud. Notably absent, and probably avoiding us on purpose, are the main parents who dogged us every day. That's fine; I'm days away from never seeing them again anyway. Plus, if they saw the performance tonight, there's no way they could criticize what was presented. The show was really fantastic. The kids will post it on youtube by morning, I'm sure, where it'll garner hundreds of hits with comments like, "That was the best *Oliver* ever!" (Brag, brag!)

Kids fly by, clutching bouquets of flowers, posing for pictures with their grandparents and families– their still garishly made-up faces open and alight with joy. Ah, post-show high. There are enough happy pheromones in this place to revive the sullen dead.

When the crowd finally thins out, Lisa and Larry rush towards us and grab us in one of their famous group hugs.

Lisa teases, "Can we have your autographs?" while Larry enthuses, "Man, that was great, you guys! So I guess it was all worth it in the end, right?"

I look at Jackson, the puffy gray bags under his eyes, the lean, haggard look on his face. I take in the outward manifestation of the hell we were ground through, and I say lightly, "Oh, I don't know about that."

Larry seems embarrassed that I didn't just go along with his happy pronouncement, but I'm too bruised. I know I should just let it go and revel in the happiness spinning all around me, but I just can't.

"Sorry, Larry," I say. "Just keeping it real."

I feel Jackson squeezing my shoulders as Larry says, "No, no, I get it. Hell, we watched you live it! But guys, you deserve to enjoy this night, because that was freakin' awesome!"

We all burst out laughing together and Jackson says, "I'm turning into my father; I just want to go home to bed! Let's shoo the stragglers out and get the frig out of here."

I seize my chance.

"You guys go ahead, I'll lock up. Jackson, there's no reason for both of us to stay, and you're the one who's been performing for two and a half hours." I nudge him towards Lisa and Larry and say, "Can Jackson hitch a ride with you?"

Lisa and Larry, as if on cue, surround him like two cops taking someone into custody and grasp him by each arm. Jackson stands limply between them like a captured man. He looks just about as beat, too, like he's been running for too long, and is kind of pleased to have someone take over at last.

"I shouldn't leave you alone to lock up by yourself, Kel..." he begins in halfhearted protest, but I brush him off.

"I won't be alone. Tony's probably still up in the booth," I say.

"Nope," Jackson says. "He told me he had to bolt. I saw him leave, like, twenty minutes ago."

"Probably took those stage crew kids out for ice cream and a nice rub down," Lisa says sardonically out of the side of her mouth.

Larry shoots her a warning glance, and I say, "Well, Angelo's probably still here. Angelo!" I call out to the empty theater.

Angelo pokes his head out from inside the booth and waves down at us.

"See?" I say. "Plus, I have the protection from the sleeping princess." I gesture towards the last row of the theater, where Lillette sleeps in her favorite position: head thrown back, mouth opened like she's reaching for the high note in an aria.

Before Jackson can try to protest, Lisa and Larry start pulling him up the aisle. He smiles sheepishly at me, and I say, "I love you, Jackson Graham."

Jackson stops and turns to Larry. "Permission, sheriff, to say good-bye to the missus?"

Lisa and Larry drop his arms and he strides over to me. He places his warm hands on either side of my face and kisses me softly, like he knows I'm still tender from all our battles. His kisses always breathe new life into me when I'm feeling depleted. Now is no different. As tired as I feel, Jackson still sends me. Melts me. Could have me right here.

"We did it," he says, still cupping my face. "And I wouldn't have gone through this with anyone but you."

I can only grin back like a dope. Or dopily, if that's a word. Okay, it's not a word, but it describes exactly how I feel.

"Me, too," I say. "Now go. I'm right behind you guys. Save a warm spot in bed for me."

He gives me a final hug and I watch them go. The only sound left is the snuffling and snoring from the conked out maiden in the feather boa.

—m—

Once I make a sweep through backstage to secure and lock up the pen for the night, I walk toward the back of the theater to the booth.

It's probably kind of petty of me at this point to put the iPod back, but what the hey. So I'm petty. I don't want this problem, literally, in my hands anymore. And if this doesn't earn me my

Brave Warrior badge for going back to the creepy hallway not once, but *twice* tonight, then I don't know what will!

I stand directly below the booth and look up.

"Angelo!" I call as softly as I can. Luckily, Angelo pops his head out right away and looks down at me.

"Hey there– you up in the clouds!" I giggle. "I forgot something in the main building. I'll be right back."

"Right-o," he says with a thumbs-up.

"Shhhh!" I stage whisper. "Lillette." I point to the snoring Lillette, passed out nearby and say, "She's sleeping. I'll come right back for her."

"Got it," he whispers back.

—∿—

I am grateful for the gust of wind that greets me as I cross to the main building. The rush of crisp air does a thorough job of peeling away any leftover layers of tension that I may have been harboring and I feel instantly lighter.

The parking lot has all but emptied, save for a few kids. Lit by the peachy glow from the ancient Samuel P. Chester Academy lampposts, the kids clown around, jostling each other while they wait in front of the sports complex for their rides.

But then, there, in the dim light by the maple grove, I spot a single figure lurking in the shadows. Definitely male. Is that Forrest? Looks a bit like Forrest. I can't tell for sure. Whoever it is retreats behind a tree and for a moment I hesitate. A tiny flicker of uncertainty seizes me and I stop. I finger the smooth iPod tucked into my coat pocket and wonder again if I should just scrap the whole thing and go home.

With a defiant toss of my head, I march forward toward the main building.

I need to do this. For separation. For closure. For taking control of how we end it here. Noelle and her silly iPod are no longer my problem.

Casting a furtive glance back at the maple grove, I see whoever it was has disappeared. Good. Home to bed, kids. I grasp the cold metal handle of the heavy, etched door and slip inside.

As always, the painted likenesses of Headmaster Hank and his ancestors greet me benignly from their framed positions on the wall. Buoyed by the illusion that ten big, burly men accompany me into the building, I smile back at their frozen faces and scoot quickly over to the creepy back hallway. Looking down the blackened corridor, I can see the dim orange glow shimmering there at the end.

"Just a hop, skip and a jump, Kelly," I console myself. "Familiar territory. Piece of cake."

Surprisingly, I notice I don't feel afraid. Maybe it's because I now know the promise of light awaits. This thought perks me right up. Maybe I have grown into a "brave warrior" after all.

Terribly pleased with myself, I begin walking carefully down the hall, eyes focused on the weak shaft of light up ahead.

Snap. Drat it and damn it all to hell– what the heck is that? I think I hear the dead girl crying!

Instantly deflated, I stop maybe ten feet before the entrance of the stairwell and freeze. Apprehension grips my heart and steals any courage I had moments ago. I listen so hard my inner ears start to hurt. I absolutely hear it– soft, soft, weeping for sure. But that's not the only sound. A deeper bass line, a male voice, steady, low. As I inch closer, the voice becomes clearer.

Poised just a few feet from the entrance to the stairwell, I lean against the wall for support. I can just make out his words: "...will mature you. Years from now, when you speak of this..."

Speak of what? Who's talking? Is this some ghost guy, coming to the weeping girl's rescue?

"...and you shall– be kind."

Wait a sec. I recognize those words. They're from a play, I think. Yeah, they are. "Years from now, when you speak of this, and you shall; be kind." That's the famous last line from the play *Tea and Sympathy*. Every acting student knows it.

The weeping stops and it gets completely quiet. I tiptoe closer, my heart thumping loudly in my ears.

*Tea and Sympathy.* That play. That play ends with the headmaster's wife seducing a student at a private school. Oh no.

Not thinking, just reacting on automatic pilot, I round the corner to the stairwell and stop with a jolt. In the ghostly light, sitting on the top step of the landing, is Tony, with someone's head in his lap.

My mind clicks an indelible picture, and in shock I blurt, "Holy shit."

A pale, oval face, surrounded by long colorless hair, lifts from Tony's lap and gasps. Tony half rises, pulling his pants up to his waist with a noisy jangle of his belt and yells, inexplicably, "What?!"

All three of us stare at each other, all three of us are frozen. But only for a split second, because then, suddenly, the pallid face of Noelle is tripping down the stairs towards me and my arms float up to receive her. She hurtles past me, crying, alive-girl crying, and I shout, "Noelle, wait!"

She trips and stumbles, arms stretched out before her as if she is about to take flight, but then she falls to the ground with a dull smack. Tony starts to scramble down the stairs just as I reach down to lift her back up, and I have her, I have her, but she breaks free, slips through my fingers like a ghost and dashes down the hall.

Stunned, I turn back towards Tony, who is hastily buckling his belt, and I screech, "Oh my God! What were you doing?!"

I instantly close my eyes; I know what they were doing. I'll never be able to forget the sordid image. I bark, "Are you insane? How could you do that to her?"

Tony sits down hard on the bottom step, and hangs his head.

"You freak! What the hell– you *freak!*" I sputter as I look down at him.

So holy snap and crap it was Noelle. Noelle crying about this for God knows how long.

"How could you?" I seethe. "You animal! Have you lost your fucking mind?!" I keep lobbing questions at him, but he doesn't answer me.

He lifts his head. His mouth opens as if he's going to speak, but then it snaps back closed again. He opens his hands beseechingly and shakes his head.

"Answer me, Tony," I say, glaring at him. "How could you use her like that? She's a student, Tony– hello? A kid— a minor!" I sink down onto the floor. "And she was *crying*, Tony. She was *crying*."

"She was crying because she's in love with me," he mumbles. He clasps his hands desperately between his knees. It almost makes him look small.

"It doesn't matter," I say sharply. "You can't do that to her!" My brain starts fast-forwarding and I blurt, "I have to report this, Tony. I mean, I think I have to call the police."

Tony's head snaps up suddenly and he pleads, "No, no, don't do that, Kelly. I have a family."

I jump up. My eyes flash and I yell, "Then why did you do this? What the hell were you thinking?"

When he doesn't answer again, all my pent-up tension and festering hatred for him swells in my chest and I spit, "No answers? I'll tell you the answer, Tony. The answer is you'll be *so* fired. *So* fast. You thought you were untouchable– thought your Teflon-cool had everyone fooled. I knew you were a snake! You can't have sex with students!"

He still doesn't move. He drops his head to his knees and covers his head with his hands.

With disgust, I sit down next to him and hiss "Listen Tony– how you feel now? It's not half as bad as you're going to feel when everyone finds out. Let's see—there are the adoring parents, the headmaster, your *wife*..."

He stands up abruptly. "Your word against mine."

"What?"

"I'll deny it," he says defensively. "You can't prove it."

I stare up at him incredulously. "Tony, I *saw* you. And Noelle will tell!"

"No she won't." He takes a step towards me, his body looming over me. "Because it didn't happen. You don't know what you saw."

I leap to my feet and literally stand up to him. "I saw you with your pants down, and her head in your lap!" I shout. "I saw her giving you a..."

His arm thrusts out suddenly and he grabs my neck.

"Shut up! I didn't do anything. She wanted it," he says hoarsely.

I claw at his hand and squeak, "Tony! Stop! You're hurting me!"

I stumble as he spins me around and backs me up against the wall, holding me there. His face next to mine, he whispers, "You shouldn't have left her alone with me." Abruptly, mercifully, he drops his hand.

I rub my neck, my eyes darting around quickly, looking for an escape. I shouldn't have left him alone with her? This is *my* fault? What kind of crazy is this?

Adrenaline pumps through my body so fiercely that I start to shake and my teeth chatter. I shrink against the wall, my fingers searching the rough surface of the hard bricks.

Tony stares at me and says, "She's in love with me. I can't do anything about it." He squints as he slowly brings his face closer to mine. Our eyes lock, but then his eyelids droop as he languidly drags them away to stare at my mouth. I am biting my lip frantically to stop the chattering. For some reason this makes him smile and he throws back his head and barks out a sharp laugh. Clapping his hands together he says, "Oh, I get it now. You're jealous! You're actually trembling for me! You wish it was *you*."

Even in my terrified state the absurdity of that statement makes me want to slap his face, but I'm too scared. I want to make a run for it, but he has boxed me in.

He points at me and snickers, "You always wanted me, I could tell. You and that crackpot Lillette-the-Loon were always staring at me. I got you all hot and bothered, huh? Now I get it!"

I slip my hands into my coat pockets so he won't see them shaking. I feel the slippery surface of the iPod buried there, and my face must register something because Tony looks at me closely and says, "What?"

He steps nearer and shouts, "What?!" as he pulls my hands from my pockets.

I hold my trembling hands up in surrender and say, "Nothing. Nothing, Tony. You know what? You're right. About everything. So, you know, let's just forget all about this, okay?" I make a move to casually walk away.

He smacks my hands to the side, grabs my jacket and thrusts his hands into my pockets. I stiffen against the wall as he roughly rummages through them and pulls out the iPod. His eyes grow wide as he stares at it dangling helplessly in his hand.

He barks, "Where did you get this?"

He recognizes it? My mouth drops open, but no sound comes out. I've forgotten how to breathe.

He repeats, "Where did you get this?"

It's *his?*

My breath comes in tiny rasps, but still no sound. He turns his back and rants, "This isn't yours, Kelly– it doesn't belong to you." He jams it into his pocket and spits, "Take, take, take. That's all you and your wimp husband do. You think you can take everything that's rightfully mine? I was here before you and Jackass, and I'll be here when you're gone." He turns back in a rage and grabs me by the hair. I scream as I bend forward and try to grab his wrists.

Suddenly, there's a loud scraping sound, the low rumble of brick on brick. At the top of the landing, a bright light pierces through the murky haze and I see the unmistakable rotund silhouette of Angelo.

As I squint against the light, Tony spins around and drops his hands.

"What's going on down there?" Angelo's voice booms above us. Lit by a powerful flashlight clutched in his left hand, Angelo stands before a dark cavity that has appeared in the wall. Swinging the light, he descends down the stairs towards Tony and me.

Tony does a psycho switch of mood and says coolly, "Hey, Angelo; it's nothing. Just me and Kelly Graham doing a little acting scene from the play, right Kelly?" He looks at me, and winks– his face entirely composed, like we were just discussing Shakespeare.

Angelo stops six or seven steps above us, eyes scanning back and forth from Tony to me. The light illuminates the entire stairwell, and cannot hide the terror on my face. Although I manage to shrug my shoulders and say, "Yeah, yeah, everything's fine," Angelo locks eyes with mine and they tell him everything he needs to know.

Without warning, like a human cannonball, he launches himself through the air and lands on Tony, knocking him on to the floor.

"Angelo! Angelo! What the hell are you doing?" Tony says as they tussle. Angelo lifts the flashlight and tries lamely to hit Tony. Tony grabs it easily and says, "Knock it off, Angelo! Cut it out!"

Tony wrestles Angelo into one of those wrestling holds he used on the stage crew boys and barks, "Give up? Give up, Angelo!"

Grunting, Angelo freezes for a moment, and I think it's over, but then Angelo suddenly bucks him and lands a blow to Tony's side. Incensed, Tony scrambles to restrain Angelo's flailing arms and flips him onto his back. Angelo struggles, but is no match for Tony. Tony rolls on top of Angelo and pins him with his long legs. Angelo grabs at the flashlight at his side and swings it ineptly at Tony's head. As they grapple, Tony wrests the flashlight away and raises it over his head.

"No!" I scream. I fly forward to grab Tony's arm, but he flings me off like a speck of dirt and slams the flashlight down onto Angelo's head. Angelo's glasses shoot through the air, and then he lies still. So still. Too still. His silver bandana lies crumpled near the top of his head; his glasses, broken on the floor.

"Why didn't you stop? Why didn't you stop?" Tony cries astride Angelo's immobile body.

I rush forward to pull Tony off Angelo, but Tony rears on me and grabs me around the waist. The flashlight clatters to the floor and with his teeth bared he screams, "It's all *your* fault!"

Then, with the force of a thousand demons, he hurls me against the wall. My head bounces on the unforgiving brick, and my breath leaves me in a simple puff. I hear it go, I feel it leave me forever, then everything is black.

# VILLAGE OF HARDING COVE
## POLICE REPORT
### Transcript from Taped Conversation with Miss Lillette Brewster:

"It's on? What? But I don't see a microphone. Oh, yeah, never mind, now I see it. It's just that a have a little phobia about really tiny mics. I thought I was being bugged once in my ponytail...

Yeah, sure. I can start from the beginning.

Well, I was in the theater. That's the Little Theater at the Samuel P. Chester Academy on North Ridge Road. Oh? You've got that already, okay, good.

I must have fallen asleep after all the excitement of opening night for *Oliver!* This happens to me a lot. I'm hyper wide-awake one minute, then blah, out like a light.

Narcolepsy? What is that? Like a narc? Or narcotics? Hey, I don't take narcotics! I have never taken drugs; I'm high on life! And for you to suggest... What? Oh. Sorry. I thought it meant you thought I took drugs, and I... back to the facts? Yessir.

So when I opened my eyes, Forrest Keller was standing over me. He told me he snuck into the lobby to wait for me because he hadn't seen me leave the building and wanted to make sure I got to my car safely.

Did you hear what I just said? Forrest Keller, the boy so many think of as a troublemaker, was actually doing a very considerate thing. He can be very caring. He just gets a bad rap... hey, isn't that a word you use a lot down here, like, 'he took the rap?' Isn't it funny that I never used that word before, and now I'm using it at a police station?

Right, sorry. Yes, so Forrest said that while he was in the lobby, he heard someone crying. He thought it sounded like it came from the lighting booth, so he went up to check it out.

He said he actually thought it was *me* crying at first, so he was surprised to find Noelle Pratt sitting at Mr. Glynn's desk sobbing her eyes out. He asked her what was wrong, but she ran back down the stairs to the lobby. That's when he noticed the wall was open.

Now this is where I come in. Forrest came into the theater looking for Noelle or someone, *anyone*, there to talk to. He saw me sleeping and woke me up. He told me Noelle ran away crying for some unknown reason, but that didn't surprise me. I saw that girl crying all the time– almost as much as me! Anyway, Forrest was all excited, telling me there was a big open hole in the wall of the lighting booth and he wanted me to come up to see it.

So, we go up to the booth, and let me just tell you, it was like a scary Tim Burton movie up there. Strange, spooky tools were hung on the walls, like the design team was led by the Bogeyman. And sure enough, the wall at the far end was open. Which was totally weird because it's a brick wall! Made out of real, heavy bricks! But it opened to a genuine secret passageway with all these rickety steps. We took a flashlight off the wall and decided to see where it led. It was so dark and gloomy in there, but Forrest was a perfect gentleman and helped me down the creaky steps. See what I mean about how really caring he can be?

I know, I know, back to the story, gotcha.

We went down, down, down, with the dust swirling in front of the flashlight, and when we got to the bottom, the tunnel went straight. As we crept along, we suddenly heard echo-y yelling, so we just followed along 'til we got to more stairs. We went up and up, like, a lot of stairs, but the yelling had stopped. I could sort of hear someone crying, and I froze inside. You see, there was this rumor going around that there was a ghost girl living at the academy, but my uncle told me it wasn't true. When I heard that crying, though, I thought, 'What if he was wrong?' But that's just when we arrived at another hole in a brick wall. It was in the main building, on, like, a landing. And that's when we looked down the stairs and saw Kelly and Angelo laying on the floor.

That rat, Tony Glynn– oh man, I hate his guts! He was sitting on the floor sobbing like a baby. I ran down the stairs, and that asshole ran away. I know I shouldn't say asshole, but that's what he is! Asshole! Asshole! Asshole!

I'm sorry. This has been very hard for me.

I started screaming and screaming for Kelly and Angelo to wake up, but they wouldn't. Forrest had started to run after Tony, but I yelled for him to come back and call 911. We were both shaking so hard, but Forrest managed to press the numbers on my cell, then he wrapped my boa around Angelo's head to stop the bleeding.

And Kelly, well, you know.

Wait.

Keep this thing on. Because I just want to say, to *state*, for the record, that I'm glad you found that coward, Tony Asshole Glynn, riding in his car with Noelle. I hope when you arrested him, you stripped him of his tool belt, because that's his favorite thing in the universe. He wears it with all those wrenches and screwdrivers hanging down like twelve penises dangling from his waist.

Don't turn it off! I've already said asshole, so I may as well say penis, too, and go to hell for the whole lot.

But cheese and rice, he deserves everything he gets. Cripes, I hope he rots in jail for how he hurt so many people!

I may say asshole and penis, but I will never take the Lord's name in vain.

I'm done now. Thank you."

Ow. My head. My neck.

My eyes flutter open, but I close them again quickly against the light.

I smell cherries.

I turn my head slowly to the left and come eye level with six cherry ChapStick's, lined up perfectly in a row like they were waiting for me. As I part my lips, I feel the familiar waxy coating encasing them like a protective overcoat.

"Jackson?" I venture.

"Hi." He's suddenly next to me. I feel the warm grip of his hands enfold mine and I blink at him. Everything hurts. I squint my eyes and try to point upwards towards the painful light.

He strokes my cheek and says, "They want the light on. Here." I feel the palm of his hand slide across my forehead and it feels so good.

I try to lick my lips, but my mouth is like sand.

"Water?" I croak.

A straw is slipped between my teeth and I take a long sip.

Jackson draws my hand up to his lips and kisses each knuckle. He slowly brushes his lips back and forth across my folded fingers.

"You're okay, Kel," he says. "We're at Lincoln Medical."

My eyes adjusted, I gaze around the room. Just past the cherry ChapSticks stands a long silver pole. Suspended from the pole is a blue box with a long, clear tube snaking over the top sheet and into my hand. Looking down, I see the sliver of a needle poking into my skin, bound in place with tape.

A nurse bustles in and goes right over to the blue box. Pressing some numbers on its calculator face in a rapid succession of bleeps and blippity-blips, she smiles and turns to me. "How are you feeling, Mrs. Graham?"

"Okay," I say. "My head."

She nods and says, "You have quite a bump. And you've suffered a concussion, but you'll be just fine."

Jackson pulls my fingers away from his mouth so I can see his hopeful little smile. He looks wiped.

"Have you told her?" the nurse asks Jackson.

I raise my eyebrows in alarm, but the funny smile on Jackson's lips dispels my fear.

"Tell me what?" I ask, as I shoot Jackson a look.

"Uh, no, not yet," Jackson tells the nurse, ignoring my question. "Soon."

I am suddenly feeling markedly better. I glance down at the back of my hand, knowing that the tube and the needle and the tape attaching me to the blue blip-blip machine has something to do with it.

"I didn't want to give you too much, but this will help with the discomfort," the nurse says as she pats the blue box. "She looks good," she remarks to Jackson as if I'm not even there.

When she's gone, Jackson squeezes my hand gently and says, "Do you remember what happened?"

"Tony." I say immediately.

Jackson nods. He grows still and very quiet, as if he's searching for what to say next. I become aware for the first time of the hospital noises outside my door: voices, the rumble of carts, the shrill sound of phones.

"They got him," he says simply.

I'm suddenly flooded with a vision. "Angelo?"

"He's fine. Tony knocked him out, and he needed some stitches, but he's good. He was treated here, too, and is already home, resting." Jackson looks down for a moment. "He tried to save you, Kel."

"I remember," I say solemnly.

"But it was Lillette and Forrest who discovered you and Angelo. They called 911, and Lillette even made them let her ride with you in the ambulance." He smiles again. "I hear she raised quite a ruckus."

"I'll bet," I smile back.

"Oh, look!" he says. "Angelo sent this." He lets go of my hand to reach for a brown teddy bear with angel's wings. Crumpled aluminum foil rings its little head like a sweatband. Just like Angelo wears!

I start to laugh, but a searing shot of pain licks through my head and back. Jackson grabs my hands again and says, "Try not to laugh, Kel. They said you'll feel sore as heck for a while. But you're okay."

He lifts a stack of paper off the nightstand and pats them together. "And here are a bunch of e-mail get well wishes. Everyone and their aunt sent you one. I have to read this one first, though. The Prof made me promise. It's kind of weird, but he said you'd get it."

He clears his throat and reads, "'Kelly, I have your Brave Warrior medal here. I will pin it to you personally when you are up for visitors. Be well, dear heart, Your Prof.'"

I bite my lip as I feel the sting of tears leap into my eyes. I always cry with the Prof!

"Jackson, how long have I been here?"

"Two days."

"What happened with the show?" I ask with alarm.

Jackson grins. "Glad you asked, Kel. The headmaster wanted to cancel Saturday night's show, but the kids went ballistic. Like, *all* of them. But they were led primarily by our sweet little Amber, who insisted we continue. Seems someone had filled her head with a lot of theater lore and she was adamant that the show go on. It was her war cry on every e-mail, and through every text message: 'The show MUST go on!' She rallied Thomas, Delaney, Jasmine, Marta, Erik and Blake together, and they met with the headmaster and some parents and convinced them to go ahead with it."

His blue eyes dance and twinkle and I say, "The show must go on? Uh, I don't know who could have promoted such a concept..."

"Well, the show went on, amid all the turmoil of the cast trying to take in the fact that you and Angelo were injured, and that it was done at the hands of Tony." He spits the last part out like he's trying to rid himself of a mouthful of venom.

He composes himself then says, "It was good, Kel. Everyone really banded together. Lisa stayed with you, while Larry ran the lights and I played. Even the parents were helpful." He trails off, then becomes quiet again.

I try to get my mind around all this information, but my brain isn't interested in dwelling on any of it. Noelle crosses my mind, but just as quickly, she disappears.

Jackson starts to get all squirmy as he fumbles through his jeans pockets looking for something.

"Kelly, I have something else to tell you." He's all over the narrow hospital bed, twisting and turning while he searches.

Finally, he pulls out a tiny piece of paper and begins unfolding it.

"What?" I ask. "Are you becoming like Lillette– putting notes in your pants pockets instead of your shoes?"

He gives me the strangest secretive smile and says, "No– I'm following *your* lead. I wrote this, uh, poem for you, to, uh, tell you something."

"Spill it, Mr. Graham." Lord, I've never seen him so nervous. He gives his ear one of his famous little tugs, and says:

"Kelly, Kelly, theater girl,

Deep inside you grows a pearl.

One plus one does not make two,

One plus one makes someone new.

One plus one was you and me,

Now one plus one will equal three."

Now *this* is the kind of math I understand. Because I already suspected. I slide my taped, tubed hand over my barely sloped belly and ask, "In here?"

Jackson's eyes flood with tears as he bows his head and gives a wobbly smile. "Yes. You're due in November."

I try to steady my breathing, as it's suddenly taken off in a gallop.

A sweet pea.

"Is the baby all right?"

"Tucked in safe and sound," he says.

"Jammin' Graham," I say, as I gently rub the curve of my belly.

"Uh, no," Jackson says with a laugh. "More like a *Pam* Graham."

A girl!

Probably a girl with curls. In fact, most definitely a curly-haired girly-girl.

I grab Jackson's hand and we lace our fingers together. I feel a warm surge of tenderness flood through me.

"Okay, only, not Pam," I say.

"Well, then, what? What should we call her? Samantha, maybe? For 'Sam Graham'?"

"Stop with the rhyming," I murmur, feeling a wave of sleepiness come over me.

"How about 'Kelly,' after you?"

I carefully shake my foggy head 'no.' My daughter doesn't need to be a brave warrior. She's going to be a princess.

"Then how about a name that's related to theater– or music?"

I grin a lopsided smile.

"Maybe," I drawl. I feel myself slipping away, like I'm kind of tipsy. Not a good state to be in to name my child. I'm liable to approve naming her Paris Hilton. Or maybe Lady Gaga. Ooh, that's perfect. My own baby Lady Goo Goo Gaga.

"Maybe Sarah, after Sarah Bernhardt," I hear Jackson say from far away.

"Mmmm, maybe."

As I start to peacefully drift off, I remember Noelle's anguished face. Wait...

# End of June
## 3pm
# Samuel P. Chester Academy Parking Lot

Amber runs across the parking lot shouting excitedly, "Mrs. Graham! Mrs. Graham!"

I'm on my way back to my car, where Jackson waits for me. I turn and see her running towards me; her shiny ponytail sweeping back and forth behind her head like a pendulum. She holds a piece of paper aloft, waving it in the air like it's one of Willy Wonka's golden tickets.

As she catches up to me, she leans against a chichi looking car and tries to catch her breath. Thrusting the paper towards me, she pants, "Nobody died."

For a bemused moment I almost say, *You mean other than my spirit and my innocence?* But I maturely squelch that thought and say, "You're right, Amber; nobody died."

"It's so good to see you're okay, Mrs. Graham," she says as I take the wrinkled paper.

My stomach drops. It's The Chart. My nemesis.

I look at the tiny Amber-perfect check marks in their tiny, perfect boxes. The empty death box– void of the check mark that could have been me.

I reach to embrace her tightly. I didn't do one hundred percent right by Amber, and for that I'm truly sorry. "It's so good to see you again, too, Amber," I say warmly into her hair. "You look terrific."

She pulls back from our hug and says, "Thanks. So do you think the curse is lifted now?" She looks at me hopefully, so full of trust.

"There was never a curse," I start to explain carefully. But then I stop. This is how I got myself into trouble in the first place. I try a new tack. "Yes, Amber. Yes, I think the curse is lifted. I think it's over because the prophecy ends when life trumps death."

"You mean because you didn't, um, um..." she looks around like she's searching for another word, *any* word, other than "die."

"No, I didn't die, Amber, but that's not what I was getting at."

"What do you mean?" she asks.

I pull her away from the Ferrari and start to walk through the parking lot towards my Nissan. "Well, this is the first production I've ever worked on where a new life was created. I think that the new life will eliminate the death part, leaving the old curse null and void."

As we walk, colorful patches of vibrant-hued flowers line our path. They sway gently in the breeze like hula dancers. Who thought to make even the parking lot look so pretty? It's like being surrounded by a living, breathing carpet of color.

Amber looks at me uncomprehendingly, and then says suddenly, "Are you talking about a baby? Do you mean, like, a new baby?"

I smile at her and nod in that drippy, goopy way I've seen pregnant women before me nod. Now I know first-hand why their faces go all melty.

"*Your* baby?" she says as she casts a quick glance down at my belly.

"Yes, my baby."

A smile spreads across her face and she jumps at me for another hug. Her glasses smush to the side a little as she squeals, "That's great, Mrs. Graham!" She looks down at the paper holding The Chart and says, "Then I guess we don't need this anymore."

"No," I say.

She starts to carefully fold it in half, but then stops herself. "I've got an idea!" she exclaims. "How about we start a new chart, Mrs. Graham? Like, a positive one. We can call it 'The Terrific Three' or something!"

"No chart, Amber."

"But it could list three wonderful things that always happen when you rehearse a play!"

"Such as...?" I ask guardedly.

She gives me an impish smile, then rests one hand over her heart and raises her right hand. "Such as, one," she flicks her index finger up. "Someone's self-confidence will grow." I see Thomas prancing across the stage. "Two: someone will be transformed," Delaney's face flickers through my mind. "And three, someone will be born."

My brain flashes on front-page headlines about a sudden outbreak of teenage pregnancies at the exclusive Samuel P. Chester Academy, and I gasp. I can clearly see Jasmine, Taffy and Sienna waddle by with swollen bellies and I bark, "No! No chart. Period."

Am I getting wise, or what? Wasn't that short and to the point? I have to start practicing being this simple and clear on an ongoing basis if I'm going to be a mother, don't I? Now is as good a time to start as any, for pity's sake!

Amber drops her arms to her sides in resignation and says in agreement, "Okay. No chart."

I watch as she purposefully rips the paper into shreds. She pockets the scraps and gives me a tentative smile. "Does this mean you're coming back? All we hear are rumors..."

A sweet, slow, sugar breeze wafts by, fragrant with the scent of lilacs and honeysuckle. I raise my face to the sun and say, "Yup. We're coming back."

Time for my third hug from the normally reticent Amber. She squeezes me so hard I'm afraid the baby's going to pop out right here in the parking lot.

As I extract myself from her happy grip, I motion towards my car, where Jackson sits in the driver's seat. Sporting a jaunty blue cap that makes him look instantly older, he tips the cap at us in his most gentlemanly "afternoon ma'am" fashion and smiles. He calls the hat "The Dad Cap," and when he wears it, I never, ever, think about lice.

Jackson rolls down the window and rests his arm on the door.

"Hi, Amber. How's every little thing?"

Amber waves back, "Hi, Mr. Graham. Congratulations on every *big* thing. A baby! Wow! And I'm so glad you're coming back."

Jackson cuts me a sidelong glance as I scoot into the passenger seat next to him.

"So the cat's out of the bag, huh?" he says as he smiles at Amber. "Well, we couldn't leave the group high and dry now, could we?"

Having just come from picking up our new contracts with Headmaster Hank, it's official. We've been rehired to direct two productions next year, with new guidelines hammered out and typed up into our agreement.

Some of the stuff the contract includes:

The return of Lillette? Absolutely. Angelo? Of course. His heroic act of trying to save me was even recognized in the newspaper, not to mention all over the web. If he hadn't discovered the secret passageway that led from the lighting booth to the main building that night...well, it does no good to dwell on it now.

Our new contract also includes a new tech guy. And guess who qualified for that position? Our own dear Larry. With his knowledge of all things electronic, he'll be perfect.

Who didn't make the cut? That's right– Tony. You can't work in the theater when you're facing twelve to fifteen in prison.

The crazy parents? As there is no real definition as to what constitutes crazy behavior, we have it in writing that we can 1.) have closed rehearsals, 2.) have veto power to say in what capacities parents may assist us, and 3.) have the authority to limit the number of activities a student may be involved with that could conflict with their commitment to the show.

That was the long, chewy way of saying that the Headmaster backs us up for real and in writing this time, and will be there to support us.

I think he's taking this stance for a bunch of reasons. The first one being he's probably so relieved I'm alive and didn't add another ghost-girl to his already haunted academy. And two, the reason I like best– and the one I hope was foremost in his decision to keep us on– is that he thinks we're decent people who know how to do our jobs well. I imagine he's relieved to have Tony gone, and I *know* he is horrified that all this occurred on his watch, but in the end we said "yes" to Headmaster Hank because we didn't want to let the kids down.

For the most part, it was a positive experience for the kids, but I will always feel I failed Noelle. I failed her because I wasn't as good as Sister Aloysius at figuring out what was wrong. It wasn't enough to have doubt; I should have acted. Even if I wasn't absolutely certain, there were enough weird things going on that I should have gone to the Headmaster to at least air my concerns. I know better now.

Headmaster Hank told me Noelle is in therapy. In fact, it was recommended that anyone involved with the production go for counseling. What Tony did to Noelle was just the most tangible manifestation of his control over all of them. They were intensely loyal to Tony– he had a grip on their fragile teenage psyches like a cult leader. The fallout was devastating. Chip and Allen had to be deprogrammed to see that what Tony was doing was immoral and wrong. Not to mention a crime in all fifty states.

They confessed to knowing Tony was having sex with Noelle, but like pathetic little minions, kept his distorted secret and even stuck up for him.

Initially, when this first broke, some of the parents invariably sided with Tony, too, and even sent in letters of support. I say "invariably" because I have read enough reports of educators accused of sex abuse in the newspapers to know that a certain percentage of parents will back the teacher, no matter the facts. And if he's known as "the popular teacher," it's apparently harder for them to think it may be true. The parents just can't make the leap that he may have been popular because he was a wily, manipulative snake. It would mean they'd have to acknowledge that they themselves missed the cues that he was a predator, and who wants to admit to that?

It was only once other girls came forward to say how seductive Tony had been with them that they changed their tune.

I still shudder. And I feel bad I didn't do enough to protect them. Especially Noelle.

"Tony the Tiger." That was the nickname Tony gave himself and told Noelle to call him. The pink iPod was just one of his gifts to her. A new cell phone was another. The police uncovered an entire encyclopedia of explicit sexts between Tony and Noelle that show him for the slime he was. Tony the *Tiger*? More like Tony the Turd.

It's been a lot to take in. But we Brave Warriors soldier on. I reach across Jackson to wave a final good bye to Amber and say, "Have a fun summer, Amber. We'll see you in September." Amber backs away from the car and reaches into her purse. Pulling out an extra-sharp pencil and waggling it in the air, she yells, "I'm ready for the next show!"

Jackson yells back, "Yes, Amber, but are *we*?"

She laughs and says, "Yes– you have me! And I can babysit, too!"

We back out with a final wave. I watch out the side view mirror as Amber becomes smaller and smaller, until she blends in and becomes just another delicate flower waving in the breeze.

One more stop to go...

—ᴡᴡ—

The grave is small, and is covered with moss. Time's hand has scrubbed some of the hard edges and blurred the marker a bit, but I see her name clearly: Clara Rose Beckett.

Born: January 18, 1914. Died: April 25, 1931.

I place the single pink rose on her grave and stand up slowly. The baby kicks and Jackson slips his arm around my thickening waist. We stand in silence, lost in our own thoughts.

"She'd be in her nineties now, Jackson, if she had lived."

Jackson tips his head down on top of mine and I feel him nod into my hair.

I sigh. "Thank you for indulging me, Jackson. I just had to see her for myself."

I close my eyes. My fascination with Clara Beckett's untimely death has now morphed into a kind of kinship with her: We both shared a dimly lit stairway where we both came to harm. And that's not all we share.

When Headmaster Hank looked through the archives and found an old yearbook picture of her, we all gasped: curly locks, upturned pug nose; a Keri Russell wannabe just like me.

The freaky coincidence that our accidents occurred on the same date in April, in the same stairwell, has also weighed heavily on me. Separated by eight decades, I'm not sure what to make of it. I mean, how can all these coincidences be explained? It makes me wonder if Clara and I are, perhaps, linked in a more otherworldly sense, too. Could I be a reincarnation of her spirit that had to go through this again to change the outcome? This time her spirit lives, and she gets to live out the life she missed?

These are disturbing thoughts for a non-believer-in-ghosts person, such as myself. I was raised Catholic, so I was taught your spirit is either in heaven with God, or in "aitch-e-double-hockey-sticks" with the devil. Ghostly spirits don't float around disturbing the living. When we bury someone, they are truly "laid to rest." It's over.

But I'm plagued by questions now about the afterworld. And about life in general. For example, does this mean that balance is now restored to the creepy back hallway, in some yin/yang fashion: one dead girl/one alive? Or am I just trying to give order and explanation where one doesn't exist, to help it make sense to me?

Not that anyone used that stairway much to begin with, but I'll bet no one uses it now. They should just board the damn thing up and bury those secret passageways, too. The only people using them were Tony and the stage crew kids– scurrying through them like a pack of rats, mining the tunnels for long lost "treasure"– read: "tools." And of course, poor Noelle, who took refuge there to cry out her sorrow.

I'm sure Angelo and his guys on the custodial staff could have the whole thing sealed off in a New York minute. I know it would put *my* mind at ease.

Jackson interrupts my thoughts and says, "It's the circle of life, right here, Kelly."

I focus again on Clara's grave. Jackson is right. Here is one girl, tucked into the earth; and here is another, tucked deep inside me. I stand, a link to both worlds.

"Clara Rose," Jackson says.

"Yes," I murmur. "She had a beautiful name."

"No," he says. "I meant for our baby."

For a moment it sounds karmically right. But then I'm seized with a feeling so strong I push myself away from him and say, "No, Jackson. I don't want our baby to have her name. It's like keeping *my* problem alive, and I don't want this thing perpetuated."

I take this as evidence I have thoroughly learned my lesson. No more teasing about ancient curses and tempting forces beyond our control. Good stuff and bad stuff will happen all on their own without me trying to play director all the time.

I'm not messing with the cosmos anymore. It is beyond my comprehension, so I'm keeping my life plain and simple from now on. Our little girl will have enough to face in her own life without us putting this on her.

We wander slowly back to the car, our fingers laced together like one heart. The noble gravestones peer down at their charges like mothers looking over their carriages.

The balmy June breeze ruffles the grass grown over the rounded mounds of the graves, and I'm grateful to be here, grateful to be alive.

We're meeting with Lisa and Larry later for an idle movie night. They'll crank up the ancient VCR player and we'll just veg. That's the plan. I feel a tiny stab of dread that it should be more; that after today, I should do something more. But this is all there is. See? Green grass, blue sky, man, woman, unborn child. Simple.

As Jackson shuts the car door, I hug myself with a little shiver. Goosebumps prickle my arms and spread down my legs. I glance back at Clara's gravestone. Don't they say you get goosebumps when someone walks on your grave?

—⁓—

As we drive away from the cemetery, Jackson asks, "So what play do you want to do in September?"

I almost laugh. I have been so preoccupied with my heavy spiritual musings, that it's the furthest thing from my mind. But I guess it always comes back to the theater for Jackson and me, no matter what.

"I don't know," I say. "We did a comedy last year, so maybe a drama?" I shrug. "What do you think?" A few powerful plays rain through my mind: *The Crucible, The Diary of Anne Frank, A Doll's House.*

Jackson says, "I think we should write our own play."

"You do? Really?"

"Yeah. We could write one about all the stuff that goes on behind the scenes when you're in rehearsal for a play."

"Sounds kind of boring," I say with a smirk.

"Boring?!" Jackson all but explodes. "Are you kidding me? We could write it directly from the experiences we just had rehearsing *Oliver!* It would be chock full of high drama!"

I consider it for a moment. I think briefly about all the frustrating, wacky, impossible things that happened.

"Nah," I say finally. "It's too implausible. No one would ever believe it."

# Acknowledgements

Thank you to Lisa Cahn: a chance meeting at a garage sale, of all places, brought your talents right to my doorstep. Thank you for sharing your editorial skills.

To my fellow Thespians: Bill Cannon—my Captain, my Papa; Donna Murphy, Lisa Werner, Jeff Bennett (true Prof and editorial savior), Jessica Gutteridge, Ron Stroman—inspirations all.

To my teachers and mentors: Joanna Merlin, Mary Hall, Judi Beck Tracy—I think of your lessons still.

Endless gratitude to Molly Prep for your photography, artistry and brilliance. Thank you Katie Fletcher for sharing your talent!

To the best Tech Directors I have ever worked with: Tim Trotter and Yuriy Zacharia, my heroes– thank you for all the fun and for all you teach me.

Special thanks to all my inspiring students (stars—everyone of you!) both past and present, and to the wonderful parents, teachers and staff at the many schools I work in– and who, of course, bear no resemblance whatsoever to the characters in this book.

To Phyllis Beck—Emotional terrain Sherpa: thank you.

Many thanks to my pals and fellow cartoonists in the Berndt Toast Gang: Bunny Hoest, Joe Giella, Janine Manheim, Adrian Sinnott, Pauline and Stan Goldberg, Sandy Kossin, Roberta Fabiano, Ray Alma, Simmy and Sy Barry, Helene Parsons, John Reiner, John Pennisi, Carmen and Tony D'Adamo, Jeff Fisher, Rhoda and Dan Danglo et al.

Heartfelt appreciation to my family and friends– most especially to Mom and Dad, a/k/a Helen and Frank Murdock. And to Lynn Gambarelli, Andrea Holmes, and Leah Martin for insightful talks and unending support.

To my grandfather, Frank "Red" Murdock—actor extraordinaire: Although we never met, I carry on your work. Your 1926 Actor's Equity Card sits on my dresser—a reminder of you and an explanation for why I am who I am.

And finally, to my magnificent, vibrant, creative family: Kerry and Molly— you are everything.

Helen Murdock-Prep is a Theater Educator, Artist, Cartoonist, Writer and Actress living in New York with her family. She teaches the Pre-College Program in Musical Theater at Adelphi University, among other schools. She sings constantly.

19545034R00211

Made in the USA
Middletown, DE
24 April 2015